To Peter,

THE CALLING
OF THE
KEY

DONALD JONES

If I can acheive only a
fraction of what you have — I'll
be more than satisfied.

THE CALLING OF THE KEY

by

Donald Jones

Excalibur Press of London
13 Knightsbridge Green, London, SW1X 7QL

Printed and bound in Great Britain
Published by Excalibur Press of London
Typesetting and origination by CBS, Felixstowe, Suffolk
ISBN 1 85634 050 3

Chapter One

Two years had passed since. Two long and lonely years during which time he had suffered constant heartache and sorrow. But finally the time had come when he found himself faced with no alternative but to accept the harsh reality. She was not coming back to him, no special miracles were to be performed for the sole benefit of John Williams. Life with its great challenge had to be taken up; somewhere from within he must rediscover the strength to continue, to emerge from the depths into which he had sunk, almost drowning in his own self pity.

'In sickness and in health.'

He stared steadily at the neat headstone which bore her name, the feeling of sadness erupting once more inside him, and tears came to his eyes. It was always the same when he came to visit her, he was unable to control his emotions, or the increasing anger at the unfairness of it all.

Why did it have to be her, why not someone else? He had asked himself these questions a million times before, but would never, could never, understand the reasoning.

His memory went back to the day when they had stood so close together in the tiny chapel on the far side of the world and repeated the vows, pledging lives and love to one another. The words of the naval chaplain still so clear in his mind, as if the ceremony had been only yesterday. But twenty years had gone by since that day.

He felt empty without her, a vacuum now existed inside his heart, void of all feeling for the outside would.

The doctors and eminent specialists, with their combined expertise and access to up to date resources, had been powerless to prolong her life and provide some ray of hope. Nothing they attempted was in any way successful in combating the evil cancerous growth which ate greedily at her very existence, causing her to waste away before his eyes. No words of encouragement could be spoken, no deed done, to rid her of the absolute certainty that death lay impatiently waiting. To this she had resigned herself so bravely, with a strength he himself found it impossible either to comprehend or equal. Even during the last few hours of her life, a relatively young life spanning a mere thirty seven years, and with pain an everpresent companion to her, still she had found it in her heart to worry about him.

"Who's going to look after you when I'm gone?" she cried, "You've got nobody." That one sentiment in itself, epitomising the bond of love between them, and as he had to sit by her side witnessing her suffering, totally inadequate to ease her burden in any way, was in its own sadistic and twisted way, almost as painful to himself.

When the inevitable day arrived and the extreme effort became too great a struggle for her, she slipped quietly away. The slender grasp of Angela's fragile hand in his gently released its hold of life; this was to be their final moment together.

'Till death us do part.'

The passing of Angela Williams becoming one additional statistic to be entered upon the Maker's scroll, her name inscribed in his register of life, never to be erased or forgotten.

On that day, not only had he lost the best wife any man could wish to find, but was also deprived of the best friend he had ever had, the one going hand in hand with the other.

Her death had almost proved too much for him to accept. He tried to find solace and escape in alcohol, in the contents of numberless bottles. But no matter how many weeks or months he 'lost' by its effects, there was to be no changing the truth; he was alone. His only solution was more drink; his life seemed to revolve and take place in another dimension, where everything and everybody was in a permanent haze.

It was only on very rare occasions that he ventured far from the confines of his home, which he had inadvertently turned into some kind of shrine to her memory; photographs adorned every room, as if she were watching over him. The only place he visited was her graveside, and always late at night. Somehow, through the haze of alcohol, he had convinced himself that it would be at this time her celestial spirit would be at its closest, and he expected to hear her familiar voice beckon from the darkness.

If only they had been blessed with children, but even that small favour had been cruelly denied them. If only Angela had not developed the growth inside her body, a young and vibrant body he had worshipped........, and if only she could still have been here by his side, in a continuance of their lives together.

It was as if everything he yearned for in life could be encompassed by those two words 'if only'.

He now realised that he must have been close to insanity; but eventually the passing of time, and then the registered letter he had received two weeks ago, brought about a reluctant acceptance of the truth. He decided to pull himself together; there had to be a meaning to his life and, if there was, he wanted to be ready to face it.

Instinctively he fingered the small key which lay in the depths of his pocket, the small key which had arrived tucked in the registered envelope, and the cause of the transformation in himself. For that at least he had to be thankful, he had been balancing on the edge and this at least had brought him back with a shock.

How he now wished with another 'if only' that the activities he had been involved in all those years ago had not taken place. But as with the death of his wife, they were also the truth and, like it or not, he had no choice but to accept it.

The well known saying was an eye for an eye, a tooth for a tooth. Did it apply to his own particular circumstances? Could it mean a life for a life? Was it possible that this sudden reappearance of the key, which brought back with it the past violence in his life, was to be the beginning of a penance which he was now expected to undergo?

A delayed payment which now had to be made.

Absurd as it appeared on the surface, and after more than twenty years of total inactivity, there was a distinct possibility of his being recalled to the section. The whole idea was nothing short of ridiculous, he had not heard from them at all during that period of time, nor had he handled any type of firearm whatever, even making feeble excuses so as to avoid the many 'shoots' his friends arranged here in the country.

A cynical, saddened smile appeared at the thought of it all. His past had returned to haunt him. How many of the inhabitants of this close-knit community where they had chosen to settle down, would understand or even believe that the quiet affable man who lived in their midst had eliminated eight men from the face of the earth. They would scorn the idea and treat the informer with the ridicule such rubbish deserved; that kind of thing does not happen in real life, at least not here in Durham.

Marriages were supposed to be built upon the strongest foundations of a mutual love for one another, coupled with complete trust. The two ingredients moulded together, forming the steady foundation from which love could blossom and grow even stronger with the passing of time.

Then why had he never told Angela?

It had hurt John; this was the one thing he had kept hidden away from her, never being fully sure that she would have understood. Could it have been possible that, apart from the fact he had signed some vague and additional section of the Official Secrets Act, which only a privileged few were aware of, he was too ashamed of what he had done?

Returning to the present, he raised his eyes to the heavens. The rather ominous presence of a large mass of black-looking clouds hovering directly above caused him to wrap the large fur collar of his sheepskin coat more tightly about his neck, the movement a futile gesture at warding off the intensity of the cold. It was a bitterly cold mid-February morning, the thermometer would be showing well below freezing point, the earth underfoot as hard as concrete. The severity of the weather being more than ably aided and abetted by the force six winds blowing hard across the land from the direction of the North Sea, itself only a matter of a few miles away in the distance. Fresh falls of snow accompanied each renewed gust, some heavier than others, but each as eager as another in penetrating any unprotected area of flesh. Icy fingers probed at vulnerable barriers, searching eagerly for any possible weaknesses. Delicate crystal-shaped snowflakes danced mischievously about his feet, swirling crazily around the many rows of regimentally placed headstones by which he was surrounded, each one upright as if ready for inspection, the immediate scene faintly resembling myriads of drunken dervishes actively engaged in some childish prank. Walls of snow were climbing upwards, already completely covering the marble bases en route to their summits, as if intent on obscuring all visible signs of recognition to the outside world.

Crouching on one knee, he brushed away the loose snow in front of her headstone and placed the small bunch of flowers on the cold earth, the water inside the ornamental vase being solid ice.

"I'm sorry, flower," he whispered, his voice tailing away in the sound of the wind.

Sitting alone in the warmth and relative comfort of his car, Bob Looker, proud proprietor of the village's one and only taxi service, looked out of the window and observed the sad and dejected figure of his friend some fifty yards away inside the cemetery grounds, the sagging shoulders evidence enough of the grief the man still suffered, and in turn reflecting an uneasy discomfort in himself, as he too recalled the morning of her funeral. Angela Williams had been a strikingly beautiful woman, causing more than one of the male population to turn their heads and cast a second approving glance. But other than a polite smile and friendly acknowledgement, there was never any further encouragement on her part.

The old saying about time being a healer of wounds certainly did not seem to apply in the case of his friend, because if ever a man grieved for the loss of his wife, he did.

"'E must be bloody frozen standin' about out there," he said to himself, lighting up yet another cigarette amidst a further bout of coughing and spluttering, "Jesus, a'm goin' ta have ta give these bloody things up or a'll be lyin' alongside 'er."

Bob was forever promising his wife that he would give up the 'evil weed', but promising her was as far as it ever got, he did not possess the willpower to do it.

When the Williams's first moved to the village and became part of their small community, they had quickly formed a firm friendship, their likeable manner easy to get along with. But since the funeral, John had sentenced himself to the life of an almost total recluse, avoiding any visual contact with the rest of humanity. That was apart from the old couple who had been his neighbours since moving here, Tom and Mary Stead, who had taken the responsibility upon themselves to act as guardian angels to him. They tended his needs and made sure that he ate a regular meal, even when he was so drunk he did not realise they were there.

The old girl, she had to be eighty if she was a day, was one of the village 'characters', being the kind of person who could instil fear into children and adults alike with just one stare of her beady eyes; she had perfected this over the years. Bob himself had been subjected to one of these and had felt the cutting edge of her tongue on more than one occasion, the latest less than a month ago, when he had dared approach her to enquire about the state of John's health and frame of mind. Most people were aware of his late night treks over to the cemetery, but most were sensitive enough to leave well alone and not intrude into his privacy. Yet there were others who openly stated that the man 'had a tile loose', or had 'flipped his lid', and it was worrying for someone who cared.

" 'E's not crackin' up, is 'e Mary?" he had asked her.

She snorted in apparent rage and presented him with one of

those famous looks, her right eye suddenly developing a nervous twitch.

"Silly sod!" she cackled, moving towards him in a threatening manner, causing Bob to take a step backwards. " 'Corse 'e's not crackin' up as yer so nicely put it. Some fine bloody friend you've turned out ta' be, askin' daft fool questions like that. Da' yer think 'e's a loonie or summat? Should be put in a special room in Winterton, eh? 'S that what yer want fer 'im, is it?"

"Jesus Christ Mary," he protested,"A'm only askin' cos a'm worried about the man. It isn't natural the way 'e's goin' on, now is it?"

Mary had looked hard into his eyes, then her whole manner changed, there was no further need for her tyrant image, she knew Bob was a good friend. "Me'n ma' Tom's lookin' after 'im alright," she replied, "we're takin' good care of 'im, and as lang as we de', then 'e'll come to ne' harm."

" 'A know that, 'a know that," he said, "but 'e's nearly always permanently drunk, and 'e's wanderin' about the graveyard late at night. That isn't the behaviour of a rational man, now is it?"

She muttered something under her breath, then answered. "If it's tha' drink yer worryin' yersel' about, then don't. As far as that goes, 'e knows well enough when ta' stop, 'e can control it if 'e wants to. Anyway if a' remember right, there's more than 'im in this village that's fond of the odd tipple. Yer ain' wife is very partial to it, cos a've seen yer 'elpin' 'er across the road many a time, 'er net 'avin' the legs ta stand on so ta' speak." Bob had to smile to himself, as old as she was, she never missed a trick and her tongue still had the cutting edge of a new razor.

8

" 'E'll be alright, just yer wait 'n see," she added in a more understanding tone of voice, "everythin' takes time, that's all. Some things just 'appen ta take longer than others, but 'e'll come through in the end, just ye' wait 'n see if a'm not telling' ye' the truth."

Those final words had stuck in Bob's mind, " 'E'll come through in the end, just ye' wait 'n see if a'm not tellin' ye' the truth." It certainly appeared as if the old girl's prophecy was right, because whatever it was that had contributed to this sudden about turn in John's behaviour, had to be for the best. Outwardly his friend's appearance was as it always had been in the past, well turned out and clean-shaven. But on a careful study of his features, the combined effects of the last two years had taken their toll. The intake of alcohol and self-imposed seclusion being the major contributors to the fact.

Glancing at his watch, he suddenly realised that if his friend did not want to miss the train, they were going to have to set off soon. The snow was falling steadily and it did not take too much to close the road into the city. Sounding the car's horn to attract John's attention, he pointed to his watch and indicated for him to return to the car.

Turning somewhat unwillingly away from the graveside, John slowly began to retrace his footsteps in the snow; it was time to go. On nearing the taxi, an awareness of doubt and apprehension flooded over him. Fear caused his stomach muscles to tighten in premature anticipation of the unlikeliest of possibilities, like taking a step forward into the unknown. What feasible explanation could there be? He was twenty years older and well out of the way of things of the kind they required. What could they possibly hope to achieve by his apparent recall? The very presence of that small key assured him at least that there was a recall.

A deep depression added fuel to the fear; he did not want to leave the safety of this village they had both grown to love. It was their home, a home they had built together during the past fifteen years; everything in it was symbolic of their lives. John had been born and brought up in a nearby coastal colliery, but Angela had been raised in the more genteel way of life in the South West. To her, this move to the North East of England had equalled the great migrations of the past, into the far reaches of the wilderness. It did not take her long to lose the yearning to return to 'civilisation' and, like himself, she quickly developed a fondness for the area and its colourful inhabitants. The friendliness of the people about her, with their truly distinctive accents and outward ways, was something she had never experienced before, but she soon came to terms with it.

After enrolling in the Teachers' Training College for a refresher course, and being successful, she gained a position at the local junior school. Not being able to bear children herself, she opted for the next best thing. Time and time again she returned home with the troubles of her little 'bairns', and time and time again she went out of her way to help them as much as she could.

Having no qualifications to speak of, John found himself a job driving for one of the local haulage firms and their combined wages were very good - not that money worried him unduly. As long as he had enough in his pocket for a good night out and to 'stand his round', he was more than content. Life was progressing very nicely indeed.

The financial aspect of their marriage was well managed by Angela, this being one of the areas she excelled in. Her hobby was to dabble in stocks and shares, but always in a small way and if, at the end of the day, there was a profit to be gained, she was satisfied.

"You have to know the right time to make a killing," she used to tease him. Each time she uttered those words, he winced a little: if only she knew. All in all life was good to them, they were very much in love and, as an added bonus, they were financially sound. Just how sound he was not aware until after her death when the insurance company paid out on her policy, not that any amount of money could ever replace the woman he had lost. "We have to make preparations for the unexpected," she had stated, "you never know what's in store for us."

John remembered her astonishment at the substantial amount he had had in his own bank account at the time of their marriage, enough to purchase their small two bedroomed bungalow outright. The time for honesty had been then, but he lied to her by saying the money was left to him by some uncle. She had believed him then, as she always did; there was no reason not to. In plain truth, the money had been a kind of bonus for services rendered; the killing of four men for the section had been rewarded.

"Oway man!" said Bob, "Get yersel' in before yer freeze yer goolies off altogether. It's time we were on our way to the station, yer've got a train ta' catch."

John nodded in acknowledgement and climbed thankfully into the seat next to his friend. The warmth inside was more than welcome, his body began to thaw out and his fingertips began tingling.

"Yer ready for the off?" asked Bob.

"As ready as I'll ever be."

Staring hard into the face of his passenger, Bob smiled sympathetically, both understanding and respecting the feelings of the other man. Things were still far from being right with him and it showed.

The short journey to the railway station passed without any further communication between the two men, Bob engrossed in driving as carefully as possible in the conditions and John staring blankly out of the window at the whiteness all around them, with the countryside covered in a shroud of false purity.

"You alright mate?" asked Bob, after stopping the car outside the main door to the ticket office.

John stared for a while at his surroundings, then a soft smile appeared at the corners of his mouth. "Corse I'm alright," he answered, "it's all this fresh air, I'm not used to it, that's all."

"Yer sure about that?"

Opening the car door, John stepped out once again to face the elements, involuntarily shivering in the cold.

"Yer comin' back 'ome again, aren't yer?" persisted Bob, passing the large hide suitcase from the back seat.

"I'll be back, don't you worry about that," replied John, "it's just that I feel as though I 'ave to get away from it all, get myself sorted out once and for all........Anyway how much do I owe you for the ride?"

"Nowt, no charge for this 'un, but the next one 'll cost yer double, OK?"

"Thanks Bob, that seems more than fair to me. Now get

yourself off back home before you get snowed in, it's gettin' heavier. Tell you what, get the sledge out and take the kids over the moors, they'll love it."

"Right-o," answered Bob as he closed the door, "take care o' yersel' and a'll see yer when yer get back 'ome. We'll 'ave a few jars together."

With an added wave of his hand, he reversed the car into an arc, then slowly drove away from the station.

"That we will," answered John to the rear of the now disappearing vehicle. Taking a firm grip on the suitcase, he walked carefully over the few precarious yards to the station entrance and, after purchasing his ticket to London, he made his way onto the south bound platform. No instructions had accompanied the key, but instinct told him where to go, not that he expected the left luggage lockers to still be in the same place after all these years.

They had taken the trouble to contact him, there would be someone waiting, of that he was certain.

There were only a handful of fellow travellers and they were huddled in various corners and doorways in an attempt to keep warm away from the winds that whistled wildly throughout the full length and breadth of the station.

Within ten minutes the sound of the diesel engines could be heard in the distance, heralding the arrival of the impressive looking Inter City 125 express, surprisingly only a few minutes late. The falling snow had obviously failed to delay it much; as if it was eager to deliver him to his destination in all possible haste.

"It bloody well would be," he said to no-one in particular.

The distinctive sound of the public address system being switched on interrupted his thoughts, followed by a couple of

13

blistering coughs as the announcer cleared his vocal chords.

"The train now approaching platform two is the twelve fifty eight for London, calling at Darlington, York and Kings Cross stations only. Passengers for Sheffield and Leeds change at York."

A second 'click' signified the end of the information, the informant no doubt satisfied with his oration to the masses and more than keen to return to his statutory mug of British Rail tea.

Thinking along almost parallel lines himself, John remembered the flask of coffee Mary had careful prepared for the journey, more than liberally laced with brandy.

"It'll 'elp ta keep the chill out o'yer bones," she had said with a wink, "them trains 're draughty 'oles alright."

Before leaving his home, he had placed his arms around those frail shoulders, hugged her closely to him and kissed her withered cheek affectionately. This old woman and her husband had been his strength, caring for him when he had most needed it, easing him through the heartache and pain of losing Angela and, in general, offering a shoulder to cry on whenever he felt the need.

"Thanks Mary," he had said, "you 'n Tom have been as good to me as my own mum and dad, had they still been alive today. Without the two of you, I very much doubt whether I could have made it. You kept me going, when all I wanted to do was lie down and die. I'll never forget either one of you, and that's a promise."

His mouth felt parched and the need for something stronger than laced coffee was in him but he had made up his mind that he would not weaken, and about that he was adamant. Since opening the envelope and getting over the initial shock of seeing that key again, he had forced himself to reduce his intake of alcohol. He also appreciated the fact that he could not give it up immediately, that there would have to be a gradual decrease.

Although he had to admit that he drank almost to the extreme, he was definitely no alcoholic, and he convinced himself that if he really wanted to abstain then, with willpower and determination, he could prevail. Boarding the train with a comparative reluctance, he sought out an empty table, not relishing the idea of spending the next few hours in the company of some compulsive talker, who would surely tax his nerves.

John felt the need to be alone with his thoughts.

The task proved to be easier than he imagined, like the station, the train was woefully short on passengers.

'People with any commonsense at all would stop indoors on a day like this', he thought sarcastically.

After first removing the flask and carefully placing it on the table before him, he hoisted his suitcase up onto the luggage rack. Next he removed his heavy overcoat, folded it neatly and placed it on the vacant seat opposite, hopeful that it might deter anyone from thinking about sitting there. He settled down for the journey.

Staring through the moistened windows at the deserted station, he was troubled by a sadness he could not free himself of; the whole situation he now found himself in seemed so unreal. It was as if he had became detached from reality, having to act out some strange role he did not want, but from which there appeared to be no escape. At first he had thoughts of completely ignoring this obvious invitation, of locking himself away behind closed doors, hoping that he would be forgotten and somehow keeping the rest of the outside world with its troubles at bay. But thinking about it was as far as it had gone; he had never had a choice from the beginning. They knew, and he knew also, that once beckoned, he would respond. And here he was!

The guard's whistle sounded and immediately the sound of doors being slammed shut followed. Throttles were opened and the revolutions increased noisily. The train began its journey south, wheels gently rumbling over the points with a gently swaying of the carriages from side to side. Once clear of the railway sidings, they travelled over the old viaduct and into view of the Cathedral and Castle which stood so magnificently side by side dominating the skyline for miles, towering majestically over their united domain as they had done throughout the centuries.

Large white snowflakes were now cascading from the heavens onto the earth below, covering the many trees which lined both banks of the River Wear, to present the most picturesque scene, the like of which would have graced any festive card. He would remember this scene for a long time to come. With every rotation of the steel wheels under him, the impetus of the train increased and the distance between himself and the security of his home became greater. There was to be no turning back.

Unscrewing the top of the flask, he carefully poured a cup of steaming liquid, the strong aroma of brandy sifting through his nostrils. Carefully he took a sip, the flavour excellent; at least there was something he would enjoy about today's trip. As he gazed absentmindedly into the white void outside, the popular words of a well know ballad came into his mind.

'*I'm going to leave old Durham town, I'm going to leave old Durham town,*' Only one thing seemed wrong with those sentiments, that nothing was said about returning. John hoped this could not be some kind of omen, but he also realised that if the absolute ridiculous was about to happen, and they were expecting him to rejoin the section, then anything was possible. As the train forged its relentless way forward, gradually the combined effect of the heated compartment and the regular intake of Mary's very special coffee made his eyes heavier. Unaware of it, he lapsed into a deep sleep and unconsciously slipped back in time.

Back to where it had all started, almost another lifetime.... the beginning.

Chapter Two

The year was 1965, when the world and its neighbour were too interested in the much publicised war in Vietnam to concern themselves unduly with the insignificant campaign Britain happened to be engaged in against the communist guerilla forces of the Indonesian people, taking place in the hazardous jungles of Borneo.

John was twenty two years of age and serving as a leading mechanical engineer on board the frigate *H.M.S. Falcon*. At that particular time the ship was involved with the campaign in Borneo but, owing to her size, she was restricted to illuminating as many of the inland waterways as possible during the hours of darkness by firing 'starshell' over the jungle. It was hoped that this action would deter any guerilla activity or the ferrying of arms and supplies downriver to their forces. Reports occasionally filtered through to the ship's company of the odd skirmish here and there, involving either the Royal Marines or the contingent of Ghurkas who were also assisting. The main threat to the Marines did not come from the guerillas, but from the sodden terrain of the jungle itself, with dysentery and sickness being the main enemies. The Ghurkas and the guerillas were equal to one another in these conditions, with the tiny Ghurkas having perhaps the better of the reported confrontations.

Approximately once every fortnight, half a dozen small inshore patrol boats, or *'kumpits'* as they were more commonly known, would leave the rivers and rendezvous with the *Falcon* to replenish with fuel, fresh water, food and ammunition if needed. These *kumpits* were skippered by British officers of junior rank, sub-lieutenants or even lowly midshipmen, and crewed by ratings belonging to the Malay Navy. These little brown-skinned men were always armed to the teeth, like Mexican bandits on the rampage.

It all seemed rather ridiculous to John as he observed them scampering about, waving their guns in the air as if expecting an imminent attack. To his dismay, it was onto one of the larger *kumpits* he found himself seconded. Because one of the two engine room ratings had to be admitted to *Falcon's* sick bay, suffering from suspected appendicitis, the Engineering Officer had selected him as his replacement. "Only temporarily," he smiled, as John clambered unsteadily down the rope ladder into the small boat, an extra change of clothing stuffed into his bag. "Thanks very much sir, I might enjoy the change." It was meant to be a light hearted comment, but what a change it turned out to be.

The patrol boat he unwillingly became part of was at least thirty years old and her captain was a young 'subby' called Leonard Fotherington. Only an officer of obvious breeding could possess a name like that. On setting foot aboard her, he was handed a weapon and four extra clips of nine millimetre bullets.

"This is the Sterling machine gun, or the SMG, whichever you prefer," explained the officer, "it's yours for as long as you're with us. Get to know its function inside out and become familiar with reloading it in the dark; you may find that you need it. But whatever you do, don't go and shoot yourself with it, it could prove rather embarrassing."

John did not feel the need to reply to the officer's weak attempt at witticism, he was not to know that the recipient was a classified marksman and had used the Sterling quite a few times on the firing range, discovering that when fired it tended to pull from left to right.

'Jesus Christ, what've I dropped into this time', he thought, 'this fella can't be serious'.

It appeared to John actually that they all took everything seriously and that, if the need ever arose, they would be more than willing to anticipate trouble. There were six Malays on board, including his opposite number in the engine-room, and they seemed amused at having him join their ranks. One of them, obviously their self-appointed spokesman, sauntered over to him and pointed at the Sterling.

"No woman up jungle Johnnie," he said, showing yellow teeth, "plenty of bang-bang though."

John shrugged his tanned shoulders and smiled, everybody was 'Johnnie' to them.

'Little bastard,' he thought.

It took a further hour to complete replenishing, in that time John had a good look at the enclosed engine room; it stank of diesel. The only operating he would be called upon to do was to knock the large gear stick into forward or reverse; the throttles were controlled by the subby up on the bridge, a matter of four rungs directly upwards.

"Cast off," called the subby, "stand by with those fenders until we're clear of the ship's side."

Twenty minutes later they entered the mouth of the river, the other *kumpits* going their separate ways. All lights were extinguished and they slid quietly amongst the overhanging trees in complete darkness. Once hidden from the open sea, John found himself in a different world altogether, the weird sounds of the jungle echoing through the night. He half expected to hear that familiar Tarzan call pierce the stillness and see him swing across the river on one of those handily placed vines.

The young subby quickly explained to him what was expected. He was to alternate every four hours with his counterpart, who surprised him by eagerly shaking his hand. The first 'watch' was spent on the bridge, diving down into the engine room whenever the officer decided to do an about turn. When he was not actually in the engine room, he was to take charge of one of the two Bren guns mounted on either side of the bridge superstructure. For the second 'watch' he was to take up his 'action station' at the stern of the little vessel, his cover was two four feet stacks of empty ammunition cases filled with sand, the Sterling machine gun was at the ready.

"You ever fired a Bren gun?" asked the subby.

"A few times sir," he replied, then with an added degree of satisfaction, he continued, "represented Naval Command against Combined Services. I got the highest individual score."

"Ahhemmmmn," answered the subby, "good."

Hours of sleep were limited; if he happened to be on watch between the hours of midnight and four a.m. he was allowed the four hours until eight o'clock, and *vice versa*. He was to share one cramped cabin situated just aft of the bridge with the other engine room rating, whom he nicknamed 'Wanky'.

'Just great,' he thought, 'trust me to win first prize on a jungle cruise with a bloody chink as a bed-mate.'

He felt as sick as the proverbial parrot and silently cursed the engineer on board the *Falcon*, who would more than likely be sitting in the wardroom sipping at a gin and tonic. Officers do not drink they sip, and when they, too, got drunk, it was always down to high spirits. Only members of the lower-lower-deck get drunk, because they do not know any better.

At exactly ten p.m. that first night, and subsequently every night after, *H.M.S. Falcon* opened up with her main armament, firing starshell. The only appropriate place to be to fully appreciate its effects was directly under it, as they happened to be. Everything, no matter how small or insignificant, was immediately illuminated in its sheer brilliance. John likened it to being under the floodlights of his favourite football team at Roker Park in Sunderland; but this particular game would go on a lot longer than an hour and a half, and there would be no few pints and off to bed after it.

One thing worried him about the starshell: if they themselves were able to see everything so clearly, then they too must be sticking out like a sore thumb, sitting ducks for the enemy. He suddenly felt very vulnerable even if he did have the impregnable protection of the ammunition cases to cower behind. His imagination began to run wild and he visualised hoards of little brown-skinned men hiding behind every tree, all pointing their large weapons in his direction. When the flares had slowly drifted down amongst the vegetation of the jungle and extinguished themselves, as brilliant as the night had been seconds before, the sudden darkness was every bit as vivid, until thankfully the next round of starshell burst into the night. It was when the night was suddenly lit up that they hoped to surprise any guerilla movement or rafts being floated downstream ferrying supplies to the guerillas, but nothing was ever seen.

John attempted to sleep when he came off watch at four a.m., his eyes sore from peering into the undergrowth, but he had very little success, spending the entire four hours tossing and turning in his communal bunk. There is nothing less hygienic than waking someone up, then taking his place between not very fresh sheets, but there again submariners did it all the time and they did not complain.

Coming onto the bridge, he noticed the young subby looked as shattered as he himself felt, sprawled in his 'command' chair grasping an enamel mug of dirty brown liquid. It looked as if it had been scooped straight out of the river, with the leaves and twigs removed.

"Mornin' Williams," he greeted, "mug of tea?"

"Thanks sir,...could do with it. I'm absolutely knackered; couldn't get to sleep at all."

The subby's whole attitude seemed to have changed overnight; pouring out a mug of identical coloured liquid, he passed it to John.

"With us being the only two British on board, we'll fend for ourselves as far as our meals go. But once the fresh meat runs our, I'm afraid we're all in the same pan together. I hope you like curry, because these guys curry just about everything you could imagine."

Throughout the day they relentlessly patrolled their own stretch of river, up and down smaller tributaries running off at different angles to the main stream. All of this appeared to be a waste of time as far as John was concerned, his attitude differed entirely from that of the subby and the rest of the crew. If anything he was guilty of being rather lackadaisical about the whole matter; no-one had bothered to explain the politics of the thing to him, so it was difficult for him to appreciate that there was conflict taking place around him. He had neither seen nor heard anything to substantiate what the others believed, therefore he did not really accept it. The others were forever watchful, and trying in their own way to convey their fears to him, but it did not work. After three or four days living amongst them, they came to accept him and he them and friendships began to develop, each with its own distinct character. Obviously being in close contact with 'Wanky', John felt closer to him than the others, but all in all they were a pretty good bunch.

H.M.S. Falcon with its home comforts now seemed a thousand miles away and, if it had not been for her nightly starshell spectacular to remind him, the ship could have been.

On the sixth morning of their patrol, just as the beautiful dawn was about to break through the trees, there was sudden excitement amongst the men keeping lookout on the bows. One of them had spotted a raft drifting towards the boat; there were three figures on board, and they too had obviously seen the small patrol boat because they were frantically paddling the raft towards the river bank.

The subby thrust the twin throttles into the full ahead position and the little boat reacted almost immediately, surging ahead as if eager to prove herself capable of more than cruising for hours on end at a paltry three knots. Given the distance between the raft and the boat, however, there was only going to be one winner in this race, and they were still some hundred yards away when the three figures gathered whatever supplies they had on the raft and made off into the jungle. It was then that John saw that they were armed with rifles and that now made things seem a lot more serious to him.

By the time the small boat closed in on the raft, in mid-stream because of having too deep a draught to get any closer to the river bank, the three individuals were long gone. The jungle was so dense that there could have been fifty guerillas hiding not twenty feet away and they would not have been visible. One of the more senior Malays, the one who relieved the young subby on the wheel when he decided he needed to

25

sleep, grabbed a megaphone and began to shout into it in the direction in which the three had disappeared. John's heartbeat had increased and he realised he was being carried along on a wave of high anticipation; something had actually happened, those three men were actually their enemies.

"Order them to return to the river," shouted the subby, "or we'll damn well open fire."

'Open fire!' thought John, 'what the bloody 'ell we going to open fire at?'

The Malay crewman relayed the officers message over the megaphone and then they all waited for the response, weapons pointed in the general direction of the escape. No response came, not that John expected any.

The *kumpit's* main armament comprised one almost obsolete oerlerkin, left over from World War One, but the Malays were only too keen to show its effectiveness. All eyes focused on the subby and, after what seemed an age, he made his decision.

"Open fire!" he yelled.

Every weapon on board began to fire simultaneously, bullets screamed through the air, decimating the jungle vegetation in the immediate vicinity. Palm trees were almost stripped of their branches as round after round was spent harmlessly for absolutely no result. After a couple of frantic moments, the pungent smell of cordite filled the air around the crew, but there was no-one to be hit. John himself had spent the whole magazine of the Bren gun spreading an arc, but feeling quite foolish having to fire at nothing in particular. Not so the Malays; they were acting as if their very lives depended on it, the barrels of their Sterlings smoking.

"Cease fire!" screamed the subby, making himself heard above the din.

They remained stationed there for almost an hour, but the three men on the raft were gone. Before continuing the patrol, the subby ordered the raft to be destroyed, and the gunner on the oerlerkin made short work of it, reducing it to match wood in a matter of a few seconds, leaving no evidence of its ever having been there.

Placing the throttles into the familiar 'slow ahead' position once again, they carried on as before, patrolling their stretch of the river. If nothing else had been achieved that morning, they had at least prevented supplies reaching the guerillas for a while and had shown they meant business.

Shortly after one a.m. the following morning, during *Falcon's* spectacular, the bridge windscreen was shattered by automatic gunfire from the riverbank. Fortunately no-one was hurt in the attack, but the subby's pride took a dent; it was as if the guerillas wanted to prove to the men on patrol that they in their turn could destroy the little boat at any given time.

At the time of the firing, John was asleep in the communal bunk and he almost fell out of it with the shock. Groping for the Sterling in the darkness, he stumbled out of the cabin and ran aft to his action station, the brilliance of the starshell almost blinding him.

But it was all over and done with within a split second.

The next few days were uneventful. He was a lot more wary than previously, beginning to take things more seriously than at first, his eyes scanning the undergrowth nearby. He longed for the day when it would be time for his return to the *Falcon,* to be able to take a shower, to climb into a clean bunk with fresh sheets and not have to share it with anyone, as well as washing down his tot of rum, with a half dozen cans of Forrest Brown Ale. He could almost taste it. At present he did not smell too good at all and his teeth seemed to be coated with a layer of creosote, not to mention the fact that he was beginning to worry about his new diet of cold curried everything; it was beginning to taste quite palatable.

From time to time contact was made with the *Falcon* by means of an ancient radio, powered by an even more ancient generator which ran on kerosene. One this occasion, through intermittent crackles and interference, they were able to make out that they were to proceed to a 'safe village' just south of the Indonesian border. There they would find sufficient stores for a further five days patrol. The subby took note of the safe village's chart references and marked it out on his own map which he kept on the bridge.

It took almost two hours for the young officer to navigate their way to the village, but then he brought the small boat gently towards the decrepit-looking landing stage. There were no signs of life to be seen; the village appeared to be deserted. "Tie up," the subby ordered, and two seamen jumped onto the jetty and secured the hawsers. The young officer seemed worried. "There's supposed to be supplies," he said, "and there's supposed to be somebody in charge of them. Surely the *Falcon* must have confirmed this, we wouldn't have been sent all this way for nothing."

It was at that moment fate decided to take a hand in John's life. He heard the sound of a splash in the water coming from the stern section. Walking slowly towards the rear of the boat, he peered cautiously around the storage locker, only to find the five gallon drum which the kerosene was stored in bobbing away from the ship's side. It had been stored away as usual in the wooden pannier and held in place by rope, but the rope had frayed and snapped, depositing the drum into the flowing river.

Swimming did not bother John at all, but swimming in a river where there were quite a few snakes was a different matter altogether. Admittedly he could not see any of them at that time, but this was not to say there were not one or two slithering about amongst the nearest reeds. Rather than look like being a British coward and ask 'Wanky' to go in after the drum, he removed his sandals and dropped carefully into the murky water. Swimming watchfully after the wayward drum of kerosene, he grasped it by the handle and swam back to the side of the boat towing it behind him but found it too heavy to lift it back onto the upper deck with only one hand. His mouth opened and he was just about to call out for 'Wanky's' assistance.....when it happened.

All hell seemed to break out above him!

There were several long bursts of automatic fire, mixed with hideous and pitiful screams of pain and suffering and suddenly one of the Malay crewmen fell unceremoniously over the side, splashing into the water only a few feet away from where John had frozen half in and half out of the water. Blood immediately stained the area around them, splashing on John's body and face; he shuddered with horror.

Then as suddenly as it had started, the gunfire ceased, and then he heard the voices above him. To say that he was frightened had to be the understatement of the century, he was petrified; he dare not move nor look up in case they, whoever they were, were standing directly above him and he was to be next.

More voices followed, followed by an ear piercing scream of pain.

'Jesus', thought John, his heart pounding as if fit to burst.

One voice was distinct from the others, this voice was yelling in some kind of broken English similar to that used by the 'chinks', but it could not be them.

Another scream, but this time he heard a curse, and this curse was in proper English. It had to be the subby, but what was happening to him he dared not try to imagine.

A couple of minutes passed, and between the shouts and the young officer's screams, John was beginning to calm himself down. One thing was certain to him, he could not remain where he was, stuck like a limpet mine to the side of the patrol boat. Looking over to the far river bank, he soon ruled against attempting to escape by swimming over; he was sure to be seen and, in any case, he had been lucky so far in coming into contact with none of those fearsome water snakes. He was never quite sure what made him decide to climb on board the stern, whether it was his intention to try and help the subby, or the fear of having a snake clamp its teeth into him.

Releasing his grip on the handle of the kerosene drum, he allowed it to slide back into the water, then he pulled himself slowly between the bottom guard rail and the deck of the boat. The first thing he set eyes on was his very own Sterling machine gun, he remembered placing it between the ammunition cases to see what was going on in the village, and being as surprised as the subby had been when they found nothing.

'We should 've fucked off then,' he decided. Sliding himself along the hot deck on his stomach, he found a temporary haven between the cases; never was he more pleased for their cover, and overjoyed at grasping hold of the Sterling. All the time he took to get out of the water, until he stood up with the Sterling firmly in his hands, the subby kept on screaming in obvious agony. John did not have any idea what he was going to do, but he realised he had to try and help the officer some-how; it seemed as if he were the only one who could. Stalking along the upper deck, he made his way agonizingly slowly towards the area of the bridge; sweat poured from his body and his hands felt too weak to take the weight of the weapon. Carefully peering around the bulkhead, his eyes took in a horrible sight, one which he would never forget as long as he lived; that quite possibly not too long. The bullet-ridden bod-ies of the Malays, including that of his new friend 'Wanky', were scattered over the deck which was literally covered with their blood. If anything acted to make him determined to do something, it was that sight; they had not just been shot, they had been slaughtered.

Three men, their butchers, stood with their backs to him, totally ignorant of his presence amongst them. Sweat stained their jungle garb as they towered above and threatened the young subby lying on the deck, one of the men was shouting at him and prodding the bloody tip of a machete into a ragged bullet hole in the young officer's stomach, twisting it a little as it entered. This was the cause of the screams.

"Why you basta'ds 'ere?" he yelled, cutting into the wound again, "Why you cum 'ere....this our land?" John decided that he had to do something before it was too late, he could not let the subby suffer any longer. It was down to a plain simple matter, kill or be killed, because he had no doubt they intended to finish the job once their entertainment was com-plete.

As he stepped away from the bulkhead and out into the open, the subby's eyes met his and hope flickered in them through the mist. This served to act a warning to the three guerillas, they swivelled as one in John's direction, their eyes falling on the threatening presence of the Sterling which was pointed at them. It was then they completely surprised John by dropping their own weapons on the deck as if they were suddenly red hot, and placing their hands on top of their heads, indicating surrender. He stared long and hard at the bodies of the Malay crewmen and the young subby's blood slowly pumping his life over the deck, then into the eyes of the men responsible for all this carnage.

"You bastards must be jokin'," he shouted, "fuckin' jokin'." Without any hesitation, he pulled the trigger and kept the pressure on. There were approximately twenty two nine milli-metre bullets in the magazine clip, and they ripped into the bodies of the three guerillas, their clothing torn into shreds by the impact. John stood over their lifeless forms, the barrel of the Sterling smoking, no feeling of guilt or remorse at having killed them.

Then, kneeling down beside the young subby, he gently touched his shoulder. "Sir," he said quietly, "you still with us?"

The officer's eyes flickered open and he tried to smile. "I'm still here," he said, his voice strained, "now for fuck-sake get us out of here before any more show up." But they were not to be that lucky, bullets began to ricochet all around them, pinging off the bulkheads and going out into space. Lying flat on the deck, John peered carefully around the bridge housing and looked down the landing stage to the closest of the build-ings. Two more guerillas were standing firing their automatic rifles. Whether or not they had been there all the time, John did not know. It was to be hoped they were not the front runners belonging to a second group.

"The Bren," gasped the subby, "use the Bren."

John had not thought of that. he was too busy trying to find an extra magazine for the Sterling. Crawling over until the Bren was directly above him he began to pull himself up by the butt, when suddenly he felt a terrific pain in his right leg and he collapsed into an untidy heap next to the officer. Blood poured freely from a hole about six inches above his knee, but there was no exit hole, so whatever went in was still there. The air was thick with bullets, splinters from the wooden deck flew everywhere, it could only be a matter of seconds before another one hit either the subby or himself.

Dragging himself back to the Bren, his leg almost useless, he pulled himself up once again, taking the full weight of his body onto his uninjured leg. Both guerillas, now confident of a kill, were out in the open and running towards the boat; their rifles at the ready. When they became aware of John's head reappearing and the long barrel of the Bren moving in their direction, they decided to make a hasty about turn and ran towards the cover of the nearest hut. The smaller of the men made it, being the faster of the two as well as the more fortunate. His guerilla friend was not so lucky, the larger .303 calibre bullets almost cut him in half, hurling his body off the jetty into the river. John then concentrated his fire on the hut where the smaller man was hiding, sending long bursts into its fragile walls, not knowing whether or not he had actually hit him.

'Time we wasn't 'ere,' he decided.

Ramming the throttles into the forward thrust, he expected the little boat to move quickly away from the landing stage, but nothing happened. The engine revolutions increased loudly, but the boat remained where it was. It was not in gear!

Somehow he agonisingly clambered through the hatch and

almost fell down the four rungs of the ladder into the engine room, seemingly taking an age before he was able to knock the gear lever forward; blood from his injured leg flowing freely over his sandal into the bilges. By the time he returned, the young officer had managed to sit himself upright, his hands grasping at the nasty looking hole in his tanned stomach.

"The ropes," he grimaced through clenched teeth, "we're still tied to the jetty."

"Bollocks," cursed John, "I wish ta' fuck we was well outa' here."

There was no time for the appropriate 'leaving harbour' procedure, so he scooped up the blood stained machete and, moving as quickly as he could, slashed through both bow and stern lines. The little boat was free. Still there were no signs of life coming from the hut. Maybe he had hit the remaining guerilla, but there again it was possible that the guerilla had made good his escape and was on his way for help. If there did happen to be other guerilla groups in the vicinity, then there was no doubt they would have heard the gunfire and would be coming to investigate it.

On moving the throttles this time, he was very relieved when the boat began to move away from the landing stage, away from the jetty of death where the ten men, maybe even eleven, had lost their lives in a vicious encounter. The small body of the Malay crewman bobbled about in the boat's wake as they passed by him, but much as he wanted to, he had neither the strength nor the time to lift it on board.

With one hand concentrating on steering the boat, he delved into the first aid box and brought out a handful of lint padding; he handed them to the officer.

"Press these over the hole," he instructed, "an' keep as much pressure on as you can, it should stop the bleedin'"

Sub-Lieutenant Fotherington looked into John's eyes and did exactly as he was told. "Thanks Williams," he whispered weakly.

John then removed a large bandage from the box and wrapped it tightly about his own wound. "St. John couldn't get 'ere," he said, trying to smile, "so 'e sent me instead."

The little boat was forging its way through the murky waters, but John realised that he did not have a clue where they were. He looked at the subby, but he had closed his eyes and his head lay at an angle.

"Which way do we go?" he shouted at him, "Come on subby....which bloody way outa' here?"

The officer's head lifted slowly and his eyes flickered open again, looking desperately around the bridge.

"We safe?" he asked quietly, "We safe yet?"

"Corse we're not safe yet," replied John, "we'll not be safe until we get back to the *Falcon*, but I don't know which way to go. Do I just follow the river downstream?"

The subby nodded his head, "Yes, follow the river."

Realising that he would not get much help from the officer, he rammed the throttles to their maximum, the engines were going to be well and truly tested by the time he was finished with them, there would be no stopping for any pedestrians this time. Neither being a coxswain nor a seaman rating, he decided that as long as he steered the boat down the middle of the river, they should not be in any danger of running aground; that was definitely the last thing he needed right now. Three long and painful hours, the river twisting and turning one way and then the other, and the pain in his leg throbbing in time with the old Perkins diesels below, and then at last it widened and they were out into the open sea.

H.M.S. Falcon was still where he had last seen it, as if time had stood still, and the last thing he remembered seeing was all those inquisitive faces spread along the upper deck staring down at him.

He was airlifted from the R.A.F. station on the tiny island of Gan in the Indian Ocean within three days, having had the bullet removed from his leg by the surgeon on board the *Falcon*. On arriving back at Lyneham in Wiltshire, he was placed in an unmarked ambulance and taken to a private home somewhere in Kent, where a doctor awaited his arrival. The whole situation more than puzzled him at the time, he wondered why he had been flown back to the United Kingdom, when surely the British Military Hospital in Singapore was nearer.

And where was the subby? Why all the secrecy surrounding his own whereabouts? It was three months before the limp disappeared altogether, he was almost as good as new. During this time, apart from the regular visits from the doctor and physiotherapist, one other person came to interview him, a Commander Ward belonging to the Admiralty hierarchy. His visits resembled more of a question time with an interrogator, wanting to find out exactly what sequence of events led up to the confrontation with the guerillas. Photographs of a dozen different villages, from a dozen different angles, were shown to him.

Were any of the villages the one they arrived at?....... No.
Are you positive?.......Yes.
They opened fire first?.....I was in the river at the time, but it

definitely looked that way to me.

Did Sub-Lieutenant Fotherington study his charts before going into the village.....Yes.

How many guerrillas were there?........I saw five.

How many guerrillas did you kill?......Four. Three with a Sten gun and the fourth with the Bren gun.

At the end of the day, it appeared to John that, after taking into account his version of what happened and adding it to the one taken from the young subby, it was finally decided that Fotherington had unfortunately erred in his calculations. Not only had they entered the wrong village, they had entered the wrong village on the wrong side of the border, a navigational error of approximately five miles.

Commander Ward never informed him of his final conclusions, but it appeared that both Governments were aware of what had taken place, of the unfortunate loss of life suffered by both sides and, rather than risk a possible international incident, they had decided to sweep it under the carpet. The families of the six Malay crewmen would never be told the truth about the deaths of their loved ones; all because some inexperienced officer had been in error.

Sub-Lieutenant Fotherington, after recovering from his wounds, was given a medical discharge and returned once more to civilian life, after being persuaded to sign an undertaking never to make the incident public. A similar statement was produced for John, which he too signed. If they wanted to evade responsibility, who was he to argue?

Commander Ward's interest now centred upon John himself and he attempted to investigate his innermost thoughts. How had he felt after killing four human beings? Did he worry about it? Did he lose any sleep? Were there nightmares? Why

37

did he decide to shoot the man on the left before the one on the right? What did he feel as he held onto the boat and heard the firing above? Was he proud of what he had done? After all everyone could not have done what he did, he had saved an officer's life. Could he kill again? This line of questioning seemed sadistic and unreasonable to John, and eventually he ceased to co-operate since his only reason for doing so was that the officer represented authority, and from the age of sixteen he had been taught to respect authority.

A person could only take so much rubbish.

"Look sir," he said, after one of the Commander's sessions, "I don't know what you want of me, or what you're after. All I can say is that when I was in the water and heard all the shootin' going on above me, I was shit frightened. If I'd a' had the lungs to swim all the way back to the *Falcon* underwater, then I would 'ave done just that. I did what I had to do so's I could get out of there in one piece.....I didn't fancy the idea of endin' up lyin' alongside those other poor bastards. As far as me killin' those four men goes, and savin' the subby's life...then fair enough. No, I have not lost any sleep over it..it hasn't bothered me. All I was really bothered about was myself...you've heard the old saying 'fuck you Jack, I'm alright'......well I am."

Well he had it off his chest at last, he now fully expected the Commander to go off it and explode into a rage; but he did not. Closing his large file, he nodded his head at John and smiled.

"Good enough," he said.

He then explained to John that he was in charge of a new and experimental section which had just recently been sanctioned by the authorities, with direct responsibility to combat the ever increasing threat of terrorism. Only men of exceptional quality were to be considered as part of his 'team', men who would unflinchingly obey his command, no matter what they thought. In his considered opinion, after their series of interviews, John could eventually become an integral part of the operation.

Was he interested?

The Commander held out his hand to John.

For some unknown reason, John Williams accepted both the offer and the officer's handshake. There was something about the older man which appeared to be genuine, and in any case it definitely sounded a bit out of the ordinary.

Once the Commander had left the premises, he went into the library and found a dictionary.

"Integral," he said to himself, "that's a new one on me."

Chapter Three

After being reclassified as medically fit to return to duty, with all visible signs of his limp having totally disappeared, John left the comfort of the private nursing home, dressed inconspicuously in civilian clothing. His uniform, plus the remainder of his kit which he had left on board the Falcon, had been forwarded to the Royal Naval Barracks at Chatham.

Pleased as he was to be out of the place, he admitted to himself that he would miss his long walks in the extensive woods which formed part of the home, and the fresh smell of the English countryside that went with it.

Although he was now an official member of the Commander's newly formed section, the pretence was that he was joining the staff of the Commander-in-Chief, Home Fleet, which was regarded throughout the service as a highly enviable posting to acquire.

On arriving at the barracks and completing the tedious 'joining barracks' procedure, he was eventually taken to a small detached office block standing quite some distance from the rest of the main buildings.

"Your cabin's at the far end," instructed the duty Petty Officer, "an' a very nice one it is an' all. How'd yer manage to get yourself a fair old number like this? I wouldn't mind gettin' on the C-in-C's staff myself."

"Got to know the right people, that's all," replied John with a wink.

"Hummph!" exclaimed the P.O. and began to walk back towards the main gate, "Got to be shaggin' the right people's more like it."

After settling in his neat little cabin, he lit the coal fire, took a shower and turned in for the night. He had the feeling that tomorrow was to be the start of something important.

Early the next morning, freshly shaved and dressed in his number 8's, under the supervision of an old Chief Gunnery Instructor, he was taken to the far extremities of the barracks, where an underground firing range which had not been in use for over ten years had been converted for his induction training. It contained an array of weapons ranging from the handgun and rifle to the more damaging Remington pump-action shotgun, the type favoured by the American Police force as an anti-riot deterrent. Hardboard figures were placed in strategic places, in various poses, these represented the 'opposition'. Every day for the next month, apart from Sundays, was spent in the Chief's company on the range, until he became effective with each weapon and the cutout figures had been shot to pieces.

"Speed and accuracy, laddie," was the old man's constant advice, "speed and accuracy. When the day comes, and mark my words it will, I want you to be ready and able to face up to the challenge."

John admitted to himself that he had willingly, if not eagerly, accepted the Commander's offer, but he was still unaware of what it entailed. He often wondered about the fact that, apart from himself, no-one else had made an appearance and the office block still remained unoccupied.

Where were the others?

Were there any others?

When the Gunnery Instructor had satisfied himself with John's prowess, he reported his findings to the Commander.

"A natural, Sir," he explained, "every now and then one

crops up. He possesses one of the best 'eyes' I've ever come across, possibly *the* best."

"Good," nodded the officer, "and his temperament?"

"Perfect. He'll do just fine for you, Sir."

This report more than satisfied Commander Ward, what with the explicit account given by Fotherington on his actions against the guerillas in Borneo, coupled with the feelings he himself had about the man, he knew that his choice would prove to be the right one.

Things were beginning to take shape. The section was now complete as to personnel. Each one was selected and highly trained in his own particular field of competence, each one a specialist. In addition, an informer belonging to the terrorist group had been uncovered, his greed for money obviously stronger than his political beliefs. It was almost time for the encounter, but it was up to the Commander to decide when the section was ready; there could be no possibility of failure.

The second stage of John's education was taken on by an impressive looking Physical Training Instructor, and he taught the art of self preservation. Not the more traditionally used methods, but an unsophisticated kind which made use of every dirty trick in the book and some which the P.T.I. had come up with himself. The honourable art of fisticuffs went out of the window and the ancient laws of the jungle came in.

In this department of life, John had previously regarded himself as more than adequately provided. During the seven years he had been in the 'mob' he had served his apprenticeship, sometimes painfully, in many of the finest arenas in the world. From the notorious Gut in Malta, to Boogie Street in Singapore and downtown Wanchai in Hong Kong, his defences had been well and truly tested by Americans, Australians and even our own British Forces when there was no-one else. As will happen with any worthwhile trade, he suffered setbacks and indignities in the early stages of his learning. But, as with any good wine, he gradually improved with age and experience. It was like life in general: you either adapted and came to terms with the problems, or you suffered the consequences of your folly. John's thoughts about it all were a little premature, the P.T.I. introduced him to levels of street fighting which were almost unbelievable, even highly questionable; but at the end of it he was wiser for the visit.

The second stage completed, the third and final one commenced. Because, to all intents and purposes, he was still a serving member of the Royal Navy, an adequate front had to be provided for him. It was decided that he should attend a crash course to familiarise himself with the basic principles of Naval Law and its disciplinary procedures. He had removed his beloved 'propeller' insignia, designating the engineroom branch, and replaced it with the 'crown' representing the dreaded Regulating branch.

If his mess-mates could see him now, strutting about dressed as a Leading Regulator, they would not believe their eyes. But then again, they could hardly believe their eyes the last time they saw him, being hoisted on board in a stretcher, bodies and blood all about him on the little *kumpit*.

"You bearin' up under the strain?" asked the old G.I. with a wry smile, "It's not everybody becomes a Regulator overnight."

44

John looked down at the brand new gold coloured crown adorning his uniform and shrugged. "Not too keen on this side of things, I can't get used to people sneerin' at me when a' walk past," he admitted. "You got any idea of what's goin' on, Chief?"

The older man nodded sympathetically, understanding John's feelings of anxiety and understandable curiosity.

"Listen son," he said, "a hell of a lot's gone into organising this operation. You'n me's just a couple of the smaller cogs in a much bigger wheel, part of a team hopin' to stamp out terrorism and the bastards behind it all. Commander Ward is our leader and it's all brand new to us as well.....Somethin' like going with a virgin for the first time, we 'ave to feel our way gently into things before makin' our move. We don't want to get our fingers snaffled off before we get anywhere...now do we?"

This was the longest speech he had heard from the Chief, but at last the purpose of the training he had undergone was beginning to unfold itself to him. How could be have been so ignorant as to the evident facts? The reason why he was the only one to use the firing range became clear to him now.

Because he had killed before, he was expected to do it again. The time for disclosing all the facts to him came a few weeks later, almost three months to the day since he had left the nursing home.

"Morning, Williams," said the Commander, after John had been summoned to his office, "sit down and make yourself comfortable." Opening a large brown envelope, he removed a file and studied its contents for a few moments, eventually nodding his apparent approval. "I've nothing but glowing reports on your progress," he said, "you've done better than

I dared hope for. No doubt you're anxious to find out what it is you've become involved in and what specific role you have to play in it. At last I am in a position to enlighten you. As I explained at the very beginning, our section has been authorised to stamp out this growing threat of terrorism before it gets a good hold in this country."

Passing a photograph to John, he continued, "I want you to study those features very carefully, until you become so familiar with them you would be in no doubt whatever that if you came face to face with this man, you would know him instantly." Whilst John concentrated his attention upon the face in the photograph, the Commander carried on with his explanation.

"All personnel selected to become part of this section were thoroughly screened before being considered for acceptance and each man is a specialist in his own right." He paused, then added, "In your own case John, it's your undoubted talent with the handling of firearms. You've more than proved that already."

Switching his attention from the face in the photograph, he looked into the officer's eyes. He now realised fully just how serious his new involvement was going to be; the likes of it were unknown to him. He was no longer to be Jack the lad, getting pissed with the rest of his mates on a run ashore in the lowest of dives and a quick leg over with some loose living damsel before jumping into a taxi back to the ship.

That life was gone forever, but what of the new one?

"As you will no doubt be aware," continued the Commander, "there's been an increasing number of bombings in the London and South coast areas. A number of innocent people have already lost their lives, more have been horribly injured and maimed for life. These include women and children whose only mistake was being in the wrong place at the wrong time; families have been torn apart by these so-called freedom fighters from the Middle East. Their demands are for our government to release ten political prisoners who are being held in prisons throughout the country. They think that by murder and threats they will make us bend to their demands.... but they're wrong, our resolve will become all the greater. That is why we have been given the go-ahead to use whatever means are in our power to effect the elimination of this threat.''

John's study of the face in the photograph was complete. It was of a man of middle-eastern appearance, aged somewhere in his late twenties or early thirties; a couple of blemishes on his right cheek and a slight scar across the bridge of his nose. He had a shock of black hair and moustache to go with it. But the thing that struck one most forcibly were the man's eyes; they were deep blue, somewhat odd for such a dark skin, they seemed to stare right into John's own, as if issuing a challenge to him.

"I'd recognise him sir," he said, "no doubt about that."

Replacing the photograph in the file, the officer looked intently at the younger man's face, as if attempting to read his mind. "John," he said quietly, "that man is an animal. Intelligence reports show him to be responsible for the deaths of at least two dozen people; it's our responsibility."

Commander Ward stopped speaking, as if to allow time for John to digest what was being told to him. An air of expectation filled the room, the clock on the wall ticked away as if it were as big as Big Ben. "If you have any doubts whatsoever, or qualms about what has to be done, then now is the time to speak out before you become involved any further."

It was true, he had heard all about the bombings and had felt revulsion at the deaths and hatred for the people responsible. But actually to be placed in a situation where he himself would be confronted by them was another matter. Surely this was a matter for professional people, the Special Branch or even the renowned Special Air Services. Then he realised what the Commander's speech had meant, it was with just such a professional body that he was now involved and he felt ashamed of his doubt. Here he was, chosen from countless others only too willing, being given the opportunity to punish the evil-doer, and he was hesitating over his answer.

"I've no doubts sir," he said positively, "none at all."

It was on the morning of November the fifth; John was again called to the Commander's office.

"Until this moment we have been powerless to halt this reign of terror," said the officer, "but owing the diligence of others, the situation has changed...we now know the bomber's next venue."

The next statement was almost expected, as if John had had a premonition. "I want you to kill that man," said the officer, "on no account must he be allowed to escape retribution. The informer is under the misapprehension that all we want to achieve is his apprehension, but apprehension alone is unsatisfactory.....he must be eliminated."

So there it was, and now he knew for certain. He had had a feeling that he was being prepared for such an operation, and he was right.

"Can you kill this man, John?"

Surprisingly enough the suggestion did not shock him and,

after glancing at the photograph of the terrorist once again, he fully realised there could be no other solution. But when he came face to face with him, could he kill again?

Borneo had been a different situation altogether, he had killed on the spur of the moment, without too much time to think about the consequences; but this time he knew in advance. The wise words of the old Gunnery Instructor now seemed very relevant. Had he known what lay ahead?

"Never forget laddie, a target is a target. Do not allow yourself to consider the human element."

It was at that moment he became aware of a strange voice in the room, as if some third person were present with them, and it was this third person who was speaking on his behalf.

"Yes sir," it said, "I'll do it."

No ifs or buts, he had definitely heard this third voice commit him to killing this bomber, and it was only then that he realised that the strange voice of this intruder was his own. The responsibility now rested squarely upon his shoulders, but the question still remained......could he actually do it?

"When sir?" he asked quietly.

"Tonight John."

John's mouth almost opened in disbelief.

'Fuckin' hell,' he thought, 'Tonight!'

Next came the details of the operation. The terrorists' next target was to be the large crowds expected to gather at the site of the annual bonfire held on Plymouth Hoe. There had already been a meeting with other section members, the wheels were already in motion, he had been the final cog. Had he refused, then a replacement was on standby to take his place; all situations had been covered.

"All things have to be considered," said the Commander,

"the lives of our people are too important to gamble with."

There had been no time for John to wrestle with his conscience. Maybe this had been the whole idea; the longer he had to ponder over the rights and wrongs of it, the more possible for him to change his mind. It was not the kind of thing one does every day.

This was to be his first encounter with the key. It was to open a specified locker in the left luggage compartments on Waterloo station. The number completely unforgettable, number thirteen....unlucky for some, but unlucky for whom? After lunch, and smartly dressed in his number two uniform and raincoat, he handed in his blue coloured 'special duties' station card to the duty quartermaster at the main gate and walked out of barracks, *en route* to that most famous of all Naval cities. It was as if, like Sir Francis Drake centuries before him, John Williams' future was bound up with Plymouth Hoe. When the crucial moment arrived, he only hoped that his own actions would be as positive and successful as those of Sir Francis; but only time would tell.

Commander Ward had left Chatham immediately after his meeting with John, one of the section had been detailed to follow the young man and report his movements, as a precautionary measure only. A lot rested upon the young shoulders of John Williams, but the Commander was positive that his selection of him would be fully justified. The Minister responsible for the section's being had been a little worried about entrusting so much to one so young; twenty three years of age was considered still relatively young. Nevertheless the Minister had bowed to the officer's wishes; the young man

50

had not been too young in the jungles of Borneo. He had acted then like a seasoned veteran, and the Commander expected nothing less on the Hoe tonight. November the fifth was an important date in the British history and it would certainly be so for the future of the section.

On his arrival at Waterloo station, John made his way directly to the left luggage department and located the number thirteen locker. Pausing momentarily before turning the key, he thought over what it was he had agreed to do. Nine months ago all he had cared about was making sure he had plenty of money to have a good time with his mates and let the rest of the world go fuck itself. Now here he was, four dead men under his belt and on his way to kill the fifth. He did not feel like a killer, and he was sure that he did not look like a killer; reality was very different from films. One thing was certain; if when the time came for him to pull the trigger he froze....then that would be the last thing he ever did in his life. The olive-skinned man with the piercing blue eyes would surely have no qualms whatsoever about killing one more. One of the many details outlined by the Commander was that the terrorist always carried an automatic pistol in a harness under his left arm.

'Jesus Christ,' he cursed to himself, 'what the fuck 'ave I let myself in for this time?'

He turned the key in the lock and opened the door. Inside was a brown coloured holdall, the likes of which thousands of matelots possessed. Carefully removing it, he found it to be quite bulky and suddenly became self conscious about its contents, as if everyone on the station also were aware of it.

"What you need to carry out the operation will be inside the locker," the Commander had informed him, "do not let it out of your sight."

John was now physically equipped for his part of the mission.

Five minutes before the Plymouth train was due to depart, he made his way to the platform and handed his ticket to the collector, who appeared to look strangely at him. Did he know? Did everybody know all about what he was supposed to do? It seemed to John that everybody in the whole world knew what he was carrying in the holdall.

"Go on son," smiled the ticket collector, "the train won't wait all day, not even for Jack."

"Yeh, thanks," replied John.

Once on the train, after it had started its journey westwards, he went to the nearest toilet and locked the door behind him. Placing the holdall on the wash-basin, he unzipped it and peered inside.

'Jesus!' he thought, 'they're not takin' too many chances, might as well 'ave given me a bazooka.' Inside was a Sterling machine gun with a full clip of ammunition strapped to its barrel. It didn't take too much of a marksman to hit someone close up with one of these.

Before leaving the safety of the toilet, he gave the weapon a thorough examination; it was in perfect working order. All that was required was the slightest pressure on the trigger mechanism.

Throughout the remainder of the journey, the holdall and its deadly contents remained between his feet on the floor of the carriage. Although he had travelled this same route many times before, today it seemed twice as long.

On arriving at Plymouth, he walked out of the station and into the dark night air, the cold making him shiver involuntarily. "N.A.A.F.I. club please," he informed the driver, as he clambered into the awaiting taxi.

"Yer off to the bonfire, Jack?"

"No bloody danger," replied John with a smile, "if I can see it through the windows of the bar, then that's close enough for me. Too many screamin' kids runnin' all over the place..... can't stand the little sods."

This seemed to amuse the driver and he drove away from the station car park. The car moved through the busy streets of Plymouth, negotiating the rush hour traffic; John watched the crowds of people on their way home after a day's work. How many of them could hazard a guess at the reason he was visiting their City?

'I've got to pull mysel' together,' he warned himself, 'before I balls things up for everybody.'

"Here we are," the driver interrupted his train of thought, "that 'll be four bob to you." John paid the fare, giving him an extra shilling tip, and climbed into the darkness. The N.A.A.F.I. club was at the bottom of the Hoe, with a walkway leading up to where the bonfire was built, its silhouette clear enough to see on the skyline. Small groups of people were already making their way towards the site, children running about obviously having a good time and expecting an even better one when all the celebrations got under way.

'I wish it would rain,' thought John hopefully, 'then everybody might go 'ome.' No such luck, it was a crisp and clear night with a biting wind, hardly a cloud in the sky.

"No second thoughts, John?" a voice from behind spoke.

Turning, he was surprised to find Commander Ward standing behind him, a slight smile on his lips. At least he was not on his own.

"I'd be lyin' to both of us if I said that I wasn't," he replied honestly, "but when the time comes, I wont let either of us down."

"Back up has been arranged." the Commander said, "Although you may feel you're alone out there, I assure you friends are close at hand. We've received information from our informer within the last half hour; everything is going as planned. Our man will be wearing one of those donkey jackets, the type favoured by our counterparts in the Merchant Navy, and the explosive device will be carried in a small duffle bag..... Believe me John, the device will be powerful enough to kill a hell of a lot of innocent people here tonight. But the bomb is someone else's problem, all you have to do is concentrate on its carrier."

"Right sir."

"One thing that I must stress to you," continued the officer, "and that is before you take any action, you must be positive you are well away from the immediate vicinity of the crowds. Be patient, eventually the opening will present itself to you and when it does, it's up to you. That's all I have to say, John, good luck."

John nodded and walked away from his superior and entered the N.A.A.F.I. club to wait. Someone would be in touch when he was needed so, after ordering a rum and coke from the bar, with the full bottle of coke going into the glass, he found himself an isolated corner and settled down. He did not know how long he would be there, but nothing looked more out of character than a matelot sitting in the bar without a drink in front of him. The one would last.

It was seven fifty when the commissionaire came into the bar and announced that there was a phone call for a Leading Regulator Williams in the foyer. This was it.

"Williams here," he said into the phone.

"He's on his way, dressed as expected," replied some strange voice on the other end, "should be there in about five minutes.....Good luck mate."

The phone went dead.

John walked away from the phone booth, the holdall firmly grasped in his hands; he went into the 'Gents' and found an empty cubicle. Once again he unzipped the bag, this time removing the weapon to fix the full clip of nine millimetre ammunition into place. Drawing the spring loaded bolt, he made the Sterling ready and put the safety catch on. Fastening the buttons of his raincoat and turning the collar up, he jammed the old white cap firmly on top of his head, not wanting it to blow off at an inopportune moment. He took a deep breath to steady himself, left the toilet and, after saying goodnight to the commissionaire stationed by the door, walked out into the cold November air.

He had decided on his course of action and hoped he was a good enough actor. Swaying from side to side he was like just another drunken matelot already at this early hour well over the top. This was not an uncommon sight in any Naval city or town where 'Jack' had long since become part of the scenery; and as long as the sailors behaved themselves reasonably well then no-one bothered too much. In any case there were always the Naval patrols to keep them in check, if things sometimes tended to get out of hand.

There were large crowds heading all in the same direction and he mingled amongst them easily enough, making his way slowly uphill, singing as he went. Dozens of children were already in the mood, running wildly about the Hoe, a couple of them even bumped into the stupid looking sailor who could not even walk straight. It was all good fun for them and they had a laugh at his expense. As he was nearly halfway between the club and the bonfire, there was an almighty 'Whoosh!' which filled the air, and the bonfire was suddenly engulfed in flames. For a second John's heart missed a beat, until he realised that it was simply that the bonfire had been lit. Until that precise moment, he had failed to see any sign of the bomber, but he became aware of his presence then. The crowds had halted as one to stare at the bonfire with flames already clawing their way towards the figure of the guy perched on the top. Everyone excepting one; a solitary figure dressed in a donkey jacket and carrying a small duffle bag over his left shoulder, seemed intent on reaching the site, weaving his stocky body in and out of the stationary crowd.

'There you are you bastard,' thought John with a mixture of relief and anxiety. Lengthening his stride a little, but ensuring he was not too noticeable, he set off in pursuit of his quarry. It took a few minutes for him to reach the place where he had last seen the terrorist, who had already begun to mingle with the crowd gathered around the perimeter ropes. Suddenly John lost sight of him and a feeling of panic came over him.

'Jesus, where's 'e gone?'' he cursed to himself.

The crowds were getting noisier by the minute as the first of the fireworks were lit; rockets zoomed up into the sky, cascading into brilliant arrays of colour.

'OOOhhs!' and 'AAAhhs!' were all around him.

John stopped and stared about in despair, the crowds milling about were making it difficult to locate the bomber again.

It was no good, he was nowhere to be seen. He had lost him.

After what seemed an age, but which could only have been a matter of seconds, he suddenly saw the small duffle bag again. The only snag was that it now lay discarded under one of the many bench seats placed here for the night. Instinctively, he moved towards it, unsure of what he intended to so, but knowing what the bag contained and that it had to be removed as soon as possible. At that moment a stranger moved into his path, smiled at him and indicated with his head in another direction. Turning that way, it was as if suddenly a weight had been lifted from his shoulders. There in the distance he saw the donkey jacket heading into the darkness and comparative safety of the old lighthouse, approximately four hundred yards away. Nodding gratefully to the stranger, who had to be another of the Commander's team, he set off in pursuit. The bomber must be under the false impression that his mission was almost complete, that all he had to do was wait for the big bang and he could be on his way to plan the next one.

How wrong he was.

John felt a trickle of sweat work its way down his back. This time it was different from Borneo, this time he knew exactly what he intended to do, each step he took brought him closer, each word of his song another second nearer; his act had to continue for just a little while longer.

Donkey jacket had taken refuge by the wall surrounding the lighthouse, providing himself with an excellent vantage point. Another blow was about to be struck against capitalism. One more step towards the freedom of the oppressed nations. What did it matter to him if hundreds, or even thousands, of innocent victims were killed; finally the ends justified the means.

As he got nearer, John felt a relative calm come over him; the sound of his singing rang out into the darkness.

"We're a shower of bastards, bastards are we. We'd rather fuck than fight, we're the dockyard cavalry......"

He was doing the famous old Naval song proud, always one of 'Jack's' favourites. The distance was now down to thirty yards, he was inside the killing range of the Sterling but he wanted to be positive, because the slightest error on his part and it could be goodbye to Mrs. Williams' only son.

"Hi-ya oppo," he shouted at the dark clad figure, "fancy a drink d-ya?"

The features on the olive-skinned face never altered.

"Oway man, 'ave one wi' me," slurred John, staggering slightly;

Still no reply, the man in the donkey jacket seemed intent on ignoring this intruder, staring blankly past him in the direction of the bonfire.

The distance between them was down to less than fifteen yards, close enough for what had to be done, the terrorist must be expecting the explosion at any time. A few more unsteady steps and John let the holdall fall to the ground, grateful that he had put the safety catch on.

He persisted with his offer.

"Are yer goin' ta 'ave a bloody drink with me or not?" he slurred impatiently.

Donkey jacket was obviously intent on completely ignoring this untimely intrusion, hoping that the drunken nuisance would soon be on his way before the device detonated. If not, then the death of one more ignorant sailor would soon determine that.

"Looka', there's a bottle o' brandy in me' bag," said John, "and a'm not goin' ta ask yer again."

This had to be the crucial point, turning away from him had

to make him completely vulnerable, but he had no other choice. Crouching to unzip the bag, he rummaged about inside pretending to find the imaginary bottle, but his right hand soon located the stock of the weapon, and at the same time he removed the safety catch with his thumb.

"'Ere it is, I've found it," he shouted, "brandy for the boyos!"

"Piss off you English bastard....while you 'ave the chance."

At least donkey jacket had acknowledged his presence, the ploy seemed to have worked. Acting as if totally unaware of the insult, John indicated with his free hand in the direction of the crowds.

"Did yer see that little fella' sittin' on top o' that bonfire?" he asked the terrorist, his right hand firmly grasping the Sterling, forefinger poised over the trigger.

"Well the reason that 'e's 'aving 'is arse burned," he continued, "is because just like you, 'e tried blowin' up people for a livin'."

It was at that split second that the terrorist realised his mistake. His hand went towards the gun inside his coat.

But he was too late, too late by far.

The Sterling appeared from inside the holdall as the final syllables left John's lips, coming to rest in his left hand. It was steadied and fired in one fluent motion.

A short cry of desperation came from the terrorist as he realised death was upon him, the first of the bullets ripped their way through the flimsy fabric of he coat and into his heart. The force of the impact flung him bodily backwards into the wall, where he stood for a second before sliding to the ground, the darkness of his blood staining the grass around him. Walking over to his victim, the barrel of his weapon still smoking and drifting into the night sky, John looked down into the face of the terrorist.

The deep blue eyes stared back at him and then closed forever, a short cough brought frothy blood streaming from between his lips.

And now it was five. He had not hesitated; when the need had arisen, his actions had been positive.

Realising what had happened, he turned quickly in the direction of the bonfire, half-expecting to find the entire population of Plymouth bearing down upon him. Surely everybody had heard the firing; but amazingly the mass of people had heard nothing, they were still laughing and shouting in their excitement. The noise had blended in naturally with the sound of the fireworks.

A strong smell of sulphur hung in the air and John turned once more to look at the still body lying on the ground.

'Live by the sword, die by the sword.'

Unclipping the partially used clip of bullets, he replaced them and the Sterling into the holdall, zipping it closed again. Turning his back on the dead man, he walked towards a familiar looking silhouette standing alone some sixty yards away. The shepherd was out tending to his flock, ensuring all were safe and accounted for.

"Is it over with John?"

"It's over sir." Tonight had been the section's initiation; bonfire night celebrations would never be the same again.

'Remember remember, the fifth of November. Gunpowder, treason and plot!'

Chapter Four

During the long and tedious journey back to Chatham in the Commander's car, John had to sit quietly and endure endless chatter about the huge success of the operation, how every minute detail had gone according to plan, the exhilaration was almost too much for the officer to control. But for himself there was no feeling of jubilation or satisfaction at what he had done; maybe this would come later, but at present he felt nothing but emptiness.

It was a welcome relief when Monday morning came around, after a restless and uncomfortable weekend. On reporting to the Commander's office, he was taken aback by the expression on his face.

"Mornin' John," he said, pointing to the chair opposite, "everyone connected with the section is absolutely delighted with Friday night's outcome, and rightly so. Now our informer friend tells us that there is still a dangerous terrorist at large. He fears that with the unaccountable disappearance of his comrade, this second man will go to even greater lengths to attack more vulnerable targets."

"Surely if this fella' knew about the first terrorist," said John, "then he must also 'ave known about this second one as well."

The Commander nodded in agreement.

"I've already put that to him, with the promise of yet more money," he replied, "and he has assured me that he will be in touch as soon as he finds out anything definite. Until then the whole of the section is to be placed on standby, ready to move at a minute's notice."

John spent the majority of his time on the isolated firing range, which he now had authority to use without any supervision, although the old Chief Gunnery Instructor still turned up every now and again to offer a little advice.

"I hear that you done well son," he said and never mentioned it again.

Three weeks went by, then information was received that it was believed that the second terrorist had fled the country and returned to the Middle East, where it was thought he was to recruit others to assist him. John was granted seven days' leave.

"Go home and relax," said the Commander, "but remember...not one single word about the section or its function."

This was a welcome release for John; he had not seen his parents for over twelve months, it would be nice to be with them again.

The leave did not come up to his expectations, things appeared to have changed somehow and he found himself unable to relax. It was not the surroundings, and the beer was as excellent as ever, but he could not settle. Even his parents had noticed the change in him.

"Yer 'aven't gone an' put some young lass in the family way, 'ave yer?" asked his dad.

" 'Corse I 'aven't," smiled John.

Always straight to the point, his dad. No frills or posh accent, a miner of the old brigade since the age of fourteen; who called a spade a spade. During the past five years, since John was old enough to frequent public houses, the two of them had shared a special relationship. Not a father and son relationship, but more like that of two brothers. This time though it was all so different, as if he had retreated into a shell; the experiences of Borneo and Plymouth had changed his whole outlook on life. On the fifth day, the local policeman called at their home and instructed John to get in touch with his Commanding Officer as soon as possible. After walking half a mile or so to the nearest public telephone box, he managed to get through to the Commander's office.

"Our missing friend has turned up," the officer informed him, "instructions will reach you tomorrow morning. The items you will require to carry out your task will be on hand and back up will once again be in assistance.....Good luck John."

Instead of going back to his home, he walked through the farmer's fields and scrambled down the cliffs onto the beach where he had spent so much of his time as a boy. It was December, and the easterly winds coming off the North Sea were not too kind to anyone foolhardy enough to venture out on a day like this; the sea whipped into some kind of frothy frenzy and crashing onto the rocks. The weather did not seem to affect John, his mind was too busy on the possible events of tomorrow. It must appear natural to the Commander and all the others that he would carry out the necessary killing, regardless of how he felt about the situation. The fact that he might be troubled by his conscience did not enter into it. He was now, as far as they were concerned, a hardened killer. Why not again? It had to get easier from now on; five down, how many more to follow? It was dark when he eventually returned home, and was immediately sorry for causing his parents to worry about him. His explanation of the phone call was that because he was now in the regulating branch, which in its own way was the police force of the Navy, one of his many duties now included apprehending sailors who went absent without leave and then often deserted. This was the reason he had to return earlier than expected, a prisoner had to be collected from patrol headquarters in London and escorted to the detention centre at Plymouth.

This was to be his new way of life; he had chosen it freely and now there was no alternative but to deceive his parents. The ordinary boy from the collieries who had even failed his eleven plus exam, who had left the mines before his sixteenth birthday to join the Royal Navy and see the world, was now an entirely different person.

A registered envelope arrived shortly after eight a.m. the following morning, inside was the small locker key and a brief note of explanation. Our informer had located the second terrorist hiding out in some disused barn approximately six miles south of Ashford on the main London to Folkestone road. It was also known that he intended fleeing the country by means of the Dover to Calais cross-channel ferry. John's responsibility was to prevent him doing so. By six thirty the same evening he stood beside the number thirteen locker on Waterloo station and, after hesitating once again, he opened the door, a feeling of apprehension building up inside him. No holdall this time, only a bunch of car keys and a further note explaining where the Commander's car had been left for his use; requirements which he would need were inside the boot of the car.

'Fancy trusting me with that,' thought John.

The one and only car he had ever owned was a twelve year old Morris which just about remained intact until he had passed his driving test. When he reached the Commander's car he found a map in the glove compartment and he soon pinpointed the position of the barn, located by a small 'X' drawn in red ink. The Commander had decided that the operation should commence at four a.m. the next morning; why he had chosen that particular time John did not know, but he was the man in charge of things.

Easing the car smoothly forward out of the station car park, he joined the busy mainstream of London traffic. After driving about for over an hour, by some minor miracle he suddenly found himself moving away from the capital and travelling in the right direction. Navigation and map reading were never two of his better qualities.

The weather was taking a turn for the worse, the South of England had been experiencing heavy rain over the past few days and more was falling again, the windscreen wipers barely able to cope.

After a while curiosity got the better of him and he stopped the car in a deserted layby, climbed out and opened the boot. Inside, wrapped in a blanket, was a short-barrelled pump-action shotgun, a really lethal weapon. There were seven cartridges with it, more than enough to do what was needed; if he had to rely on the seventh, then he was surely in a bit of trouble. A dark blue boiler-suit and a pair of size ten wellington boots were also for his use; at least they had considered the weather conditions.

It was nine p.m. when he drove into the town of Ashford; only a further six miles to go and ample time in hand. His stomach reminded him of the fact he had been travelling all day, so he chose a suitable restaurant where it was possible to keep an eye on the car. At ten thirty he returned to the car and drove out of the town, keeping a careful check on the mileage. The barn was reported to be six miles further on. He had to remain inconspicuous and he came across the perfect place to stop after five point four miles of driving. It was a large layby situated well away from the main road, with the added advantage of a column of trees with their overhanging branches providing a little extra cover. Halting the car under the limbs of an old oak tree, he stopped the engine and switched off the lights. Outside, the rain seemed to be getting heavier, the constant drumming on the car roof producing a warm feeling of security inside. Relaxing, he felt himself becoming a little drowsy but he knew that, before he could allow himself the luxury of a couple of hours' sleep, he had to first locate the barn and make a positive sighting of the second terrorist.

After a few more minutes, he reluctantly climbed out of the car and put his overcoat on; it was definitely unsuitable for these conditions. Making sure that the vehicle was secure, he began to walk back to the road in search of the barn. He walked slowly, staring in every field, and each time some vehicle came towards him he hid from sight. There was almost total darkness, the dense cloud formation obliterating the moon and making his task all the more difficult. The only sounds, apart from the lashing rain, were the occasional flutter of wings as he disturbed some impatient owl or nervous wood pigeon.

After about ten minutes the outline of a building appeared in the darkness. His heartbeat quickened in hopeful anticipation; both co-ordinates and distance were near enough; this could be the place. Climbing over a three bar gate, his foot suddenly slipped and he straddled the gate, almost castrating himself. He lay in the darkness until the nausea had passed, cursing everybody he could think of who had made him come here. After checking that all his essentials were still intact, he carried on limping towards a small copse of trees to the right of the building.

Feeling more than a little exposed to the possible danger, he wished what he had decided to bring the shotgun with him, but it had been too risky just to reconnoitre the surrounding area.

'If this is the right place,' he thought, 'an' that bastard happens to see me before a' see 'im, then I could end up gettin' my goolies shot off altogether.' Pleasant thoughts!

Reaching the last of the trees, he found himself confronted with a clearing of about thirty yards to the building, which he could see was definitely a barn. Staring intently into the darkness, he searched every foot of it, hoping for some sign to indicate the terrorist's presence, but there was nothing to be seen. After ten minutes of intense concentration, his eyes sore with the strain, he began to doubt the location. Moving his aching legs to ease the stiffness and aid circulation, he unconsciously provided himself with a new angle of vision, and suddenly saw a chink of light.

'Thank fuck for that,' he thought.

It had to be too much of a coincidence for it not to be the man he was seeking, but still a positive sighting had to be made; too much depended upon it. Things could prove rather embarrassing if he suddenly burst into the barn waving the shotgun and it just happened to be some young couple enjoying themselves. Crouching, he ran to the side of the barn and peered in through a small space between the wood. At first all he could see was straw littered all over the floor, but as he waited, he saw a shadow moving and then a dark-skinned man came directly into vision. He looked so like the terrorist on the Hoe it could have been his brother; yet again, like Chinks and

Japs, they all looked alike to him. A positive sighting had been made. 'Time to go,' he decided.

A few hundred yards away, the warmth and dryness of the Commander's car beckoned to him, all he had to do now was to return to it and wait. Running carefully, and being extremely careful climbing the slippery gate, he returned to the car. It was only then he realised just how cold and wet he was, his overcoat was so sodden it weighed almost as much as the camel it was named after. During the tension of the last half hour or so, he had not been aware of these trivial discomforts, but now he was.

Once inside the car, he started the engine to get the heater going. Fifteen minutes of hot air blasting through the interior of the car and the windows were completely steamed up, with the atmosphere like a sauna. John relaxed, his eyelids became heavier, weariness began to win the battle over his body. Glancing at his watch, he found it was just after midnight, almost four hours before he was to make his move, ample time to get some sleep. There was no chance of him oversleeping, most sailors had in-built alarm systems in their brain because of the unearthly watches they kept whilst at sea.

He switched the engine off; the sound of the rain beating out its tune reminded him of the steady but monotonous rhythmic beat of the ship's engines.

He closed his eyes.

Something had woken him up! What was it? How long had he been asleep? He found himself swamped in brilliant light and he froze, not able to move a muscle. Through the panic, he was gradually aware of a gentle tapping on the car window, and suddenly the light went out, leaving him in total darkness. It took a few seconds for his eyes to adjust, but gradually he was able to distinguish shapes and then he became conscious of a large wet looking face staring in at him, the mouth belonging to the face was talking. He wound the window down. Outside in the rain stood an elderly policeman leaning on his bicycle, steady drips of water dropped from the rim of his large helmet onto John's right shoulder. The brilliant light had come from the torch he was carrying, which now shone onto the ground.

"Jesus," groaned John, "you just about frightened the life outa' me."

"Sorry about that sir," replied the policeman, but I was wonderin' if everything was alright. Couldn't have rested in my bed if a' hadn't.''

"Yeh, I'm OK," said John, "it's just that I've been travellin' all day and I was about knackered, so I thought better to be safe than sorry, so I was 'avin' a couple o' hours kip."

The old man nodded in apparent agreement.

"You're perfectly right there," he answered, "it's just as I was wondering. I'll be leavin' yer in peace then, sorry to have disturbed you, but like you said yourself, better to be safe than sorry."

"That's alright, I feel more awake now anyway.....I'll be on my way before much longer."

"Well then," smiled the policeman, "it's off 'ome for me now that my shift's finished, and I'll not be sorry when I sign off for the night. It's not the ideal kind of weather for riding a bicycle around country lanes."

One very damp officer of the law bade him goodnight, mounted and pedalled off into the darkness. Checking his watch, John found it was one fifteen. At least he had managed a little sleep, but still almost three hours remained. Only now a small problem arose. He had told the policeman that he would be moving on shortly; it had been an instinctive and defensive reaction. If that old man had anything of a suspicious nature, and he decided to return and found him still here, it might make him ask questions. The operation had been moving along smoothly, then the aged guardian of the law had appeared out of the darkness and made things awkward. It was up to him to make a decision and, rightly or wrongly, he made up his mind that the operation would take place earlier than planned. After all, he knew where the terrorist was hiding and he felt that he did not need the assistance of any back up team, and in any case he could worry about that later. Climbing once more out of the car, he opened the boot, donned the clothing provided and unwrapped the shotgun.

'If P.C. Plod comes back now,' he thought, 'I'm right up shit creek without a paddle.'

One of the lessons which had stuck in his mind during his school days, was that the shortest distance between two points was a straight line so, pointing himself in the general direction of the barn, he took to the fields immediately. This unfortunately turned out to be entirely the wrong decision. Because of all the rain the fields resembled a quagmire and he made agonisingly slow progress. The short cut in fact, took him almost twice as long as it had taken by road. After what seemed an age, he found himself at the edge of the small copse of trees; the clearing still looked as daunting.

So far so good.

Edging his way to the glimmer of light, he peered in and instantly observed the terrorist putting a sleeping bag alongside the glowing fire.

'Gettin' himself nice an' cosy for the night,' thought John cynically.

But the terrorist's next move caught him completely by surprise. He began stuffing the sleeping bag with straw until it outwardly resembled someone occupying it. After convincing himself of its authenticity, he stepped away and smiled, suddenly saying something in his native tongue.

John stood astounded at the man's actions, but not half as much as he was when a second man came into view and both started to laugh and gesticulate as if the sleeping bag was being shot to pieces. Each man then picked up an ugly looking automatic rifle and checked it was loaded; they were smiling and talking to each other as they did so.

Suddenly the reality of what was going on came through to John; the two men inside were obviously preparing for an ambush of their own making, and the only person on their hit list had to be himself. Somehow they knew he would be coming to the barn; and not only that, they knew that he fully expected only one terrorist to be present.

'So much for our bloody informer,' spat John, 'the bastard's gone 'an dropped me right in it.'

It was time for him to steady his nerves, to put his thinking cap on. Either that or his running shoes, because the safest place for John Williams to be was a long way from there.

He allowed time for his brain to take command; the facts slowly unfolded themselves. It was painfully obvious they expected him, and it could be taken for granted they would also know what time he was supposed to arrive. The one thing in John's favour was that because of unforeseen circumstances he was here over three hours early. Because of the diligence of the local constabulary, there was still a possibility he could complete his mission, but instead of having only one man to dispose of, there were now two.

What worried John more than anything else was how they knew. There was an awful stink about the whole thing and he wanted to find out what it was. He watched the two men light up a strange looking cigarette and pass it back and forth. It had to be one of those 'magic cigarettes', long and tapered at both ends, when it was inhaled the lit end flared a little. Hopefully it would not be too long before the effects of the cannabis had them floating high on some astral plane, leaving mere mortals like him bogged down in the rain.

There had to be some way he could enter the barn without being noticed and, after fifteen minutes of probing about in the dark, he discovered a few loose planks which, after being carefully adjusted, allowed him enough space to squeeze inside. He found himself completely hidden from view by a twenty foot wall of straw, bales of it stacked one upon the other, and once inside he replaced the planks, not wanting to cause a draught of cold air which might possibly warn the terrorists of an intruder.

Peering carefully around the straw, he was able to see both men clearly, they were totally ignorant of the danger in their midst.

'Right you pair o' bastards, we'll see who's goin' to surprise who,' he thought.

Preparing himself, he waited for the opportune moment to present itself to him; after all time was on his side.

It was not long before one of the terrorists seemed to be nodding off, his head began to sag forward onto his chest; the minute stub of the cigarette fell onto the floor, the magic effects taking over. The second man looked at his comrade and laughed, nudging him with the barrel of his rifle, but there was very little response.

Standing away from the fire, this second man stretched himself and looked about the barn. Suddenly he began to walk towards John, his rifle swinging to and fro in his hand, and he was humming some strange tune to himself. Deciding that the time had to be now, John almost stepped out in front of the approaching terrorist but, before he had time to move, the man stopped and loosened his trousers before squatting to the ground.

A bodily function which we all have to obey had came to John's assistance, so he decided to strike whilst things were going his way. No better opportunity would present itself to him than this; number one terrorist was floating somewhere close to oblivion and the second one was definitely indisposed for the time being. It was still, the quiet before the storm which was to follow.

Moving from his cover, he began a slow walk towards the nearest man, things crystal clear in his mind, feeling in total control of the situation. These men were not human beings, they had lost that standing by acting as rabid animals and neither pity nor remorse should be shown to them. Along with their comrade on the Hoe, they too were responsible for the many deaths and mutilations, sharing guilt and retribution alike.

He had walked seven steps before the terrorist concentrating on relieving his bowels somehow realised the danger, his spine visibly stiffening. Spinning around, somewhat awkwardly, he stared into the gaping hole of the shotgun's barrel and made a vain attempt at grabbing the rifle which lay by his left foot.

The twin explosions from the shotgun sounded almost simultaneous, the charges hitting the terrorist squarely in the chest and ripping his upper body to shreds as bone and muscle tissue were decimated. Such was the terrific force, it hurled him bodily into the air and smashed him against the barn wall, his life's blood gushing from the gaping wounds.

Swivelling to his left on the balls of his feet, John now faced the second man, who had just experienced the worst kind of rude awakenings. His bleary eyes almost popping out of their sockets in sheer disbelief at the sight of his friend's grisly remains, the effects of the drug well and truly shaken off with the realisation that death was awaiting him. He began to whimper to himself, as if accepting the inevitable that these were to be his last moments on this earth, praying to his 'Allah' and hoping for deliverance. Never again would he see his loved ones, or the country he now gave his life for.

John pumped the firing mechanism twice more and fired in rapid succession, the impact almost tearing the terrorist's head off, blood and brain fragments were scattered all around. It was as if the man's body was controlled by some unseen puppeteer, jerking violently in its final throes of death, until it slumped to the floor in a bloody mess.

'Almost too high,' John scolded himself.

Everything was still once again, he removed his finger from the trigger. That accounted for numbers six and seven.

It was highly unlikely that anyone could have possibly heard the gunfire, because of the weather conditions outside, but there again anything was possible. The back-up team, wherever they were at this time, would be unaware of what had taken place, so any assistance from that quarter was out. It was left up to him to finalise things here inside the barn, leaving as little evidence as possible of what had actually happened.

Over in the far corner of the barn stood an old Dormobile van, he ran over and checked it over. Inside he found four cases of assorted clothing and, surprisingly enough, a half dozen gift wrapped presents, maybe for their families living in the Middle East. Tucked away underneath a tool box was a smart attache case, full of neatly stacked bundles of crisp five pound notes; it seemed to be a fortune to John, more money than he had ever seen in his life. Inside the glove compartment were two passports and a pair of tickets for the following morning's ferry to Calais. The keys for the van were still in the ignition, and not only did it have a full tank of petrol, there were two five gallon drums for standby.

Jumping into the driving seat, he drove the van over to the body of number two terrorist and then dragged the remains of the other man over to join that of his comrade in death. After liberally covering both bodies with straw and soaking them in petrol, he left a trail of petrol to the tank of the van. Collecting the shotgun and attache case in one hand, and the two automatic rifles in the other, he kicked a burning ember from the fire into the straw covering the bodies, igniting it immediately. A fitting funeral pyre to end it all. It was time to leave.

Running to the door of the barn, he kicked it open and went outside into the driving rain, stopping momentarily to look back once more into the barn. Then he set off at a gallop towards the main road.

'Balls to the theory about a straight line bein' the quickest way,' he decided. Moving as fast as the slippery conditions underfoot would permit, plus all the extra weight and the cumbersome wellingtons, he finally arrived back at the car absolutely breathless. It was reassuring to find that the old policeman had not decided to return; hopefully he would be tucked up in his warm bed. Whilst he was unceremoniously removing his wet overalls and footwear, throwing everything untidily into the boot of the car, he was stunned by the sudden ferocity of the explosion which lit up the sky. The fuel tank, plus anything else they had hidden away inside the barn for future use, had most definitely gone up.

He started the engine and rammed the car into gear even as he slammed the door. With a spinning of the rear wheels as they sought traction on the wet surface, the car suddenly leapt forward and sped off down the road he had just run along, his racing gear change would have done credit to Stirling Moss.

After two miles he eased off the accelerator pedal and settled down to a steady fifty miles per hour. Once again it was over, and on this occasion he did experience a certain amount of satisfaction. But he also had to acknowledge the truth, and the truth was that but for that particular old warhorse of the Constabulary, the eventual outcome might have been very different.

He owed his life to P.C. Plod.

Chapter Five

On arriving at the barracks gate, he had to endure patiently the customary banter by the duty quartermaster and his gate staff. The usual candid remarks about him being a dirty lucky bastard, not only having the good fortune to be on the C-in-C's staff, but using the boss's car to do his courting in.

"That's the way it goes," smiled John, wishing they would open the gate so he could drive in.

"Bloody good number yer've got," shouted one of the sailors as he drove past them, "don't you know it's an offence to get yer leg over in a Naval vehicle?"

It was an excuse for everybody to have a good laugh and to help break the monotony of being on guard duty throughout the night.

'If you only knew the truth, pal,' thought John, as he waved to them through the rear mirror.

Commander Ward was visibly shaken as he entered the office; he had spent hours pacing from one side of the room to the other, hoping for some kind of information, but none had come through.

"What's wrong?" he demanded, "Why aren't you at the barn?"

Placing the attache case and the two passports on the table, John turned to the officer. "Something went a little wrong with our plans sir," he said, "but it all came out right in the end."

John then went on to explain the sequence of events leading up to his return to the office, finally opening the passports and handing them to the officer. The Commander carefully examined them, a bewildered expression came across his face, a mixture of embarrassment and relief; and he sat silent as if attempting to find the reason for the apparent blunder.

"It appears to me as if they tried to turn the tables on us," he eventually said quietly, "I can only blame my ignorance and inexperience for not realising the possibility of such a move. They used the whole situation to their advantage and it almost worked for them. The terrorist in Plymouth was obviously expendable to their needs and they were quite willing to sacrifice his liberty in return for the funding of their political cause. It was the financing they were after all along, and my own stupidity presented them with you as well as some kind of bonus before they fled the country. Money and revenge, what more could they ask for?"

The dejected sight of the Commander fumbling nervously with the two passports brought a feeling of sympathy from John; he felt the need to reassure him. "Anyway sir," he said with a smile, "not only did we get two for the price o' one...we got our money back as well."

"I'm terribly sorry John," he answered, "everything could have gone so wrong tonight, but because of your initiative the section may have a future after all. If, after this shambles, we are able to learn by our mistakes, then we have to thank you for it." Passing one of the passports back to John, he added. "This was our so-called informer; he knew our every move."

The face in the passport belonged to the terrorist who had been killed with his trousers down around his ankles, definitely not the most dignified way to depart this life; "Serve the bastard right," said John.

"Go and get yourself some sleep," said the Commander, "I'd better be in touch with our overlord in London and explain the details of tonight's outcome."

This time John fell into a deep sleep, no faces turning up to haunt him, no more struggles with his conscience; he had done what had to be done.

'Fuck 'em all,' he thought.

It was late afternoon when John was summoned to the Commander's office and on entering he soon became aware of the officer's uneasiness.

"I've just received an unedited version of a report which will be in the evening newspapers, and by morning the nationals will be carrying it," he said, "It states that the remains of two bodies were discovered in a disused barn which was gutted by fire. Initial thoughts suggested that they belonged to two 'gentlemen of the road' who were thought to be sheltering from the rain, but after an examination by forensic scientists it now transpires that the two men were part of an activist group responsible for the recent spate of bombings. Experts have confirmed traces of an explosive substance being present at the scene, substantiating the claims that the men were indeed terrorists." The Commander paused for a moment, and looked up at John.

"It's the final paragraph which worries us," he added, "it gives an explicit description of a young man seen in the vicinity at the approximate time, even down to your Geordie accent."

"I thought I'd lost that," complained John.

"It's still there," smiled the Commander, "like a trademark, it will take some getting rid of."

"What happens now ?" he asked.

"There's been a lengthy discussion about you John," replied the Commander, "and it had been decided that you must disappear for the time being. It's unfortunate that the description, even down to the colour of the car you were using, was so vivid. The Minister conveys his congratulations to you and readily acknowledges the significance of your achievement, but in the interest of both the section and yourself, you are to be posted abroad until this thing blows over. If it was to become public knowledge that the section existed, there would be such a massive hue and cry from every do-gooder in the land; we would be finished."

Within seventy two hours, Leading Regulator John Williams was sitting a little uneasily in the lounge of R.A.F. Changi, in Singapore. It had been decided to send him back to the Far East for the time being, because the crew of *H.M.S. Falcon* had since returned to the United Kingdom and so the chances of him meeting anyone who knew about his Borneo experience were slim.

Before leaving England he had had to concoct some feasible lie to explain to his parents why he was once again leaving the country. It had been another emergency he had said, and in this new role he now played, they seemed to come thick and fast. What their reaction would have been if they had known the real truth behind his 'deportation' he dreaded to think.

Master-at-Arms 'Andy' Andrews, in charge of the Regulating branch belonging to the barracks of *H.M.S.Terror,* had been cordially invited to a meeting with some Rear Admiral he had never seen before. During this 'meeting' he was politely requested to ease this new rating who would be joining his staff into the ways of the branch. No reason was forthcoming, and he knew better than to pry. He fancied remaining in Singapore until his twenty two years were up and he could retire with a nice pension. There were a lot worse postings than *H.M.S. Terror*, and had he objected then he would have surely been found one. After the meeting Andy made a few discreet enquiries about the secretive Rear Admiral, eventually concluding that no-one was certain, but it appeared that he was involved with the Intelligence branch of the service.

"Ours is not to reason why," he reminded himself, but he decided that a watchful eye would be focused upon this certain young man.

The new member of the regulating branch was very conscious of the almost casual way he was treated by the Master-at-Arms, especially since such men were almost law unto themselves and caused fear amongst the lower ranks, and even officers at times.

Although sceptical to begin with, the Master gradually found himself more and more satisfied with Williams' work rate and his willingness to learn. As well as being quite an intelligent individual, he was a likeable person and very easy to get along with; but that certain air of strangeness always hovered about him. It did not matter how many times he asked a leading question, they were always evaded with an almost natural skill which left the questioner unsatisfied. After three months had passed, John had progressed sufficiently to work side by side with the rest of the Regulators, a tribute to his endeavours to learn. It was after this period of time that the

Master took it upon himself to set aside any initial misgivings he had about John by inviting him to his home and to meet his family.

One thing could be taken for certain in the Royal Navy and that was if someone ever extended this kind of invitation to you, you had been accepted.

It was during this visit that John met the girl who would soon become his wife, his obvious instant attraction to Andy's daughter when being introduced to her was mutual. Throughout the meal, their eyes were in constant contact; Angela was a beautiful girl with hair the colour of a raven's wing which went half way down her back, over deeply tanned shoulders. She had a slim athletic body which she knew how to move in just the right way, her ample breasts swinging gently before her, so that John felt hot with excitement.

All men differed in their preference for one part or another of the female anatomy, some even favoured the anatomy of other men; in his own case it was most definitely breasts.

During the following months his visits to the Andrews household became more and more regular and inevitably their feelings for each other became stronger by the day. The Master did not whole-heartedly approve of this, not because of anything to do with John himself, but because of the uncertainty which surrounded his presence amongst them. When John and Angela were alone, they were both aware of their special relationship and what they now meant to one another, an entirely new experience for both of them. For once in his life, he found himself willing to restrain himself sexually. He did not want to endanger the situation; so he did as she wished.

Times were happy for him and he was well content with his life, more than he had any right to be; back now into the normal way of living in the midst of normal people.

He was mistaken about this.

It was during the early hours one morning in June that the Master came into his room and awakened him. He had received urgent orders that John Williams was to report to Singapore, dressed in civilian clothing, where he was to meet another officer who would relay further instructions to him. The Master had also been ordered to say that Williams had been despatched to Government House in Hong Kong as part of an official escort to the visiting British Consul.

"What you mixed up in, son?" pressed the Master.

"I'm sorry Andy," he replied, "that's the one thing a' can't tell you. I was beginnin' to think they'd forgot about me....but a' was wrong."

"You be coming back?" pressed the Master.

"Couldn't tell you.....a' haven't a clue where I'm going."

The orders were for the Master himself to transport John to Raffles hotel, in Singapore itself; there he watched the young man being ushered inside by the same Rear Admiral he had met previously. Whatever it was John was involved in, it had to be extremely important to warrant such treatment. It was also becoming more likely that this same young man would soon become his son-in-law, he had never seen his daughter blossom so much as when she was in his company. He blamed himself for this development, he had presented him with the opportunity to meet her. Had John been an authentic member of the branch he would have welcomed it, and even encouraged the idea. but the presence of that dark cloud of uncertainty bothered him, now more than ever.

"Give Angela my love," had been John's parting words.

"I will, son," answered the Master.

Once inside Raffles John was told he was to return to England, and before long he was taken to the airport at R.A.F. Changi, passing the infamous Changi prison where so many allied soldiers had suffered and died at the hands of the Japanese. The dark pitted walls and observation towers were a constant reminder of the atrocities of the past.

Within the hour he was seated by the window of a R.A.F. Comet and airborne, the island of Singapore behind him. His mind was dulled with the disappointment at having to leave Angela, not knowing if he would return, or whether his journey back to England was to be permanent. Thoughts of their last meeting came into his mind, how finally, after hours of gentle persuasion, she allowed him to unfasten her flimsy white bra, releasing the fullness of her breasts to his grasp. She had moaned with the pleasure of his gentle massage, her dark-tipped nipples becoming hard and erect in their eager response, the sight of them being everything he had imagined. Unfortunately this was as far as she would allow him to go, though there was the feeling that more could possibly follow in the not too distant future.........and here he was at thirty two thousand feet going in the wrong direction.

On his arrival at Lyneham, near Swindon, he was not too surprised to see Commander Ward waiting for him in the departure area.

"Hello John," he said with a smile, and surprised him by offering his hand.

It was an unexpected gesture, because officers do not go around shaking hands with members of the lower ranks, but John felt the genuine bond between them was as strong as ever.

"Hello, sir, thought you'd forgot all about me."

"No possibility of that happening," replied the officer, "and

I'm sorry to have sprung this on you out of the blue, but a situation has arisen where we find ourselves requiring your assistance.''

That one sentence explained everything to John, it was immaterial what the Commander had to say from then on......., they needed him to kill someone again.

'What you mixed up in, son?' the Master's voice came back to him.

He had become a pawn in some game of political chess, to do with as they wished. The Commander led him to an empty room where refreshments were spread out on a table by the window, in the background R.A.F. personnel were scurrying about refuelling and preparing the Comet for its return flight to the Far East.

"The Special Branch, working in conjunction with the American C.I.A., have apprehended a man called Robert McIvaney,'' began the officer, "he is known as one of the top political assassins in the world, already reputed to be responsible for at least two dozen eliminations in as many countries.''

John looked a little bemused, not fully understanding what this could have to do with him. The Special Branch; the C.I.A., assassins and political eliminations; what could this possibly have to do with an anti-terrorist organisation. And in any case, the Commander had said this man had been apprehended, and as far as he knew that meant he had been caught.

The officer, sensing John's confusion over the matter, carried on with his explanation, handing him a freshly poured cup of coffee at the same time.

"We know that McIvaney accepted a contract from an unknown source to assassinate someone here in England, but no-one knew who his target was to be, so our two countries decided to work together until his objective became clear. McIvaney was 'allowed' to enter this country through Heathrow Airport in one of his many excellent disguises, and under the alias of Robert Wilson. From the moment his feet touched British soil, the Special Branch had him placed under constant supervision.''

The Commander paused to take a sip from his china cup, and carefully selected one of the many assorted biscuits from a large flowered plate in the centre of the table.

''To cut a long and complicated story short, and not wishing to bore you with the intervening details, the officer continued, ''his target was to be the Prime Minister herself, and as many of her cabinet as possible. McIvaney had successfully concealed a highly explosive device in the York Minster where a Remembrance Service was to be held, knowing that the P.M. and other high ranking dignitaries would be attending. He even managed to acquire a copy of the seating arrangements; how he came to be in possession of that highly confidential information is still a cause of some concern.''

''At this moment McIvaney is locked in a top security cell in York police station, with armed guards keeping an eye on him around the clock, and he's awaiting transportation to London where a delegation of officials from other interested countries wish to interview him. He is a very important prisoner, and Special Branch have a right to their moment of glory because of their prize catch.

At eight o'clock tomorrow morning his transfer will commence, an unmarked black Jaguar will pull up outside the main doors of the police station and two armed Special Branch men will escort him.....one on either side.''

"But what's this got to do with me, sir?" asked John.

"Your job is to eliminate McIvaney before he is able to get into the car," stated the Commander.

"But why, sir?" complained John, "Surely if he's been caught and there are plenty of other countries after him as well...we don't 'ave to kill him."

This was the one and only time John had ever questioned an order.

"Williams," the officer responded curtly, "we are not in a position to decide the rights or wrongs of the situation. The decision was made for us by someone in authority high enough to by-pass both the special branch and MI5; they are both totally ignorant of the plan. The politics are way above our heads but, as with anything else, we in this section are sworn to obedience and, as I've already stated, the decision has been made. Is that clear?"

It did not really matter what John felt.

"Yes, sir," he replied, "I'm sorry."

"Good man," smiled the officer, "we've located a derelict building, adjacent to the main doors of the police station, which will present you with an unobstructed view. The distance is in the region of three hundred and forty yards, quite possible for you, but I must stress the time factor. Because York is full of armed Special Branch officers, there is only time for one attempt. It has to be good....but I know you can do it, John."

Remaining silent, John contemplated the prospects of having to hit a walking target at some three hundred yards plus. As the Commander had implied, it would have to be a good shot; one of his best.

After he had freshened up, the officer handed him over to two men who were to drive him to York and instal him in the derelict building.

"Good luck, John," he said.

For the whole of the journey north, his two companions remained silent. Whether by choice or otherwise was immaterial to John; he had more than enough to occupy his thoughts. It was three a.m. when they eventually arrived, coming to a halt in some darkened alley. Alighting from the vehicle, John stretched himself and looked up into the grey sky of the early morning, dawn was not too far away. One of his travelling companions went up to a door and gave a pre-arranged knock. 'All very dramatic,' thought John.

The door opened almost immediately and a third man appeared and quickly ushered them all inside, leading them up two flights of stairs, along a corridor and into an empty room. Well, almost empty, for over in the corner resting against the wall, was a .303 Lee Enfield rifle fitted with telescopic sights...the sniper's weapon.

One of the trio spoke.

"When it's finished, run back along the corridor and drop the rifle out of the window," he said, "we'll be there to catch it. After that it's up to you to get out of here and make your way to the railway station, where a dark blue Zodiac will be waiting to get you out of it. Go up to the car and ask the driver if he knows the way to the airport.....he'll know it's you."

"'Ere, you'll be needin' this," the other man added, passing a solitary .303 cartridge to him.

Before his new companions left, they produced a flask.

"Coffee."

"Thanks," replied John gratefully, "I could do with it."

"Bill 'ere will be downstairs all the time, keepin' an eye on

88

things......Don't worry, yer' not on yer' own in this.''

Alone in the confines of the little room, John's thoughts concentrated on the task ahead, and on how he had travelled thousands of miles to assassinate an assassin. Strolling over to the corner of the room, he picked up the rifle and carefully carried out his customary inspection of the weapon, not that he expected to find fault with it. It was a beautifully balanced rifle, and extremely accurate if used correctly, accurate and deadly.

Just over three hundred yards away, in some uncomfortable police cell, the man he had come to kill should be asleep at this precise moment, or would he too be lying awake pondering over his future?

Sitting with his back to the open window, John drank most of the strong coffee and then rested his eyes, though all the time fully conscious of his surroundings. At seven thirty, with the sun's rays streaming into the bare room, he stood up and massaged some feeling back into his limbs. It was a fine morning, with very little breeze, and the city was beginning to make its way to work, mostly by bicycle.

The blue coloured doors of the police station stood prominently in the distance, a solitary police constable standing unobtrusively to one side, occasionally engaged in casual conversation with some passer-by.

Picking up the rifle, John took up a stance well away from the window, going down onto his left knee and placing his left arm through the sling, then tightening it by grasping hold of the stock. Next he snuggled the butt into his right shoulder and levelled the rifle; it remained in a fixed position. Slowly he began the delicate operation of lining up the telescopic sights onto the letter 'O' of the word 'POLICE' placed ominously above the doors. Three hundred and forty yards was quite a distance, his alignment had to be positive as there could be no margin of error.

Satisfied with his preparation, he carefully replaced the rifle back in the corner of the room. It was seven thirty eight.

At seven fifty seven, he once again took up the rifle and placed himself three feet inside the window, so as not to expose the barrel of the weapon to possible detection. Once more he completed the routine of becoming 'ready', only this time he placed the live cartridge into the breech and locked the bolt into place. Just as Commander Ward had said, at precisely eight a.m. the unmarked black Jaguar pulled up at the kerb, directly opposite the doors of the police station. John estimated that it would take nine or ten strides for the men to reach the car. The large double doors opened and three figures were clearly visible inside. They began their walk.

Inhaling a deep lungful of air, John held his breath and concentrated the sights on the left breast pocket of the man in the centre, visibly handcuffed on either side. Prisoner and escorts were now almost halfway to the waiting car. John began breathing out slowly through pursed lips, his body completely motionless except for the slightest movement of his right index finger squeezing very gently.

The three men had reached the car; one of he escorts placed his hand on the door. John pulled the trigger.

The terrific velocity of the .303 bullet whistled through the intervening air space and thundered into the unprotected heart of Robert McIvaney, the force of the impact throwing all three men to the ground in an untidy heap on the pavement. That now accounted for number eight.

Inside the small room, the echoes reverberated around the four walls and the sound was deafening, like the noise from the *Falcon's* main 4.5 armament. Whilst out on the streets below pandemonium had broken loose, with the two blood spattered bodies of the Special Branch men frantically attempting to uncuff themselves from the dead weight of their prisoner. People were scurrying in all directions, most not fully realising what had actually happened but being carried along in the hysteria of events.

John picked up the flask, ran the length of the corridor and looked down into the yard below, before dropping both rifle and flask into the waiting arms of his colleagues. Within a matter of seconds the men had concealed the rifle in the boot of the car, climbed inside and were leaving the scene. Now it was up to John himself.

There had been no necessity for him to hang around to verify the accuracy of his shot, he knew that from the moment he pulled the trigger that it had been true. Careful to look calm though he didn't feel it, he walked down the flights of stairs and left by the front door as if nothing untoward had occurred. No-one seemed to take any notice as he emerged from the empty building, all were too busy rushing in the opposite direction to the police station. He mingled naturally with the confusion and within a couple of minutes found himself on board a bus, the driver hanging onto the platform rail and looking towards the melee of bodies outside the doors of the police station, as angry Special Branch officers were rounding up all passers by.

"Jesus!" exclaimed John, with an appropriate look of astonishment on his face, "What's goin' on over there?"

"A 'aven't a clue lad," replied the driver, "but whatever it is, 'a daren't get behind me' schedule, it's more than me' job's worth.''

"You goin' anywhere near the train station?'' asked John.

"Stop right outside it.''

The conductor reached up to the bell and gave the driver the customary two rings to move off and within four minutes John had got off in front of the railway station. A casual search of the car park and he soon located the dark blue Zodiac he was to be taken away in.

"Excuse me,'' he said to the man sitting behind the wheel, "any idea where the airport is?''

" 'Corse I have,'' he smiled, "climb in, I'll take you there myself.''

The City of York with its famous Minster were soon left behind in the distance. A strange reason for the first visit.

Forty eight hours later, and feeling completely exhausted, John arrived once again in the humid heat of Singapore, and once again he sat patiently for someone to come and pick him up.

"We'll allow a reasonable time to let the storm subside,'' the Commander had explained just before the flight took off, "then we'll have you back in the fold where you belong.''

He had been congratulated on an exceptional piece of marksmanship under difficult conditions. Although the Special Branch were devastated at their immense loss of pride, there was more than sufficient relief in other high quarters to balance this. John's train of thought was interrupted by the sound of a familiar and friendly voice.

"It's a bloody funny Navy that sends a Master-at-Arms out to fetch some jumped up killick,'' said Andy, pretending to be a little aggrieved.

"Hello Master," smiled John wearily.

"Back with us, are we?"

"Looks that way for the time being."

The Master knew better than to try and extract anything from John, but wondered if it could be possible that his sudden disappearance coincided with the reported shooting back in the United Kingdom. Surely not; that was far too high a league for someone like this young man to be mixed up in. The newspapers and overseas radio stations were making such a commotion about an extremely dangerous assassin being shot dead in the streets of York; it was like the gangland killings which took place in America.

"You been back to the U.K. John?" he asked.

John walked towards the exit as if he had not heard the question.

"You a marksman, John?" persisted the Master.

"A marksman, Master?" repeated John, " 'Corse I'm not a marksman...I'd have the crossed rifles on me sleeve if I was. No..I'm no marksman."

"No-one knows who the piper is," said Andy thoughtfully, "but when he plays his tune, we all come running."

John Williams was back amongst friends, with one of them being more than a little suspicious about his sudden trip away from the island.

Three months later John and Angela were married and, thanks to her parents generosity, they spent their honeymoon in the beautiful city of Penang in North Malaya, where John's delighted expectations of his new wife were fulfilled.

It was on his return that the Master informed him he was to get in touch with a Commander Ward back in England. His new-found happiness suffered an abrupt setback. Andy Andrews had had reservations about the couple getting married; he put forward the age old excuses against getting married 'just yet'. About how in his opinion Angela was far too young to take such a great step; they had not known each other very long. But nothing he said changed their minds. What other argument could he put forward? He could prove nothing and, in any case, would his daughter have believed him? When he saw the expression on his new son-in-law's face change from happiness almost to despair, he knew he had been right all along. He was involved with something he didn't want others to know about. The Master made up his mind that, come hell or high water, when John was through talking to this Commander Ward, he was going to get to the bottom of the matter.

"Williams here sir."
"Ah, John," said the Commander, his voice clear over the thousands of miles which separated them, "I hear that congratulations are in order."
"That's right sir...thank you."
"Well John," continued the officer, "this now creates a bit of a problem for us. When the section was formed, a decision was made and I'm afraid there's no choice but to abide by its ruling. We are only to recruit suitable personnel who had no marital commitments, in case of any unforeseen circumstances arising from the nature of our work. Because of your marriage I find myself with no alternative but to report you ineligible for any future operations, and it pains me to have to do it, because if given a choice I would have preferred to make

you an exception to the rule. But the Minister vetoed my proposal, insisting that we stick strictly to the ruling, although he too is extremely sorry to be deprived of your services because they've proved to be invaluable to us in the past.''

John could not believe what he was hearing; could it possibly be true?

''What you've done for the section in particular and the country as a whole,'' continued the Commander, ''can never be publicly recognised. So, as a kind of severance payment for services rendered, and as a way of conveying our gratitude to you, a substantial amount of money had been deposited in your bank account....., call it a wedding present if you like, to invest in your future. Finally, although I know there's no necessity, I am duty bound to remind you officially that you are still sworn to secrecy by the Official Secrets Act, and your silence is of the first importance; but I know that the secret of the section's existence is safe with you.''

It took a few seconds for John's brain to register just what it was the Commander was informing him. He was saying that John was FREE. Free to live a normal life in the company of normal people, not having to concoct excuses about where he had been and what he had been doing.

''It's safe sir,'' he replied quietly, wanting to shout with glee.

''Only one more thing, John,'' added the officer, ''you have the choice of remaining where you are and staying in General Service, or if you wish you will be granted a honourable discharge and be out of the Navy within seventy two hours. It's entirely your decision.''

It did not take long for John to make the decision.

''I'll stay, sir.''

''So be it,'' said the Commander, ''goodbye and good luck,

Leading Regulator Williams."
And that was that!

"Everything all right son?" enquired his father-in-law.
"It is now, Andy," he smiled broadly, "it is now."

Chapter Six

The train drew slowly into Kings Cross station, gently colliding with the oversized buffers signifying journey's end and, after quite some time, he was once again back in London. Luggage in hand, he stepped from the carriage and onto the platform. Everything had completely changed since the day he had first arrived here at the tender age of sixteen on his way to join the Naval training school of *H.M.S. Ganges* at Shotley, near Ipswich. The distinctive smell of the aged and obsolete steam trains were gone, and in its place the sickly stench of the modern diesel engines and a kind of mini-shopping precinct at the station entrance.

As he approached the taxi rank with its endless line of hackneys awaiting fares, memories of many a Monday morning scramble came to mind; the frantic dash of partially aroused service personnel and the ensuing race to the nearest taxi. The faces differed from one week to another, but the numbers were almost guaranteed, all returning to their ships or bases, whichever the case might be. Smiling sadly to himself because it had all been so long ago and a lot of murky water had flowed under the arches of London Bridge.

On arriving at Waterloo station, he removed the small key from his pocket, but as he neared the place where he thought the left luggage department was everything had changed, as at Kings Cross. He stood for a few minutes undecided, not sure of what he should do next.

"Mr. Williams, sir?"

John turned to the speaker, finding himself face to face with a tall, well built young man of pleasant appearance, somewhere in his mid-twenties.

"Yes," he answered, "that's my name."

"The Commodore sent me to collect you," the young man informed him, a smile spread itself across his face, "he said you'd come. I've had quite a wait..but the main thing is that you're here now."

Looking into the face of the younger man, John paused momentarily, then said, "Told you I'd come did 'e, well he bloody well knew more than I did.....because I wasn't too sure about it."

The young man laughed.

"He was very confident," he replied.

"You said the Commodore," said John, "Commodore who?"

"Ward......Commodore Ward."

John was visibly taken aback; surely it could not be the same man.''I believe the two of you knew each other in the past,'' added the young man, observing the look of surprise on John's face.

It was him! He would have to be well into his sixties now. The Commander of old had risen to the rank of Commodore, almost an admiral; the section must have done all right by him.

"Well then," said John, returning the smile, "we can't keep the old sod waitin' now..can we?"

Relieving John of his case, the well turned out young man indicated for him to follow.

"He also said that I'd recognise you by your accent.....Geordie isn't it?"

"As a matter of fact it isn't," corrected John, "I come from Durham and, am pleased to say, not a Geordie."

John had to admit to himself that during his years in the

Navy, anyone from the North East of England got the name either 'Geordie' or George', and at the time this was generally accepted by one and all.

"You all sound the same to me sir........foreigners."

John was beginning to take a liking to this brash young man who somehow reminded him of himself some twenty years ago; how time passes you by.

"By the way sir, my name's Steve Bright."

"I'm pleased to meet you Steve....I think."

This droll comment brought another laugh from the young man, who was striding in and out of the busy commuters all in a terrible hurry to get home. Steve Bright had enough time to make an early decision about this man from Durham and, behind the apparent friendliness of the exterior, he could see the deep sadness in his eyes. There had been a buzz going round the section for the past few weeks, as there always was regarding one thing or another, rumours of a certain man who had been in at the initial founding, returning once again. Taking into consideration the relative age of the Commodore and this John Williams, plus an instinct he now had, it was more than likely that this was indeed that person. If this was so, and the Commodore had found it essential to bring him back to the section after this time, then something important had to be in the wind and, if it was true, then he Steve Bright wanted to be included.

"Climb in Mr. Williams, sir, and make yourself comfortable," he said, opening the door of a gleaming black Daimler, "it won' take us long to get there."

"The section based in London now?" asked John.

"Been here for years, so I'm told," replied Steve, "we've got an office block just off Victoria; not that far from New

Scotland Yard, but they never invite us over for tea.''

Once again John found himself being driven through the busy streets of London and, staring out of the car's windows, he was aware of the rain pounding against the glass, the heavy storms of the North East now far behind him. It always did appear to be two topcoats warmer south of Doncaster. He seemed preoccupied with the weather, but in reality his mind was in a turmoil.

At the same moment, Commodore Thomas Readfern Ward stood silently by the window in his third floor office complex which, apart from serving as an office, had a small self-contained living area for the many times he decided to remain here in London. He had only moments previously left a heated discussion with the Minister who was responsible for the section's activities, the Minister not too enthusiastic about the idea of having recalled his former operative. There was argument for and against the Commodore's wishes, but finally the Minister relented and succumbed to pressure. The man from Whitehall had willingly acknowledged John's past record, his courage and dedication had been of the highest quality, the files more than substantiated that.

''But all of this took place a long time ago,'' the Minister had argued, ''and our latest up-date on him reveals that he now hides himself away from the rest of society. That fact, coupled with the evidence that he has never recovered from the loss of his wife, must bring his reliability into question.''

The Commodore had not relented in the slightest, his faith in John never wavered for a moment, he himself had selected him. In the intervening years he had always discovered adequate replacements, but neither for effectiveness nor capability were they comparable. Men like John Williams were a rarity, a one-off with natural ability, and if somehow you happened to come across one, then you did your level best to hang onto him. Since his wife's death, John had, without being made aware of the fact, once again been placed on the active list and thereby made officially available for operations. The actual likelihood of such a need ever arising were thought minimal. But due to the circumstances the officer now found himself in, the necessity had suddenly arisen.

Observing the arrival of his Daimler, he watched with mixed emotions as the two men alighted from the car........the past and the present together. Twenty years had certainly changed the man, and the Commodore thought he noticed a slight limp; this was to be expected, time stood still for no man. A feeling of nostalgia mixed with companionship came over him, from out of the past stepped an old friend and a colleague who was returning to the fold. He had many years of memories associated with the section, but that chilly night in November stood out as the single most decisive moment. Had John Williams failed then, the whole future of the organisation could have suffered; he had a lot to be grateful for, but he also realised that he was doing John no favours in what he was about to ask of him; it could so easily cost him his life.

The sound of footsteps could be heard coming towards the door and a gentle knock followed.

"Come in," he called.

The two men entered the room and old acquaintances from

years gone by now stood and faced one another once again. It was at that moment that Steve Bright realised there was indeed something very special between these older men, something well out of reach of the rest of the section. This Geordie was obviously highly regarded by his superior, and the likelihood that he was indeed the first 'eliminator' was increasing by the second. There was a silence in the room as they stood and looked into each other's eyes, Steve was unsure of what to do next; the Commodore solved the situation.

"Thank you, Bright," he said, "you can leave us now."

This was John's first meeting with the officer since the day he had killed Robert McIvaney in the City of York. "Hello John," said the Commodore, finally breaking the silence and offering his outstretched hand.

"Hello sir," replied John and, as he did all those years ago, he accepted it.

It was firm then as it was now, a mutual feeling of respect for the other man going into the handshake and immediately assuring the older man that the old bond between them was still strong.

"I was deeply sorry to hear of your loss," said the Commodore sympathetically, "it must have been an awful blow to you; because I've never married I'm not in a position to appreciate how much."

John only nodded.

Commodore Ward was conscious that it obviously still pained John a great deal; this would be his greatest barrier to overcome if he wished to persuade him into accepting the operation. Walking over to the drinks cabinet, he poured out two generous measures of Navy rum and handed one of the glasses to John, who stared deeply into the dark-coloured liquid.

102

"No doubt you're wondering why I've sent for you," said the officer, "and I've too much respect for you to attempt to camouflage the situation. Now, as in the past, something has developed which I find requires your special kind of assistance."

John sat himself in one of the impressive-looking easy chairs and looked up at the grey haired old man standing in front of him. Deep down he knew as much, but at the same time thought just how ridiculous the whole thing had to be.

"It's been too long for me to 'ave to start all over again," John replied, "and in any case what's the good o' using me; you must have other people better than me now."

"Had I any alternative John, then you can be assured I would have taken it; I fully appreciate only too well what this intrusion means to you."

Whilst John remained silent and took a sip of the rum, the strong alcohol warming the inside of his stomach, the Commodore walked over to his desk and took a large portfolio from the top drawer, removed two photographs and placed them face down on the desk-top.

'Jesus Christ,' thought John, 'not this trick again; this is where I came in.'

Commodore Ward returned to where John was and sat in the matching chair next to him.

"When this section was formed all those years ago and we were instrumental in its birth, our prime responsibilities were to combat terrorism and everything it represented, at that particular time being instigated by Middle Eastern pressure groups. As the years have progressed, so has the threat; and now that threat comes to us from the I.R.A., more dangerous than ever before. It was as long ago as 1968 that the first home-made device exploded on mainland Britain, and since then the situation has steadily worsened. The financing of their needs seems to pose no stumbling blocks, they receive large donations from both exiles and sympathisers all over the world, the main suppler being the American-based Noraid fund. This supplies the means to purchase the most up-to-date weapons for their fight against British rule. The great majority of these American-Irish have never even set foot upon the soil of their ancestors, the nearest they have been to Ireland being a re-run of the film 'The Quiet Man'. If I seem a little embittered towards them, it's because I do not believe that they're fully aware of the reality of the situation we're up against, that the majority of the Irish people are peace loving, with a strong desire to remain part of the British Isles.''

The Commodore went on to describe several occasions on which the section had been directly instrumental in scoring victories over this unseen adversary, the latest incident being the seizing of a large cache of arms and explosives; a definite blow to the I.R.A.'s morale.

Finally he came to the significance behind John's recall.

''We have received information identifying the main headquarters of all I.R.A. activities in this country as a well frequented night-club in the heart of Portsmouth, whose clientele in the main are members of the armed forces. This establishment is owned by two brothers, but actually financed by the war council in Ireland, and it's from there that all arrangements were made for the transfer of the last shipment. There are strong rumours of a further cargo, one almost double the size of the one we seized, an attempt to recoup losses and regain some lost pride. Our aim is to remove this shipment as well, cancelling out the whole British connection along with it. If we could be successful in this venture, it would certainly prove to be one of the greatest blows we have been able to deliver in recent years; it would take them a long time to re-establish their network all over again.''

John sat and listened to the Commodore's words, noticed the obvious enthusiasm in the man's face and understood the need to do whatever was necessary to strike a blow against this evil which hid in the shadows of innocent people. He was one of the 'bring the boys back home' brigade and honestly believed that after the initial bloodbath they would soon opt to rejoin the flag.

"Now we come to your part in all this," added the officer, "that is if you decide to take it on; nothing will be forced upon you John, and nothing less thought of you. It's your decision, and yours alone."

John nodded, and looked the old man straight in the eye.

"Well, let's hear what you've got for me," he replied, "then we'll see about it."

"I want you to go to Portsmouth and somehow get friendly with the two brothers in question," explained the Commodore, "gain their confidence and find out anything which might help us destroy their organisation. Once the shipment has been seized, and if things go as I hope they will, it will then be up to you to eliminate the brothers."

John listened calmly, but in all honesty could not believe what he was hearing.

"Do I get this right sir?" he asked bemusedly, "You actually want me to get pally with these two known killers, whose main hobbies include blowin' people away. If they've really done only half of what you've told me, then they're not a couple o' fools and they'll be able to smell out a rat a mile away. After they lost that last lot o' arms, they're sure to be bloody careful who they even talk to, never mind bein' matey with."

The John Williams of twenty years ago would not have dared question the Commodore's wisdom, he would have accepted what was told him and carried it out to the best of his ability.....but this was not the same John Williams of old. It would have been difficult enough for him to rejoin the section after such a long absence, even if all that had been required of him had been a 'straight kill' as in the past, but this operation seemed to be nothing short of insanity.

The old man had anticipated the look of utter disbelief which had appeared on John's face, and decided that it was time to show him the two photographs.

"Your immediate reaction is perfectly understandable," he smiled, passing the first of the photographs to John, "but it might not prove to be as difficult as you imagine." The face meant nothing to John; nothing stood out to him. It was of a man aged somewhere in his late thirties or early forties, black curly hair tinged with quite a bit of grey: bushy eyebrows above vacant-looking green eyes. The name on the photograph was Timothy Patrick Reagan; something else which meant absolutely to him.

Shaking his head slightly, he replaced the photograph on the arm of the chair, and accepted the second one from the Commodore.

This face was something entirely different and took him completely by surprise, no need for a second look.

"Michael," he said quietly, "Michael Reagan."

"Yes John," confirmed the officer, "Michael Reagan.....I understand you know him."

106

The face brought back many memories for John, all of them good; of laughter, countless drinking sessions and true companionship in their youth. The clear eyes with the 'couldn't give a fuck for man nor beast' look about them, and the mouth which seemed to smile a permanent smile. Michael had been completely grey by the time he reached his twentieth birthday, it was his 'Jeff Chandler' look which attracted him more than his fair share of the opposite sex. On many a run ashore, when they were not battling side by side in some local dive, he would take to the dance floor; he was the most energetic rock 'n roller most people had ever seen, and other dancers made plenty of space so they could stand and watch in awe. The two of them had met on the very first day of their time in the Navy, living in the same dormitory during training, with their beds next to each other. During the loneliness and homesickness of those traumatic first few weeks, they had sought each other's company in an attempt to combat it together; it was the first time either one had been away from home. They were both just turned sixteen years old, and, from the day they met, their friendship grew and became stronger. After completing eighteen months training, the drafting authorities even managed to keep them together for the next five and a half years; then fate took a hand and John was sent to join *H.M.S. Falcon* and Michael went into the submarine service. Nine months later Commander Ward had offered John his new way of life.

"It's true John," said the officer, as he retrieved Michael's photograph and put it back with the other into the file, "Michael Reagan and his brother were recruited by the provisional I.R.A. during the month of February, 1970, and in December of '77 took control of 'The Four Leaf Clover Club' in Portsmouth.

107

We have had them under scrutiny for the past six months; one of our operatives even managed to get a job in the club itself. I'm relying on your past close friendship with Michael to get you the necessary foothold we need to provide us with a way into their organisation." The Commodore paused momentarily, then continued, "It wasn't until I became aware of Michael Reagan's Naval career that I decided to search the records and came up with this uncanny coincidence. It's strange how certain paths open up when you least expect it; now you must realise my need for your return."

From the moment he had received the key through the post, John had known that at the end of the day he would do exactly what was required of him. The matter was now out of his hands; he knew that he had to find out the truth about his old friend....no matter how distasteful it turned out to be.

"All right, sir," he said, "I'm in."

The following two weeks seemed never ending, but at the finish he realised the significance of it all, and in a way he was grateful to the Commodore for giving him the chance to become involved in something once again, because his life had been going nowhere.

On the first morning he had been put through a thorough medical examination by the section's appointed Medical Officer, a small wiry character with the largest and also the coldest hands he had ever had the misfortune of 'coughing' into. The doctor's diagnosis was that, for a man of forty four, John Williams was in reasonable condition; with heart and lungs strong and the remainder adequate for whatever was required. The only apparent weakness he found was a slight deterioration in his eyesight, but that was to be expected in a man of his age. At six feet in height and weighing thirteen stones ten pounds, John was well proportioned, with only the slightest sign of excess weight around his midriff. Before Angela's illness, they had both been regular players of squash and badminton, enjoying many hours of friendly competition; she had looked beautiful in her skimpy white outfits and the thought of her brought back a sadness which he had to fight off.

After the medical examination, phase two went into operation; he was entrusted to the care of some sadistic physical training instructor who had to satisfy himself that John's bits and pieces would not fall off under stress......this he did. Every limb in his body ached, he must have been crazy to submit himself to this amount of punishment; if he had had any sense whatever he would have told the Commodore to stuff his operation and returned to the calm and tranquillity of his home.

Five days later the punishment stopped, the P.T.I. was satisfied that John would not drop dead on the job and passed him fit to proceed.

It was then the viewings took place. He was put in a locked room and shown specific video recordings of actual scenes from the aftermath of I.R.A. bombings and assassinations. No television network would ever have been given permission to show these to the general public; the carnage caused by a 'nail bomb' or an explosive device placed under some unsuspecting person's car was beyond description or comprehension, almost like some scene from a local abattoir, the remnants carried away in black plastic bags. In the darkness of the room, he felt the gradual emergence of hate towards these evil people who were responsible; it was now becoming something personal. Very different from sitting in the safety of your home far away from these true life atrocities and listening to the news reports on the latest I.R.A. murders. Television and radio did exceptionally well under the circumstances but, due to necessary restrictions placed upon them, were unable to convey the real message to the ordinary men and women in the street. It was not possible to convey fully just how devastating and utterly revolting these so-called liberators of the I.R.A. actually were.

If it turned out that Michael and his brother were involved, he could surely feel no remorse over the necessity of having to destroy him; and if that meant death by his hand, then so be it.

After the viewings were over, the Commodore entered the room and produced more still photographs clearly showing the brothers talking with a man known as Rudi Schumaker, one of Europe's principal arms dealers. They had been taken recently in Madrid and gave rise to the suspicion that another arms deal was about to be carried out.

"If possible, John," said the Commodore, "we would prefer it if Mr. Schumaker were taken out of the game as well."

"If the opportunity presents itself," said John, "then he'll go."

"Only one more for you to look at, then you've seen everything."

John knew this face too; it was Rose, an ex-Wren who had become some kind of obsession with Michael. He could never understand the obvious attraction or the hold she had over him, but it did not matter where they had been, Michael always returned to her like some love-sick pigeon.

"She's living with him as his common-law wife," added the Commodore, "that's if we still have such a thing in today's society; people now have 'live-in lovers' and their resulting off-spring are now known as 'love children'.....at least it sounds a lot better than the truth.''

So they had never married after all. It had come as no surprise to anyone when Rose had announced that she was pregnant but, all credit to Michael, he vowed to do the right thing by her. Fortunately or unfortunately, whichever view you happened to take at the time, she fell down the steps of the cinema and miscarried. Rather than providing Michael with an escape route, this accident had only served to bring the two of them closer.

Thinking back over the loving relationship he shared with Angela, and their desperate yearning for a child, John was now in such a position to appreciate how such a turn of events could have that effect. It brought him to ponder over the forthcoming meeting between tried and trusted friends, and the kind of reception he would receive. Would they still welcome him after all these years and the changes in their lives? Even before they met, an invisible barrier had been erected between them, one consisting of violence and deceit; and if somehow they found out about the true reason behind his sudden visit, it could prove to be fatal to him.

The following week was spent on the underground firing range with the section armourer scrutinising his every move, the general public walking about above them and totally unaware of what was taking place under their feet. After the initial re-accustoming himself to various weapons to 'get the feel of things again', he eventually selected a .38 calibre Colt Python revolver, specially fitted with a shortened 2½" barrel which was constructed with a heavier type of metal, producing an added strength as well as reducing 'muzzle jump'. All in all a very effective and deadly weapon, though John doubted he would derive much pleasure from its use. It did not take long for his natural ability to come to the fore; his old skill was very much in evidence. The re-cocking and trigger mechanism were expertly adjusted to suit his personal requirements and he found this made the weapon extremely smooth and produced a much quicker firing rate.

"I've got to admit that's pretty fair shooting, Mr. Williams, sir."

That same voice he had heard behind him on Waterloo station was there again. John had just completed a rapid succession of six shots, three sets of twos as was recommended; five had entered the heart-shaped plaque, the sixth a trifle adrift, but close enough to cause someone considerable discomfort.

"You spyin' on me, young man?" asked John, with a slight smile, "I have to admit it's not bad; but it still doesn't compare with you.....you see I've been doin' a little bit of spyin' of my own."

It was natural enough for John to smile at this young man, he was definitely a genuine kind of person with a pleasant enough manner. The compliment he had paid him was the truth, Steve Bright was an excellent marksman, obviously the Commodore still chose his team wisely.

"Mr. Williams, sir," said the young man, "I know the reason you were sent for..and I promise you that you'll be able to rely on me."

"What do you mean....I'll be able to rely on you?" asked a bewildered John.

An uncomfortable look appeared on the face of Steve Bright as he realised that the Commodore obviously had not enlightened John on the part he was to play in the forthcoming operation.

112

"I'm sorry sir, I thought you knew," he apologised, "when I realised who you were, I asked the Commodore if I could work with you in whatever it was he had sent for you to do......he agreed, I'm to be your back-up."

"Times have certainly changed," smiled John, in an attempt to ease the other's discomfort, "I was always used to working on my own....but maybe the company will do me good."

"I think we'll get along just fine," beamed Steve.

"By the way," said John, "is it common knowledge why I'm here, because I was under the impression the whole thing was supposed to be hush-hush?"

"Apart from the boss and the two of us, the rest are in the dark," replied Steve, "most people are guessing hard, but no-one knows anything for certain. They're all a bit puzzled by you suddenly turning up out of the past, and you've been the topic of a few wild rumours; I will admit that."

"You ever had to kill anybody, Steve?" he asked seriously.

"No sir, I haven't," the young man replied, "but if the need arises....I'll do what I have to."

"I don't doubt that for a minute," added John, "but there's one thing I want you to remember and that is, when the time does come, the fact that you're in this section almost guarantees it will.....be positive. An old instructor of mine used to drill it into me, always make certain of your kill.....because you might not get a second chance. We're not here to observe the niceties, we 'ave to be able to kill another person without the fear of bein' bothered by conscience. Do to the I.R.A. as they have done unto countless others, it's the only way to survive; there's no room for self recrimination or doubt whatever."

This speech was one of the longest John had ever delivered to anyone about anything. He was usually a man of as few words as possible, but he felt that it had helped Steve to understand the situation and he became more at ease with himself.

"I don't want to 'ave you thinking that I'm lecturin' you son," he added, with a smile, "but I think a' know what you're going through.......After all, the old man 'ere's been through it all before and, I might add, was the first to do so."

"You ever been to York?" he asked, a little pensively.

"York?" asked John, "Where the fuck's York?"

After a concentrated two weeks' training, John Williams was once again judged ready to face up to the outside world and its adversaries; he was ready to go.

"Do not, under any circumstances, become too involved with these people," instructed the Commodore, "and always remember what they're guilty of. I realise this is new ground for you and that it will take time to adjust....but be extremely careful and don't rush headlong into things. I will rely on you to use your own initiative; it's always stood you in good stead in the past and I've no doubt it will see you safely through this. Young Bright will remain in the background, he is there to assist you whenever the need arises. He may be a little green, but I've no doubts or reservations about using him........certain things he does remind me of you yourself, and that must be a plus factor; he'll prove to be a valuable asset to have with you."

John was then handed an envelope containing two thousand pounds expenses, more would be made available if needed; the cost was of no consequence. Finally, after shaking hands with the old man, he walked out the undistinguished looking

114

building and climbed into Steve Bright's little sports car.

Once again he belonged to the section.

Arrangements were for the young man to drive to Portsmouth, but to drop John off at Havant, where he was to spend the night with his in-laws. He would then travel independently the following day and register at the same hotel as Steve. They were to be discreet in their communication with each other, no physical link between them had to be suspected.

The drive to Havant proved to be a minor nightmare as far as John was concerned. The little sports car was a far cry from the large Volvo parked in his garage, and sat so low to the ground that it produced an uneasy feeling of having his rectum scraped along the tarmac at speeds approaching one hundred miles an hour.

It was a much relieved passenger that alighted from the vehicle outside the Andrews residence, extremely grateful to be still in one piece. Had the section's Medical Officer placed his stethoscope on John's heart at that precise moment, he would have despatched him back to Durham with all possible haste; a suspected seizure in the offing.

'Jesus, 'e's a bloody nutter,' he thought, after watching the car roar off into the darkness.

It was almost nine p.m. and, after gathering up his suitcase, he walked slowly to the front door; ringing the bell, he soon heard the sound of footsteps.

"Bloody hell!" exclaimed his father-in-law, as he opened the door and found John standing outside. "Lillian!" he called over his shoulder, "Come 'n see who's visiting us."

Grabbing the suitcase from John, he wrapped his free arm firmly around his shoulder and led him into the house. Lillian came into the hallway, curious to find out what all the com-

115

motion was about. She looked tired and frail, the loss of her only child had surely taken its toll on her. The instant she recognised the visitor, tears flooded into her eyes and she came to him, reaching up to kiss his cheek.

"Hello flower," he said.

"It's lovely to see you John," she said, wiping her eyes, "come into the sitting room where it's nice and warm."

The pair of them ushered John into the room and took his coat and scarf, closing the outer door to keep out the cold of the winter night.

"It's only a flyin' visit," he explained, "thought a'd just surprise you before you had time to bolt the door on me."

A comfortable feeling came over him at being with them once again, as if he sensed Angela's presence. The last time he had seen his in-laws was at the funeral and that had been a most sombre time for everyone concerned.

"Never mind that for now," smiled Andy, "a nice glass o' rum is called for to warm the cockles of yer' heart. I know that you're quite partial to the odd tipple....and it just so happens that I've got a couple o' bottles of 'neaters' stowed away for such an occasion."

"If only you'd have let us know," his mother-in-law chided him, "I could have prepared a nice hot meal for you, I bet you haven't had one all day."

Excusing herself, she disappeared into the kitchen; returning after a few moments with a plateful of sandwiches. The next couple of hours were spent with the three of them reminiscing over the past, with one person foremost in their thoughts, bringing both joy and sadness in her memory. There was a regular supply of the excellent navy rum and it began to have an effect on John; he was feeling more relaxed and at ease

116

with himself than he had for a long time.

"How've you coped John?" asked Andy, with obvious concern in his voice.

"It's been all downhill," admitted John, with a slight shrug of his shoulders, "but I think I've turned the corner at last....things can only get better."

Sometime shortly before midnight, Lillian stifled a yawn, apologised and went up to her room. This sudden reappearance of her son-in-law, although he was always more than welcome in their home, had rekindled the past and with it a renewed sadness in her heart.

More drink followed Lillian's departure and a lot of idle banter passed between the two men, the topic of conversation naturally revolving around their times in the navy. The room was thick with the atmosphere of rum and *'Old Holborn'*, as the fumes belched freely from the end of Andy's walnut pipe. After a particular lengthy spell of silence, the old Master-at-Arms looked into the eyes of his son-in-law and finally came out with what he had bottled up inside him for the last twenty years.

"Listen son," he said, "normally wild horses couldn't drag you away from that bloody North East of yours, so what's the real reason behind the visit? It would be nice to think you've come all this way just to see two old codgers like us...but I've a strange feeling that it's more than just that; the same kind of feeling I had when you suddenly turned up in Singapore. What're you up to John?"

Deep down in his heart, John wanted to tell him the secret he had kept so long which weighed heavily on his mind. Could it be possible that the time was right to tear away the barriers of officialdom which had restrained him all these years; to break from the rules and regulations of the Official Secrets Act by which he was bound. Now at last, here in the warmth and friendliness of this small room, in the company of a compassionate friend and ally; the alcohol swilling around inside his brain was urging him to unload his story and to bring release. After long thought, he made up his mind.

"You're right Andy," he began, "but it's the same as it was all that time ago, I still can't tell you; I'm sorry. A lot of confidences would be shattered, not to mention the Official Secrets Act, and by saying that alone I've said too much."

"So you were mixed up in something cagey after all," the old man replied, nodding his head in confirmation of his suspicions, "I bloody well knew it all along. How come you're back amongst it all.....that is if you were ever out of it?"

John sat deep in thought, and Andy waited patiently for his answer.

"When I was sent out to the far east, it must 've stood out like a sore thumb that I didn't know the first thing about how the regulating branch operated, and at that time a' didn't know if you knew what I was involved in, or not."

The old man shook his head.

"As a matter of fact son," he said, "I wasn't told anything about you until I got summoned to a meeting with some high 'n mighty rear-admiral, who I managed to find out later had something to do with the intelligence service; he quietly advised me to treat you with kid gloves until you found your feet. When you get that kind of 'request' from such a person...you do exactly as you're told; otherwise it could have cost me my pension."

"Well one thing cropped up which they hadn't bargained for," said John, "I met and married the most beautiful and

118

caring girl in the world; this threw a spanner in their works, and I did it without even realising that I had. Because I then had an immediate dependant, I'd made myself useless to them; a condition a' didn't know about was that I was supposed to stay 'unattached'. From that day I was a bona-fide member of the regulating branch, and you 'ave to admit that I didn't do too bad a job of it. It was a few weeks ago when they got in touch with me again; unbeknown to me, once Angela died, I was officially put back on the active list.......now they find they need me.''

''That satisfies an old man's curiosity,'' said Andy, blowing a large cloud of tobacco smoke into the air and watching it swirl its way up to the ceiling, ''but whatever it is you're mixed up in.....be careful.''

The partial truth was out and John felt a little guilty at betraying the trust placed in him, but at the same time he realised that he had not divulged anything of real significance or which could endanger the operation.

Andy stared at his son-in-law with a new found admiration; getting out of his chair he poured out another two generous measures of rum.

''Last one, then it's off to bed we go,'' he announced, ''Lillian 'n me, we loved our little girl more than anything in the whole world. When the two of you said you wanted to get married, I'll not lie to you John, there was this shadow over you which worried me and I had reservations about the whole thing. There was no reason I could put to her to turn her against you, not that it would've mattered because she loved you so much, so I gave my blessing with reluctance. Nevertheless, since that day you became part of our family and in the years you were together, you more than proved yourself to be a bloody good husband to her. You cared for her when she needed your strength to get through each day and, for that alone, we'll always be grateful to you.....you'll always be part of our family.''

''Thanks Andy,'' replied John sincerely, ''you two are the only family I've got left, so it looks as if we're stuck with each other. Before I leave in the mornin' there's an envelope I want you to keep for me; inside's my will. I know this sounds a bit melodramatic, but it's necessary and, because I've no immediate family left alive, I've named you 'n Lillian as my next of kin. All of this is just a precaution and nothin' for you to worry yoursel' about and, if things go as planned, then you can give me it back..then we'll sit down and finish off the rest of that rum, OK?''

''OK son,'' agreed Andy, ''but as I've already said, be careful how you go. It's a bloody evil world we're now living in.''

Deciding that he was worn out and would like to turn in for the night, he bade Andy goodnight and climbed wearily up the stairs. They led him to the room in which he had so often slept with Angela; he felt again how much he missed her. It was the first time he had slept in the room without her.

Chapter Seven

He slept soundly, the amount of alcohol he had drunk the night before had guaranteed him that much, and now he was almost ready for the short journey into Portsmouth. Lillian had roused him earlier with her usual cup of strong coffee, as she had done on previous visits. The only difference was the absence of Angela snuggling up beside him and squinting over the sheets. Lillian's face was drawn and she looked older than her years; his sudden reappearance had rekindled so many sorrowful memories which she had tried so hard to keep under control.

"Come on John, rise and shine," she said, with a smile which did not fool him.

"Lillian.......I'm sorry flower if my turnin' up out of the blue's caused you any distress; I never thought," he apologised, "I'm an inconsiderate sod.......I shouldn't a' come."

"Nonsense," she rebuked him, putting on a brave face, "it's lovely to see you again, you know that,........only when you walked through that door last night, somehow I half expected our Angela to be with you. I'm just a silly old woman who can't forget her."

"Do you know something," he said, "I used to spend hours.....days, just sittin' in her favourite chair and looking through all our old photos. But one day I realised that if a' didn't buck myself up and somehow snap out of it, a'd go round the bend.....in fact I was almost halfway there. We 'ave our memories of her, no-one can ever take them away from us; but we've got a life to get on with, too. I'll never forget her as long as a' live, she's the best thing that ever happened to me.....but I'm determined to start all over again, I know that she wouldn't begrudge me that."

Lillian brushed a tear from her eye and smiled.

"You've a wise head on your shoulders, John Williams," she said, "anyway, enough of this, we've still got you haven't we.....and it's about time for breakfast, so get your lazy self ready."

With that she turned and left the room, closing the door behind her.

After dressing, he glanced at the brown coloured envelope which he had 'borrowed' from the Commodore's desk, the contents of which were to be entrusted to Andy's care. In the event of his death, everything he possessed was to be sold and the sum total, together with what he had in the building society, which included Angela's death premium, was to be donated to the National Research Foundation for the fight against cancer; hopefully somebody somewhere would discover a way to cure this evil disease. With the sale of their home, the almost new car in the garage and all the other odds and ends, the final count would be somewhere in the region of eighty thousand pounds.

His own parents had died in the last ten years and the Andrews were financially all right, so the money could be used to ease the burden of others. In a way he realised that he was indebted to the Commodore for restoring his reason for living, he was to become instrumental in striking a blow against a different king of cancer; the kind caused by the killers and supporters of the I.R.A.

Removing the Colt from its protective case, he found the cold metal reassuring to his touch. He then put it into the inside of his left boot and found it was a snug fit; tight enough not to dislodge itself when he walked around the room. The next five minutes or so were spent practising his 'quick draw' method, his right hand going to the top of the boot and bringing the revolver to bear on different fitments about the bedroom. He realised he would never be greased lightening, but there again the need might never arise for a quick draw. As long as the gun was there, he had a chance; and that was all he wanted.

Under normal circumstances Andy would never have dreamed of just coming into the bedroom, but on this particular morning he decided to be different. He tapped on the door and walked straight in, at the precise moment the Colt had left John's boot; the .38 revolver levelled itself on his heart.

"For cryin' out loud!" he spluttered, his face draining of all colour, "You trying to finish me off altogether?" John in turn was totally embarrassed, feeling as though he had been caught playing like a little boy.

"Sorry Andy," he apologised, "I wasn't expectin' you."

He turned away from his astonished father-in-law and carefully put the weapon back in its case, together with the two boxes of cartridges and the four inch silencer which accompanied it.

"No need for apologies son," said Andy, his face serious, "it was my own stupid fault......I should've waited. I know you said you were back with them, but until I saw that gun, I didn't fully appreciate just how involved you were........who is it you're up against John?"

"Who're we all up against Andy......the I.R.A."

The old man looked astounded. "The I.R.A........here?"

"They're all over the bloody place, people just don't realise it....but with a bit o' luck we're goin' to fuck 'em up a little."

"Jesus Christ, you be bloody careful," said Andy.

"I've every intention of bein' bloody careful just like yer said," smiled John, "now forget you saw the gun, an' let's get downstairs and 'ave some breakfast."

Breakfast in the Andrews home had always been a grand affair and today was no exception, the full works, bacon, sausage, eggs and fried tomatoes, with toast and marmalade on the side. But, keen to get away from the bedroom, John could not do it justice and, after picking away at it for ten minutes, he left most of it untouched.

Poor old Andy bore the brunt of Lillian's displeasure.

"It's your fault you old fool," she scolded him, "keeping him up till all hours and pouring that revolting drink down him.......no wonder he can't eat his breakfast."

John was quietly thankful for this plausible excuse, but the real reason behind his lack of appetite was the tension building up inside him. Inside this house he was safe from possible danger, this world was apart from the world of the Commodore and all his cronies; but he would soon leave the sanctuary and face up to the evil of the real world outside. He had never thought of himself as being a brave man, apart from his experience in Borneo, and that was the result of absolute fear. His other 'achievements' had been because of a mixture of slyness and cunning. He had killed eight men for the 'good of his country', but on each occasion he made sure he was in a position of minimal risk. This time it was to be different; he would be fully aware of his enemy, and some time soon he was going to have to face them.

If he was to get started, it was no use delaying things any longer.

"Any chance of a lift into Pompey?" he asked Andy, " 'Cos

if you're busy I'll get a taxi."

"Of course I'll take you......it'll give me a chance to get away from another tongue lashing from Lillian."

After collecting his luggage and coat, he returned to the dining room. His mother-in-law had never asked the reason for his short visit and for that he was thankful. Feeling particularly close to her at that moment, he kissed her cheek and embraced her affectionately.

"Take care of yourself, sweetheart," he said. "I'll pop back for a few days before a' go back home again."

Fingers crossed that nothing would prevent him from doing so.

During the car journey, there was an uncomfortable silence, as if neither man knew what to say to the other. Andy's thoughts were concentrated on his son-in-law and the shock of discovering that he had a gun in his possession. Normal everyday people did not realise this kind of life existed outside the safety of the cinema or their television sets, it was totally unreal to them. Everyone knew of the threat of the I.R.A., but they all just hoped it would somehow disappear and come nowhere near them and the people they loved. Now that Andy realised a member of his own family was directly involved in the fight against them, he felt closer to him than ever before.

John was half listening to the weather report over the car radio: the extreme North and North East, as well as the whole of Scotland, was being ravaged by blizzards. Heavy falls of snow had occurred in these areas for the past week without any sign of a let up; most minor roads were completely blocked and smaller villages were cut off.

He looked at the clear blue sky, with just the slightest signs of frost on the grass verges; it was as if he was in a different country. Andy brought the car to a stop in the main drive of the impressive-looking 'Queens Arms Hotel', an appropriate name in the circumstances, where John and his companion had arranged to stay; Steve should be settled in by now. Climbing out of the car, John put his case on the ground and reached into his pocket for the sealed envelope, giving it to Andy.

"Well me old mate," he smiled, and held out his hand, "this's where I 'ave to say ta-ra to you for the time bein'. Don't go worryin' yourself about me and before you know it, you'll be givin' me that back. When you do.....we'll sit down and finish off that bottle o' neaters.....OK?"

"That's a promise I expect you to keep," replied Andy, "I'll not say anything else because you know how I feel about things, but if ever the need arises and you find you need help......call me."

John watched as the car drove off, bluey white exhaust fumes trailing after it. Picking up his case, he walked into the hotel reception area with the look of a man who was accustomed to the expensive life and could afford it.

"Here for a holiday are we, sir?" enquired the receptionist with a smile which showed off her evenly matched teeth; "Durham," she added, noticing the address he wrote in the guest book, "I hear it's rather cold there."

"That's the reason I'm down 'ere," he said, purposely dropping his 'h's, "to get away from the blizzards."

"Well I hope you enjoy your stay with us," she said, "I've had you put in room twenty-two; it's at the front of the hotel and has a very pleasant view overlooking the park."

With a smile still, she rang a small bell at her side and a young boy appeared from out of some cubby-hole under the stairs.

John stepped back and allowed the boy to pick up his suitcase and at the same time cast an approving glance at the receptionist. She was immaculately dressed in a black two-piece suit and white lace blouse, very attractive and easy on the eyes; aged somewhere in her mid-thirties he guessed.

Acknowledging his approving inspection, she turned to the boy and said, "Take this gentleman's luggage up to room twenty-two." Turning her attention once again to John, she added, "If there is anything I can do to make your stay more pleasant, please let me know."

"Thank you, I will," he answered.

He followed the boy, taking the lift to the second floor. The room itself turned out to be very comfortable, only to be expected for the price they charged; not that it mattered to him, the Commodore was footing the bill.

"Smashin'," he said to the boy, and tipped him with a pound coin.

After ushering him out of the room, John closed the door and unpacked his belongings. Not wishing to alarm the cleaning staff who might rummage through his things, or alert any uninvited guests to the fact he had a gun in his possession, he decided to put it in the hotel safe until such time as it was needed. After placing the gun and its accessories, plus fifteen hundred pounds, in a small briefcase he had inside the larger case, he returned to the foyer and saw that it was put in the safe.

The remainder of the day was taken at a leisurely pace; he put on his overcoat and went for a walk, spending most of the day visiting places which reminded him of years gone by. Nostalgia seemed to be playing more and more of an important part in his life, he somehow preferred the past to the present; the past seemed so much less complicated. Gazing around he became aware of the noticeable absence of that familiar Navy blue uniform; once these streets had been crowded with sailors hustling and bustling about the place. Times had changed and sailors now were allowed ashore in their 'civvies'.

As the evening closed in, bringing with it the much colder night air, John retraced his footsteps back to the hotel. When he walked through the guests' car park, he noticed Steve's red sports car. He had not seen his young colleague about, but did not doubt that before too long he would be in touch; they had to be careful not to be connected with one another. On entering the lounge bar, he casually looked round at the three customers already inside, each one sitting alone and browsing through a newspaper or magazine.

"Bacardi and coke please," he ordered, as he moved against the short bar-rail, "quiet night?"

"It's nearly always like this during the winter months," replied the barman, "not many visitors about; and too expensive for the reps to stay here."

Thanking him for his drink, he signed for it to be charged to his account and walked over to one of the vacant seats by the large bay windows which overlooked the well-kept gardens. After an hour of sipping his way slowly through another two drinks, he finally decided enough was enough and collected his room key from the night porter in reception. There could be no advantage in appearing to discover the nightclub owned by Michael and his brother accidentally on his very first night back in Portsmouth and, as the Commodore had said, there was no immediate haste. It was two a.m. when the sound of the phone ringing awakened him and he realised that he must have fallen asleep whilst watching some uninteresting play on the TV, which was still switched on and buzzing loudly. He switched off the television set and lifted the phone.

"'Ello?"

"Mr. Williams, it's Steve.......sorry if I woke you, but I thought I'd better check with you."

"That's alright son," replied John, now fully awake, "I was 'alf expecting you to give me a ring......how are things goin'?"

"I've just came from the club....it's quite a plush affair. Both Reagan brothers were there and I'm told that it's not often they aren't. When you decide to pay it a visit, be a bit careful because they've both a rather large bodyguard apiece and believe me they look bloody evil; I intend checking them out.....you can guarantee a pair like that will certainly be known to us."

"I was thinkin' of trying it out in a couple o' nights' time," said John, "the trouble's findin' something to fill the time in with until then.....but I don't want to rush things. I'd rather 'ave Michael recognise me, than me 'im."

"I agree," replied the young man, "by the way, you shouldn't have too much trouble getting into the club. Although it's supposed to be strictly for members, I found that a little bit of the old palm tickling will get you in."

"Right then, son, I'll see to that. You get yerself back there tomorrow night and just keep an eye out for anything that might interest us...O.K.?"

"I'll do that," acknowledged Steve.

"By the way, Steve," said John bringing the conversation to a close, "do me a favour will you and call me John, you make me feel ancient with this 'Mr. Williams'......goodnight."

The following two days took on a similar pattern to the first,

John spent most of his time wandering about the streets of the City, going into the odd pub for a glass of lager or two....generally passing the hours away. At ten p.m. on the third night of his 'holiday' he was dressed for the part and stood outside the doors of *'The Four Leaf Clover Club'*.

'Right then,' he told himself, ' 'ere we go, into the lion's den.'

He knocked loudly on the green door, after all he was on his holidays with plenty of money in his pocket, so why should he be reserved. It was opened by a smart looking man wearing a tuxedo, the normal attire for such employees.

"Yes sir," he asked politely, "can I help you?"

"Hopefully," replied John, putting on one of his warmest smiles, "I was wonderin' if there was any chance o' me getting in?"

"Are you a member, sir?" asked the doorman, knowing full well that he was not.

"No, I'm afraid I'm not," admitted John, "I only came down 'ere a few days ago for a bit of a holiday and one o' the guests stayin' at the same hotel as me said that the club was one of the best places around."

"Well sir," added the doorman, "I'm sorry but you've either got to be a member, or have a member sign you in; that's the law and you wouldn't like us to break the law, would you?"

" 'Corse I wouldn't," answered John, then making a show of hesitancy, he added, "surely there must be some way around these rules of yours; I've been bored stiff so far and a'd really fancy a night in here."

The smart looking doorman seemed to ponder over John's suggestion, as if trying to reach some monumental decision.

"I'll tell you what sir," he finally said, after deliberating the problem, "ten quid will get you inside as well as making you a member; plus a second ten quid for me sponsoring you....I promise you it's all above board and good value; we're well known as being the best club in the area."

Removing his wallet from his inside pocket, John peeled off two crisp ten pound notes from the many inside and handed them to the doorman. "That'll do for me," he said.

"Thanks," said the doorman, accepting the money, "all that's needed now is for you to sign the members' book and put your home address in it and as long as your name's on the register you can come in any time you like."

Scrutinising the address, he smiled at John.

"From Durham eh," he stated, "I like Geordies myself, but we've had a few of your lot down in the past that 'ave caused us a bit of aggro. The owners insist that members and their guests must behave themselves, or they have them ejected....and they've got the right pair upstairs who thrive on doing just that....but you don't look the type to cause any trouble, am I right sir?"

"Well to answer your first question first," replied John cordially, "yes I'm from Durham, but I'm not a Geordie; and you're right, I don't like bother of any kind....all I want to do is to be able to come in and have a quiet drink, maybe even find myself female companionship; you see I'm more of a lover than a fighter. I'd rather find mysel' in a violent clinch with some lovely woman than an 'orrible bloke with whiskers."

"Well then," laughed the doorman, "if it's loving you're after, there'll be plenty of that about a little later on."

With that, the door to the outside world was closed behind him; at least the first hurdle was cleared...he was inside the club. Climbing the flight of stairs which led to the lounge, he heard a woman singing, she was singing one of his favourite country and Western songs. Inside was as Steve had described it, lavishly furnished in various shades of green, undoubtedly the Irish connection.... at least they were not attempting to conceal that aspect of things. John thought he could have been forgiven for thinking he was on the film set of *'The Men of Sherwood Forest.'*

Strolling casually over to the bar and surveying his surroundings at he same time, he sat on one of the stools at the bar. Although it was only a little after ten p.m. and the pubs outside would still be open, there were quite a few customers inside; the majority of them sitting with their attention fixed on the singer seated behind a piano. But he could see no sign of the brothers and their 'minders', but there was plenty of time; as night-club hours went this was early.

"Bacardi and coke," he ordered as the barman approached, producing one of his better smiles; the barman was wearing a dark green suit which could easily have been mistaken for something out of Robin Hood.

It had to be a gimmick, just the kind he would expect of Michael; there again it appeared to be very effective. All it needed to complete the scene was some tiny leprechaun playing a penny whistle to the tune of *'Danny Boy'*. John's attention focused on the singer, the sound of her voice was lovely and her diction so clear; a far cry from the modern singers who use all kinds of contraptions to hide the fact that they can't sing. She was a very attractive, if not beautiful, young woman in her mid-twenties, with blonde hair which came down to her smooth white shoulders, she had deep blue eyes and brilliant white teeth. As she sang she switched her attention from one person to another, giving the impression that she was singing to each of them individually. When her gaze came to rest on John, he felt himself smile at her, it had been an automatic reaction, but her eyes soon moved past him to her next victim.

"Lovely isn't she," said the barman, noticing John's smile.

"She is at that," he agreed, "in fact she's gorgeous."

The barman introduced himself as Tom and told him he had worked at the club for the past five years and that she was the best resident singer they had ever had; John decided that ruled him out, thinking back to the Commodore saying that the section had an operative working on the inside.

"People come here just to sit and look at her," added Tom, "but there's a rumour going round that she's a bit of a 'lesby', if you know what I mean. It's hard to believe, but there again she's never shown the slightest interest in any man."

"Gerraway!" exclaimed John, genuinely shocked, "I can't believe that."

"Well I don't know if it's the absolute truth," said Tom, shrugging his shoulders a little, "but there's a bloke here who works for the boss, and he's been tryin' it on since she came here; but she's took no notice of him at all...There again with Lurch, nobody can blame her, he's bloody horrible."

"Lurch," repeated John, "what kind o' name's Lurch?"

Tom laughed. "He's called Lurch after the weird lookin' bloke in the 'Adams Family'....you know them, they're a family of monsters that used to be on the telly. Well Lurch is named after him, and believe it or not, we 'ave another one just like him called 'Herman'; he's named after the one in 'The Munsters'......you must have seen them on the telly, everybody has."

133

"Yeh, I remember them," said John, laughing, "is it what people call 'em to their faces, or do they call them by their proper names?"

"No, they both love it...think it's great," replied the barman, "one of the owners. Timothy Reagan, he christened them years ago and it just stuck; they even call themselves by it; as a matter of fact I don't think I can remember their real names. But there's one thing I do know, and that is to be very wary of both o' them; they're alright if you steer well clear of them, but if you happen to cross them......."

Tom left the sentence unfinished, but shook his head as if in mourning.

"That bad eh?" asked John.

Tom nodded his affirmation. "That bad," he repeated.

Turning his attention again to the young woman who was now being applauded for the end of her song, John shook his head as if in dismay. "What a bloody awful waste of good womanhood," he said sadly, and took a drink from the glass in front of him. From the corner of his eye, he saw Steve enter the room and take up a stool on the side of the bar opposite; well away from himself. It was midnight when the singer came to the end of her final song, to much loud applause and whistling; John himself joined in the applause but managed to control himself as far as the whistling went.

She stood up, stepped away from the piano and gave a slight bow of her head; her flashing smile of acknowledgement concentrated on the whole room. After the appreciation had waned a little, she stepped from the small stage and walked across the dance floor, disappearing through a door at the far end of the room marked 'Private'. He had time enough to cast an admiring look in her direction, and he liked what he saw. She would be somewhere about five feet seven or eight, slender body, narrow waist and shapely legs which were in full view, the side split in her dress reaching her thigh. But time had not changed him and, as usual, it was her breasts which came under the closest scrutiny; perfectly shaped and not so large as to be ugly, with ample cleavage, to get the clientele uncomfortably adjusting their dress. Her small nipples could be easily seen protruding through the thin material, which was one of the few items in the room not coloured some shade of green. He decided that if this woman was indeed a lesbian, then there was no justice left in the world. It was a long time since the sight of a woman had made such an impression on him and he began to feel a little guilty about his thoughts; as if disrespectful of Angela's memory.

Two men entered the room by the same door the woman left, one was undoubtedly one of the pair of 'monsters' Tom and Steve had told him about; he had to be six feet five inches at least and weighed about seventeen stone. The second man was Timothy Reagan, but of Michael there was no sign.

'Jesus!' thought John, looking at Timothy's minder-cum-body-guard.

''Another Bacardi and Coke,'' he asked Tom, ''and 'ave one yersel'.''

John continued his friendly banter with the barman, who must have enjoyed his company because as soon as he was free from serving a customer with a drink, he returned to where John was and carried on their conversation. It appeared that both of them were football enthusiasts and their talk revolved around the present state of the game. Tom crowed about his team, Liverpool and their regular success for almost two decades. With John, it was the ever increasing plight of his own team, Sunderland, seemingly continuously involved in relegation battles and, in the latest and most disastrous season, slipping down into the third division for the first time in their history.

"You a scouser then, Tom?" he asked.

"Originally.....but I've been livin' here in Pompey for the past seventeen years, but I still follow the reds and when they play along the road at Southampton I always get my scarf out o' mothballs and go and see them."

"It's easy to follow a team like that," moaned John, "but you've got to 'ave a lot o' bloody willpower to watch one like mine....at times they're pitiful; but the regular supporters turn up Saturday after Saturday, hoping that one day we'll end up with a team as good as yours........but a' doubt if it'll ever 'appen in my time."

Timothy and his henchman sat at a table near the door which gave them an ideal vantage point from which they were able to observe the whole room, they sat talking quietly, occasionally sharing a joke which made them both laugh. Drinks were taken over to them by a pretty young waitress, there were quite a few of them circulating about the room and something else was said to her which had all three bursting into laughter, with Michael's brother making a playful grab at her, which she expertly evaded.

Three young men and two girls appeared on the stage, accompanied by extra microphones and speakers.

"Ready for blast off," announced Tom. John finished the remnants of his drink, and said, "Time for me to be makin' a move...I'm not keen on the noise."

"Me neither," said Tom, with a smile, "but I've got no choice. I've been getting into a system where I can switch me

136

ears off and just concentrate on the bar, it's a lot better that way........will you be coming back?''

"Yep, I'll be back tomorrow night," replied John, "Now that a' know where it is, a'll be a regular visitor till it's time to go home again."

"Right then, I'll see you tomorrow night, or I should say tonight......goodnight to you."

"Goodnight Tom."

With that John nodded to the barman and walked out of the room, collected his coat and walked back down the stairs to the main door.

"You leavin' already sir?" asked the doorman, "not enjoying yourself."

"Yes I enjoyed the young woman singin'," said John, "but I'm feelin' a bit tired, so I decided it's time a' was in me' bed......but I'll be back."

"I'll bid you goodnight then, smiled the doorman, "and look forward to seeing you again."

"Definitely," replied John, "and goodnight to you."

Outside the club, the night was freezing cold but clear, and he inhaled a lungful of air as he walked away. He was now conscious of his surroundings, and tomorrow was another day; but he wondered why Michael hadn't made an appearance and hoped that the shipment was not going ahead earlier than they had anticipated.

Once again it was shortly after two p.m. when Steve rang him. This time he was sitting up in bed and watching a video with Charles Bronson playing the lead, as usual ridding the streets of America of undesirables.

'If we 'ad somebody like him on our side, I could go 'ome,' he thought.

"What did you think of the place?" asked his young colleague.

"Very nice, just like you said......anything happen when I left. Did Michael show up?"

"No, the place soon got crammed to watch that group...they were very good, you should have stayed, you'd have enjoyed them. Michael Reagan never came in until one thirty five.....I wonder where he'd been? Ten minutes later, the brother left the club with one of the waitresses and Michael just sat there on his own......I left a few minutes after Timothy and came straight to the hotel. You think anything's happening yet?"

"I've no idea," admitted John, "but it must be gettin' close to the time. We'll just have to see how things go.....I've got to 'appear' from out o' the past, but the problem is that it has to look natural.....I don't want to just walk up to him and say 'Ello, Michael..guess who."

"You'll sort it out," said Steve.

"There wasn't any sign of a woman with Michael, was there?.....about the same age?" asked John, thinking of Rose.

"No, none at all.....when his brother left, he just sat on his own."

"I'll make my move tomorrow night somehow," said John, "somethin' will turn up."

"You be careful."

"You can bet on that."

The following night he was welcomed by the doorman as if he was a long lost friend...Steve was already inside the club.

"Chancing it again sir?" he asked with a smile.

"I am at that," replied John, returning the smile, "That young woman singin' again?"

"Chris?....Yes she's here. Don't tell me you're taking a fancy to her."

"A waste of time by all accounts," answered John, "The barman reckons she's a bit strange......'ave to admit she's lovely to look at, but the girl's got a great voice as well."

"They all say she's odd," agreed the doorman, "but I don't believe it myself.....all she needs is a good man to sort her out."

"Pleasant thoughts," said John, as he walked up the stairs.

He got a warm welcome from Tom too. If he hadn't known better he would have been completely fooled by the outward appearance of the club and its employees; but it was what was under the surface which mattered. A glass of Bacardi and coke was put in front of him as he sat on the same stool as the previous night.

"Have the first one on me," said Tom.

"You shouldn't 'ave," said John, "but thanks all the same."

Inevitably, his attention rested again on the singer, the words of her song now well known to him.

"Memories,......all alone in the moonlight"....and she sang them with obvious feeling in her voice; the entire room was captivated.

"You takin' a bit of a shine to her?" whispered Tom.

"No" he lied, "it's just that there's something about her. Maybe it's because I can't really believe that a woman who looks as feminine as she does is strange....but whether she is or isn't she's definitely worth lookin' at."

Tom nodded his head in total agreement. "The boss knew what he was doing when he signed her on, the punters love her," he said, "just look at yourself....that's proof enough; she's a goldmine to this place."

One of the bodyguards, the one he had seen with Timothy, came sauntering across the room and sat directly in front of her, leering into her face.

"That's Lurch, the one I told you about last night," said Tom quietly, "he never gives up......right ugly lookin' bastard ain't he."

The young woman was doing her level best to ignore the obvious distraction, but on the rare occasion her eyes accidently met Lurch's, she coloured in embarrassment. It must have been an immense relief to her when her final number was finished and she could escape his unwelcome attention; but by this time both brothers had entered the room and Lurch had gone over to stand alongside his 'twin'.

Michael was instantly recognisable; slightly more portly than he had been, but there was no mistaking him......and in a funny sort of way John was looking forward to meeting him again, the anticipation was rising inside him. He was grateful for Tom's conversation because it made things that much easier.

Ten minutes after leaving the stage, the singer reappeared dressed in her normal street clothes, walked across the room and sat on the stool next to John.

"Gin and tonic, Tom," she asked in a quiet voice, "I need it to calm my nerves."

The barman poured out her drink. "I see he gave you the treatment again." he said to her, "you want to complain to the boss....tell 'im you'll walk out of here if he doesn't warn 'im off."

"What good will it do," she asked, "it's all part of the game to them....I only wish that I didn't need the money."

"Never mind, Chris," said Tom, with a sympathetic smile, "one day something will turn up for you and you'll be able to walk out o' here.....tell them to stuff it."

Then turning his attention to John, he added, "Chris...I'd like you to meet John, he's here all the way from Durham and I know he's dyin' to meet you."

Chris turned her head and looked into John's surprised eyes.

"Hello John," she said, "are you on holiday?"

John felt momentarily tongue-tied; he had been discreetly listening to the conversation, then suddenly Tom had introduced her to him.

"Ahhemmnn...." he coughed a little to clear his throat, "yes....came down a few days ago."

"Are you staying long?" she asked, smiling at his uneasiness.

"I'm not sure....a couple of weeks or so; there's no real hurry to get home."

"Talking of home," she said, checking her watch, "it's almost time I was on my way. My taxi will be coming shortly."

Unknown to John, Timothy's eyes had followed Chris to the bar and he noticed John being introduced to her; not only that .....he noticed that she smiled at this other man and began to talk to him. That in itself was something out of the ordinary, normally she evaded any kind of contact with men as if they all carried the plague. Timothy knew about Lurch's obsession with her too, how he worshipped the ground she walked on; and that Lurch had never had the slightest encouragement...she obviously detested the sight of him.

Timothy decided to have some fun at Lurch's expense.

"Hey, Lurch," he said, "see your girl friend's bein' chatted up by that fella' at the bar...not only that, she seems to be enjoying it as well; must prefer his company to yours.......can't see why, he's a fair bit older than her. But there again, some women like the older man.....they seem to know how to use it better than the younger ones; it's not the wham-bam thank you ma'am with them, their hearts couldn't take it."

He stifled a smile at the rage building up inside the giant of a man.

"There again," he added fuel to the fire, "you can't really blame 'er, he's not a bad lookin' fella."

Without any warning, Lurch hurried away from the table in the direction of the bar, his face like stone and his pride hurt.

Michael had heard Timothy goading the bodyguard and he knew what would inevitably follow; some poor innocent bloke at the bar was in for a nasty surprise.

"Timothy," he said, "I wish you wouldn't take the piss out of Lurch....you know he can't take it. We want punters to come into the club, not get carried out of it; it's not good for business."

"It's only a bit o' harmless fun, Michael," protested his brother, "it helps to break the monotony.....anyway it's only another Brit bastard that's goin' to get a thumpin'."

Michael turned in his seat to see the person who was in trouble, but he couldn't see him clearly because of the immense span of Lurch's shoulders. Lurch reached the bar at the precise time Chris had announced that she would have to be leaving..and he clumsily barged between her and the stranger.

"Double whisky!" he snarled at Tom, " 'n be quick about it."

The barman was accustomed to Lurch's manner and he knew the signs well enough; someone was in for trouble.

"Comin' right up, Lurch," he said, attempting to smile.

John felt more than a little aggrieved at the way the large man had barged in between Chris and himself, and he could see what kind of mood he was in.

'Keep calm and say nowt,' he advised himself; hoping that once Lurch was given his drink, he would return to where he came from.

As the big man was handed his drink, he suddenly pivoted and crashed into John, the entire contents of the glass going over his suit. The move was so obvious to anyone who was watching, Lurch's intentions were crystal clear.

"Mind yer' bloody self," he now snarled at John.

"Sorry pal," apologised John, in a clear voice, "but a' didn't move....you bumped into me."

Lurch's face was getting wild with rage. "You did, yer' lying bastard!" accentuating the word 'bastard'.

It was then John realised something was amiss, there was trouble in the air.....Lurch was purposely goading him; his heartbeat began to quicken, it had been years since he had been in a fight.

"If a' did, then a'm sorry," he apologised once more, but this time in his best North Eastern accent, "a'll tell yer' what.....let me buy ya' another one to take its place, OK?" Out of the corner of his eye, he noticed Steve move away from behind his stool and take a couple of steps forward.

'No Steve,' he thought desperately, 'for fuck's sake keep out of it.'

It looked as if Lurch was in no mood to be pacified, he was after blood, and it looked like John had the appropriate group.

143

"Yer a bloody Geordie aren't you," he spat, spraying saliva into John's face, "I hate fuckin' Geordies."

He was being insistent.

John fully appreciated the predicament he was in, the large threat loomed directly over him and he accepted that he was either going to have to defend himself, or cower away into the darkness; and he had never done that in his life. He intended that he would pick his moment, the best form of defence is to attack, and the massive man standing over him would not be expecting that to happen.

"No a'm not a Geordie," he added, mentally preparing himself for what was to come, "as a matter of fact a' come from Durham......but there again it's easy enough for anybody to make that mistake."

Observing everything that was taking place at the bar, Michael had a clear view of the stranger at the bar....only he was not too sure that the man was indeed a stranger. He was positive he knew that face from somewhere; from out of the past......the Navy, a long time ago.

"John!" he said, standing from his chair, "Timothy, I know him.....he was the best friend I had in the mob; we've got to stop that mad bastard before he hurts him."

The two brothers made across the room....but they were too late.

"You're still a fuckin' Geordie," insisted Lurch, "and do you want to know something else.......there was never a Geordie until some drunken Scotsman went berserk one night and fucked a pig....you lot were the outcome.'' With that he burst into laughter, people in the club who were not already aware of the pending confrontation, soon were now.

John decided it was time; Lurch stood so close to him that he could smell his body odour.....he didn't only suffer from bad breath and B.O., his manners were not all they should be. The big man stood with his legs slightly apart in an arrogant stance which dared John to do something about the insults.....and he did just that.

Clenching his fist as hard as he could, he smashed it upwards into Lurch's unprotected testicles, feeling the satisfaction as the contact ran itself all the way up his arm. His own thirteen and a half stones went into that punch; weight coupled with momentum produced a fair number of foot pounds of force into the large man's most sensitive parts. The effort behind it almost lifted Lurch off his feet, he was caught totally unaware. With a strangled scream of agony, both of his hands went to protect his damaged parts and left the remainder of his mighty torso vulnerable. John took full advantage of the situation.

Grabbing the massive head of his would be assailant, an ear in each hand, he steadied it for the merest fraction of a second before smashing his forehead onto the large bulbous nose in front of him; it burst open like some over-ripe tomato with blood spurting in all directions. As the battered bodyguard began to totter, the temptation was too great for John; a perfectly timed uppercut brought from almost floor level nearly separated Lurch's head from the rest of his body. This monster of a man crashed backwards onto the floor like some mighty oak being felled, blood streaming from nose and mouth. He was definitely one hell of a size, whether upright or horizontal. Standing over him, John had the feeling of accomplishment David must have felt on the day he slew Goliath.

Steve Bright had seen John's every move, standing to one side and not sure of what he would have done had his older friend taken a beating; but it didn't happen. He shook his head in admiration and returned to his seat at the bar.

'The old sod still knows a trick or two,' he thought to himself.

"John!" a voice called.

Turning, John stared into the sea of faces, searching out the caller.

"John Williams," the same voice said, "I knew it was you."

It was Michael.

The two men stared at each other.

"Michael?" asked John after a short while, then with a knowing smile, he added, "Michael Reagan......bloody 'ell it's you."

The Irishman, with a large smile on his face, nodded in acknowledgement and the two old friends embraced each other.

"I'm sorry about this," apologised Michael, looking down at the prostrate form of Lurch, "this fucking great idiot's beginning to get out of hand."

John also stared down at Lurch, then back at his old friend, with a puzzled expression on his face. "You know 'im Michael?" he asked.

"Unfortunately, yes......I'm afraid he works for me, or should say me and my brother; we own this place."

"You.....own this club?"

Michael nodded and turned to the slightly smaller man by his side, then he completed the introductions. "John...this is my

146

brother Timothy, Timothy this is John Williams, one of the best friends I've ever had, and it's years since I last laid eyes on him."

"About twenty two to be precise...but it could've been yesterday," added John, "but I'm definitely impressed.....owning a night club; you've done bloody well for yourself, mate."

Timothy extended his hand and John shook it; but he was aware of the lack of feeling in the grasp of the other man.

"Any friend o' my brother's alright by me," said Timothy, with a strained smile.

Sounds from floor level caused all three men to look down at the bodyguard, he was beginning to regain his senses; tenderly feeling his battered face.

"I've never seen Lurch put away like that by any man before," said Timothy, shaking his head, "boy, did you do a fair job on him."

"Get up!" ordered Michael, "If you can't learn to control yourself better than this.. then you're out...understand?"

The large man looked distinctly embarrassed. "Yes Mr. Reagan," he mumbled, "I'm sorry."

"You got more than you bargained for this time, didn't you," added Michael, then turning his attention to the second of the bodyguards who was standing nearby, he beckoned him over. "Get him onto his feet and take 'im into the back room to clean himself up.......he's a bloody disgrace."

"Yes Mr. Reagan," said Herman, still shocked by the punishment his friend had taken at the hands of this older man, who now turned out to be the boss's friend. Helping Lurch to his feet, he kept a wary eye on the man who had inflicted the damage; he must be about twenty years older and quite a bit smaller. Had he not seen it for himself, he would not have

147

believed it was possible; he knew how strong his friend was, he had seen him in action too many times before.....but this man had disposed of him without so much as raising a sweat.

Remembering that before the trouble began, he was talking to the woman, John turned to face her; but her stool was empty, she had gone.

"Come on upstairs," said Michael, "you can borrow one of my shirts....yours has Lurch's blood all over it."

"Thanks mate," smiled John, "and if a' remember right...the last time we had a night out together, you borrowed one o' mine....'n a' never got it back."

"Well," laughed Michael, "more than likely it would've been mine in the first place....we always wore each other's clobber in those days.......happy days John, happy days."

"You really own this club, Michael?"

Michael looked about the club and nodded with apparent pride. "That I do," he said, "about twenty years ago I got disillusioned with bein' in the mob and bought myself out. It was just after I went into the submarine service......Jesus, did I make a cock up there. I couldn't stick that for long, sharin' bunks 'n going for weeks without a proper bath or dhoby...so I thought, fuck this for a lark and handed over two hundred quid to get out. It turned out to be the best two hundred I've ever spent. I was pig sick of the do this and do that....officers treatin' the lower ranks as if they were shit and thinkin' themselves a cut above normal people......But now I'm the boss, and it's me who tells others what to do; it's a great life if you don't weaken."

Michael paused for a moment and turned to look at his brother, putting an arm round his shoulders. "I eventually went back home to Ireland and became just another Irish layabout.....but

148

that's when things began to change for the better. Me'n Timothy here pooled what money we could beg, steal or borrow and took up gambling and, after winnin' a little and losin' a little....just managing to keep our heads above water....we scooped the big jackpot at the races and things then went from good to better. I 'ave to admit that it was my brainwave to come back here to Pompey, set up a club and cream all the matelots....it couldn't fail, and it hasn't. Wherever you've got servicemen, especially the Navy, you'll find men more than willin' to part with their money on having a good night out....we provide them with that and take their cash away from them into the bargain......everybody's happy with the arrangement."

Tom coughed quietly, to interrupt the two old friends, and pointed to a tray full of drinks. Michael smiled in acknowledgement and handed one to John, then one to his brother, then took one for himself.

"Thanks Tom," he said then, raising his glass, added, "to long lost friends, may they never become lost again......it's great to see you mate, you don't know how much. You've got another surprise in store for you when you come up to the flat......'n I know she's going to get a shock when she sees you as well."

"She?" asked John, "Who's this she?"

Michael laughed, he still had that impish look about him when he laughed; his eyes sparkled. "You remember Rose from the wrennery....well that's who she is, and I still can't get rid of her."

"You don't want to get rid of her," butted in Timothy; John noticed the disdain in his voice.

"Wouldn't swap her for a beauty queen," laughed Michael, ignoring his brother's attitude, "not that I've had the chance,

149

mind you." Then his manner seemed to change a little and he looked into John's eyes. "You married mate?" he asked.

John paused for a moment, sadness coming into his eyes...there was no necessity for him to act out this part. "I was until two years ago, to a fantastic woman.....then she upped and died on me.....cancer. After that 'appened, I almost went to bits, 'cos a' was left with nobody.....no kids or nothin'. Things went from bad to worse, a' couldn't keep off the bottle and eventually lost me' job through it. It's taken all o' this time to straighten myself out and get things back together again, so I decided to come down here for a holiday and a bit of a change.....I spend hours thinkin' of the past....so I thought why not, 'n here I am. If it wasn't for some fella' stayin' in the same hotel telling me about this place, more than likely I'd 'ave stayed another couple o' days then moved on to Plymouth......there's no hurry for me to get back to Durham; anyway it's snowin' up there."

"And that big bastard tries his best to put the boot into you," spat Michael, "Jesus mate, I'm sorry," he added with compassion in both his face and voice, "but there's one thing certain from this moment on....you're goin' to have a bloody good holiday......I'll make certain of that. Come on, we'll go up and you can see Rose again.....boy, is she in for a shock when I walk in with you."

"I'm pleased you two're still together," said John, "you were good for each other....did you ever marry?"

"Never seemed to get round to it," laughed Michael, "and she didn't insist."

John followed Michael across the room and through the door marked 'private' where the woman had disappeared; it turned out to be the artistes' changing room and there was a second door inside which led into a corridor, where yet another door led up two flights of stairs to the living accommodation.

"Your brother live up 'ere as well?" asked John.

"Yeh, he's got a bedroom across from ours," replied Michael, "not that he spends much time in it. He's knockin' off one of the young waitresses at present....and I 'ave to admit she's quite tasty, wouldn't mind having a crack at 'er myself...but you've got to be careful you know." Then giving John a wink, he added, "never do your courting on your own doorstep.......there's nothin' like a bit o' young stuff to keep the sparkle in your eye and a spring in your step."

"So they reckon," smiled John, "I might give it a try one of these days....it certainly couldn't do any harm."

"It would blow the cobwebs out of your system, me old mate," laughed the Irishman, "you just let me know when you're ready and I'll line somethin' up for you.....I've still got a few contacts, you know."

"You always 'ad," said John, "but a' was takin' quite a fancy to that singer of yours, until that big ugly bastard stepped in to spoil things...she soon scarpered."

"I can't tell you how sorry I am about that," said Michael, "we keep the two of 'em about as personal bodyguards....it was Timothy's you gave the treatment to. Normally just the sight of them hoverin' about does the trick.....but you certainly give 'im one hell of a shock."

"To tell you the God's honest truth," replied John, "I was bloody terrified of him, 'n for one horrible moment I had thoughts of wakin' up in some 'ospital bed....but I got lucky, that's all."

Michael laughed loudly, they neared the door to the flat. "You forget I've seen your luck at work in the past, it's helped me out of many a scrape which was my own fault.....some things you never forget; like old times and old mates, especially when they were good." Then as if remembering what John had said, he added, "so you fancy our Christine do you.....well I can't say that I blame you, she's a smasher alright; I wouldn't mind a dabble there myself.....but the girl doesn't seem very interested in the male sex; but there again I 'aven't noticed her chatting up any o' the girls either. That's the reason Lurch must 'ave taken an instant dislike to you....he's fuckin' crackers on her, but she makes it obvious that she hates his guts.......a John Wayne he ain't."

Before opening the door, Michael's manner seemed to get a bit serious. "Rose might possibly be a bit worse for drink," he explained, "she sometimes gets one or two too many......but there again there's not much else for her to do, bein' cooped up inside the flat all night by herself......if you remember, she's not your typical night-club kind o' woman."

"That's OK mate, there's no need to explain anythin' to me.......I've been there mysel', and a' know the feeling."

John was ushered into a spacious living room, lavishly furnished with everything anyone could wish to have, and an expensive looking cocktail cabinet and bar in the corner which was well stocked; it did not appear as if Michael tried to keep temptation out of Rose's way.

"I've tried to give her everything she wanted." said Michael, "as she doesn't get out very much." Then raising his voice, he called, "Rose....come 'n see who I've brought to see you."

Sounds of crockery and cutlery being handled could be heard coming from another room and it suddenly stopped; a few seconds later the adjoining door opened and Rose walked in. Smiling at Michael as she entered, her concentration soon

152

focused itself upon the newcomer as she stared into his face. Initially, there was no response, then gradually her expression changed and a smile of recognition came into her eyes; the slight smile became a big one.

"It's John Williams, isn't it?" she said, "I wasn't sure at first, but that face soon came back to me..........after all these years."

"Hello sweetheart," said John affectionately, genuinely pleased to see her again, "do you know...you still look the same as you did that day Michael 'n me found you'n that Brummie friend of yours on the beach at Southsea."

It was a lie, but what harm could a little white lie do; it seemed to be appreciated by Rose, she was obviously pleased at his words. She came across the room and kissed him on the lips, the distinct smell of alcohol was present; and he gave her a hug.

"Thank you kind sir," she said, "even if it's not true, it sounds nice....you always did have a way with women."

John appreciated the fact that the welcome he had had from both Michael and Rose was as genuine as anything could be. It was as they hoped; an outwardly genuine meeting of old friends..........another important obstacle cleared. Then, noticing the blood on his shirt, Rose stepped back and her hands went to her mouth in dismay. "What have you been doing?" she asked, "Are you hurt.....the blood...what's happened?" Her eyes searched Michael's face for an answer.

Michael laughed uncomfortably. "It's alright Rose, it isn't John's blood....it's Lurch's. He picked on John at the bar.....and before he knew anythin' else, he was flat out on the floor. I saw him go flyin' and went over to see what was going on....and it was then that I found out who it was who did the flattenin'......our John 'ere. That reminds me pet, go and get him one of my clean shirts, he can't go about like this....you'll wash his out for him, won't you?''

"Of course I will," she replied, the look of concern gradually disappearing from her face, "you're going to have to warn that monster....one day he'll bring trouble onto you....both of them should be kept in cages."

"I will...I will," answered Michael, "I promise you...but uncouth as they are, they're handy to have around at times."

That seemed to pacify Rose, and she went into what John surmised was the bedroom and returned with one of Michael's immaculately pressed shirts. Removing his own stained one, he replaced it with Michael's.

"Leave your coat off mate," said Michael, "you might as well have some supper with us...you made plenty, Rose?"

"There's more than enough," she smiled, then peered in the direction of the outer door, she added, "where's that 'dear' brother of yours? Will we be having the pleasure of his company?"

John sensed a definite dislike in her tone of voice towards Timothy. Michael laughed, a little embarrassed; Rose and Timothy had never seen eye to eye about anything.

"No," he answered, "he's gone off with the sexy Brenda. We'll not see much of him before midday tomorrow."

"Good," said Rose, with obvious satisfaction, "you pour some drinks, Michael, the supper won't be long....we have to celebrate the return of our prodigal friend....the one good thing that's happened in a long time."

The meal turned out to be a pleasant surprise; John remembered that Rose had served her time in the Wrens as an officers' cook. During the meal, he retold the tale about

Angela.....almost reducing Rose to tears of sympathy.

"It must have been terrible for you," she said, "losing some-one you love very much. I don't think I could go on living if I ever lost Michael."

After that the drink flowed freely and the hours passed; it was past four a.m. and each one of them at one stage or another had stifled a yawn.

"Well folks," said John, standing up and going for his coat, "it's time I was in my bed. I've got to thank both of you for the best night I've had since.......well you know when. It's been like a tonic no doctor could prescribe...and but for that Lurch bloke it might never have happened; and for that I thank you both very much."

Michael and Rose got to their feet, both with a little diffi-culty.

"You're not gettin' away that easy," slurred Michael, "how long are you stayin' here in Pompey?....You can't leave now that you've found us....we're mates, the three o' us."

"I've never really thought about it," answered John, "time means nothin' to me. There's no job to go back to....so why should a' care. My house is bein' looked after by me' old neighbours, so I've got nowt to worry about on that score. I just intended stayin' a couple o' weeks and seein' how things went."

"That's great, just bloody great," said a jubilant Michael, "because, my son, we're goin' to have ourselves a ball. We'll show these young Jack Tars what a good run ashore is all about.....we've spilled more than these young 'uns can drink."

"Great," said John, "we'll start tomorrow night O.K.?.....Can you get the time off from the club?"

"Time off," laughed his friend, "I'll go absent without

leave.....Timothy will 'ave to keep an eye on the place.....anyway we can always finish off here.''

John fastened his coat and walked over and kissed Rose on the cheek. ''Thanks flower,'' he said, ''for the shirt..the meal...and for listening. I'll be seein' you.''

''Hang on a minute,'' said Michael, I'll get you back to your hotel....use the car.''

''Bloody 'ell mate, you're not in any state to drive,'' said John, ''it's O.K. I'll make me' own way back.''

''It's O.K. my arse,'' answered Michael, ''I'm not going to drive you...not that I couldn't, mind you. I'll give Herman a buzz..he'll take you, that's what he gets paid for.....where you stayin'?''

''Queen's Arms,'' replied John, ''I only 'ope they 'aven't locked me out.''

''Queen's eh,'' said Michael, impressed, ''you must have a few bob, it's supposed to be a bit exclusive in there.''

''It's not too bad at all....once you've taken the coals out o' the bath,'' said John with a smile, ''but if a man can't spoil 'is self on holiday, when can he?''

''I agree with that,'' said Michael, ''if you've got it...throw it about.''

He went over to the far side of the room and pressed a button on the wall and, within five minutes, a bleary-eyed Herman knocked on the door.

'Jesus,' thought John, 'what a pair o' bookends Herman and Lurch would make.'

''Herman,'' instructed Michael, ''I want you to drive my old mate 'ere to the Queen's Arms Hotel.''

''Yes Mr. Reagan,'' replied the big man, without as much as a whimper of protest.

"I could've walked," said John, "don't want to put anybody out."

"You're not puttin' anybody out," insisted Michael, "the boys get bloody well paid for what they do, and they don't mind...do you Herman?"

"I don't mind Mr. Reagan."

It was like listening to some battery driven robot answering his master.

"I'll see you both later," said John, smiling at Rose and Michael, "and to tell you the truth....I'm about knackered, not used to these late nights."

"Well you're going to get used to them again," laughed Michael as they shook hands.

Herman led the way back through the club, but instead of going down the main flight of stairs, they went a different way which brought them into a large basement garage with space enough for three cars, though only one stood there: a brand new Mercedes. The big man opened the rear door for John to get in, then he climbed behind the steering wheel of the luxury car, opening the garage doors by remote control. Before John knew it, he was back out of the lion's den and on his way to the hotel.

"How's yer' mate?" he asked the back of Herman's head, as he climbed out of the car.

Herman turned and looked hard into John's eyes. "He's not too good....'is nose's broken and he's not sure about his jaw. His balls are swollen as big as a pair of pomegranates.....'n about the same colour."

"Good," said John, walking away from the car, "serves the big bastard right."

Chapter Eight

At midday, the deep penetrating buzz of the digital alarm clock which guaranteed to awaken the heaviest of sleepers, aroused John to a new day. Stretching over, he switched it off in an attempt to ease the incessant throbbing taking place inside his head; last night had been quite a session in one way and another. As he lay and relaxed in the comfort of the large bed, he recalled the sequence of events which had taken place the previous evening. Things had gone very much to plan, the accidental meeting with Michael which he feared would prove to be the greatest barrier, was accomplished better than he had dared hope, thanks to Lurch's fanatical obsession with the female singer. He smiled to himself as he conjured up a vision of her in his mind, she oozed femininity and no-one could blame the big man for falling under her spell; the majority of men would, including himself.

Nothing untoward had occurred which could possibly place a shadow of doubt over his presence in the club, the fight had proved to be a blessing in disguise. He still felt the satisfaction of what he had done: the physical contact and the sight of those eyes rolling about in their sockets before Lurch crashed to the floor had done more for his self-confidence than anyone could imagine. Picking up the internal phone, he asked reception to have two cups of strong black coffee sent up to his room; it would take both of them to remove the fur from his tongue. Whilst waiting for them to arrive, he decided to take a shower, hoping that it might revive him a little; the throbbing was almost reaching its crescendo. After spending a couple of minutes under the streaming hot water, his head resting against the shower wall, he was disturbed by the sound of the phone ringing.

'Jesus!' he complained to himself, 'there's no rest for the wicked.'

Stepping out of the shower with reluctance, he wrapped one of the oversize bath towels about his waist and trudged through into the bedroom, a trail of water behind him.

"Hello?" he answered.

"Mornin' Mr. Williams," said a cheery sounding Steve Bright, "everything go alright last night when you disappeared with your old mate?"

"Not bad at all son......apart from 'aving somebody goin' berserk inside me' head with a sledge 'ammer, yes I can say things went particularly well. We're on our way, so be extra careful from now on."

"That's great," said the young man enthusiastically, "and I have to congratulate you on the way you handled that big bastard last night.....it was a lesson to me not to underestimate the so-called age barrier. I bet he's not feeling too cocky this morning."

"I was a bit lucky," replied John, "'e wasn't expecting it, that's all...Anyway, did you manage to get a check done on the two of 'em?"

"Yep, I did," confirmed Steve, "the computer read out's in front of me.....I'll just give you the relevant details. First we have your mate from last night, Lurch...real name is William Henry Kennedy, aged thirty-three. Originated from Glasgow, but has spent most of his life in the South. He's been in and out of prison for various assaults and a couple of GBHs and was once questioned about the murder of a police officer in London...but lack of evidence allowed him to go."

160

"Sounds like a nice boy," said John sarcastically.

"Next we have the one called Herman....real name Terence Smith, a 'Brummie', and thirty one. He's got convictions for GBH and attempted robbery. It was when both of them were inside Dartmoor that they struck up their friendship....and they've been inseparable ever since."

"They're a pair o' bad 'uns alright," said John, "but not in the same league as the I.R.A. How did they get mixed up with Michael and 'is brother?"

"About four years ago they walked into the club and got into a spot of bother with the regular bouncers.....the two of them cleaned out half a dozen of them. The brothers were so impressed, they made them their personal bodyguards...and they've been that ever since. If they didn't know then that the brothers were involved with the I.R.A. then they must know now....and it obviously doesn't bother their conscience. To me, this makes them worse that the I.R.A.....they're doing it for the money. At least the other bastards supposedly have a cause to fight for."

"I agree," said John, "we're in with a bad crowd, Stevie boy....things could get very serious."

"I've been in contact with the Commodore," added the young man, "he says to tell you that they're all tarred with the same brush and have to be disposed of accordingly."

"I know son.....the tally's goin' up every day."

"I'm here to help", said Steve, "just tell me what you want doing and I'll do it....don't take too much on yourself."

"I know that," replied John, "when it's time, you'll hear me yellin'."

The sound of knocking on the door brought an end to their conversation. It was one of the hotel staff with his two cups of coffee, his eyes flickered about the room as if he expected to see a visitor.

"She's in the shower," said John, with a wink and closed the door on him.

He gulped down the strong black liquid, emptying both cups; at least his headache was beginning to ease a little and he was almost ready to face the outside world again.

Before he left his room, he carefully arranged certain items of his clothing in both wardrobe and drawers, because he was quite sure that he would be checked out by Michael's organisation. He also pulled out a few strands of hair and placed them in position so that if the drawers or doors were opened, the hairs would fall inside. It was not his own idea to do this, he had seen someone do it in a picture years ago; and it had worked alright for him.

On walking into the reception area, he found the same immaculately dressed woman on duty.

"Good afternoon Mr. Williams," she said sweetly, "your guest not leaving?"

"What guest's that flower?"

"I was distinctly informed that not only did you have a guest in your room, but she was in the process of taking a shower when the porter arrived with your coffee. It's against all hotel regulations to have a guest stay overnight without permission.....we have to be very careful of the reputation of the hotel."

John laughed. "No flower," he said, "I'm afraid 'e's carried the wrong tale to you.....I told 'im that I wished I'd had a female in the shower...it might've helped me feel better because I was sufferin' the after effects of last night." She laughed, relieved.

"It must have been wishful thinking on your part Mr. Williams," she said, appreciating his sense of humour, "but remember, only registered guests are to be in your shower."

"There's not much chance of that 'appening, is there?" he said, with a slight shrug of his shoulders.

"You never know," she replied, and continued writing on her note pad.

John had enjoyed that little bit of friendly banter with her, there was no harm in it, and you never knew what a little bit of friendly banter might lead up to; he was beginning to feel more like his old self again. It was just after two o'clock when he reached the club, after he had forced himself to eat a small lunch; the door was opened by an old woman with a sweeping brush in one hand and a yellow duster in the other.

"Yes," she asked, "can I 'elp you?"

"My name's John Williams, I'm a friend of the owner, Michael Reagan.....will you let 'im know I'm here?"

Turning her back to him, she moved the duster into her other hand and relayed the message by the internal phone. John could hear Michael shouting down the receiver as clear as if he had it held to his own ear.

"Let him in woman," he shouted, "tell 'im to come up through the club and to the flat."

John nodded to the cleaner. "It's alright pet.......I just about 'eard him."

"It's a bloody wonder they didn't hear 'im down in the dockyard," she grumbled, replacing the phone and readjusting the balance of her tools of the trade. As he neared the top of the stairs, he was surprised to hear the sound of singing coming from inside the large room, and on opening the door he was pleased to see the singer sitting at the piano. Even without the spotlight on her she still looked lovely; her face was fresh and clean, making her look younger than her years. Her attention was distracted as he entered and she stopped singing in mid-verse; her eyes sought out his and she smiled at him.

"Hello," she said, "you've caught me out trying a few new numbers.........I want to thank you for what you did last night. I hate that man, my flesh crawls every time he looks at me....he makes it so obvious what he wants. If I didn't need the job so badly I would leave.....so in a way you did me a favour."

"I was surprised when I turned round and you'd left," he said, ".....and disappointed. It's not often that I get the chance to talk to a lovely young woman like yourself and to ask her to have a drink with me....maybe you'll allow me to buy you one some other time?"

He did not feel the necessity to go into his 'Geordie' accent with her, as a matter of fact he had lost most of it years ago; but when the need arose he could easily switch back to it.

"I'd love to," she replied, giving him a smile, "if you happen to be here tonight, I'll take you up on it."

She held out her hand to him and he shook it somewhat awkwardly, he had not shaken too many women's hands. He enjoyed the moment of contact between them and held it just a little longer than necessary.

Chris blushed a little, aware that John was admiring her beauty. "It's John isn't it?" she said, "I remember Tom telling me your name....well then John, if I don't get back to learning these songs, there won't be any show tonight......and you wouldn't want to get me into trouble, would you?"

John coughed at her innocent choice of words, it would be a pleasant thought indeed. "Ahhhhhemmn," he replied smiling, "no Chris....I wouldn't want to do that. I'll let you get on

164

and I'll look forward to buying you that drink later tonight."
Just as he was about to walk away, she called out to him quietly, as if afraid anyone else might overhear her.

"Be very careful of that man," she said, with a worried look replacing her smile, "after what you did to him last night, he'll be after his revenge, and it won't matter to him that you're Michael's friend...you hurt his pride more than anything else."

John nodded to her, grateful for the concern. "I'll be careful..thanks," he said.

As he walked into the corridor of the living accommodation, he was met by Michael. "Come on then, my old son," he said, "you been chattin' up the lovely Christine? Complete waste of time there John, as far as she's concerned, a little bit o' the other is definitely out....I think it will have healed up by now."

Although he disliked what Michael had said, John made a show of enjoying his joke.

"You might be right, oppo," he said, "but what a challenge eh?"

"It would be just like you to prove us all wrong," said Michael, nodding his head, "can't blame you for givin' it a go.......Anyway, Rose was supposed to be having a look out with us, but she's a bit under the weather. I woke up with a hell of a hangover myself..but what makes you bad makes you better."

A large drink appeared as if by magic, shoved into his hand.

"Get this down you," said Michael, "we've got a lot o' years to catch up on."

John downed the drink and a second one appeared to take its place; it was going to be one of those days.

"Where do you fancy goin'?" asked Michael, "you name it.. and that's where we'll go."

"Tell you what," replied John, "let's go along Southsea front and 'ave a drink in the 'Fes Bar' before closin' time."

"Fes Bar it is then," laughed Michael, "we've had our fair share of bother in there haven't we.......Remember that night we both got a bloody good hidin' from those long-haired yobbos, just because I 'appened to take a fancy to one of their weird looking birds?"

John remembered that night well enough, some big bastard and a few of his friends had almost strangled the life out of him, he'd had to have a change of trousers after they'd eventually let go of his larynx.

As they entered the downstairs garage, Herman appeared from out of the darkness. "What do you think of the motor?" asked Michael.

Nodding his approval, John said, "Definitely a class car mate, you must be doin' alright for yersel'......rakin' in the old shekels as they say."

"That's what the good life brings you my son," replied his friend with satisfaction.

Herman politely opened the car door for them and Michael must have noticed the look of disapproval on John's face.

"Sorry about this mate," he said, "but whenever I go out, Herman comes with me...a kind of insurance policy you might say. He watches over me....and Lurch stays with Timothy, but you've put the dampener on that for a couple o' days."

"Not to worry," said John, as if not caring whether the big man accompanied them or not, " 'e can do the driving while we concentrate on doin' the drinkin'."

Herman drove the car to Southsea and parked it next to the

pier.

"It's always dead this time of the year." said Michael, observing how few people there were about, "and 'Jack' doesn't come ashore until later." Then he cupped his hands to his mouth and mimicked, "All hands going ashore muster on the quarterdeck for inspection," and going into his American version added. "Liberty guys to glamourise, gather by the after smoke-stack."

"We did quite a bit o' mustering in those days," said John.

"That we did," agreed Michael, "and who'd a thought that twenty years later, we'd be startin' all over again?"

"It's funny how things turn out," muttered John quietly.

Hurrying down the two flights of stairs into the 'Festival Bar', they just managed to get a last drink before closing time.

"There's only one drink for us in here," stated Michael, "we must've drunk buckets full of the stuff.....Two pints of brown and mild landlord please, put the bottle of brown in the glass first and swill it about with the half o' mild."

They stood side by side at the bar which ran the length of the room, reminiscing about old times and acquaintances of years gone by.

The rest of the afternoon was spent driving around the area, revisiting places which had some significant memory or other for either one of them; but as soon as it was opening time again, their 'run ashore' began in earnest. Their plan was to drink one pint of brown and mild followed by a rum chaser in as many of their old haunts as possible; those that were still there. Michael was obviously enjoying himself more than he had for a long time; it was as if he has escaped the leash and fully intended making the most of it; the troubles of the I.R.A.

and the British Government were forgotten for that one night. More brown and mild followed more rum chasers, and more rum chasers followed the pints of brown and mild; it was never ending, with one pub looking very much like any other. When nine p.m. came around, both men were well oiled, or so it seemed to onlookers, including Michael's bodyguard. Twice during the evening John had gone into the toilet, as someone drinking heavily is inclined to do on a regular basis, and there made himself vomit in order to get the alcohol out of his system. John thereby remained in contact with his senses, but Michael didn't. His speech was getting incoherent and his legs appeared to have a will of their own; of course John falsely acted likewise.

"Excuse me Mr.Reagan," said Herman, more and more worried about Michael's condition, "don't you think it's about time I took you back to the club....your brother will be worrying about you?"

"Fuck the club!" slurred Michael, with a laugh, "I've left brother Timothy in charge, because it just so 'appens that I'm out on the town with me' old mate who I haven't seen for years.....Anyway, Herman, why should we worry, you're 'ere to look after us, aren't you?"

"Yes Mr. Reagan, I'm here," he replied meekly, looking daggers in John's direction.

As the night progressed and more and more drink followed, Michael found it extremely difficult to remain upright, and John was keeping up his act, after another two visits to the toilet.

"You alright, oppo?" he asked Michael.

" 'Corse I'm alright," he giggled, hanging onto John's arm, "we'll have to do this more off'en, it's great........you're not goin' to fuck off back to Geordieland are you?''

''Not for a while mate.......get that drink down ye' neck.''

Herman was looking distinctly miserable, after all, here he was in the company of two men who tried their best to drink Portsmouth dry; they could hardly stand on their own two feet, and all he had had to drink was two half pints of lager. At twenty nine minutes past ten, Michael's head slowly came to rest on the formica table top, and he fell into a deep sleep....he was finished for the night.

During all their years of friendship and the many drinking sessions they'd had together, this was the one and only time John had ever seen Michael actually flake out.

''I think 'e's about ready for 'ome,'' he slurred to Herman, '''n I'm about fucked as well....drop me off at the Queen's will you?''

Herman would have loved to have told this Geordie bastard to find his own way back to the hotel, but he knew the wrath he would suffer if he did; his eyes betrayed his true feelings.

He nodded affirmation and grunted under his breath.

Fifteen minutes later John was inside his hotel room, the same night porter had handed him his key with that knowing look, which indicated that there was no doubt in his mind Mr. Williams was enjoying his stay in Portsmouth.

After locking the door behind him, he swilled his face with ice cold water and then began a careful study of his room; not one solitary hair was in place. He had had visitors.

Collapsing onto his bed fully clothed, he too fell into a deep sleep.

Herman had great difficulty in carrying Michael's almost dead weight up the back stairs into the flat, it was fortunate that they did not have to go through the club itself; he laid him on the large four seater sofa and went in search of his brother.

"Jesus Christ," said Timothy, looking down at the stupid smile on Michael's face, "where the fuck has he been?"

"He's been out all day with that long lost mate of his," explained Herman, "and they've never stopped boozin'...boy have they downed some between them. We've been in and out of nearly every pub in the city..some I didn't know even existed. I dropped 'is mate off at his hotel, he's just about managed to crawl inside."

Rose entered the room and took one look at Michael's prostrate form and immediately burst out laughing. "You can tell he's been out with John," she giggled, "times haven't changed that much......proves he's still human after all."

Timothy looked at Herman and nodded.

"Get him into his bed," he ordered, "then get yourself down into the club with me. That fuckin' Geordie's only been here a couple o' days and he's already put Lurch out of action, as well as gettin' Michael pissed out o' his mind....he seems to pose more of a threat to this organisation that the whole of the British army."

"Hopefully he might piss off back 'ome soon," said Herman.

"Michael never let anything slip, did he?" demanded Timothy. "Nothing out of order...never mentioned what we're up to?"

"No Mr. Reagan, I was standing close by all night....he said nothing."

"Good," replied Timothy, "I've been in touch with Davy Conalan and he checked out Williams' room at the hotel....he came up clean."

170

Rose had been listening to the conversation taking place.

"You mean to say that you've had John's room searched," she shouted at the Irishman "what did you expect to find?"

"For one thing I'm not explainin' a damn thing to you," snapped Timothy, "but in our position, and that means yours as well, we have to be doubly careful in everything we do, or who we get involved with. We can't risk Michael 'ere goin' out and getting himself pissed every time some old friend turns up outa' the blue...it's too dangerous."

"John's more than just a good friend to Michael," she insisted, "and you'll do well to remember that."

Timothy shrugged his shoulders, and said, "Alright Rose, if that's how it is....then that's how it is."

There was no love lost between the two of them, and neither cared that the other was well aware of the fact. It was Michael who was the mediator and managed to calm things down between them when they argued, which was quite often.

"Get 'im to bed!" he snarled at Herman.

It was eleven a.m. the next morning when Michael rang John.

"Jesus," he shouted, "how bloody much did we get through last night? I can't remember a thing after about nine o'clock when Herman was tryin' to persuade me to go back to the club. We had one hell of a night out didn't we...boy what a head I had when I woke up this mornin'. Rose fixed me one of her special remedies and I don't feel too bad now......are you up and about yet?"

"No," lied John, "I'm still stretched out in bed, 'n a feel as if the Marine band's playin' *Hearts of Oak* inside me' head, and the drummer's goin' berserk."

Michael was having a good laugh at the other end of the phone.

"You know what they say," he said, "don't drink it if you can't take it."

"I'm out of practice with this kind of life," replied John, "it's all right for you...you've got the club, you're at it every night."

"Don't you believe it mate.....anyway where you goin' to-day?"

"I'm not sure," answered John, "it'll take me a while to get mysel' pulled round. Whatever it was Rose made for you must 'ave done the trick...you sound chirpy enough."

"I have a little bit of business to see to," explained Michael, "I'll be away for the rest of the afternoon.....so it will give you all day to get yourself ready for the club tonight, OK with you?"

"That'll do fine," agreed John, "I'll have a lazy day lyin' about the hotel...I think I'll take a sauna and sweat the evil brew outa' my system, ready for a refill tonight."

"See you then, John."

"That you will, me old mate."

As soon as John heard Michael replace the receiver, he dialled Steve Bright's room.

"Steve Bright here."

"Listen son, it's John. I've just been talkin' to Michael on the phone and he tells me that he has to go away for the rest of the day on business...do you think you could keep an eye on 'im? He'll be leavin' the club shortly in a dark blue 'B' reg Mercedes....and I should imagine Herman will be drivin' it."

"I'm on my way," said the young man, pleased to be getting involved, "by the way where did you get to last night?"

"Don't mention last night, son.....I'm still sufferin' the consequences."

"Serves you right," laughed Steve, "you're too old for the high living."

"On yer bike," said John, "and be careful."

When John rang the bell of the club, the door was opened by the same doorman wearing the same smart tuxedo, but his time he also had a wide smile on his face.

"Mr. Williams, sir," he greeted, "you're to go straight up. Mr. Reagan says to tell you he won't be long. I'm sorry but I didn't realise that you and him were good friends." Then dipping into his pocket, he held out his hand. "Here's your money back," he added, "your membership's free."

John refused to accept it. "When I came in here the other night," he said, "'a didn't even know Michael Reagan was in the country...never mind bein' the owner of the club. It came as a hell of a surprise when I found out, and as far as the money's concerned....keep it and 'ave yourself a drink on me."

There he was again, being extravagant with the Commodore's money.

"Thanks Mr. Williams, it's appreciated.....by the way the name's Bill, I fill in 'ere to help out at home; it's an expensive hobby. running a family."

"I can imagine," said John.

"Listen," added the doorman, "if you ever need me, just give a shout. I heard all about what you did to Lurch...you told me that you were a lover not a fighter."

"I am normally," smiled John, "but these things tend to 'appen now and again."

"He deserved everything 'e got....and more besides," said

173

Bill, "but you be very careful..watch out for him."

Someone else was not a member of the Lurch fan club, they were mounting by the day. Chris was at her seat behind the piano, the sound of her voice gave the impression of warmth and affection; her song *'Help me make it through the night'* had the entire male audience willing to do just that. He wondered if she would accept his apologies for not being in the club the previous night, but there again she would no doubt get plenty of offers like that and not take them too seriously.

She saw him enter the room, her eyes met his and she smiled at him, giving a slight acknowledgement with her hand; and more than just a casual observer noticed it.

"Bacardi and coke comin' up sir," said Tom, as he sat on a stool facing the stage.

"Thanks Tom," answered John.

"You seem to have made a good impression on Chris," said the barman, "seein' is believin', and I definitely saw that smile she gave you as you came in.. and that little wave. Maybe what they say about her is a load of bull and all she needs is the right man to prove it to 'er.......wonders will never cease."

John smiled to himself, it did a lot for his ego to think that he was being successful when many others before him had tried and failed.

"I didn't get the chance to congratulate you on the fine demolition job you did on Lurch, added Tom, "I've been waitin' years to see someone do just that..Jesus, what a bloody shock yer gave 'im."

Sipping at his drink, John noticed Michael threading his way through the tables towards him.

"Business finished with?" he asked.

174

"It wasn't much," replied Michael, then added, "all ready 'n raring to go?"

" 'Corse I am.....all done up like a dog's dinner and waitin' on the starting line for the off."

"I've given brother Timothy the night off," smiled Michael, "seein' as how he had to look after the shop last night by himself...the reason being I was too pissed to stand up. We can manage by ourselves can't we?"

"That we can," replied John.

They took their seats at the owners' table and the continuous flow of drinks began; as soon as their glasses were empty, full ones suddenly changed places with them.

"Michael," complained John, "you're goin' to 'ave to let me pay my turn...I can afford it. I don't want people to think I'm only here to sponge off you, takin' too much for granted."

"Bollocks to all the people," snorted Michael, raising his glass to imaginary onlookers, "you're my mate...my guest in my club, and you're not payin' for anything. Anyway I get the stuff for practically fuck all. There's a little old man I know who has a little boat 'n he goes back and forth across the Irish Sea, just to keep me supplied." He touched his nose and winked, "It's all in the game John.....keep one step in front of 'em, make as much money as you can, and fuck the rest."

"I agree mate," said John, "what 'arm does a little bit o' fiddle do now and again......payin' taxes and this bloody V.A.T.'s a load of goolies...get what you can out o' life, that's what I've always said. Now that I've been reborn, I fully intend to start and enjoy myself again.

"And I'm gonna help you do just that," said Michael.

Occasionally John glanced over at Chris, and every now and

again their eyes would meet, with that same smile at each other. She was looking beautiful again tonight, the top three buttons of her blouse open to reveal her healthy cleavage and ample amount of white flesh either side. The animal inside him was beginning to stir, it had been a long time since he'd had any sex and the need was returning.

"You can't keep your eyes off her, can you?" observed Michael, smiling at him, "I can see the sheer lust in them myself....but 'onest mate, you're wasting your time there..she's supposed to be one of the 'anti-men' brigade. If it's a leg-over you're fancying, well I can promise you I'll fix you up with somethin' about nineteen or twenty and you won't be disappointed.....I can guarantee that."

"I just enjoy lookin' at her," replied John, a little on the defensive, "don't know what it is about her.....and yes, I've heard what she's supposed to be...but she's still got that some-thin' which attracts me to her......maybe it's those big blue eyes."

"You lyin' bastard," laughed Michael, "big blue eyes my arse, the only thing you're ogling are those big tits of hers....you'll never change. You see a big pair of knockers and you want to get your 'ands on them.....you always were a tit man."

The flow of drinks continued and the talk between the two friends was enjoyable; John had to admit to himself that he still enjoyed Michael's company and it was difficult for him to imagine Michael being involved in something as evil as the I.R.A.; but the evidence against him was positive.

At precisely midnight Chris finished off her last song, stood up and gave her customary little bow; the audience in the immediate vicinity must have had one hell of a view. She stepped from the stage and crossed the room, stopping at their table, and looked directly into John's eyes.

"Does the offer of a drink still stand?" she asked, presenting him with one of her better smiles.

Michael looked astonished, as if his ears wouldn't believe what they were hearing; his mouth half-opened in amazement.

" 'Corse it does," replied John, standing up from his seat, "you wouldn't mind this young lady joinin' us for a drink, would you mate?"

"It would be an unexpected pleasure," answered Michael graciously.

"If you'll allow me a few minutes to get changed," she said, and walked away, her shapely hips swaying gently as she went.

"Jesus Christ and Mother Mary save me," exclaimed Michael, "am I hearin' right....did our songbird actually ask you to buy her a drink?"

John smiled at his friend and shrugged his shoulders, feeling more than pleased with himself. "Somethin' like that my old son," he said.

"I do not bloody believe it," gasped Michael, still in a state of shock, "in the six or seven months she's been workin' here, she hasn't had anything to do with anyone who had a toggle and tool. You've been in here a couple o' times and you've got the bloody woman chasin' you.......If the impossible does happen, and you somehow get into her bed, will you tell me just one thing......whether or not she's a true blonde, I've wondered about that because there's no signs of any dark roots."

"Sir!" answered John in mock horror, "I hope you realise

that you are talking to a gentleman and us gentlemen never reveal the intimate details of such delicate things....but in your case, if it 'appens...I will."

"You be very careful," teased Michael, "because if the rumours about her are true, then watch out for her bouncin' handbag...you might just get more than you bargained for."

"Well then," laughed John, going along with Michael's humour, "if it's true, you'll be the second one to know about it.....If you see me walkin' in a funny kind o' way, then those rumours must've been right all along."

The two of them were still having a laugh and a joke about it when Chris reappeared at their table.

"What are you two laughing at?" she asked.

"Private joke, Chris," smiled John, "nothing of importance."

As he held the chair for her to sit down, Michael stood up.

"I hope you two will excuse me," he said, "I have to pop upstairs for a little while......shall I tell Rose that you'll be stayin' for some supper, John?"

John was unsure what to say, Michael, the sly bastard, had tried to drop him into the mire.

"That's alright," said Chris, "I'll not be staying too long....I need my beauty sleep."

John nodded to Michael. "If Rose doesn't mind," he said, rather disappointed.

"She'll be delighted," beamed his friend, "keep an eye on the place for me, if you're not too busy.....I'll be back in two ticks."

"I'll flog it to the first Yank who comes along," replied John.

As Michael disappeared through the door marked private, Chris looked into John's eyes.

"I think he's teasing you a bit," she smiled.

"I think you could be right."

"Was he teasing you about me?" she asked.

"He's tryin' to say that you must obviously feel safer with a father figure." he lied.

"Not at all....it's just that I like you and there's not too many men I can say that about."

"I'm pleased," said John, "because the feelin's mutual.....I took an instant liking to you the first night I came into the club."

"Michael must think a lot of you," she added, her cheeks reddening a little, "I've never seen him like this with anyone before.....you seem to have changed him overnight."

"Years and years ago we were very good friends....in the Navy together," he began to explain. "then, as with the way of things, we lost contact with each other.....Suddenly, after all this time, I decide to come down here for a bit of a holiday and by sheer coincidence I find out that he owns this nightclub. Not only did I have the good fortune of finding two very good friends from the past in Michael and Rose.....but it also gave me the chance of meeting you."

When Michael walked into the flat, Timothy was already waiting inside.

"Well," said Michael, "did you do what you felt you had to....did you have him checked out?"

Timothy nodded his head. "I'm sorry if this bothers you, brother," he said, "but you know it has to be done....in our position we have to be absolutely certain about who we get mixed up with. If we weren't and your old mate turned out to be somethin' a little more than he's supposed to be, we'd a'had our balls chewed off by the Council back home..'n rightly so. I've been in touch with Jimmy Leck in Newcastle and gave 'im your mate's address...he'll do the necessary, and if we get the all clear on 'im then by all means go ahead and have a bloody good time with him while he's here....with my blessin'.''

This seemed to satisfy Michael, he realised that Timothy was right; the safety of the organisation here was paramount, it had taken so long to set the network up. At last, things on other fronts were beginning to proceed again, another arms deal was due to be settled within a week or so, once the money to finance it arrived from Ireland. Then they could give the go-ahead. He hoped that nothing would go wrong with this deal, or it could possibly mean severe repercussions from the War Council; after the last fiasco Timothy and he were being scrutinised. The loss of that last arms shipment had cost the I.R.A. dearly, not only in hard cash but also in personnel; at least six loyal patriots were now imprisoned because of it. He had to ensure success....it was demanded of him.

''Two of the boys will be arrivin' in a couple o'days time,'' announced Timothy, ''they'll be collectin' one of my special packages to deliver to London. It's about time we reminded the Brits that this is our game 'n we can plant our bombs just about wherever and whenever we decide to and they can't do a fuckin' thing to stop us. By the time they get all their so-called explosives experts and Special Branch on the scene, the boys'll be back in the Emerald Isle enjoyin' a pint o' Guinness......and laughin' at the bastards.''

There was a deep rooted hatred of the British in Timothy, at times he found it extremely difficult to keep up appearances here in the club and socialise with them. To him, this club represented his own little part of the old country, and he was its elected ambassador of death and destruction....'the bomb maker elite'. He had always relied a great deal on his instincts, and those instincts now warned him that everything was not right with John Williams; it would not surprise him to discover that Michael's old friend from the past was a member of the security forces. He had made up his mind from the very beginning, when he had seen the professional way this man had dealt with Lurch, that a close watch was going to be maintained on him. If his doubts were, in fact, found to be justified then he, Timothy Reagan, would blow his head off and laugh as he did it. Meanwhile, the subject of Timothy's intense consideration was having a very pleasant time talking to Chris, and the I.R.A. was the last thing in his mind. Michael returned to the table.

"Sorry for taking so long," he apologised, "I'm sure the two of you will have missed my company."

"I'm not complainin' mate," said John, "much as I value you and your company, this lovely young woman more than compensates for your absence."

As Michael took his seat, more drinks arrived as if by magic.

"They're very efficient in here," he smiled, "have you noticed?"

"I'm beginnin' to think Tom over there's involved in E.S.P.," replied John, "the second there's an empty glass on the table...it suddenly changes to a full 'un."

"They're the best glasses to have," said Michael.

It was the turn of Chris to stand up from the table.

"Please don't think me rude," she said, "but I must

dash...thanks for the drink, and the company; I enjoyed both, we must do it again soon."

"It's my pleasure," said John sincerely.

As Chris made her departure, Michael turned to his friend and gave a knowing smile. "You play your cards right there," he said, "and you might just get your shoes under her bed."

"Figuratively speakin'," said John, with a wry smile at the pleasant idea, "I'm just about old enough to be her father. She looks as if she's in her mid-twenties, 'n 'ere I am in my late thirties, or thereabouts."

"Late thirties my bum," laughed Michael, "you old sod....you're the same age as me, forty four goin' on forty five, and our Christine there is twenty six. I know because I interviewed her for the job and noticed her date of birth.....there's not that much difference, anyway she might be one of those birds who prefer the older type men; a bit of experience never goes amiss....so they say."

It was at that moment that Timothy decided to make an appearance; he came to the table and shook hands with John, presenting at least the outward signs of friendship. The three of them spent the remainder of the night together, drinking quite an amount and listening to the guest group, which although different in appearance to the one he had seen climb on the stage the other night, were almost identical in sound.

Behind the trio at the table, and never too far away, stood the two huge bodyguards. It was Lurch's first public outing since his undignified and humiliating encounter with John, a strip of plaster covered the bridge of this nose where it had been broken. John could feel the intensity of those bruised eyes burning into his back, he accepted the fact that he had made himself an awesome enemy.

When it was time to close the club, he once again accompanied Michael upstairs; Timothy having made his excuses and left with the same young waitress as before. It must be one of the perks of owning the club. Going into the flat, they found Rose asleep on the sofa, the remains of an empty drink on the floor by her limp arm.

"I'm sorry mate," apologised Michael, obviously embarrassed, "I didn't want you to see 'er like this....she promised me she would go easy on the stuff, especially as you were here. It's gradually gettin' worse, it's been going on for years.....'n now she can't help herself."

John felt sorry for his friend. "There's no need to explain anything to me," he said, placing his hand on Michael's shoulder, "we all 'ave our crosses to bear; and takin' refuge in the bottle is something I know all about."

After quite a lengthy spell of silence, Michael did his best to rouse Rose, but to no avail; she was well out of things.

"Can you manage her alright," asked John, "or do you need a hand?"

"That's alright, mate," smiled Michael appreciatively, "I've had quite a bit of experience in getting her into bed.....began yonks ago. Once upon a time all I had to do was mention the word bed, and her eyes would light up. Now the only time they light up is when she's full o' booze."

John felt the urge to offer a sympathetic word, but what was the use.

"I'd better not stay," he said, "and she need never know I come up and seen 'er...I could do with 'n early night, all this drinkin's catchin' up with me."

"Thanks mate," replied Michael appreciatively, "hang on a mo' and I'll get Herman to take you.....I wouldn't want you

to walk, you might go and get yourself mugged, and that
would give Pompey a bad name."

It was two fifty five when John walked up to the reception
desk and asked for his room key; the night porter giving him
another of his looks.

"Enjoying your stay, Mr. Williams?" he asked politely, with
a smile on his face.

"Yeh, not too bad at all," replied John, "but there's not too
much night life about, is there?"

Looking out of his bedroom window the following morning,
he watched the snow falling from the heavens; there was a
light covering on the paths and the roads; it would not be long
before the gritter lorries came and turned it all to a dirty
coloured mush. He decided that it would be a pleasant morning for a stroll, the crisp fresh air would do him good, and he
would have time to think about what he was involved in.
Things had happened so quickly since he had stepped from
the train at Kings Cross, he felt as if he needed breathing
space to collect his thoughts. Although he reluctantly accepted
the fact that his friend Michael was involved with the I.R.A.
and there could be no disputing the evidence stacked up against
him, he found it extremely difficult to dislike the man. After
all these years, the strong bond of friendship still existed
between them and, if ever a man experienced friendship like
that once in his entire life, then he was fortunate. Outwardly it
was the same friendly Irishman of twenty years ago, but John
realised that inwardly a different man now existed; one who
belonged to, and was owned by, the organisation of the I.R.A.
Michael carried out their wishes, even to the point of slaugh-

tering innocent men, women and children. He passed the next two hours meandering about the city centre, unconsciously wasting away the time. It was as he left one of the big stores, where he had bought a small present for Michael and Rose as thanks for the welcome he had had, that he became aware of a familiar figure attempting to conceal his whereabouts from him. How on earth he hoped to achieve that successfully, with that tell-tale plaster on his nose, was beyond belief; but John acted normally, as if unaware of his tail.

The temperature was beginning to fall and the wind was increasing by the minute with large snowflakes whipped about the street; the sky was becoming noticeably darker and threatening.

"Well Lurch," said John to himself, "if you're goin' to follow me about, it's goin' to get a bit nippy."

On the far side of the road was a bus picking up passengers and, just as the last one was about to climb on board, John ran across the busy road and jumped on as well. He found a seat where he could observe the large ungainly figure of Lurch scrambling to a red Ford Granada which was parked close by. Lurch found that trying to run proved to be a painful experience, 'down below' was still very tender and discoloured; he intended to make the person responsible answer for one or two things, not the least being that Chris seemed to have taken a fancy to the older man. Sitting on the bus watching the Granada keep an even distance behind, John wondered if they suspected him. Or were they just being careful and keeping an eye on his whereabouts? It began to worry him a little. Things were beginning to look a little threatening, but the only course of action open to him was to play out his part and see what events turned up. The bus stopped outside the dockyard gate, the towering masts of *H.M.S. Victory* vaguely visible through the now heavily falling snow. Shielding himself from the elements, John stepped from the running board and ran as fast as the conditions would allow towards the ferry landing stage. Once again he was lucky with his transportation problems, the bowman on board the ferry to Gosport was about ready to cast off as he leapt onto the deck. This should make things a little difficult for the 'shadows'. It took approximately eight minutes for the little ferry to battle its way to the other side of the river, the bows rising then crashing into the angry waves, cascading brine over the passengers foolhardy enough to remain on the upper-deck, of whom John was one.

The last time he was in Gosport there used to be a small cafe by the bus terminal. He wondered if it would still be there so, as soon as the ferry got alongside the wooden jetty, he made his way towards the town. The cafe was still there, the outer buildings had changed their shape and it was larger now, but a cup of coffee and refreshments could still be had.....he walked in, and joined the queue at the counter. When he had been served with a cup of the strong liquid and a bacon bun, he chose a seat at a table near the window. If they decided to follow him across the ferry, he wanted to know about it. Things were beginning to resemble some kind of childish game with them following him all over, but he knew that there were no childish stakes in the particular game, possibly only death to the loser.

It was difficult to see outside the cafe's windows, because of the condensation, so he rubbed a small circular peep hole to give himself a view of the ferry walkway. He did not have to wait long before he saw both men walking side by side towards the town, the few people that were about moved out of their way. Each one was an awesome sight in his own right, but together they were absolutely terrifying; only an idiot would think of getting in their way. They reached the main road, exchanged a few words and separated, Lurch with his obvious limp going to the far side of the street, and Herman in the direction of the cafe. Easing himself down into his chair, John picked up a discarded newspaper from the adjoining table, opened it to shield his face, and hopefully presented the impression of being engrossed in its contents; but at the same time kept an eye on the looming figure of the big man. He had the comforting knowledge that the only way Herman was likely to see him was by actually entering the cafe itself, and he doubted if he would do that.

Pausing outside the cafe, Herman tried to peer through the steamed up windows, but without success and, after a couple of frustrating minutes for John, the big man moved on up the street. Allowing a couple of minutes for Herman to get clear, John returned his empty plate and cup to the counter and left the premises. A quick scan of the vicinity revealed nothing, the visibility was almost down to zero, it was getting towards blizzard conditions. There was no point in him waiting about, so he retraced his footsteps back to the ferry landing.

"Come on then, hurry it up," shouted a faint voice from the distance.

John hurried his steps and clambered back onto the ferry, almost losing his balance on the slippery deck, one of the deck-hands catching him and helping to right himself.

"You're bloody lucky," he shouted into the wind, "the coxswain says that this'll be the last ferry until the conditions improve, and it'll take quite a while fer' that to 'appen."

187

It looked as if Herman and Lurch were going to have to visit the sights of Gosport longer than they had bargained for. There must have been a force six wind blowing, not too much for the larger ships belonging to the Queen's Navy to battle against, but certainly enough to punish that small ferry. John decided it would be much wiser to go down below into the passenger lounge and to cast aside his spirit of adventure for the time being; he was too cold and too wet to think of being 'sea faring'.

Arriving back on the Portsmouth side, the crew finally managed, with the aid of numerous fenders, to get the little ferry tied up to the jetty without damaging the vessel.

"Fuck that fer' a lark," shouted the coxswain, as John carefully stepped ashore. He took a taxi back to the hotel and entered his room with a quiet feeling of satisfaction. It had turned out to be an eventful morning and the knowledge that Herman and Lurch were stranded for the next few hours comforted him. No sooner had he discarded his wet clothing than the phone rang.

"Steve here.....I was sitting looking out of the window when I saw this thing that looked like an abominable snowman walk into the hotel; then I realised it was you John."

"You can't beat takin' a walk out in the middle of a blizzard," replied John, "we do it all the time up in Durham.....it 'elps to blow away the cobwebs. Anyway, young man, did you come up with anythin' interesting about Michael?"

"Something very interesting indeed," answered Steve, "I followed him to a place called Hayling Island and you'll never guess what....................your old mate's got himself a young bird shacked up there, and very tasty she is too. That minder of his sat outside in the car the whole time twiddlin' his thumbs, at least, I think it was his thumbs he was twid-dlin' with; whilst his master spent the better part of two hours 'visiting'."

"You positive about that, Steve," asked John, "there's nothin' else involved in this...............she's not just a front?"

"I'm positive," confirmed the young man, "after they left I made a few very discreet enquiries in the neighbourhood and found out that he's been visiting her for nearly two years....not only that, he pays the mortgage on the house. What is it about you old gadgies that seems to attract these good lookin' bits o' stuff...what's the secret?"

"You have me there, young man," replied John, "unless its the undoubted charm and sophistication we obviously pos-sess."

"Must be that then," laughed Steve, "I'll carry on as usual...eyes peeled 'n waiting to hear from you."

"You do that son... and be careful; I've a feelin' in my water that things might just start to 'appen."

At more or less the exact time the two colleagues were having their conversation inside the Queen's Arms Hotel, Timothy Reagan entered the basement of the nightclub and unlocked a little room which was only used by himself. He was the only person allowed inside the room, he had the only key; this was his empire. Inside were all the equipment and ingredients he required to assemble one of his special devices, devices which had become one of the I.R.A.'s most effective weapons. Noth-ing crude or unsophisticated would satisfy Timothy, an im-mense amount of pride and care went into their making, so much so that even if one of them was discovered it was almost impossible to defuse it. The bomb would be ready for collection when the two 'carriers' arrived to pick it up and then, at a predetermined time, it would detonate somewhere in the midst of the capital. It was Timothy's greatest dream that some day one of his powerful devices would be placed near enough to the Houses of Parliament to wipe them all out; for him to be recognised as the most famous patriot who blew the British Government to pieces.

Meanwhile, over the sea, but in Gosport not in Ireland, two thoroughly miserable and dejected bodyguards were cursing the existence of one certain Geordie. It was plain enough to them that he had gone out of his way to make them look ridiculous. Somehow he must have seen them, but they could not understand how because they had taken extra care, just as Timothy Reagan had instructed them. To make matters worse, the ferries had stopped running and they were stuck in Gosport until the weather cleared up enough to allow them to operate again.

John was relaxing inside his room, unconsciously watching the television without really being aware of the programme, when the 'phone interrupted the peace; it was Chris.
"Hello John," she said, "I haven't disturbed you have I?"
"You couldn't disturb me if you rang in the middle of the night," he replied.
"That's nice of you," she said, "the reason I've rung you is because tonight is my night off and I was wondering if you'd like to come over and put your trust in my cooking......nothing

190

special, of course, but I think that you'll enjoy it.''

''I'd love to,'' replied John eagerly, ''I'll just give Michael a ring 'cos he's expecting me.....but I know he'll understand.'' After giving him her address, she said goodbye, and rang off. Michael was very understanding.

''You lucky bastard!'' he yelled down the phone, almost damaging John's eardrum, ''How you've managed that I'll never know; but never mind, you enjoy yourself and remember what I asked you to find out for me......is she or is she not a genuine blonde.''

''I'll see you sometime tomorrow,'' said John, ''but as far's the other thing goes, I 'ope you realise that you're talkin' to a chapel lad and one who doesn't go in for that sort of thing......a cup of coffee, a couple of sarnies and a few well chosen hymns, that's all I'm lookin' forward to.''

''Well I hope that's all you bloody well get,'' laughed Michael. At seven fifteen the taxi arrived to take him to her address, he was feeling more than just a little apprehensive, because after all it was a kind of 'date' and he hadn't done this for over twenty years; he thought his courting days were behind him. The snow had eased a little, there was a good cover on the ground but, as he expected, the gritters had done their job and the roads were clear. On ringing the doorbell to her upstairs flat, he became more unsure of himself. Why had she chosen him to invite for a meal, when by all accounts she could have her pick of most men, and that included the majority of service personnel in the area. He thought over the sequence of events which had taken place since he arrived in Portsmouth; it was Chris herself who had made all the running; she had struck up the initial conversation and had definitely been the first one to smile. Now she had gone even further by inviting him to her home; and much as he would have liked to think otherwise, all of this did not seem right; something had to be wrong about it all. Could it be possible that behind that beautiful exterior, she was just that little bit more than the club singer? Could it be possible that she actually worked for the brothers lock, stock and barrel; and this visit was just another one of their ways to check on his authenticity? He decided that he would have to tread carefully and watch what he said; hopefully to discover that all his doubts and suspicions were unfounded.

The door opened and Chris came to meet him, her smile as genuine as any smile could be. She was wearing a tight white sweater which accentuated the shape of her breasts, the lack of a bra was evident, her small nipples reacting instantly to the freezing air and becoming erect. The faded denim jeans looked as if someone had painted them onto her because they were so tight and, as he followed her up the flight of stairs to her flat, her buttocks moved in unison with every step she took.

'Get thee behind me, Satan', thought John, as the passion inside him began to stir.

''Thanks for coming,'' she said over her shoulder, ''it's a horrible night to be out there.''

As soon as he entered the small, but immaculately clean room, all of his prior doubts were suddenly realised, and he instantly became embarrassed at certain thoughts which had passed through his mind, as to why such a young and beautiful woman would go out of her way to be that little extra bit nice to him. Already seated in the comfortable chair by the imitation log fire, with a large drink in his hand, was none other than Commodore Ward.

"Hello John," he said, "sorry about the necessity of this charade, but we felt it to be absolutely essential.....had you known it might possibly have jeopardised the entire operation before we managed to get a foothold in their door; thanks to you we've done just that."

Finally things were put into their true perspective. John remembered being informed that the section already had one of their operatives working on the inside; this was Chris. His inflated ego, which had been boosted out of all proportion, now felt completely and utterly deflated, and any romantic thoughts he had about Chris were suddenly dispersed.

"The pretence of the two of you becoming close has to continue and be encouraged," explained the Commodore, unaware of John's embarrassment, "the Reagans and anyone else involved with them must get the impression that it is genuine.....a great deal depends on it."

John glanced over in Chris's direction and saw that if anything, she was as embarrassed about things as he was himself, her faint smile acknowledging her guilt at having to deceive him.

"I wanted this little get-together to update you on what is happening elsewhere," continued the Commodore, "there is rising speculation that this second arms deal is almost certain to get the go-ahead in the very near future; all information substantiates this. Both of you.. especially you John, must be alert for anything which might have a bearing on this; the smallest detail I want to be informed of."

"As far as I'm concerned," said John, "nothing out of the ordinary had happened apart from 'aving my room searched, which I expected; and being tailed all over the city this morning. More than likely they're just bein' extra careful because of this 'old mate' suddenly turning up out of the past...but we know they'll never be able to connect me with any of the security services, no matter how far they go back....there's nowt for them to find.''

A concerned expression came over the old man's face, the deep furrows in his forehead became even more pronounced than normal.

''If either one of you have the slightest idea that they suspect anything,'' he said, ''then I want you both out of it immediately, because I don't intend losing you..... We can pull them in any time we want; but the shipment would be the icing on the cake.''

''If it ever comes to that,'' said John, ''you have my word that no matter how I feel about my past friendship with Michael, I'll kill him....and his brother; their days are numbered.''

Chris had remained silent up to this point, listening carefully to what was being said.

''Surely no one can suspect us,'' she interrupted, ''John and I'll carry on with our little affair, until something positive turns up.''

The Commodore smiled at her. ''The most important thing is for you both to be careful,'' he said, ''anyway our overseas contact informs us that Rudi Schumaker is presently in Amsterdam, he's busy buying weapons from known dealers throughout Europe; but as of yet we don't know of any delivery date. Whenever this is decided, the arrangements and deal will be supervised by the brothers; this is their show.''

Chris busied herself pouring more drinks, she seemed to be more at ease now.

''How's young Bright shaping up?'' asked the Commodore.

''He's a good lad to 'ave around,'' replied John, ''I like

him...I feel certain that if I need his help, he'll prove to be more than capable.''

''Good,'' smiled the old man, ''he reminds me a lot of yourself.....the same temperament and attitude; all it needs is developing.''

''Excuse me, Commodore,'' said Chris, ''but will you be staying? Only the food's almost ready, and after all I did invite John here for a meal, even if it was under false pretences.''

''I'm sorry my dear,'' replied the officer, ''but I must decline your gracious offer; I have to be back in London tonight; maybe some other time....when all this business is over and done with.''

The old man left the comfort of his chair and put on his overcoat, not forgetting to collect his rolled up brollie. He was the true likeness of the British officer and gentleman of the old school. After shaking hands with both of them, he added. ''My driver's been waiting patiently at the far end of the road, and he too wants to be back in London tonight....but no doubt for different reasons from my own.''

Chris escorted him down the stairs and let him leave by the door at the rear of the building; obviously he believed in taking no unnecessary risks. She returned within three minutes and looked into his eyes.

''I'm sorry for deceiving you,'' she said quietly, ''it was cruel. My instructions were to become friendly with you and to make a show of it....if it's any consolation, I found it very easy to do...and that's the truth.''

''There's no need for apologies, flower,'' replied John, ''I was beginning to doubt it all myself, it had to be too good to be true. The only thing that I got wrong was I thought you

195

might be workin' for the brothers.....I'm pleased about that."
Chris smiled at him, it was a heartwarming smile, and it reassured him. There was no disputing the fact that she was a beautiful young woman and, no matter how hard he tried to convince himself otherwise, he knew that he wanted her. His thoughts were interrupted by the phone ringing. Chris picked up the receiver and, after a couple of seconds, passed it to John.

"John..it's Commodore Ward here; you seem to have attracted the attention of a very large gentleman. My driver informs me that he observed him arrive shortly after yourself and that he's spent his time concealed in the doorway opposite the flat....you have an idea who he might be?"

"I've a bloody good idea sir," replied John, "don't worry about it, I'll sort it out."

"Right then....as I've already said, be careful....goodbye."

" 'Bye sir," said John, and replaced the phone. "It looks like we've got an audience outside...it's a fair bet Lurch is keepin' a vigil outside your window. What I'd like to know for sure is whether it's me he's followin', or is it he's just potty about you and jealous of me bein' up here?"

"What are we going to do?" she asked nervously.

"Precisely nothin' at all for the time being," replied John, "you invited me 'ere for a meal and it's about ready isn't it? Well we'll enjoy that, an' he can freeze to death out there for all a' care."

Walking across the room to the window, she began to close the curtains, then suddenly stopped. "If he knows you're with me," she said, "then we must put on a show for his benefit....come over her and stand next to me."

John did as he was told, he stood within two feet of her and the fragrance of her perfume drifted to his nostrils, her very presence was electrifying.

"Now put your arms around me and hold me close," she instructed.

"What?" he asked, taken by surprise.

"I said hold me close...if we're to act out our parts, then we should at least do it well."

Never being one to argue with a lady, especially one as desirable as Chris was, John obediently did as he was told.

"Now kiss me... as if you meant it," she added.

Making sure that they were in full view of anyone who might be watching the proceedings from outside, he gently placed his lips on hers and kissed her. The pressure of their bodies as they came together had him feeling weak at the knees; her breasts were pressing into his chest, the kiss lingered and her lips slowly opened.

When they finally parted, Chris turned and completed the closing of the curtains, her face flushed; her eyes averting themselves from his gaze.

"It seems as if I owe our friend outside a debt of gratitude," said John, "because it's a long time since I enjoyed anything so much."

Looking embarrassed about her own reactions to the kiss, she turned away from his eyes. "I enjoyed it as well," she murmured, "it was nice."

Outside in the street Lurch had witnessed the whole thing, and he was seething. "Bastard!" he spat, "One day you'll pay for all of this....that's a promise." It had been a disastrous few days since John Williams had turned up in the club, things were on the decline. It had been his own idea to follow him tonight, his best friend Herman had tried to persuade him against it; but he had ignored the advice, not being able to help himself. To make matters worse he had to stand quietly and endure the taunts of Timothy Reagan gloating over the fact that 'Chris was entertaining a gentleman friend'. As long as he was back inside the club by ten p.m. nothing would be said. Although he and Herman had sworn their allegiance to the Irish organisation and were paid better than they had ever been paid before, he still had his own needs to consider. He imagined them both naked and writhing together on her bed, that bastard Geordie doing everything that he himself had dreamed of doing to her; the fantasy had almost taken control of him. No man had ever given him a beating before and, to add insult to injury, she had seen it all happen. The hate he felt inside for the man with her was becoming overpowering, he fought back the overwhelming compulsion to smash the door down and kill him in front of her; that would make up for it. But he realised that he could never bring any suspicion upon the club and the activities they were all involved in; the bombings and the killings themselves never bothered his conscience the slightest. A pleasant thought would be to have one of Timothy's specials shoved right up that Geordie's arse and wait for the bang; he smiled at the idea.

Back inside the nightclub, the Reagan brothers were engrossed in their own conversation about John Williams.
"I've had a call from Jimmy Leck," announced Timothy.
"And?" asked Michael apprehensively.
"Nothing," replied his brother, "not a thing. He says he got

into the house without any bother....says it's not a bad bit of property...but it's absolutely clean. Seems as if your mate's turned the place into some kind of shrine to 'is dead missus....photos of her all over the house, reckons she was a gorgeous bit o' stuff. He also went into a couple of the local pubs and 'ad a bit of innocent chat with some of the regulars, sayin' as how he was an old mate and just happened to be in the Durham area, so he thought he'd look him up. Nobody would say a wrong word about 'im...it's just like he told it to you..'is wife used to be a teacher and he drove for a local firm until he got the push for not goin' back to work after the funeral....not that he's short of a few bob or two. It seems as if most people thought he was goin' bonkers, pissed all the time and wouldn't come out o' the house...when all of a sudden he ups and fucks off on holiday; no word where he's gone or when he'll be back.....It looks as if you were right, Michael, and I was wrong as usual.''

Michael smiled broadly at this news, he had known that it would be so.

"No brother, you were the one who was right," he said, "you did what you had to do. The possibility of a 'plant' has always to be considered, that has to be paramount to our safety.....I was acting on purely personal feelings for an old mate, and I admit I was wrong; because we have to be twice as careful in our situation.......but let's call the dogs off now.'' Timothy agreed.

"Everything's ready for the big bang," he said, "the two 'postmen' will be here sometime tomorrow to pick up their baggage. They've selected their target, and when it goes off.....boy will this one really hurt them.''

Michael Reagan had never been too willing a participant in

199

this aspect of the operation, the organising of shipments and arms deals were his main priorities. The killing of British soldiers and U.D.R. men back on Irish soil was understandable, and he could stomach that, but the wanton death and destruction his brother seemed to revel in sickened him. Being true to the ultimate cause, he had to force himself to believe that these violent means would someday bring about a victorious end, therefore he obeyed every command issued by the officials ruling the War Council.

Chris and John spent the following few hours acquainting each other with the particular ways they had each met the Commodore and became involved with the section. She had been married to a corporal attached to the Special Air Services and he had been killed four years previously whilst on an assignment in Armagh. Like John, she had no children; the reason being that her husband had preferred to wait until he finished his time in the army, which was to have been six months after the day he was killed. Married at the age of twenty, she became a widow two years later, and out of the two years and eight months of married life, she spent rather less than half of that time actually with him.

Twelve months later the Commodore approached her.

At least John had had eighteen years with Angela.

When it was time for him to leave the flat, their individual tragic circumstances had acted in a way which now brought them closer to one another, they found comfort in each other's company.

Chris rang for a taxi.

"I'm sorry you can't stay," she smiled, "but a girl has her

reputation to think of.''

It did not take long before the taxi arrived, the driver stopped outside the flat and gave a short blow of the horn; John opened the outer door and turned to look at her and, as their eyes met, something passed between them which they were both aware of.

"Goodnight, flower," he said, "thanks for sharing your memories with me...I feel more settled in myself than I have for a long time."

She watched as he walked towards the taxi, the cold air now mixed with a freezing fog which had the limbs and branches of the tree lined avenue shimmering in its eerie whiteness; and suddenly she felt drawn to this lonely man.

"John," she called.

As he turned, she ran along the path, reached up and kissed him gently on the lips; a warm and affectionate gesture with maybe the hint of a promise behind it. With a little smile, she said, "Goodnight," and returned indoors.

A quick glance up and down the road, in empty doorways, soon satisfied him that Lurch had long gone.

Chapter Nine

After a restful and good night's sleep, during which he unashamedly dreamt of Chris, John phoned the club. Michael himself answered.

"Hello me' old mate," he greeted, "I thought you'd still be tucked up nicely in some blonde's bed....How did you get on last night and don't say right leg first?"

John responded with a laugh... the 'game' went on regardless.

"Well sir," he replied, "not too bad at all, but regarding that certain favour you wanted me to find out....about that I still don't know. But there's one thing I'm absolutely certain of and that is, she's definitely all woman....I'll stake my reputation as a Harley Street brain surgeon on that being true."

"Well there's another thing that's certain," said Michael, "and that is you won't be doin' any operating on yours truly here.....but the main thing is, are you making headway with her? Is there a light at the end of the tunnel and will it be worth all the effort at the end?"

John felt a little guilty at having to talk about Chris in this way, but he had to play along with his friend's whim. Both Chris and he had agreed to play out their individual roles in the Commodore's production, he only hoped that when the final curtain descended, things had gone as planned.

"The reason I've rung you so early," said John, changing the subject, "is to ask if you and your good lady would be partial to having lunch here with me....it would be a nice change for Rose, and it'll get her out o' the club for a while."

"That's not a bad idea at all," answered Michael, "hang on for a mo' and I'll see what she has to say."

After a short interval, when John could hear voices talking in the background, his friend returned to the phone. "Would love to," said Michael enthusiastically, "it will give 'er a chance to get herself all dolled up....what time would you like us to get to that posh hotel you're staying at?"

"About one o'clock...and we'll down a couple o' noggins before we go in, and by the way mate...don't forget to wash behind yer' ears because they tend to check them in 'ere."

"Bloody 'ell, they that fussy?"

"They are," said John, "and just one other thing, oppo...leave the jolly green giant in the car, I don't want 'im frightening the residents off."

"For you mate..anything. I'll tell him to take some sandwiches and a flask o' tea," replied Michael, then his attitude changed and he added, "Thanks for asking us John, it's been ages since Rose 'n me had a day out....I'm lookin' forward to it."

The repertoire of talk between the two of them was now as it had been all those years ago, as if the intervening time had been erased and they were both still in their youth and highly impressionable. The sad thing was, as far as John was concerned, that he was beginning to enjoy their renewed friendship. He rang reception and told them he would be having two guests for lunch and asked advice on what he could order, because these two people were special to him and he wanted to impress them. Reception informed him that the Chef's speciality would more than suffice and they were positive he would not be disappointed in the meal.

At twelve fifty five, the gleaming Mercedes drove smoothly into the hotel grounds and Herman obediently opened the door for Rose and Michael to alight, both of them looked very resplendent and wealthy.

"Do you know," said John, greeting them as they walked through the doors, "if I hadn't a' known better, I'd have taken you both for Lord and Lady Portsmouth...you look that well, especially you, flower." He presented Rose with one of his nicer smiles.

"Thank you, kind sir," she acknowledged, "you don't look so bad yourself...if I wasn't with Michael, I might've been tempted." Then she pretended to be disappointed in him, "What is this I hear about you being unfaithful to me?....Two-timing me for another woman....and a young one at that?"

"Well my love," smiled John, "it was painfully obvious to me that you yourself are well and truly spoken for...so I had no choice but to seek the companionship of another. I was becomin' desperate, and a man can only take so much...and in my case I wasn't takin' anything at all..so you can see my plight."

The three of them laughed together, the atmosphere was natural.

After they were seated comfortably in the lounge, with a drink in front of each of them, John presented them with the small gifts he had bought for them. "What's these?" asked Rose.

John shrugged his shoulders. "Just a little somethin' from me to you two, as a token of appreciation for bein' just what you are...friends, and for welcoming me into your home at a time when I needed it......just to say thanks."

"Oh John," she said, "you shouldn't have. We don't need any gifts or anything else from you to know how you feel. Just having the three of us together again is enough....I've never seen Michael so happy for a long time."Misunderstanding the reason behind the lunch invitation and the gifts, Michael looked him in the eyes.

"You're not leaving us, are you mate?" he asked.

"No...'corse I'm not, they're just a couple o' small presents....if I'd a' known they would have caused all this bloody interrogation, I wouldn't of bought them."

Rose was delighted with her small bottle of perfume, dabbing a little behind her ears. "Chanel number five...my favourite, she smiled. Reaching over, she kissed him on the cheek. "Thank you John, I'll only use it on special occasions."

Michael was also pleased with his present, an expensive looking lighter.

"It's like Christmas," he said, shaking John's hand, "I'd better stick to shaking hands with you...if I kissed you on the cheek, we'd all get flung out of here on our arses. Anyway, thanks mate; now you've made me feel bloody awful because we haven't got one for you."

John whispered into his friend's ear. "Bollocks," he said.

Two drinks later, the three of them went into the hotel restaurant and, as reception had promised him, the meal was excellent. The Chef's choice turned out to be roast duckling served with orange sauce, with creamed potatoes and asparagus tips; followed by melon with ginger. This was washed down with two bottles of red wine, with brandy and coffee rounding off the whole thing. John was not one to fuss over a meal, a well done steak and a few chips would have satisfied him, but he intended to put a show on for his friends and it certainly impressed them.

"That was absolutely beautiful," exclaimed Rose, with a contented smile, "it's a pleasure to escape from my own kitchen and have a professional do the cooking for you...thank you

John."

"Don't mention it," he replied, "as long as you've enjoyed it, then it's been worth it."

Michael had been a little pensive, as if inwardly trying to make a decision. "You wouldn't fancy moving down here full time, would you?" he asked John, "if it's money that's the trouble...then don't worry about that side of things, because I'd be pleased to fix something up for you."

This development came totally unexpected to John.

"Michael, me' old mate," he said, "as far as money's concerned...I've got no problems there; and without doubt I love bein' down here with the two of you...at last I've started to live all over again. But my whole life's back in that small village...my 'ome with all its happy memories....and Angela, she's lying in that graveyard waitin' for me to go back......I don't honestly know if I'm ready for leaving it all just yet."

"Listen John," persisted Michael, "you told me yourself that you were in a rut...now could be the right time for you to climb out of it and find yourself again; and what better way to do it than amongst friends."

"Why not John?" urged Rose, "What is there in Durham?...An empty house with painful memories as well as happy ones...and it will only get worse for you the longer you force yourself to stay there."

John suddenly realised the danger signs, he was allowing himself to become too involved, the Commodore had warned him against it. But even knowing the risks and fully understanding what was beginning to happen to him, he had to agree with both of them; what they were offering him was tempting. The last two years of his life had been so lonely and now he had friends by his side, friends who obviously cared about him.

Having lost Angela was the worst experience of his life, but here was the opportunity to find happiness once again; maybe if he got to know Chris a lot better she would stay here with him.

"I'll need a bit of time to think it all over," he said, "it's a big step to take..a lot o' things to see to."

"Don't think that I'm being nosey," said Michael, pleased with the way things were going, "but how much do you think you could raise if you do decide to move down here with us?"

"I'm not sure.....I've never really thought it out," replied John, "after sellin' the house, plus all the odds and ends in the bank and building society....I should reckon somewhere in the region of about ehhh.....seventy thousand or thereabouts."

"Bloody hell," exclaimed Michael, "you're bloody rich. With that kind of capital, I'm certain that I could get you fixed up in some tasty deal which would make you a fair profit...you can never have too much money. Remember the blank weeks when we were in the mob, when we used to have a 'kitty' when we went ashore? We always started with a few bottles o' V.P. wine, then onto the scrumpy because we were skint? Well then mate, those days are finished....if you've got the cash, you can get anything you bloody well want...no bother at all."

John remained silent, pondering over what Michael had just said...it was like Eve offering the apple to an innocent Adam......would he too take the fatal bite.

'Jesus Christ, Williams,' he suddenly thought, waking up to reality, 'for fuck's sake get your act together. You're here, among other things, to kill this man sitting beside you...All of this whole situation is play-acting on your side, and nothing about it is real. The only thing that matters here is you're fightin' a war against the I.R.A. and it just so happens that your good mate 'ere is part and parcel of that evil.'

John felt his face flush a little at his own stupidity and Rose noticed it.

"I hope you're not having rude thoughts about our lady singer," she smiled, "something's just made you blush."

"You might be right," laughed John, a little uncomfortably, "passin' thoughts that's all.....but I promise you I'll think seriously about your proposition, it sounds very promising.. and the change would do me good."

After the meal was finished, John escorted his two guests back to the lounge where they indulged themselves in more drinking and idle chatter about the old days.

"Think about what we were talking about earlier," said Michael, as he helped Rose into the back of the Mercedes.

"I will, that's a promise," agreed John, giving a final wave as the car drove away.

Later that night as he was dressing, he was once again disturbed by the 'phone, it was getting to be something of a habit.

"I've been keeping a discreet eye on the club," said Steve Bright, "and I think things are beginning to move. Twenty minutes ago Timothy Reagan took two men into the club through the basement garage and I'm positive the same men are high on the 'wanted' file. One is called Hamilton and the other Coyne and, if I'm right, they are known bombers. As part of my training I had to sit for bloody hours going through photographs of known terrorists....and I remember these two alright. Before I got in touch with you, I rang the Commodore and he confirmed that Hamilton and Coyne both escaped from the Maze prison over six weeks ago. If they're here in this country, then it's for one thing.....they're here to plant a bomb, that is if they haven't done so already. We know the club is their operational headquarters, so they're either here to collect the bomb or awaiting transportation back to Ireland. The Commodore insisted that they must not be allowed to do either...it's up to us to prevent that happening."

"Where are you now, Steve?"

"I'm in a 'phone box about forty yards away from the club," he explained, "but I can see everything and nobody has made a move yet."

"You got anythin' we might use to stop them?" asked John, "mine's locked away in the hotel safe."

"Shotgun do you?"

"Perfect," replied John.

"You going to sort this out, John?"

"Looks that way," he replied, "what I need you to do, young man, is get into that little car of yours and keep an eye on the place, I'll get there as soon as I can."

"What if they leave before you get here?" asked Steve.

"Then, my son it's up to you.....do what you have to."

It took John exactly fourteen minutes to find the small sports car, he opened the door and climbed in beside his young colleague.

"Nothin' happening?" he asked.

"Not a thing," replied Steve, "They're still inside. There's only two ways they can get out of the place, and we can see both of 'em from here."

"Describe the two men we're after," said John.

"Hamilton..he's about five six or seven, stocky build; dark haired and clean-shaven....thirty nine years of age. When he

210

went in he was wearing a dark brown duffle coat and brogue shoes...I noticed them because it somehow looked odd wearing brogues with a bloody duffel coat. Coyne is a bit older at forty eight, he's over six feet and heavily built...something like yourself; he's got fair hair and has a scraggy looking moustache that looks as if it belongs on a walrus...he was wearing a black overcoat, one of those Crombie style ones. The reason their faces clicked is because these two men always work together as a team, it's their M.O.....all information collated on them says they never work alone, they were even busted out of prison together. The I.R.A. rate them very highly so, if we can take them out, it will be a kick in the tender proverbials for them.''

''If things go as I hope,'' said John, ''then the pair o' them will have the displeasure of leavin' this life together.''

''You going to kill them?'' asked Steve.

''If I get the chance,'' admitted John, ''what's the use of capturin' them again...they'll just get out of some other prison to do it all over again, it's only a matter of time with them. What's needed 'ere is a permanent solution, and you believe me son..there's nowt more permanent than bein' dead......where've you got this shotgun of yours?''

Reaching behind John's seat, the young man fidgeted about for a couple of seconds and suddenly the weapon appeared between John's feet. Picking it up, he examined it and remembered the last time he had had cause to use such a firearm; the devastation had been tremendous....it was fully loaded and ready to use.

''Your motto 'be prepared'?'' asked Steve.

''In this game it has to be, son...that's the reason why I'm still around while a few others aren't. Survival is the name of the game, Stevie boy...you heed my words and see if they're not true."

"John," said the young man, "if I ask you something personal, will you tell me the truth?"

"Depends on what it is...if it's too personal then I won't."

"Was it you....in York all those years ago; did you do that shot?"

Looking at his younger counterpart, John realised that this man was quite possibly being prepared to do what he himself had done all those years ago.

"As a matter of fact Steve...yes I did."

"I bloody knew it.....I've known it since the day I met you at the station.

"Everybody connected with the section had heard the rumour, but nothing official's ever been said......that had to be quite a shot, John."

"I might have been as good as you in them days," smiled John, "but that's enough of the past, I've been livin' too long in the bloody past..forget it."

"It's forgot."

At ten forty five there was still no sign of the two Irish bombers, so John decided that he would have to make an appearance inside the club, otherwise it might be a little suspicious.

"I'll 'ave to go inside," he announced, "they're expectin' me..plus the fact I'll be bloody pleased to get outa' here, my legs 'ave almost seized up."

"It's the old bones, they're starting to tell on you."

"Old bones my arse," said John, "how you manage to get up to anythin' with one of those young women inside 'ere, I'll never know."

"Where there's a will, there's a way....anything's possible if

212

you try hard enough," replied Steve, "you just have to be a bit flexible."

Climbing awkwardly from the car, John stretched his legs to get his blood back into circulation. "I'm sorry, young man," he smiled, "but you're goin' to have to stay here because it's quite possible that the two we're after might be in the basement and leave by the garage doors. If that happens, then you have to take them both out yourself....but make sure you do it well away from the city."

"You got the faith in me?" said Steve, obviously worried.

"You wouldn't be here if you weren't capable....... one word of advice if you have to do it; somethin' my old gunnery instructor used to drill into me. Never ever think of the human factor, these men are animals, you yourself know that...you know what they've done in the past and why they're here tonight. If you have to kill them, don't think twice about it or it could be too late.....do it. O.K. son?"

"O.K. John."

"Good lad...I'll be seein' you, so long."

John received the same cheerful welcome from Bill the friendly doorman and on entering the club he immediately looked over in Chris's direction, her voice was as clear and pleasant as ever. Tonight she wore a stunning black dress which clung to her and, as usual, she had all the men-folk almost drooling over their beers. It was as if she sensed his presence and her eyes casually searched the room until they met his, the smile was instantaneous and brought a warm glow inside him.

Suddenly Lurch loomed up large and ugly in front of him, completely obliterating his view.

"Mr. Reagan says he's sorry that he's not here to meet you," he said, forcing himself to be polite, "but he won't be long in comin' down."

Staring blankly into the big man's bruised face, John nodded and walked straight past him to the bar; he had a feeling that the episode with Lurch was not over yet.

Chris began to sing one of his favourite songs, one of the Carpenters' better known numbers, *'We've only just begun'*; could there possibly be a meaning in her words?

"I see you've been having a chat with your 'friend'," said Tom, handing him a drink and nodding in Lurch's direction.

"He did growl somethin' or other," replied John.

"Be careful of him, Mr. Williams....he's a right evil bastard and he'll hold a grudge."

"I intend to."

It was almost half an hour before Michael came into the room.

"I'm sorry mate," he said, "but two of our associates dropped in on us without warning and I had to show them some hospitality just for appearances' sake. Luckily Timothy's got them talkin' about the 'old country' and little green men with shillelaghs, so I made my apologies and beat a hasty retreat. One thing they reminded me about is that we both have to be in Belfast in a few days time for a business meeting; most of our suppliers will be there, and it's a hell of a lot cheaper to deal direct, it cuts out the middle men."

With that, he tapped the side of his nose as if indicating a bit of a fiddle on the side.

"I got your message as soon as a' came in," said John, "but I'm sure that messenger's not too keen to become mates with me."

"You're going to have to keep any eye on him," replied Michael, "I've already warned him about causing any more

214

aggro with you, but I can't guarantee that he'll do as I say...you dented more than just his pride the other night.''

Surprisingly, Rose appeared in the room and sat at Michael's private table; the two men picked up their drinks and walked over to greet her.

"Hello sweetheart,'' said John, "this is a pleasant surprise...you look lovely.''

It was true, she did look very attractive, wearing a dress which did a lot for her and revealed quite a shapely figure.

"John Williams,'' she smiled, obviously pleased with his compliment, "you always did have the knack of saying the right things. No wonder that young woman over there seems to have fallen for your charms.''

"And it's supposed to be us Irish that 'ave all the blarney,'' commented Michael.''

"Well now,'' said John, "you taught me everythin' a' know. Always give 'em a bit of the old flannel you said........it does a power of good.''

"I was right then, wasn't I?'' smiled his friend.

At this point Timothy entered the room and came to the table; the fears of having missed their 'club associates' loomed strongly in John's mind, he was unsure of what he should do next.

But he was greatly relieved to find out he was mistaken.

"I've had to come down to get another bottle,'' said Timothy, "those two have cleaned out our private stock of whiskey and now they've decided they'd like a last one for the road.''

Then looking at John, he added, "I'll be bloody pleased to see the back o' them, these visits of theirs cost us a small fortune in booze.''

"As long as all the bookwork's sorted out satisfactorily,'' said Michael, "I don't want the bloody V.A.T. man chasin'

215

after us."

"We're just ironin' out the final details now," smiled his brother, "they're a right pain in the arse."

John realised that the brothers too were involved in their own version of play-acting, making a show of not being too keen on these visits. It seemed as if the entire population was engaged in some kind of unreality. Were there any normal people left in the world?

"D'you know somethin' mate," said Michael, as his brother strode across the floor in the direction of the bar, "since you've came here, Chris seems to be a new woman...more 'alive' than she's ever been. You must have done somethin' for her, because every now and again she stares over here, and I'm sorry to say it's you she's oglin' at 'n not me."

"She's a smasher alright," agreed John, "but it's all in the mind as far as I'm concerned...there's no chance of anythin' developing."

"Don't be so naive," scolded Rose, "if you want her..and I think you do, well tell her, and you might just get a pleasant surprise."

"We'll see," he replied.

At the end of Chris's stint for the night, once again she came straight over to their table, as if allowing speculation to increase about her feelings towards John; she stopped and smiled directly at him.

"I was hoping we could finish off that meal we started last night," she asked quietly, "I can concoct quite a tasty dish with the leftovers...it seems a pity to let them waste."

"I'd like that very much," he replied.

"Lucky man," added Michael, with a wink.

"I won't be long," said Chris, "give me a few minutes to get

216

changed.''

As she left and disappeared inside the changing room, Rose noticed the beam of satisfaction on John's face.

''What did I tell you,'' she said, ''it's plain to see that she's took with you....you make hay while the sun shines; and think about what we were talking about earlier today.''

''I agree it's a pleasant thought,'' agreed John.

''I don't know how you've cracked it,'' said Michael, shaking his head in mock bewilderment, ''but you jump in with both feet, me old mate...and happy landings.''

''Well I'll just paddle at first,'' replied John, ''to test the water so to speak....but I 'ave to admit, it seems a bit warmish.''

It was not long before Chris reappeared, well and truly adorned for the bleak weather outside; wearing a full length white wool coat and matching leather boots and a deep red scarf tied loosely about her neck.

''Ready for the arctic?'' smiled John, ''you look lovely.''

''John Williams,'' interrupted Rose, pretending to be hurt, ''that's what you said to me earlier...now you're casting me off like an old blanket.''

''I'm sorry, flower,'' answered John, ''but you know who's here,'' indicating to Michael, ''and I 'ave to be a bit careful....I'm just puttin' a show on for him, so's he'll not get suspicious.''

''I'll have you know I feel the cold something terrible,'' said Chris with one of her most charming smiles and then, turning to Rose, she added, ''I hope you don't mind me stealing him away.''

''Of course not,'' replied Rose, with an equally charming smile, ''you could prove to be just the tonic he needs.....go and enjoy yourselves.''

As John stood up from the table, Michael grabbed his leg and whispered, "Keep an eye out for that bouncin' handbag..you've been warned."

"What was he saying about a bouncing handbag?" asked Chris, as they walked across the floor, "what's a bouncing handbag?"

"It's nothin', flower, honest....only one of Michael's weird jokes.

Once outside in the freezing night air, John took hold of her arm and guided her towards where he knew Steve had been waiting patiently for news.

"I'm bloody pleased you asked me back home with you," he said, "I was hoping for some reasonable excuse to get out of the club....we know that there's two of the I.R.A.'s top men inside and it's odds on they're in the country to plant one of their bombs somewhere...and they've to be stopped. I'll get you a taxi and you can get yourself off home....but the main thing is I'll need a water-tight alibi for when it's all over. Will your reputation stand up to me stayin' the night with you? Because if things go as I hope....the Reagan boys will be hoppin'."

"Of course," she replied, "after all, we're in this thing to-gether." After rummaging around in her handbag, she produced a Yale key. "Here, take this and let yourself in, you know where I live......and John, please be careful."

Within five minutes, he had rung for a taxi and she was on her way home; he stood watching as it disappeared down the road, wishing for all that he was worth that he could have been by her side and that everything had been so different.

"Jesus Christ," he moaned as he climbed inside the small sports car, "it's bloody colder in 'ere than it is outside."

"I daren't risk starting the engine to thaw me out," said Steve, blowing into his cupped hands, "in case someone got suspicious of what I'm doing sittin' here on my Jack Jones....anyway you've been warming yourself inside the club and no doubt had one or two drops of the old anti-freeze to warm the cockles of your heart."

"You want to be grateful we're not back in the North East," smiled John, "I'd a' needed a chippin' hammer to get you outa' the ice by now.....anyway you seen anything?"

Steve nodded his head. "Just after you went into the club, one of those big bastards...I'm not sure which one it was..well, he drove a dark red Maxi into the garage and it's still in there. Do you think they're fixing it up to surprise a few people?"

I wouldn't doubt that in the least," replied John, "they'll have to 'ave transport and I doubt if they'll just jump on a train.......At least we know they're still inside the club, because a short while ago Timothy came downstairs and said they needed another bottle....one for the road he said...said they were two club associates here on a surprise visit."

"We'll give them a surprise visit alright, won't we?" stated the young man.

"That we will," confirmed John, then added, "by the way, Steve, did you know about Chris?.....I'm not bloody sure who knows what, only that I seem to know very little."

"The Commodore filled me in with the details the other night...the same night he came to see you at the flat, but until then I didn't have a clue."

It was one seventeen when Timothy opened the double garage door and casually strolled into the street as if taking in the night air, but at he same time checking out the immediate vicinity.

"Here we go," said Steve.

After satisfying himself that all was clear, Timothy signalled inside and the Maxi slowly reversed from the garage; two men were inside it. A few words were exchanged between the Irishmen and then the car drove away form the club, leaving Timothy to close the garage doors behind him.

"Righto' son, let's take things easy......don't get too close, we don't want to warn them," said John, thankful that things were beginning to happen; it had been a long time since he had killed, he had to prepare himself all over again. It did not take long before the cars left the city limits, heading in an easterly direction, but keeping away from the main A3 route to the capital.

"I knew it," said Steve, "the bastards are heading for the Smoke."

"They might be headin' that way," added John, "but they're not goin' to get there....we'll see to that."

He sat silently as the young man concentrated on his driving, being extra careful not to alert the occupants of the Maxi; his eyes focused upon the rear lights.

"They're going in a roundabout way," observed Steve, "but they're definitely heading in the general direction."

"This way will suit our needs better than goin' on the motorway," said John, "once we're out in the wilds we'll make our move.....somewhere nice and quiet."

After travelling approximately thirty one miles, he made his decision and, looking over at Steve, he said, "Now will do nicely, son......move up alongside them and have a last look, just to make sure."

The little car reacted instantly, the bonnet gently lifting in the sudden surge of speed and the back of John's seat pressed itself into him as the gap between the two cars rapidly decreased. Once level with the Maxi, the young man regulated his speed accordingly and he looked past John into the faces of the two men, giving them a slight wave of his hand as he suddenly accelerated away from them.

"It's them....no doubt about it."

"Right," said John, "now to find the right place....get well in front, but not so far that we can't see their headlights....I want to make no mistakes. When I give you the word...I want you to stop and let me out.. then drive on a few hundred yards and wait."

He saw the look of disappointment on Steve's face and he respected his feelings, he himself would have been the same.

"I've got to do it this way, son," he explained, "to prove to myself that I've still got what it takes........if it turns out that I 'aven't and they get past me, then it will be up to you; I take it you're armed."

Steve nodded. "I'm armed," he affirmed, "and I understand." Then he took his eyes off the road ahead and looked over at his older colleague and added, "somehow I don't think you'll fail. They reckon once you've got it, it never leaves you...an in-built instinct."

"They do, do they...we'll soon find out," replied John, "and keep a bloody eye on the road or nobody will be stoppin' them."

Three minutes later, and ensuring that no other vehicle had overtaken the following Maxi, they approached an 'S' bend in the road; chevrons indicating a need to reduce speed.

"Now!" called John, as they rounded the first stage of the bend.

The little car came to an abrupt but controlled halt, its brake

221

lights out of vision to the Irishmen behind, and once John's feet were on the ground it roared off again; leaving him standing alone in the darkness with the shotgun grasped firmly in his hands. He sprinted back to the beginning of the first bend and took cover behind the ample trunk of an old elm tree standing by the roadside; the headlights of the Maxi rapidly approaching.

It was time!

John left it to the very last second before jumping into the road and firing twice in quick succession into the windscreen of the car, the glass shattering into thousands of tiny particles. The car went out of control, viciously veering from side to side. As it went past, John fired twice more in the direction of the rear nearside wheel where he knew the petrol tank was; it erupted in flames which completely engulfed the rear section. The Maxi crashed through a wooden perimeter fence and ploughed forty yards into some farmer's field, finally running into an embankment before slowly overturning; the flames roaring as the vehicle became an inferno. Running after it, John could hear the muffled screams of the two I.R.A. men trapped inside, it would be impossible for anyone to escape from such intense heat. Then, astonishingly, he became aware of a smouldering figure crawling slowly from the flames, and somehow agonisingly climbing to his feet; it was the smaller of the two men.

Instinctively John brought the shotgun to bear upon him, the man's hair and clothing alight; not even an animal deserved to suffer so much. No matter what crimes against humanity the Irishman was guilty of in the past, John intended to put an end to his pain. For a fraction of a second the two men stared at each other, but before John could pull the trigger, Timothy's special device detonated and the car exploded into a massive fireball. The force of the blast knocked John backwards and off his feet, where he lay dazed upon the hard ground.

"You alright John?.....Come on mate."

John opened his eyes and saw Steve silhouetted above him in the brightly lit sky, then he remembered, and with the young man's help he climbed to his feet.

"You alright?" repeated Steve, looking into John's face for some sign of recognition.

"I'm fine," he acknowledged, and felt the large swelling on his scalp. "Where's 'e gone?"

"Where's who gone?"

John's eyes scoured the area for the Irishman, eventually finding him suspended six feet from the ground; impaled through the chest by one of the lower limbs of a tree some forty feet away from the car, his clothes and hair still smouldering.

"Jesus Christ," said Steve, his own eyes following John's line of vision and coming to rest upon the gruesome sight. "Come on John, let's get to fuck out o' here smartish."

He grabbed hold of the shotgun which now lay on the ground and placed a supportive arm around John to help him back to the little sports car, its engine purring smoothly in anticipation. As soon as he aided the older man into the passenger seat and closed the door, Steve rushed around the car and leapt in behind the steering wheel; within seconds they were on their way from the scene.

"Well one thing's for sure," he said to John, "you've still got it, mate."

"So it seems," acknowledged John quietly.

"You hurt, John?"

"No, I'm OK....got the wind knocked out of me that's all....thanks for comin' for me, son."

Steve laughed nervously. "When I heard the car go up, I didn't know if you'd been caught in it, and I just ran towards it...I couldn't help it. Seeing you lying on the ground...I thought you'd had it."

It didn't take long to cover the distance back to Southsea, Steve had the little car doing almost a hundred miles an hour at times; but somehow on this occasion it didn't seem to bother John, his mind occupied with other things.

"Stop here, Steve," he instructed the young man, as they came to the end of the road which led to Chris's flat, "better be safe than sorry; I'll walk from here. When you get back to the hotel , get in touch with the Commodore and put 'im in the picture about what's happened.......If I know him, he'll be waitin' for news."

"Will do.......we've made a start haven't we."

"Kicked them right in the goolies," agreed John, "and they won't be too pleased about it."

He waited until the little car was out of sight, then slowly walked towards the flat; but he did not really expect to find anyone hanging around in the shadows. As he entered the flat he found Chris waiting for him, she was curled up in the large armchair, wearing a heavy dressing gown.

"You alright, John?" she asked, concern showing in her face.

"I'm alright, flower," he answered, with a tired smile, "it went as we hoped it would.....there'll be no bombs goin' off in London tomorrow...or should I say today."

After helping him off with his sheepskin coat, she hung it on the rack near the door.

"The two men?" she asked.

"They're dead....that's the way it's got to be."

Chris nodded slowly as if understanding. "Cup of coffee to warm you up?" she asked, "or would you like something a little bit stronger?"

"Coffee'll do fine, thanks."

Looking at her closely, he was now seeing a different Chris; not the confident young woman who placed herself at risk every time she walked into the club; this was a worried and hesitant girl who seemed unsure of what it was she was involved in.

"Did you have to kill them, John?"

"I had no choice...but even if I had it would have been the same," he replied, "These kind of men don't care what they do..they thrive on killing. Whether it's innocent people bein' bombed, or some unfortunate soldier getting shot in the back as he walks past...they think it's great." He had said about the soldier getting shot before he realised, and wished he could have bit his tongue off. "I'm sorry Chris," he apologised as the tears came to her eyes, "I never thought.....Jesus! I'm a useless bastard, always puttin' my foot in it."

After a few minutes she stopped crying and dabbed her eyes with her handkerchief.

"No John, no need to be sorry," she said, "it's just that it still hurts when I think about it....but you're right, it had to be done.....and in a small way it's as if I've helped avenge his death, and that helps."

"I understand the tears," said John sympathetically, "I've cried myself more than once..the main thing is that neither of us will ever forget what we've lost........Now then, woman, where's this coffee you promised me?"

She smiled at him and went off into the kitchen.

Making himself comfortable on the large sofa, he tenderly probed at the lump on his head and realised just how lucky he had been, because if he had been standing a few yards closer to the car when the bomb exploded, it could easily have been the end of him having any further part in anything. He also realised there was a comforting feeling inside him, he enjoyed the warmth and atmosphere of this little room and the person who lived there.

Chris returned with two mugs of coffee and sat by him, they drank the hot liquid and stared into the simulated log fire effect of the gas fire; both of them silently involved with their individual thoughts of past loved ones.

"Go and get yourself off to bed," said John "you've had a long day."

"I will," she agreed, "you be alright here on the sofa?"

"Perfect.......I'll stretch out in a minute."

"There's a few extra blankets in the airing cupboard, I'll bring them through for you....sure you'll be comfortable enough?"

"I'll be fine, stop worryin' yourself about me," smiled John.

Before leaving the room to bring the blankets, she reached over and kissed him lightly on the lips, the top of her dressing gown parted, revealing almost all of a perfectly formed breast; his heart began to race, he could feel its pounding in his throat.

"Goodnight John," she said.

"Goodnight flower," he croaked, the blood pumping rapidly through his veins.

"Flower," she repeated, "do you call everybody flower, or is it a way of life with you Geordies?"

She disappeared into her bedroom; someone else was getting

themselves mixed up about his place of origin; but Durham seemed so very far away at this precise moment in time. After rearranging the cushions as pillows, he waited for her to return with the blankets, but they did not arrive. Shortly after he heard her voice calling out to him, so he walked over to the partially closed door and peered inside. The only light in the room was provided by a small bedside lamp which made it difficult to see clearly, but clearly enough to see the still form under the covers on the bed.

"You alright, Chris?" he asked, anticipation playing havoc with his imagination.

"I'm feeling so alone," she replied tentatively, her voice trembling, "would you like to come in here beside me?"

John could not believe his ears, this was exactly what he wanted to do; exactly what he was longing to do and imagining what it was like to be near her he walked to the side of the bed, his feet wanted to sprint the short distance but he managed to control them, until he stood towering over her. Looking down at the pillow which housed that beautiful face and blonde hair, he felt himself becoming a little apprehensive, as with his killings earlier in the night it, too, had been a long time.

"Chris," he sad quietly, "there's nothing in this world I'd rather do than be in there with you.....you don't know how much I need you; but are you sure?"

"I'm sure," she replied, "I know that I need you as well."

Normally John was a person who meticulously folded his clothes before carefully putting them away, but on this occasion they were discarded unceremoniously on the floor; and he slid between the sheets to be next to her. The warmth of Chris's naked body as she moved eagerly into his arms was electrifying, their mouths found each other and a deep rooted moan escaped from her lips as their passion intensified. His hands gently explored every part of her body, from the firmness of her breasts with nipples proud and erect, to the more vulnerable and secretive areas which caused her to cry out with pleasure. It had been so long since physical love had played an active role in either of their lives. John did not want to be quick and selfish and inconsiderate of Chris's own needs, so he made love to her slowly and deliberately with a self-restraint which he had not known himself to be still capable of. When the final moment came it was a simultaneous crescendo of ecstasy, their whole bodies trembling with the release. They lay in each other's arms, both satisfied and physically drained; and fell asleep with the worries of the world locked away outside those four walls, out in the cold of the early morning. There had been no need for words of appreciation nor explanation about the whys and wherefores; for the time being at least, two desperately lonely people had found comfort in each other.

As usual, Rose was the first one to be up and about; it had been well after three a.m. before she had eventually gone to her bed, leaving Michael and his brother deep in conversation over the visit of the two I.R.A. men. She knew what these visits meant, the only time other Irishmen came here was to pick up one of Timothy's bombs, which he openly boasted about to her. Words could not be found to describe the hate she felt for him; she blamed him solely for Michael's involvement with the I.R.A. It had been five years ago, during one of the so-called visits, that she had suddenly woken up to what they were both involved with. Up until then she had believed Michael when he had told her the story about settling down and buying the club from the real owners abroad, it had been so easy. All she had ever wanted out of life was to be with him, she never once mentioned marriage; not that she had not yearned for him to ask her, but this was to be her role in life and she accepted it. But to discover about the I.R.A. was something entirely different and her immediate reaction was to inform the police, it was her duty to do so. Then she realised that there was no way she could send Timothy to jail without implicating Michael as well; all of this was totally alien to her. When she had confronted Michael with what she had found out, he had tried to persuade her that what Timothy and himself were doing was war and, although he hated doing the things they did, eventually they would win. He also admitted that the idea of killing women and children sickened him, but his hands were tied and it was necessary to achieve their ultimate goal. She had been confused and frightened about coming to terms with what had been said, taking to drinking more and more to blank out the horror and keeping herself almost continually in a state of suspended apathy. What happened outside had nothing to do with her. Turning on the wireless as she always did, to enjoy the friendly banter coming from yet another Irishman, this one being Terry Wogan, she listened to the numerous 'mystery letters' he always received.

It was ten o'clock when she heard the news which brought the account: reporting that two men had been killed when the car in which they were travelling had exploded. Special Branch forensic experts at the scene confirmed the presence of explosive substances. One body found near the scene was posi-

tively identified as being that of Sean Hamilton, a lifelong
member of the Provisional I.R.A. who had escaped from the
high security wing of the Maze prison in the company of his
close companion Peter Coyne. The charred remains of a second body was expected to be identified as Coyne, dental records had been sent for to confirm this. Evidence gathered at
the scene tended to prove conclusively that the terrorists were
on their way to London engaged on another mission of death,
but seemingly fate had taken a hand. It appeared that the
bomb which they were carrying in the car had been somehow
triggered off prematurely; the Provisional I.R.A. acknowledged the fact that two of their men had been killed whilst on
active service on the mainland against the oppression of the
British Government. Rose ran into the bedroom to awaken
Michael.

"Michael," she said, shaking him roughly by the shoulder,
"Michael, you have to wake up.....it's on the wireless about
those two men that were here last night."

He eventually stirred, emitting various moans and curses.

"Michael," she repeated, "come on, please wake up...it's
important."

"Jesus, Rose," he grumbled, rubbing the sleep from his eyes,
"what's goin' on? It's still the middle o' the bloody night."

"Those two men...the ones that were here last night," she
splurted , "they're dead...It's just been on the wireless, the
man said the bomb went off as they were on their way to
London....they know it was the I.R.A...Michael, will they be
coming here for us next?"

"What are you talking about woman?" he shouted, now fully
awake, "and take it steady...slow yourself down."

Rose related what she had heard on the news and the expression on Michael's face changed from disbelief to rage.

"How the fuck's that happened?" he asked, then leaping out of his bed and ignoring the fact that he was naked, he ran through into Timothy's room; dragging the bedclothes from the sleeping figure. "Timothy, you stupid bastard," he roared. Finding himself roused in no uncertain manner, Timothy ogled at the sight of his naked brother and Rose standing over him.

"What's goin' on?....What's the matter with you?" he queried.

"It's that bastard bomb of yours that's what's goin' on," shouted his elder brother, "as a matter of fact, it's gone off...too fuckin' early. One of those things you call your pride and joy, the one Peter and Sean were supposed to be takin' up to London.....well my son, it's gone off, blowing them both to kingdom come. The Special Branch already know the organisation's involved, so let's hope and pray there's no way they can connect us with them.......Jesus, Timothy, you're supposed to be the expert in this...how come your calculations have gone all to cock...you must've done somethin' wrong when you assembled it."

Timothy was stunned, it could not possibly be true; there was no way in which the device could have exploded before it had been activated.

"As if we weren't in enough trouble with the council over the last farce," added Michael, "now this.....how're we goin' to explain this to them, I don't know.....they'll want our balls."

"It's impossible, Michael...honest," said Timothy, "it couldn't 'ave....there's no way I've made a mistake...I'm too bloody thorough to make mistakes..something's happened to make it go off, there's no other way."

Sitting on the edge of the bed, Michael finally resigned himself to the inevitable.

"You sure you heard the news right?" he asked Rose, hoping that for some reason she had decided to play some sick joke on them, but knowing in his heart that this would not be so.

"That's it!" cried Timothy, "she's got it all mixed up....you know what she's like first thing in the mornin'...her brain's still puddled from all the booze."

"I'm not stupid!" shouted Rose indignantly, "I know what I heard, and what I heard I told Michael......they said the bomb had gone off too soon and killed the two men in the car."

All three of them were silent, the brothers only too aware of the possible repercussions.

John opened his eyes and, remembering where he was, smiled as the memory of earlier that morning came flooding back to him. Turning to face her, he found Chris's side of the bed empty and, placing his hand where she had lain, he found it still quite warm. He had slept exceptionally well, only once having awakened, but after gazing at her beauty next to him he had fallen back into a deep sleep. But something had roused him now, and he was not sure what it had been, then he heard the sound of singing coming from another room somewhere in the flat. Glancing at the small travelling clock perched on the bedside table next to him, she saw it was just after ten a.m.; it had been an eventful kind of night all round.

The sound of singing continued, so easing himself from the warm bed he stepped into his trousers and walked through into the living room.

"Chris," he called, "where are you?"

Getting no reply, he moved towards the door through which

came the sound of her voice; he opened it slightly and peered round. He soon discovered that it was the bathroom, Chris was standing under the shower, her voice somewhat muffled by the sound of the water cascading down upon her body. Although the waterproof curtain was closed, the magnificent silhouette of her body was clear to see and he began to feel like the proverbial peeping Tom. Just as he was about to retreat quietly, her blonde head appeared out from the curtain and finding him there, she gave him one of those lovely smiles.

"Good morning," she said, "we're up at last are we?....Fancy a shower?"

"Love one," he replied.

Chris laughed. "There's plenty room in here...if we stand close together," she said with a cheeky smile.

Not being one to refuse such a tempting offer, once again he discarded his trousers and opened the shower curtain; he stood admiring Chris's fantastic body. She was in the process of washing her hair, soapy lather covered her head, shoulders and breasts, giving them the appearance of magnificent snow-clad mountains. As she massaged the lather into the scalp, the movement of her arms caused those same snow-clad precipices to swing gently from side to side. She was most definitely a beautiful woman, of that there was no doubt; and a further question had now been answered - she was, after all, a true and natural blonde.

Chris rinsed the soap from her face and saw him looking at her. "Come on then," she said, "make yourself useful...you can wash my back for me."

"I'm sorry for staring," he said, "but I think you've got a fantastic body."

"No need to tell me what you think," she laughed, "I can see for myself."

"It's boilin'!" he gasped, as the heat of the water caught him by surprise.

She laughed again and came into his arms, wrapping her own tightly around him and kissing him hard on the lips.

"That's for last night," she said, "it was wonderful......I thought that I might feel guilty about it this morning, but I don't. I hope it was as nice for you."

Holding her body close to him, he kissed the nape of her neck. "It was absolutely marvellous," he replied then, tilting her chin upwards, he kissed her; the passion which had remained dormant inside them began to rouse itself once again. He massaged the lather into her breasts, her nipples immediately responding to this touch, and he slowly kissed her, moving his lips all over her body; the nails of her fingers biting deeply into his skin. Once again they made love, first under the streaming water of the shower and then again in the comfort of Chris's bed.

Afterwards, as they lay together, she looked at him in a serious manner and said, "Do you know something....I never did get my back washed."

"I seem to have been distracted at the time," he smiled.

The room was quiet and they spent the next few moments just content to be in each others' presence; John's mind then returned to the business of the earlier hours.

"Would you put the radio on, Chris?" he asked, "I'd like to hear if anything's being said about the car goin' up; and if they've realised who was inside it."

It was after eleven a.m. so they waited for the news broadcast on the half hour; and heard the same account of the incident

234

as Rose.

Michael and his brother shook their heads in dismay, having listened intently to the news report; their half-hearted hopes were shattered and their worst fears confirmed; it was as Rose had told them.

"It couldn't have just gone off," insisted Timothy, shaking his head in disbelief, "there's no way.......Somethin's happened here, Michael, and we have to find out what it is."

"Before I appear in front of the council in three days' time," said Michael, quietly subdued, "I'm going to have to come up with some reasonable explanation...somethin' that they'll believe.....and it will have to be good." Inwardly, he was becoming a worried man, too many things were beginning to go wrong. The first was the arrest of loyal supporters and the loss of the arms shipment, and now this, both coming within a relatively short time of each other; and this after years of successful operations. He had authorised both of these failed operations, and it would be of no concern to his superiors who it was who had assembled the explosives; he would be held responsible and the blame would be laid firmly at his doorstep. Two of the organisation's most valuable 'field operators' now lay scattered to the four winds, both having perished in the land of their enemies. If anything were to go wrong with his next major operation, another large arms deal, it could mean curtains for the Reagan brothers; only a certain amount of failure could be tolerated. He would have to convince them well, that this next enterprise would be successful. Once Timothy handed the money payment to the German, the deal would be struck; all Schumaker was waiting for was the go-ahead, everything else was ready for the transfer. "Nothin' had better go wrong with the arms deal," he warned Timothy, "Nothin'!"

Inside the flat in Southsea, the phone interrupted the peace and solitude.

"It's for you John," said Chris, holding out the receiver, "It's the Commodore."

"Hello, Sir."

The Commodore was obviously jubilant. "Well done John," he said loudly, "excellent job......I received a full report from young Bright in the early hours. You conducted the whole operation exactly as I thought you would, you were always thorough in the past; there's no escaping the fact that it will always remain part of your life......Even the Minister had to agree that he was highly impressed and, believe me John, he was very sceptical about me having you brought back into the section. You've come up trumps again...as I knew you would, even if you yourself doubted it at times. Fortunately, I was able to have a few words in the ear of the ranking officer leading the enquiry and persuaded him to ignore one or two unaccountable holes entering the bodywork of the car, he owes me one or two favours from the past."

"Thanks sir," said John, "but let's not underestimate the presence of a very good back-up team working alongside me.. It wouldn't have been possible without their help, especially young Steve's powers of observation...that did the trick."

"Of course," agreed the officer, "that is perfectly true, and it has been noted. I don't doubt that things will become more difficult for you from this moment in time....they will be on their guard, so ensure extra care is taken in everything you do from now on."

"I will," replied John, "I've a feelin' that things are beginning to get warmed up."

"Be careful you don't get yourself too close to the fire," said the Commodore, bringing the conversation to a close. "Goodbye John, give Christine my regards."

"Well, flower," he said to Chris, replacing the receiver, "everybody's highly delighted.....when things go right you're their blue-eyed boy; I wonder what our lords and masters would have said if things had gone the other way."

"Best not to think along those lines," she answered.

He took her into this arms, where she seemed to have spent the last few hours, and kissed her lightly. "We have to make sure that we don't slip up tonight," he said, "as far as they're concerned, they have to believe that we spent the whole of last night together and not only will we have to stick to that...we have to encourage it. We've got to add fuel to the fire, even if by some fantastic coincidence it all actually happened...I realise that we were supposed to create the impression that we've became lovers, but what has happened in reality is merging in with the make believe....and it's playin' havoc with my mind."

"You're right," she agreed, "I didn't think it possible that there was the slightest chance of me inviting you into my bed and wanting you to make love to me....it just happened, and I'm pleased it did."

A blush came to her cheeks and she turned her face away. "You're the only man who's ever touched me, apart from my husband," she added quietly, "I don't know why these things happen...but they do. It must have been because we needed each other....and I feel as if I still need you, your love and your strength. Do I shock you John?"

He took her by the shoulders and turned her to face him. "How can I be shocked because I've felt the same about you since that very first night I saw you in the club....You've brought feelings back to me I thought were dead and buried; the knowledge of just how much pleasure a man and woman can share together was lost to me....but you've helped me find it again."

"I think that it must have been our loneliness that brought us together," she said, "there was a sadness in your eyes which I recognised." Then, as if determined to change the morose mood they were falling into, she suddenly asked, "How about you taking me for a nice long walk along the seafront? Before we know what time it is, it'll be time for me to get back to the club.....after all, I've a living to make."

Chapter Ten

They both dressed for the wintry conditions outside, but before they left the warmth of the flat, John held out a restraining hand.

"Listen Chris," he said seriously, "we're both aware of the difference in our ages and I don't want you to feel obliged because of what's happened between us....What I'm tryin' to say to you is, if it's likely to cause you any embarrassment at all, then I'll understand."

She looked at him in dismay. "You can still be as stupid as someone half your age when you want to be..can't you," she snapped, her blue eyes moistening, "when two people find pleasure in each other's arms, like we have, then these so-called statistics don't come into it. I'm twenty six years of age, nearly twenty seven....not a child anymore. Neither did you just happen to come along and rob me of my virginity at a tender age; what I gave to you, I gave willingly. We're both adults with our own feelings and, John Williams....if I wasn't prepared to become involved with you, then I would have made bloody certain that our 'relationship' had remained purely on the professional basis it was supposed to.......And another thing I'd like to point out, you weren't too old for me on three occasions during the last few hours, or have you forgotten?"

Taking her lacy handkerchief out of her pocket, she dabbed at her eyes and added, "Now then, are you going to take me for that walk, or not?"

John had just experienced the uncomfortable feeling of having had his balls chewed off for being a prize idiot. "I'm

239

sorry, flower, honestly I am," he said, giving her an uncomfortable smile, "I thought that I was thinkin' of you.....there's no way I would ever want to hurt you, because I know how great I feel when I'm with you."

"Come on then you old fool," she smiled, "let's go."

Leaving the flat they found it was another freezing cold day, tiny snowflakes blew into their faces as they strolled through the park and around the small boating lake which was frozen over. Chris had her arm tightly interlocked with his, her hair blowing in the wind, and the small tip of her nose had turned red; it was a pleasant break from the more pressing problems which faced them. For a few more hours at least they could enjoy being in each other's company and forget about the I.R.A., and the Reagans, and everything evil they represented. 'If only things could stay as they are at this very moment,' he thought wistfully.

Surprisingly enough, there were quite a few others strolling along the beach, venturing out into the elements. The next few hours were spent with the two of them happy at just being together, and Chris seemed to be bubbling over with an enthusiasm she found hard to contain; so much so that it had a similar effect upon John. She had injected a new meaning into his life; at least now there was a glimmer of hope, where all before had been darkness.

It was as they turned the corner of the street on their way back to Chris's flat that John accidentally caught sight of Lurch attempting to conceal his massive frame in a doorway; with his usual high standard of efficiency.

'Bastard!' cursed John inwardly.

It was obvious that Chris was ignorant of his presence, her manner did not change; she was laughing and chattering away as she had done for most of the time. He decided against alerting her to the problem, it was best if things appeared to be normal.

'Let the big sod think he's got the upper hand,' thought John; that would soon change.

"John," she said, as they entered the flat and removed their heavy coats, "I've enjoyed myself today, more than any time during the past few years. A little cold, I admit...but well worth it; and the meal we had in the deserted cafe was lovely...did you see their faces when we walked in? It was like we were the first people they had seen for months...we'll have to go there again."

"When all of this is over, we'll go there to celebrate," agreed John, "just the two of us."

Her face had a beautiful glow about it. "Turn the fire up," she said, "and I'll make us a nice hot drink....then we can get out of these wet clothes."

He turned the controls on the fire and casually walked over to the window and peered outside into the now semi-darkness; the worst of the winter was the short days. Although unable to see Lurch, he sensed his presence outside; felt his eyes burning through the space and transfixed upon himself. John decided something would have to be done about the big man but, whatever it was, he knew that the safety of the operation would have to be priority; it could not be endangered in any way.

Chris reappeared with the two steaming mugs of coffee and placed them on the glass-topped table in front of the fire, the effects of its heat now circulating around the room.

"Make yourself comfortable, take your shoes off and stretch out on the sofa," she said, "I'll be back in a minute."

241

Doing as instructed, John relaxed, but the niggling thought of those prying eyes outside was still very much on his mind. Leaning back on the sofa, he closed his eyes. It was peaceful, it was warm, and he was in the company of a most beautiful and desirable woman who seemed to care for him; what more could a man ask for. Suddenly a feeling of guilt came rushing over him and he realised that he was being unfaithful to the memory of Angela; for some purely selfish reason he had not given her one solitary thought. He had made love, and had enjoyed making love to another woman. His mind was in torment; he still loved Angela, she had meant everything to him, even life itself. Yet he found himself with another woman; where had his love gone?

"Chris," he called, the feeling of guilt increasing. "I'm going to have to get back to the hotel and get ready for tonight. I need a shower and a shave, as well as some different clothes."

"You can always take the shower here," she smiled as she reappeared into the room, "and this time I'll promise to wash your back."

"I'm sorry, pretty lady," he replied, "but I must resist your extremely tempting offer for the time being."

Whether it was because of the look on his face, or a different sound in his voice, Chris was aware of the change which had come over him. "What is it John?..What's wrong?"

"I don't know flower...guilt maybe. A sudden feeling of guilt at bein' here with you, and wanting to stay here with you......Guilt about making love to you, and of the deep need to make love to you again. It sounds stupid, doesn't it?"

Chris came over to him and looked up into his face. "Am I the first woman you've been with since your wife died?" she asked quietly.

"You're the one and only woman I've made love to, apart from Angela, in over twenty years," he replied, "Since she died I haven't had a reason to go on living....she was my reason for living. Now I've met you and I feel that there's something very special about you, but my conscience is troubling me.....I'm bein' pulled in two different directions, and I want to go in both of them."

"I respect everything you've said," replied Chris, "because I never thought this would happen to me. My own hurt was too deep and I thought that I'd closed my heart to the outside world.....but something happened to bring us together. I've already told you that you're only the second man to have me, that in itself is something very important to me." John took her into his arms and pulled her to him, they stood together for a time, each of them comforting the other.

"I think it's possible that I'm falling in love with you, John Williams," she said, looking him straight in the eyes, "whatever you decide to do about it...I'll be waiting here."

Kissing her gently, he put his shoes back on his feet, collected his beloved sheepskin coat from the rack and left the flat. By the time he opened the front door, it was dark and there was a slight flurry of snow falling. Turning to look at her standing by the window, he gave a slight wave and caught a glimpse of Lurch out of the corner of his eye; he was still in the same doorway. Instead of returning to the hotel by the quickest route, he decided to take a roundabout way which would include the park, which would more than likely be practically deserted. The main objective at this time was to discover who it was that Lurch was focusing his unwanted attention upon, whether it was Chris or himself. Ambling along at a steady pace, he entered the park through the gates and circumnavigated the lake which hours earlier he had walked by with Chris on his arm; the thought brought a smile to his face. There was one point along the edge when he was able to glance quickly over his shoulder; he saw Lurch following him, about sixty or seventy yards behind.

'At least we know now,' thought John. He felt relieved to know that it was himself Lurch was after, it was like having an overgrown yeti stalking you; but his mind was made up and he intended to do something about it. The trip on the ferry to Gosport he had taken light-heartedly, but now it was all getting too serious to ignore. As he passed by one of the public shelters, and out of view of his follower, he darted behind it; luckily there was not enough snow on the footpath to show up his footprints. Searching the immediate area for something which might possibly help him, he found nothing; a discarded baseball bat would have been ideal, but as it was he was left to devise something himself. It took almost a minute for Lurch to reach the shelter, his heavy footsteps could be clearly heard approaching; it sounded as if the big man was walking slowly; could it be that he suspected?

John held his breath and pressed himself hard against the wall of the shelter, the steps were getting closer. If he failed here, he might as well throw everything away, because if he did fail, the least Lurch would do would be land him in hospital. John had no intention of failing, too much was at risk. The shadow loomed across the footpath as the massive shape passed by the shelter, there could be no allowances for error. Running quietly behind him, John jumped into the air and clamped his left arm around the big man's throat, gripping the fingers of both hands in the fireman's grip, blocking off the passage of oxygen to the brain. Lurch struggled and squirmed in different directions to free himself, his neck muscles straining, but John hung on relentlessly, squeezing with all the strength his body could muster. Just as he was beginning to doubt his capabilities, Lurch gave a massive sigh and his legs began to buckle, John guided him down onto his knees, but maintained the pressure upon his larynx; the temptation to finish the job was immense, but he could not do it. The massive head slumped to one side and John released the pressure, just sufficiently to allow a little air to get through, which Lurch gasped at desperately.

"You hear me, Lurch?" asked John.

There was no reply.

"You 'ear me, you bastard?"

Still no answer John gave a savage yank on his arm and the big man cried out in pain, as if his larynx was about to burst.

"I'm not goin' to ask you again.....yer' hear me?"

The large head nodded affirmation.

"Right then," said John, "I want this to act as a warnin' to you...to keep well away from me 'n the girl. I'm fuckin' sick and tired of 'aving you foller' us everywhere...like some poxy bad smell which we can't get rid of. I've had more than enough.... you understand me?"

The large head nodded that he understood.

"All o' this is gettin' out of hand," added John, "all a' wanted to do was have a bit a peace and quiet, and to enjoy my 'oliday....but you're goin' out of yer' way to fuck things up for me....I want it stopped."

Giving an extra yank for good measure, John released the pressure on Lurch's throat; the big man slumped to the ground, attempting to drag the cold air into his tortured lungs through a rapidly swollen windpipe.

"Heed my words, Lurch, call it a day," said John, and walked away. 'I should have killed the bastard,' he thought. It was going to have to be done one day. Returning to his hotel room, he stripped off, throwing his clothes on the bed, and relaxed in a hot bath which he filled to almost overflowing; it had been one hell of a day. Later he would have to face the brothers and continue his play-acting because one thing was certain, they too would have to put on their own act; to cover up their own disappointment.

'All the world's a stage, and all the men and women merely players.' Someone had once said that, thought John as he lay there, but he was not quite sure who it had been, or in fact if that was what was actually said.

For appearance's sake, he rang Michael at the club; as far as the outside world was concerned, life went on as it had done last night; nothing had changed.

"Hello there mate," said Michael, his voice seemed natural enough, "things go your way last night?"

"As a matter of fact they couldn't have gone better," he replied truthfully, "it was fantastic." The masquerade had to go on.

"She let you stop all night?"

"I've only been back at the hotel about an hour," answered John, "I had to come back to get me'self tidied up for the club...I felt a bit scruffy."

"You dirty lucky bastard," he shouted down the phone, "I hope it drops off."

"Well if it does, I've no desire to borrer' yours, thank you very much," laughed John, "anyway I've just rang you to tell you that I'll be in the club later on....and Michael, oppo, do me a favour and keep it to yourself...I don't want to spoil things just as they're gettin' under way. OK?''

''A promise, my old son,'' assured his friend, ''my lips are sealed....but surely one good turn deserves another. What about you know what? Is the fair Chris really the fair Chris...'n don't tell me you didn't take a gander while you were at it.''

''They're as fair as the hairs on a peach,'' revealed John reluctantly.

''Some bloody peach,'' laughed Michael, ''don't try eating the stone will you...you lucky sod. By the way, talking of favours, I'd like to ask you one.''

''Of course mate, just ask away.''

''You remember me tellin' you about me 'n Timothy having to go back to Ireland on some business,'' he said, ''well it's tomorrow night...and I've got a bit of a problem with Rose. She's hitting the bottle again, and the way she's knockin' it back lately, I can't take the risk of taking her in case she fucks things up for me....a lot of business is riding on how I put this deal over. What I'd like you to do for me is stand in at the club and keep an eye on her....I'll only be away the one night and she's OK durin' the day. Tom, the head barman, knows all about the security arrangements, so you wouldn't have that to worry about...he'll see to it all before he left.''

''No bother at all, Michael,'' said John, his pulse quickening as he realised that this could be the start of what they were waiting for.

''There's only one snag,'' added the Irishman, ''you'll have to forsake that lovely blonde and her peach for one night.''

''As hard as it will be,'' joked John, ''I'll willingly sacrifice everythin' in the name of friendship....but don't you dare put a strain on it by stayin' in the Emerald Isle for more than the one night.'' It was spoken lightheartedly, but it was meant to

247

lead Michael into divulging more.

"That's a promise...it'll only take the one night, I'm not too keen on these bloody trips, they bore the arse off me."

After the conversation was finished, John decided that something was in the air, and most probably it was the arms deal. Michael said he was going to Ireland tomorrow night; necessary arrangements would have to be made. The only possible weak link in the structural set-up had to be Rose and her weakness for alcohol; it would have to be manipulated to John's advantage. Picking up the phone once again, he dialled Steve's room number.

"Steve," he said, when the young man picked up the receiver, "bit of work to be done....we need the help of a surveillance team...have we got one?"

"We have," replied Steve, "and they're the best in the game...who we going after?"

"The brothers are leavin' for Ireland tomorrow night...I might be wrong but I've a feelin' this is what we're after. We've got to keep a check on their movements from the time they leave the club...how do we arrange that?"

"I'll get in touch with the Commodore, let him know what you think...and he'll set all the necessary wheels in motion."

"Great," replied John, "and the German....ask the old man if he knows where the German is as well...it might not be too much longer now."

"Right John, I'll see to it."

"One more thing I'll need, son," he added, "do we have access to some kind o' pill or powder that I can slip into someone's drink to make them co-operative and drowsy? I've got to find out what Rose knows about all of this, hopefully she'll be able to tell me...but I think she could drink me under

the table, and I want to make sure it's the other way round."
Steve laughed. "I think I can oblige with that little thing for you," he said, "you oldies used to call them 'Mickey Finns' if I remember right."

"Cheeky young sod," chuckled John, then became more serious, "I didn't get the chance to thank you for last night, so I'm doin' it now...thanks son. And I made sure the Commodore knew all about your part in it."

"It was a pleasure to work with you," replied Steve, "I reckon you're still a force to reckon with...I must admit I had my doubts at the very beginning, but not any more......Anyway I'll have to go, got a lot to do..so long, John."

The pattern of that night at the club followed similar lines to his previous visits, but the brothers appeared to be a little subdued. On one occasion, during a small interlude in Chris's stint, Timothy excused himself and went to the Gents; John looked over the table at Michael.

"If you're worryin' about leaving Rose....don't," he said quietly, "because she'll be alright with me, I'll look after her. You get on with what you 'ave to and leave her to me."

"I'm not worrying about Rose," replied Michael, "I know she'll be alright......and in any case she's looking forward to making a meal for you, returning the compliment, so to speak."
John attempted to press his friend a little further. "Is everything alright with you?" he asked, with a noticeable degree of concern in his voice, "only you seem a bit worried....not your usual flamboyant self."

"Will you stop worrying about me," said Michael, "I know that you mean well and I'm honestly grateful...but honestly, everything's tickety-boo."
Observing his brother leave the toilet, he leaned over to John

and added, "Don't say anything to Timothy...it's not his worry, and in any case I can handle it; you know me...the king of flannel."

This was as near as it would ever get to Michael admitting there was indeed something wrong and, strangely enough, John felt concerned for him. Herman and Lurch were standing in their familiar positions, and both had observed the close-up conversation between the two men but, as hard as they concentrated, they were unable to hear anything of what was being said. Lurch was too involved with trying to ease the burning pain in his throat. His eyes never left the back of John Williams, the hate he now felt was becoming an obsession with him, and he was intent on the necessity of killing him. It was obvious that he had not told the brothers about their encounter in the park, because nothing had been said, and he wondered about the reason.

Around eleven thirty, the club began to fill rapidly with a noisier type of clientele and Chris was subjected to a chorus of wolf whistles and cheers. Michael must have noticed the look of concern on John's face and he laughed. "Not to worry," he said, "I forgot to tell you that tonight is strip night in *The Four Leaf Clover Club*.....randy bastards from near and far all flock here. Once a month we hold a 'striporama extravaganza'....not only beautiful, but extremely artistic ladies showing off their undoubted talents, and with the three that's here tonight, anything goes....well almost anything."

"Well then," smiled John, "I can't deny myself the pleasure of observing this performance erotica......all in the name of art, of course."

"Of course," replied Michael, pulling a face, "although with what you've got the chance of, I couldn't blame you if you decided to give it a miss."

"It'll still be there later on," said John.

At midnight, with her stint completed amidst noisy applause and shouts of 'Get them off!' Chris was obviously relieved to escape the stage. One or two of the more enthusiastic members of the audience were being warned off by a couple of less friendly looking bouncers, of whom Bill the doorman was one. John left his seat and went to meet her as she crossed the room. "I'm going to hang about here for a while," he told her, "somethin's in the wind and I'm going to try to find out what it is."

"It wouldn't be the added attraction of the strippers, would it?" she smiled.

"'Corse not, flower, you shock me," he teased, "anyway what could I possibly see here that could compare with what I've already seen several times today? There's absolutely no comparison...you win hands down. So you want me to hang onto the spare key you gave me last night?"

"How else will you get in once the show's over?" she replied, getting hold of his arm affectionately, "the key's yours for as long as you want it......I'll not drop the latch."

John managed to catch Bill's eye and indicated that he wanted to speak to him. "Michael," he said, turning to his friend, "will it be alright if I ask Bill to make sure Chris gets to her taxi.....there's some queer lookin' bastards in 'ere tonight."

"Sure....tell Bill that I've okayed it."

Ten minute later, Chris was out of the club and on her way home; John felt relieved; for some reason he found himself becoming a little possessive towards her and did not like the thought of anyone manhandling her. The first of the strippers appeared and began her performance, accompanied by some guest pianist who could hardly keep his eyes on the keys. He was more interested in her wares than his own sheet music but, there again, John doubted if anyone in the room was interested in what tune he was supposed to be playing; and that included the many women in the audience. This first stripper was a very large girl, and soon entered into the spirit of things, there being a distinct absence of the artistic talent Michael had spoken about earlier.

"Just wait 'til things get warmed up," shouted Timothy.

"Jesus, I wouldn't mind one o' those for a pillow," he shouted back.

John had seen similar scenes before, but never in Britain; Michael must have imported the idea. There was an unmistakeable atmosphere building up inside the room, he could feel it in his bones; there was going to be trouble tonight. The second stripper was very similar to the first, but she teased the men nearest and allowed them to fondle her breasts; but her party piece was to make several items disappear, in a direction that would definitely not have gained her admittance to the Magic Circle. After this there was a small interval when the customers were allowed to get stocked up with drink; the brothers were now visibly more relaxed and enjoying themselves.

"What do you think of it so far?" laughed Michael.

"Different, if nothin' else," he replied, "the last time I saw anything like this was in La Linea, over the border from Gib.....a few of us clubbed up together to watch an exhibition."

"We might just get one of those later on," said Michael, with a wink.

252

The lights dimmed and the third of the strippers entered, she looked to be from somewhere in the Caribbean, either there or Bradford. Her ebony skin glistened in the semi-darkness, and she slithered her body from the stage onto the small dance floor like some provocative python; wriggling and contorting herself in front of a stunned company. This woman had to be over six feet tall, and so slim that her rib cage was clearly outlined; but she had breasts which would measure a good forty two inches. The whole room was awestruck, and John had to admit to himself that his heartbeat had definitely quickened since she had appeared; this coloured girl was something extraordinary. When she finished her act and left the stage, there was a deafening silence, then suddenly the place went crazy.

"More! More! More!" they shouted in unison, stamping their feet on the floor and banging their glasses on the table tops. By the smiles on the faces of the brothers, this was to be expected.

A compere for the evening's entertainment, dressed in a black tuxedo and sporting a scarlet cummerbund, jumped onto the stage and eventually restored some semblance of order. "Gentlemen! Gentlemen! Please calm down....too much noise might alert the local constabulary, and we wouldn't want that to happen, would we?"

"No we wouldn't!" they all chorused as if prompted. Then, complying with the compere's request, they all sat quietly at their tables.

"Gentleman......and ladies of course, pardon my error," added the compere, "the girls have agreed to perform an extra 'exhibition' of artistic poses, not originally on tonight's agenda.....but to provide this extra delight to the eyes, an additional charge of two pounds per head will be required to cover their expenses, all money to go to the girls themselves......Are you agreeable?'' They were.

The collection was taken, John placing his two pounds in the box along with everybody else; this brought a laugh from the brothers, and they too delved into their own pockets.

''What about Pinky and Perky behind us?'' asked John, with a smile.

This prompted Timothy to extract two pounds from Lurch and Herman. ''The girls will be grateful to you both for this extra couple o' quid,'' he laughed, thinking the idea hysterical.

''Surely it's worth a couple o' pounds of anybody's money,'' smiled John.

''The outer doors are bolted on Strip night,'' said Michael, ''and we always have a couple of lookouts just in case the law does decide to get funny about it..but we've never had any bother from them. As a matter of fact I don't doubt there's a few off duty coppers out there watchin' the show......they're just like any other horny individual. We provide them with free membership into the club and a few drinks now and again as perks, and they love it...and they leave us to get on with things.''

The three artistes appeared and began an apparently unrehearsed exhibition, gradually becoming entwined in each other's naked bodies, all three covered in some kind of body oil. As their cavorting continued and the tempo increased, the performance becoming even more daring, the audience were getting themselves more and more aroused. And then the inevitable happened. A naked man ran through the crowd and onto the dance floor where the girls were, his intentions plain enough for all to see; and he made a grab for the glistening body of the black girl.

John smiled to himself, it was like watching an action replay of what he had seen time and again in different corners of the world; he would bet good money on the naked man being a matelot. The girls screamed in mock horror at the sight and tried desperately to disentangle themselves before he became too involved with them; but our naked friend was denied his ultimate pleasure. Timothy had alerted Herman and Lurch, and suddenly it was their time to perform, they ran onto the floor and grabbed the interloper, who struggled with them, still intent on becoming part of the show. It seemed as if the remainder of the clientele took exception to the two big men interfering with their pleasure; and the expected *melee* began.

John looked across the table at Michael, and saw that he was laughing. "Just like old times," he shouted, "like bein' in the mob again."

"Jack never changes, does he," said Michael, watching the various scuffles taking place around them.

Both Herman and Lurch were giving an exceptional account of themselves, but they were beginning to wilt under the sheer volume of numbers. It was at that stage in the proceedings that a few members of the audience suddenly turned their attention upon the three of them sat at the owner's table. A half a dozen of them rampaged forward intent on inflicting bodily harm upon them, John saw a large bearded man bearing down on him; his teeth bared as if he meant to take a large bite out of him.

There was no time for finesse, John swung a right hook and hit the man flush on the point of his bearded chin; his already glazed eyes rolled up into their sockets and he collapsed in a heap on the carpeted floor. It was then he noticed a second man swinging a large fist at him and, before he could take any evasive action, it caught him on the side of the head and knocked him sprawling over the table, where he remained for a few seconds to allow his head to clear. Looking up between the table legs, he saw some gentlemen obviously taking a dislike to Timothy's head, holding it between his arms and doing his best to remove it, hoping to do a drop kick with it. Climbing back onto his feet, John grabbed Timothy's assailant, swung him round and head-butted him, causing one more of the opposition to retire from the friendly competition.

"Thanks John," shouted Timothy, feeling his head, "I thought the bastard was goin' to pull it off."

Both of them returned to the affray, and the next ten minutes or so was bedlam, with John managing to get in a few good blows, but at the same time collecting one or two in return. Out of the three of them, it appeared as though Michael had came off the worst; Timothy and John lifted him back onto his feet from under one of the few remaining tables which were still upright. Slowly the club was returning to sanity, the shouts of anger had turned to laughter, and an assortment of bodies littered the arena, some of them women.

"Jesus!" exclaimed Michael, pulling himself together and straightening his tie, "That takes me back a few years.....there's still life in the old dogs yet, and we didn't do too badly at all, did we?"

A round of drinks was brought to them and they returned to their table, surveying the surrounding scene. People who five minutes ago were intent on severing limbs, or depriving each other of their manhood, or womanhood, whichever the case, now sat together laughing and joking about having a fantastic night out.

"Does this kind o' thing happen often?" asked John, tenderly probing at his nose to find out how much it had been damaged.

"Nearly always," laughed Michael, "but I have to admit this was one of the better nights. It's that black girl, she drives them all wild...it's the animal instinct coming out. As long as nobody gets seriously hurt, then we don't mind...and it guarantees they'll all come back next time."

Timothy raised his glass to John. "I'd like to drink a toast to you," he said, "because if you hadn't o' stepped in when you did, I might have found me' head in a picklin' jar."

"Anytime Timothy," replied John, "it was my pleasure."

It was almost three a.m. when John arrived back at Chris's flat. Putting his newly acquired key into the lock, he quietly let himself in. Taking extra care so as to not make any noise, he tiptoed into the darkness of the sitting room and took off his coat. Everything was still and he turned towards the bedroom; he noticed the faint aroma of her perfume lingering in the air, as if inviting him to her. A little light could be seen under her bedroom door and, opening it carefully without a squeak or a groan, he peered inside. All that was visible to him was the back of her head, with its blonde hair spread over the pillow. Noticing the regular rise and fall of the bedclothes, he decided that she was in a deep sleep, so he carefully removed and folded his clothes before edging himself alongside her. He put his arm about her warm body, and snuggled up against it, and Chris turned to face him, her eyes slowly opening. "Sorry if I've woke you," he said, "I tried to sneak in without disturbing you."

She smiled and kissed him. "I wanted to stay awake," she said, stifling a yawn, "but I was tired out." Bringing her body up against his own, she added, "but I'm awake now."

It was mid-morning when Chris woke him, bringing him a cup of coffee into the bedroom. "Come on lazybones.....time you were up and about."

"Mornin' sweetheart.....I'd have been up and about ages ago if you hadn't of kept me awake nearly all night."

"At least now you know what you're taking on, John Williams.....any regrets?"

"No regrets, it's giving me a new lease of life," he smiled, "something to look forward to again."

"Steve Bright rang about half an hour ago," she said, "the surveillance team you wanted is on its way, should be set up before lunchtime. The Commodore says to tell you that Schumaker arrived at Dover this morning....he's driving a red BMW with German number plates."

"It definitely looks as if the deal's goin' down, and pretty soon at that." said John, "we have to be ready to move after them."

"Steve also told me to tell you that he's got that little thing you asked him to get...but he wouldn't tell me what it is."

John laughed, the news satisfied him, everything pointed to a meeting between the German and the brothers; maybe it would be all over and done with before long. Tonight, with the help of Steve's 'additive', he hoped to prise the information from Rose; it would be risky but he had to take the risk.

"Do you feel like some breakfast?" he smiled.

Closing the bedroom door, she moved slowly across the floor, unbuttoning her dressing gown as she came, allowing it to fall away from her body.

"Will this do for you?" she asked.

"Better than toast," he replied.

Later as they lay snuggled together, Chris looked up at him. "Would it help if I said that I had the same sort of doubts and fears as you," she said, "but we've got to accept the facts....My David and your Angela are gone forever, they'll never be replaced in our hearts and in our lives; but the main thing is that we're still here and we've found comfort in each other. I also know that deep down what we're sharing isn't just a physical attraction, there's something else; and I think you realise this as well.......You might have thought that I was slightly impetuous when I told you that I could be falling in love with you, but it wasn't some silly young girl's infatuation.....it's quite possibly the truth."

"If only things weren't so bloody involved," he replied, kissing her on the forehead, "but I've got to finish this job.....when it's over and done with, there's nothing I'd like better than to get myself involved again; but this time with you Chris. To get to know the real you..your likes and dislikes....where you come from and where you'd like to go...and for you to get to know the real me; not someone who kills at the Commodore's request, but a normal person wanting desperately to live a normal life again."

Chris smiled, and hugged him tightly. "I'll look forward to that day, John," she said, "to the day we can walk away from all of this."

They spent the rest of the afternoon together, but an inner tension was beginning to mount inside John; old doubts were beginning to return and he was aware that the inevitable was drawing closer.

"Do you ever worry about what you have to do?" asked Chris, sensing the change coming over him.

"I'm not allowed that luxury....it's the same today as it was all those years ago," he said, "they don't ever let go. This time it's Michael and his brother who are national risks...and that I can't deny; but the day will surely come when I'll tell the Commodore enough is enough. The only decent thing that's come out of all of this, is that I've met you."

"And me you," she agreed, "I never thought that I'd ever feel like this again.....I thought love only came once in a person's life, and that if they were lucky; but now I know different."

Before John left the flat to return to the hotel, he gave her Michael's phone number in case either Steve or the Commodore needed to get in touch with him urgently once the brothers had left for Ireland, or wherever it was they were really going.

"Promise me you'll be extra careful," she asked, as he left.

"That's a promise, flower," he winked.

At reception he collected his items from the safe and went up to his room, locking the door behind him. He removed the Colt and accessories from the case and loaded six rounds into the cylinder, tucking it tightly into his left boot; the silencer went into the right one. After doing a few irregular kicking exercises, he was well satisfied they would not get dislodged under normal circumstances.

With time on his hands, he decided to ring up old Mary and see if his home was still in one piece and surviving the blizzards, which by all accounts were over now.

"'Ello John lad," she shouted, "'ow's the 'oliday....anyway where are ye' at?"

"Holiday's smashing, sweetheart," he replied, it was good to hear her crackling old tones, "I'm down in Portsmouth, lookin' up some old Navy mates o' mine...everythin' OK up there?"

"We've 'ad a bit o' bad weather," she replied, "some people are sayin' it's the worst we've 'ad, but a' can well remember the winter of forty six...it was a bloody sight worse than this. Anyway, son....a funny thing 'appened just a week or so after you went away...I went into the 'ouse as usual, 'cos I've been keepin' the fire on so the pipes wouldn't burst in all the cold weather, and a' was sure a' could smell cigarette smoke. Well ya' know me 'n Bob don't use the things, 'cos of our chests yer know.....but a' give the 'ouse a thorough search and a'm positive there's nowt been touched. It's all 'ere waitin' for yer to come 'ome."

"Don't worry yourself, Mary, I know it's in good hands...and thanks, a'll bring you both a bit of somethin' when I come back."

"Yer not drinkin' are ye?" she asked, "a drop now and again's not too bad, but don't let yersel' go over' the top."

"I'm just about teetotal," he lied.

"a'll believe that when a' see it fer me'sel," she laughed.

Another couple of minutes of genial chatter and then they said their goodbyes..but he now knew that if things went as he hoped they would, he would never take another woman into that house; it would have to mean a fresh start completely.

Next he rang Steve Bright. "All set to go, son?" he asked.

"Raring to go," said the younger man, "I'll be parked outside the club where you know where to find me, waiting for your word. By the way, there's a small white pill under your right hand pillow....it'll do the trick for you; only there's one thing I didn't tell you about - its side effects."

"What side effects?"

"It tends to make whoever swallows it....well let's say, almost as amorous as a nymphomaniac," he stifled a laugh, "so be warned.....hang on to your essentials."

"That's all I bloody well need," replied John, replacing the phone.

At nine thirty that night, he stood outside the club and rang the bell.

"Evenin' Bill," he said.

"Evening, Mr. Williams, enjoy yourself last night?"

"It was different," he replied, "definitely different.....and I want to thank you for makin' sure Chris got to her taxi alright, I appreciate it."

"No need to thank me," said the doorman, "it was my pleasure; you two getting on friendly terms?"

"It's a distinct possibility," answered John.

"I'm pleased for both of you," smiled Bill, "she's a nice woman...too nice for this place."

"What do you mean Bill...this place?"

"I'm sorry if I've offended you, knowing how good friends you and the boss are...but I don't think this place is all it's cracked up to be."

"You haven't offended me," said John, "but I'd better get up there, they're expectin' me."

Timothy opened the door of the flat to him. "Come on in John," he said, "any after effects from last night?.....I bet you don't get entertained like that up in Geordieland, do you?"

"We don't get it in Durham either," replied John, with a forced smile. 'I'd like to see how you'd fare in a club full of miners,' he thought.

"I seem to be aching all over," added Timothy, "but thanks to you, I've still got me head on to have a headache with."

Hearing the conversation, Michael entered the room. "Hello, oppo," he said, "just in time as usual. Rose is in the kitchen putting the finishing touches to a tasty meal for you, it smells that good I'm tempted to stay here with you and have some."

Going to the drinks cabinet, Timothy poured each of them a large one. "We just have time for a quick drink before we go," he said, "Michael.. give Rose a shout, she won't want to miss out."

The brothers were ready to leave, two small overnight cases were by the door.

"You flyin' over?" asked John, matter-of-factly.

"Flying," laughed Michael, "you have to be joking mate....me flying. I'm terrified of bloody planes....too many of them seem to fall out of the sky; Rose could never even get me to go on the big wheel at Southsea funfare. No.. we're driving up to Liverpool and then it's the ferry to Belfast, slower but a sight safer."

It was at that moment Rose appeared and relieved Michael of her drink; she looked attractive in a quiet kind of way. Her hair was tied neatly behind her ears and she was wearing a white dress which clung to the top half of her then flared a little from the waist.

"Are you ready to take up your role as babysitter?" she asked John, with a smile.

"I've been lookin' forward to it all day...in eager anticipation as they say," he said, hoping it sounded like a compliment.

"Time for us to be runnin'," announced Michael, "look after the store for us John."

263

Timothy picked up the cases and walked into the corridor, where their minders relieved him of his burden; at least John knew all four were going on the 'trip'. Michael kissed Rose on the cheek, "Be good," he said, "see you some time to-morrow night," and closed the door on his way out.

Walking to the window, John looked down into the street, and a few minutes later the Mercedes with its four occupants pulled out of the garage and drove away, leaving only a va-pour trail from its exhaust. Within a few seconds, a dark coloured Rover followed; the surveillance team had gone into action.

"Off into the darkness they've gone," said John.

The meal turned out to be worth waiting for, fillet steak and all the trimmings, assisted by a litre of red wine, of which John ensured that his companion consumed the lion's share. After it was finished, Rose conjured up two large cups of Irish coffee, which they drank sitting side by side on the immense sofa. He did not have to concentrate very hard on the task of getting her drunk, she kept up a continuous flow of drinks. Once again nostalgia crept in and she spoke of old acquaintances she missed from her years in the Wrens. At eleven thirty she put an L.P. of Nat King Cole on the turn-table and turned to him; her eyes were beginning to glaze over.

"Will you dance with me John?"

He had never been a keen dancer, only ever managing to master the more rudimentary steps of the waltz and the quick-step; with more modern dancing he just shuffled about in time with everybody else. Nevertheless, if Rose wanted to dance, he would have to put his best foot forward.

"As long as you don't compare me to Michael," he replied.

"There's nothing to compare," she answered, "he doesn't dance with me anymore...or anything else for that matter, he's always too busy or too tired."

Their arms around each other, they moved about the room in comparative unison. After the third record, Rose's head came to rest on his shoulder and her body gradually moved closer to his, until both of them were aware of the presence of the other.

"Come on, sweetheart," he said, "let's have another drink...this dancin's giving me quite a thirst."

This time it was John who went to the drinks cabinet and poured out two more, one mostly alcohol and the other almost pure coke, which he kept for himself. Rose had excused herself to go to 'the little girl's room', so he took the opportunity to drop the little pill into her glass. He stirred it with his finger and it dissolved completely in a few seconds, apprehensive that she would come back into the room and catch him at it.

"Come on then, flower, drink it up," he urged her, "then we'll get back to our soft shoe shuffle......I think I'm improvin'."

Half the contents went down in one, and then Rose once more wrapped her arms around him, pressing her groin into his, rotating it gently but firmly. And this before the pill could even have entered her bloodstream.

"Do you enjoy making love?" she suddenly asked, catching him completely by surprise.

" 'Corse I do," he replied, appeasing her, "it's a very nice way of passin' the time....don't you think so?"

"I can't remember," she said, "we haven't...not for over six months now."

John sensed a kind of desperation in her voice; whether he like it or not, he was going to have to pursue this topic of conversation.

"Gerraway!" he said, in almost total disbelief, "what's the matter, you gone off the idea?"

"Me!" she replied, raising her voice, "Not me John, it's Michael....he just doesn't seem to be interested anymore."

"Maybe it's his age," he said, "he might be goin' through a difficult time...some men do, you know."

The waltz was now little more than groin to groin contact, with neither of them going anywhere.

'Jesus!' he thought to himself, 'this is one aspect of the thing I didn't bargain for.'

After the record had ended, they both finished their drinks, and John filled them up again, in the same way, minus the pill. The room was getting very warm, and he noticed Rose's eyes were more and more shiny. Time was getting on, he was going to have to begin his prising out of information before too much longer.

Rose put on another record like the last and stood in the centre of the room, her body swaying gently with the music and smoothing the palms of her hands over certain areas of her anatomy.

"Do you think I've still got a nice body?"

Something was definitely happening to Rose.

"I think you've got a lovely body," he replied.

"It might have been a few years ago...but I'm forty now you know...over the hill; forty and over the hill....I bet that's what Michael thinks."

"Rubbish," said John, "you've still got the body of a young woman."

266

A little white lie might go a long way in these circumstances, because it obviously pleased her. "Thank you kind sir," she said, and tried to curtsey, almost falling over.

More drinks followed, more dancing, and Rose's movements were definitely taking on a new kind of meaning; he did not have to be very intelligent to understand her intentions.

"When Michael left tonight," he said, "he looked worried....I know by what he told me, something's up and he wasn't lookin' forward to going over to Ireland."

Whether Rose had heard him or not, she remained silent, intent on her bodily motions against him; if they had been on a public dance floor they would have both been shown the door. Encouraging her a little, he placed his hands on her buttocks and squeezed them gently.

"Listen flower," he added, "Michael's a good mate, I wouldn't like to think that he's in some kind of bother....if he is, then I'd like to help."

Ignoring his persistence completely, she looked into his eyes, her own almost closed by now. "Will you kiss me John?"

'Jesus!' he thought desperately, 'I hope I haven't given her too much too soon.'

"When the cat's away, the mouse will play," she giggled, "I'm a mouse.......so come on John, please kiss me."

He had very little option but to do as she asked; it developed into a long passionate kiss, with Rose's tongue exploring pastures new; her hands held firmly behind his head so he could not break free. It was as if all her months of pent up passion were finally being released and he happened to be the safety valve; her whole body writhed in pleasure.

John Williams was human after all; even after attempting to concentrate on other things, he felt his body slowly succumbing to her will. Rose's hands went lower, she was almost at the point where she would be totally out of control; six months was a long time.

"How'd you get on with brother Timothy?" he asked. He realised that it must have sounded stupid at the time, but he had to apply the brakes somehow; and surprisingly enough it brought about an immediate reaction.

"I hate him!" she spat, "he's a real bastard. If only you knew the truth about him, John, you wouldn't be too keen on getting so pally with him."

'Thank fuck for that,' he thought relieved. "He seems alright to me," he said, hoping to provoke more information from her, "and he helps Michael a lot." At last her tongue was loosening, she began to talk.

"Help him you say," she laughed bitterly, "that's the biggest joke of the century.....he's the cause of all our troubles."

'Great,' thought John, 'she's goin' to tell you....don't cock it up.'

"What trouble's that, sweetheart?" he asked, a show of concern in his voice.

"I can't tell you, John...honest I can't."

"Alright, flower," he said quietly, "it's alright."

These tactics were not working, he decided to revert to his previous ones. Moving his body hard up against hers, he slowly danced her around the room and gently nibbled at her neck. Obviously these were better tactics; before long she was once again writhing up against him, her breathing louder and much quicker. Moving his right hand to the buttons down the front of her dress, he slowly undid them one at a time to her waist and looked at her breasts; she was wearing a flimsy nylon bra which fastened at the front by a small clasp. With a slight twist of forefinger and thumb, it was loose and all was revealed; he grasped one of her breasts and massaged it gently. "Make love to me," she pleaded, "please John, make love to me."

"I will...soon," he replied, then thought, 'Christ almighty, what kind of bastard are you, Williams?'

It had to be done, he had to get the information out of her and he needed to get it quickly because, passionate as she was, she would not be conscious much longer, her legs were beginning to go.

He picked her up and carried her to the bedroom.

"Is Michael in any danger?" he asked sharply. The risk was there, but he had to take it.

"It was the bomb," she cried, "all because of the bomb. Timothy must have done something wrong because it went off too soon and killed them both.....and they're blaming Michael for it......it's Timothy's fault, I hate him."

It was out; at long last it was out.

"Is that why they're goin' back to Ireland,...so Michael can take the blame for that idiot brother of his?"

Rose began to lose concentration, her eyes began to roll upwards; he thought he was going to blow his chance.

"Why are they goin' back to Ireland, Rose?"

"They aren't," she giggled, "only Michael is....Timothy is meeting the German man."

'Oway flower,'thought John, 'nearly there.'

"What German man is that, Rose?"

Giggling to herself, she suddenly sat upright. "Heil Hitler," she shouted, and gave the old Nazi salute.

"Where's Timothy meetin' the German?.....Fancy our Timothy meetin' a real live German....where's he meetin' him

269

again?''

"In Booley...some little cafe in Booley," she slurred, her eyes closing, "Boooolley!"

She stared up at him through her half closed eyes and smiled, then she lifted herself up and wrapped her arms about his neck; then went into a deep sleep. John shook her roughly, trying to get one last response from her; but it was too late, the information he had was all that he was going to get.

"Booley, Booley," he said it over and over again, hoping that the name would mean something to him; but it did not. "Where the fuck is Booley?"

It took him a few minutes for him to readjust her dress; undoing her bra had been easy enough, but trying to get her breasts back and fasten the clasp proved to be no easy task. Before closing the bedroom door, he glanced at the still form spread out on the bed and acknowledged the fact that, if it had been necessary, he would have made love to her. Looking at the clock on the wall, he saw it was twelve minutes past midnight; there was a chance that Chris might still be on the premises.

He picked up the internal phone which connected him to the bar. "Tom, it's John Williams....has Chris left yet?"

"No," he replied, "but she's getting changed to go."

"When she comes through, ask her to come up to the flat for a couple o' drinks."

"Will do," said Tom.

Within five minutes she knocked on the door.

"Where is she?" asked Chris.

"Somewhere on another planet," he smiled .

"Did you get what you were after?"

"Maybe," he told her, then thought to himself that he nearly

270

got something extra.

John told her the information he had managed to get out of Rose, but omitted all details about the tactics he had used to get it.

"The only snag is this place called Booley.....obviously this is where they're meeting to arrange the shipment. Have you heard of anything or anywhere which resembles this Booley?.....I haven't got a clue, it could be bloody anywhere." Chris repeated the name slowly, as if savouring the taste of it and trying to come up with the ingredients. She went to the bookcase and took down one of the books: it was the R.A.C.'s members' book of roads and maps. After what seemed an age of looking at names of places and then finding them on the appropriate page, she looked over at John.

"It had to be Beaulieu," she explained, "it's not far from here, in the New Forest area. If your friend Rose comes originally from somewhere in Devon or Cornwall, then with all that drink inside her, the pronunciation of Beaulieu would turn out something like Boolie."

"Chris, my pet," smiled John, "you might just be right about that......if I remember right, I think Rose was a 'Janner'.....came from somewhere near Plymouth. If you're right about this Beaulieu, well young Steve 'n me'll have to get ourselves there smartish....only thing is, I can't leave here 'til the club closes."

"If Rose was right about what she told you," said Chris, "then surely if Michael's going to Ireland, then Timothy can't meet up with this German until they drop him off at Liverpool.....he'll have to come all the way back."

"If that's so...then we have a bit of time on our hands," he said, with a sly smile, "any idea how we can pass the time?"

271

"John Williams," she gasped, "with Rose asleep in the next room, you wouldn't....would you?"

At two thirty, there was a gentle knock on the door; it was Tom.

"All's safe and secure," he said, "and I've dropped the takings into the floor safe.......once I've closed the outside door on my way out, I'll ring the bell three times. When you hear it, if you turn the key in that little black box on the wall, to the left....the burglar alarm will be set. To knock it back off when you want to leave, just turn the key back to its original position....it's easy enough to work."

"Right then Tom, we'll be OK......I'm afraid Rose's had a bit too much, she's 'retired' for the evening."

The head barman smiled, as if fully aware of the situation, "I'll bid you goodnight...or should I say good morning."

"And a good mornin' to you Tom..get yourself off home."

"See you tonight Tom," called Chris, producing a nice smile for him.

"And I'll see you Chris," he replied, returning her smile.

After Tom had left the premises and rung the bell the three times, John set the alarm, he was not to know whether there were any kind of warning light came on anywhere to enable the barman to check if the system was in operation, so he turned the key as instructed.

Peering out of the window, he watched Tom disappear down the road, until he was out of sight.

"Right, time for me to go," said John, "keep poppin' in every now and again to make sure Rose's alright. If that pill young Steve gave me is half as good as he reckons it is, then she'll be out all night....hopefully I'll be back by then and everything will be sorted out. I'm sorry, flower, but it could

272

be a long night for you."

Putting on his overcoat, he removed the Colt and silencer from his boots, and fitted them together, putting the weapon into the right hand pocket.

"Take care, John," said Chris, "I'm getting used to having you around."

"I will," he replied, "I'll switch this alarm off and, once you can see me outside....switch it back on, just turn the key to the left like the man said. When I get back, I'll ring the bell three times just like Tom did....switch the alarm off again and come down ready to get yourself off home..and I'll take over here. OK?"

It was two forty eight, he took her in his arms and kissed her.

"See you in the mornin' then," he said.

Chapter Eleven

It was another freezing cold morning, hazy mist hung like a dusty grey shroud draped over the buildings. It took him a couple of minutes to walk to the little car; opening the door, he climbed in beside Steve.

"This bloody thing doesn't get any warmer," he complained, "you been in contact with the Commodore lately?"

"On and off all night," replied the young man, "the walk helped to thaw me out."

"Where's everybody at?"

"At one o'clock this morning, the brothers met up with another man near the docks in Liverpool...he handed them a black case," said Steve, "we think the money for the deal's inside it. Michael Reagan, his bodyguard and this other geezer went onto the ferry.....surveillance verifies their departure, and a team from the Special Branch will keep an eye on them after they land on the Belfast side.....Meanwhile, Timothy and your mate Lurch got back into the Merc, with the case, and at present are on their way back down the motorway. Other reports state that Schumaker booked out of his hotel in Dover and he, too, is on the move. As you guessed earlier, it looks as if the meeting is definitely on....but the jackpot question is, where?"

"Tell you what son," said John, "get yourself back on the phone and ask the boss to check the latest positions of both parties; ask him if it's possible that they could be converging on Beaulieu in the New Forest area...if they are, then Rose has come up trumps for us."

Steve jumped out of the car and ran over to the phone box.

Within five minutes he was back.

"The Commodore's had his map out, and did as you asked......Beaulieu is definitely in their line of direction."

"Smashin'....Beaulieu, it is," said John, "you know the way?"

"Beaulieu," replied Steve, with a faint smile, "it brings back memories. It just so happens that in my youth I courted a fair maiden from those parts, but after regularly wining an dining her in the grandest of manners, it became painfully obvious that she intended hanging on to what she had; so I had to abandon all hopes of ravishing her. Yes...I know Beaulieu."

"Good," said John, "and if it took you as long to get your leg over as it did to explain everything, no bloody wonder she hung on to it....let's get there, and quick.....but not too quick, OK?"

"What are we looking for when we get there?" asked Steve, as he started the car and roared off down the road.

"Rose said a cafe," he replied, "and my experience as an ex-lorry driver tells me that the only place open during the night is a transport cafe....so that's what we're lookin' for."

The heater inside the car was soon blasting out hot air, John loosened the buttons of his coat and looked out into the darkness, a heavy frost covered everything; it was a cold morning to die.

At four thirty five they arrived on the outskirts of Beaulieu, a quick reconnaissance soon turned up the transport cafe, just as John had guessed. It was on the far perimeter of the town and well away from the nearest buildings; parked outside were two large articulated lorries carrying containers, and one three ton Luton van. No sign of either the Mercedes or the German's BMW.

"Great," observed John, "I'll get out here and take cover

behind those trees over on the far side of the parkin' area....I'll take the old shotgun 'ere for company. I want you to drive down the road to the telephone box we passed on our way in and get in touch with the boss again. Ask for the co-ordinates of the two cars just to make sure we ain't in the wrong place; and if they're coming here, ask him for an estimated time of arrival...alright son?''

Fifteen minutes later Steve returned; John propped the shotgun up against a tree trunk and walked over to the car.

''It looks as if you're right, mate,'' smiled Steve, ''they're definitely heading this way....in fact it won't be long before they get here. The Commodore says for you to use your own judgement and to do what you have to do...he also wished you good luck.''

''Right then, this is it,'' said John, ''now for our plan of action. I want you to go into the cafe and have yourself a nice mug o' tea and a bite to eat....I'll be out here. You've been out on the town and you're on your way home...use your imagination and make somethin' up, because the bloke be-hind the counter will be wonderin' why you're out this time o' the morning. When the two parties arrive, make bloody sure you don't keep lookin' at them and make them suspic-ious of you.....act as if you're knackered out, but be careful, son, I'm gettin' to be fond of you and a' wouldn't like any-thing to happen to those good looks.''

''You can rely on me, John.''

''I know that, son.....when it's over inside and the deal's gone through, they'll not want to hang around. Give them enough time to get out of the place, then go after the German; do what you have to do to stop him drivin' away, because I'll want to have a few words with Mr. Schumaker myself. I

know you've been wanting to get involved, now you are.''
John directed Steve to park the sports car in one of the dark
shadows on the far side of the container lorries.

"OK Stevie boy, time to go and do your party piece,'' said
John, "rub your eyes to make them red...and get yersel' in
there.''

With those words in his ears, Steve walked over to the cafe's
front door and strolled inside, observing one man behind the
counter and three men sitting at the tables; two of them talking together and the other one sat on his own. They all looked
up as he came through the door, but soon lost interest; that is
except the man behind the counter, he saw extra trade enter.

"Cup of tea and a couple of bacon and egg sarnies, please,''
said Steve, stifling a yawn.

"You lost, son?''

"Naw, been out for the night,'' replied Steve, "ended up
taking a girl home..and now I'm on my own way home. Saw
the lights of the cafe and fancied something to eat, it'll help
me to stay awake.''

"You got far to go?'' asked the man.

"Just this side of Havant....it'll not take long once I've had
something down me.''

"What kind of car you drivin'?'' asked the inquisitive man.

"An old MGB'' answered Steve, "I've had it all done up...new
wings and door panels, it looks brand new...my pride and joy
that car; comes before any woman.''

"That's the life,'' smiled the man, "fast car, plenty of money,
and lots of easy women willing to take their knickers off.....you
kids of today have it made; wasn't like that when I was a
young man.''

"Times change,'' said Steve.

"That they do," agreed the man, handing him his tea and sandwiches, "that'll knock you back one pound fifty."

Picking up his refreshments, Steve paid the man the one pound fifty and sat at a table near the counter trying his best to look unobtrusive. Once Steve had gone into the cafe, John retrieved the shotgun and climbed into the passenger seat of the little car, sinking as far into it as he could; and waited. It would be virtually impossible for anyone to see him in the darkness unless they actually opened the door, and that was highly unlikely. The BMW with the strange number plates was the first car to arrive, the driver got out, locked the door and walked straight into the cafe.

"Number one," whispered John.

Ten minutes later the Mercedes arrived, drove a precautionary circuit of the car park, checking on the vehicles already there, and finally halted thirty yards away from the nearest vehicle, which was the three ton van. Observing the safety procedure, John appreciated their need to be careful; they had not survived so long without taking such measures.

Lurch climbed from the driving seat and, after a final visual check, he walked around the car, opened the door and let Timothy get out; then both men walked into the cafe; the black case was in Timothy's hand.

"Two and three," said John, satisfied.

Steve casually observed first the German arrive, then Timothy and his henchman; the three men shook hands and sat together. As if having second thoughts about it, Lurch got up again and went over to the counter, standing close to Steve and ordered three coffees.

"Nothing to eat?" asked the man hopefully.

"If I'd wanted something to eat, I'd have asked for it," snapped

Lurch.

The big man's tone of voice dissuaded any further conversation, and close by a young man's heart was beating faster; but he had the comforting reassurance of the Colt tucked away under his left arm. Steve watched carefully out of the corner of his eye as the buyer and seller became engrossed in their business; Timothy opened the case slightly and the German produced a slip of paper which the Irishman read and then placed in his pocket. Both men appeared satisfied with the arrangements, nodding their heads in apparent agreement and smiling at each other. Schumaker got up from the table and walked to the counter, without so much as a look at the young man who was apparently finding it difficult to remain awake.

"Excuse me," he said to the man behind the counter, speaking in almost perfect English, "is there a telephone I could use?"

"There's one in 'ere," replied the man, "but you'll have to leave something to pay for the call."

"I understand," agreed the German, "will five pounds be enough, I'm ringing Scotland."

"Scotland eh' yeh that'll be enough," replied the man, more than satisfied. Steve strained his ears to hear what Schumaker was saying.

"Negotiations have been successfully concluded...commence the arrangements."

It was short and to the point, but Steve had heard.

Returning to the table, the German nodded acknowledgement and sat down again. A further ten minutes of conversation followed, then Timothy and Schumaker shook hands once again and all three stood up as if to leave. Once again Lurch made certain that it was safe outside, then signalled for the other two to follow him.

"Jesus," said the man behind the counter, as the trio left, "them three gave me the creeps, I wonder who they were."

"I think the bloke who used the phone has something to do with wrestling," said Steve, "I'm sure I've seen him on telly before.....it could be one of those secret deals they do....you know, to fix a fight; that big bastard looks like a wrestler to me."

"You could be right," said the man, "anyway I done alright out of it...a fiver in me pocket for a phone call."

It was time for Steve to move, he stood up and stretched himself. "Well I'm off as well," he said, "see you again sometime."

"You know where we are," called the man, as Steve went out of the door.

Outside, John had witnessed Lurch's performance, followed by the reappearance of Timothy and Schumaker, who was now in possession of the black case.

The deal had been struck!

A final few words passed between them, and yet another shake of the hands, then the parties separated and walked towards their respective cars. It was then John saw Steve walk from the cafe.

"Good lad," he whispered, "go get him."

He opened the door of the sports car as quietly as possible, the shotgun firmly in his grasp; and stepped out of the car. Remaining in the shadows of the articulated lorry, he stalked the two terrorists, closing with every step. Rudi Schumaker was well satisfied with the night's work, he put the key into the door of his car, but before he could unlock it, he felt something hard dig into the side of his head; there was no need to ask what it was.

"Let's you and me hang about for a while," a voice whispered into his ear, "I know someone who's dying to meet you."

Turning very slowly, he came face to face with the young man he had seen in the cafe, and at a glance his worst suspicions were confirmed; it was a gun. The young man then carried out an efficient search of his person, but found nothing; his business was selling arms not using them.

Meanwhile Lurch had reached the Mercedes, he opened the door and was about to step inside, when suddenly he became aware of the figure stepping out of the darkness; the ominous presence of the shotgun being pointed at him made him freeze. Noticing the sudden hesitation, Timothy turned in the direction of Lurch's eyes and he too saw the figure holding the shotgun. Such a weapon made any attempt at reaching his own gun foolhardy, it was capable of removing most of his vital organs from such a short distance. It was obvious that Lurch, with his limited brain power, had also arrived at the same conclusion; things had suddenly begun to look bleak.

It was then the stranger spoke.

"Hello lads, I thought you two were on your way to Ireland..you get lost?"

Lurch instantly recognised the voice and his body stiffened in rage.

"Don't be stupid, Lurch.....I could blow yer head off before you had time to move," said John, then raising his voice a little, he added, "now then, I want both of you to put the palms of your hands on the roof of the car."

Surprisingly enough it was only then that Timothy became aware of who he was.

"You bastard!" he spat, "You rotten bastard! I knew it all along.....knew there was somethin' fucking strange about the way you suddenly turned up...but Michael wouldn't hear of it."

"Shut it Timmy, and do exactly like a' said," replied John, "I'm in no mood to be fucked about be the like o' you......you tried hard enough to find out. Having my room searched at the hotel and even sendin' one of your cronies to check through my home in Durham....but you failed miserably my old son; and now it's time to pay for your mistakes........Hands on the roof of the car, I won't tell you again."

Both men did as they were told.

"Now I want you to listen to me," continued John, "I'm going to search both of you, but I'm a bit worried about you gettin' ideas, so......." He broke off speaking in mid-sentence and smashed the butt of the shotgun hard into Lurch's kidneys; the big man choked back a scream of agony and sank to his knees, his head resting against the door of the Mercedes. "This's gettin' to be a bit of a habit with me 'n you," he added.

The end of the shotgun's barrel was placed under Timothy's chin. "Stand still Timmy, or you'll have no head left...I'll finish off what that bloke started the other night," said John, and carried out his search of the Irishman, finding a Walther automatic pistol in his pocket.

"Tut-tut, don't you know there's a law against carryin' these things," said John, "now don't you move a muscle while I search me' mate here."

Next he placed the barrel of the shotgun between Lurch's legs and 'assisted' the big man upright once more. "You got a gun, Lurch?"

"In a shoulder holster..right side," he gasped, obviously his kidneys still pained him.

"That's a good lad," said John, as he removed that weapon as well, "Jesus, I'm like a bloody walkin' arsenal.......Right now, I'll tell you what I want you to do....slide slowly into your seats inside the car and put the palms of your hands up against the windscreen...fingers wide apart. I'll get in the back, I want to talk to you."

The two men did as they were told, and John now held the shotgun menacingly covering both men in front of him; he proceeded.

"That's better," he said. "It's a lot warmer in here, isn't it?"

A quick glance over in the direction of the German's car soon satisfied him that Steve had the situation well under control; so far so good.

"Just what is it you're after, you bastard Judas?" snarled Timothy, "you a copper?"

"No copper, Tim," replied John, "you're not even close, so don't rupture your brain tryin' to figure it out. I want you to think about something....because I'm sittin' here with you, at this particular time...then isn't it logic to accept that I know why you're here. You both belong to the I.R.A.....you bomb people and murder people, but you never do it out in the open; if you did, then some might even admire you a bit....but your lot won't risk that."

"I'm not a bomber," protested Lurch.

"Lurch, whether you're a bomber or not, you're in this up to your neck."

"But I never planted any fuckin' bombs," he repeated.

John decided it was time to progress. "My boss has been wise to your moves for ages," he explained, "and he knew that this shipment was to be the big one......this is the one he wanted. Timmy...you and Michael are finished with the I.R.A. after this, you've made too many cock-ups."

Timothy stifled a curse.

"I'll tell you one thing that might be a bit of consolation to you," added John, "you know that bomb you made...the one your two mates were cartin' up to London in that old Maxi? Well it didn't go off by itself like it said on the news report......I helped it a little. Jesus, Timmy, you shoulda' seen your mate fly through the air....."

"Oh Jesus," cried Timothy, "you the S.A.S.?"

"Don't flatter me," said John, "but there again I can understand you bein' frightened of that lot...they're the best. As I've already told you, it doesn't matter a fuck who I am. The one thing that stands out here, is that I'm sittin' with this nasty lookin' shotgun pointed at you two and, let me assure you...you're both in bad trouble. The degree of trouble depends upon the amount of co-operation I get from you, try to flannel me with a load of bullshit...then without a shadow of doubt, you're both dead meat."

John allowed them a short interval to ponder over their future, at the same time removing the Colt from his pocket.

"Right lads, time's up.....time for answers. I want you to tell me when and where the exchange's takin' place....that's clear enough, isn't it?"

Both Timothy and Lurch remained silent, their hands firmly pressed against the windscreen, but very aware of the seriousness of what was happening to them.

"I'll ask you one more time," said John, "and there's one other thing I forgot to tell you....I'm not governed by any specific rules or regulations; if I decide to kill you both here and now, nothing will be said about it, because there's only a few of us know what's goin' on....the same goes for your German friend over there."

Both men in the front of the car twisted in their seats, but made sure their hands remained where they were; they saw Schumaker standing over by his car, and they saw the second man with him.

"Piss off," snarled Lurch, "you're full o' shit...you're gettin' to know fuck all from me."

It appeared as if they were beginning to doubt the authenticity of his words, and at the same time gaining confidence.

"That's fair enough, Lurch," said John quietly. Bringing the silencer of the Colt against the big man's head, he pulled the trigger. There was a distinctive 'pphhtt' and Lurch's head snapped sideways under the impact of the .38 calibre bullet as it entered his brain, causing a fountain of blood to spray over Timothy's face and upper body.

The Irishman screamed in terror, attempting to stave off the flow of blood and at the same time shove Lurch's body away from himself, the pressure of the fountain gradually decreasing.

John then placed the silencer behind Timothy's left ear.

"You have to realise that I'm deadly serious, Timmy," he said slowly, "but I'm willing to give you one last chance to come up with the goods.....poor old Lurch has had a bad week all round, 'asn't he."

Even in the early morning cold, the windscreen of the Mercedes was beginning to frost over; beads of sweat oozed from the pores on Timothy's brow, and sweat trickled down his back.

"Right Tim, I'm runnin' out of time and patience," said

John, "and I have to get back to Portsmouth before Rose wakes up....she doesn't know I'm here."

"I don't know all the details," replied the Irishman, "honestly I don't; I'm only the messenger.....you've got to believe me."

"As I've already told you, if you refuse to answer the question, or you try and tell me a load of bullshit; that's it......and I think what you've just said comes under the second category....you want to change it?"

"Michael set it all up," he insisted, "it's him you want to ask..not me."

"I don't believe you......you know the score, Timmy."

Timothy Reagan was beginning to think that he might be able to bluff his way out of this after all; all Williams had done was to kill Lurch, who he well knew was expendable. There was no way he could afford to kill him, the information he had was too important. "I've told you all I can," he protested, "you're going to have to get the rest from your so-called friend....some fuckin' good friend you've turned out to be."

John was aware of Timothy's unfounded confidence and, moving the end of the silencer, he pulled the trigger again; the sound barely audible. The bullet shattered the passenger's door window on its trajectory from the car, spending itself harmlessly into the darkness of the winter's morning. Timothy screamed in agony and his left hand left the windscreen and clutched at the bloody mess of all that remained of his ear; the pain was almost unbearable.

"Alright! Alright! I'll tell you what you want to know," he cried, trying to staunch the flow of blood running down his neck, "but please don't shoot again."

"OK Timmy, but no more of your shit....only the truth will do."

"I've got a map," he spluttered, his bloodied hand searching for remnants of skin, "it's in my pocket....all the details you need are written on it, time and place of the exchange."

"Pass it to me," instructed John "but be very careful what you do."

The Irishman fumbled inside his coat and produced the slip of paper, passing it meekly to John; his eyes never leaving the Colt. Switching on the interior light, John quickly glanced at the map reference and recognised the two coastlines drawn; the southernmost tip of Ireland and the familiar shape of Wales. "That's better, " he said, "easy, wasn't it?"

"What happens to me now?" asked a worried looking Timothy, "once this gets out, they'll go out of their way to get me....you have to make sure that I'm safe..a new identity and everything that goes with it, I know you've done it before."

"Oh, I'll do all o' that for you Timmy," smiled John and pulled the trigger, "I've a commitment."

A look of disbelief and horror appeared fractionally on Timothy's face, as the force of the bullet thundered into his temple. "A lot of good people aren't around anymore because of you...that's for them."

Both men lay slumped at awkward angles, their eyes wide open in death; closing the car door behind him, John walked towards the two men standing by the BMW. Steve and the German had stood in silence, the pressure of the gun against the man's head unrelenting. Both had heard the sound of the car window being smashed and the sound of the bullet whistling through the air, but neither of them realised that two men now lay dead inside the Mercedes.

Two of the cafe's customers left the premises and walked over to their lorries, bidding each other farewell, unaware of the happenings close by. The sudden roar of the powerful engines of the articulated lorries was deafening, followed shortly by the loud hissing of air pressure as the handbrakes were released. A final wave to one another and then the huge lorries began to move off slowly at first until they cleared the parking area, then faster as they disappeared into the darkness; the noise of the engines gradually fading.

It was now five forty five, on a bitter and bloody cold morning.

John reached out and relieved the German of the burden of the black case and, after placing it on the gleaming bonnet of the BMW, he opened it. A small fortune in cash greeted him, in tightly packed bundles of hundred, fifty and twenty pound notes; all in all quite a substantial sum of money, no doubt a percentage of it having filtered through from the funds of Noraid.

"I must insist on the meaning of this," complained Schumaker, mistaking John for the young man's superior, "I'm a visitor to your country and am well aware of my rights; are you gentlemen members of the police?"

"You have no rights," replied John, "your name is Rudi Schumaker and you sell guns to the I.R.A...so be very careful what you say from now on. I've had just about enough bullshit tonight to last me a lifetime, something your business associates over there found out to their peril........I want you to chose your words very carefully, because I'm in no mood to be pissed about by you. First I want to tell you that I know all about your little deal, the Irishman gave me certain details; but I'm not too sure about his reliability....I need you to verify things, OK?''

Accepting what he was being told as the truth, and noticing the serious expression upon his interrogator's face, Schumaker became a little desperate.

"But this is England," he stammered, "you English do not stoop to such actions....who are you? I demand to know who you are."

"Who I am doesn't matter," replied John, "it's who you are that counts. I've already told you what I want.....I won't ask again."

Indecision appeared upon the German's face.

"Let me assure you of one thing," added John, "I've got no compunction at all about killing you.....I'll willingly settle for two I.R.A. agents and a top gun runner, it's better that nothing; so it's up to you."

John removed the Colt from his pocket and made a show of re-cocking it, then he levelled it at the German's heart.

"Alright," said Schumaker, "I'll do as you ask...the exchange of arms is to take place at eight p.m. tonight, at a place 52 degrees longitude and 6 degrees latitude.....this is approximately halfway between St. David's Head in Wales, and Carnore Point in southern Ireland. When I received the payment, the captain of the vessel was informed and the operation was set in motion."

"I heard him use the phone," said Steve, "that's what it sounded like to me...he told them to commence arrangements."

"Good," said John then, passing the slip of paper he had taken from Timothy, he added, "go over in the light of the cafe and check those figures....52 long and 6 latitude."

Steve did as he was instructed, and was back almost immediately. "They check out," he said.

290

"That's about it then," said John quietly and shot Rudi Schumaker through the heart; he was dead before his knees had time to buckle. Steve reacted instinctively by catching the full body weight of the German; a combined expression of disbelief and astonishment came on his face. It was difficult for him to come to terms with the fact that John had killed three men in the space of ten minutes without any apparent feelings at all.

"Oway son," said John firmly, rousing him from the state of apathy which had overcome him momentarily, "help me get him in the back of the Merc...keep 'em all together." He was aware of the younger man's doubts and, once the grisly task had been completed, he tried to explain things to him. "Stevie," he said, "I know better than anybody just how hard it is when you have to go out and kill somebody; to take the life of another human bein'. It's something that, no matter how hard you try, you can never forget or get used to.....but if there weren't men like you and me these bastards would go on bombin' and killin' innocent people....our people. They could do this without any fear of reprisal, or even being adequately punished for it...we don't hang people anymore, all they would get is a jail sentence...and you know how long these fellas normally stay locked up before they manage to escape to start again......You have to make readjustments to your life and to accept the fact that it's now developed into an eye for an eye situation.......Stevie son, this country's been easy pickin's long enough, it's about time we retaliated as we have done here this mornin', and as we did the other night; time for us to put the fear of God into them for a change......The German's made himself a fortune out of sellin' guns to the I.R.A., guns they use to kill our lads who are over there trying their best to keep peace between two sets of Irish people.''

John paused to allow time for Steve to think over what he had said. "This cold morning is the stark reality of life, of what really goes on. It might've crossed your mind that I'm just as bad as they are, and you might be right about that; I make no excuses for it........It's up to you son, if you can't take the responsibility for the job and everything that goes with it, then it's time for you to get out.....because this is your apprenticeship, and one day I'll not be around, then it'll be left to you. The only reason I've spouted off like this and explained myself is because I like you; you remind me of someone a long time ago.''

Standing in silence, Steve thought over what John had said, he had never heard him talk so much; first to the German and then to himself. The Commodore had stressed the need to observe and educate himself, saying John would prove to be the most effective operator he was likely to meet. A natural he had said; he was absolutely right.

"I'm sorry John," he apologised, "only it came as a shock...I honestly didn't appreciate the full implications of what's going on. You're right, it had to be done....I can accept that now.''

John smiled at his young companion, he had every confidence that he would come good. "Right then, son," he said, "get into that little flier of yours and give the Commodore a ring...put him in the picture and tell him we need the clean up squad to get rid of the Merc and its contents.....oh, by the way, your shotgun's in the back seat.''

It was fifteen minutes before the little sports car roared back along the road.

"He told me to congratulate you," said Steve, "wants to know if you fancy a trip out to sea to be in at the finale.''

"Hhmmm, I wouldn't mind," replied John, "the sea air might clean out me' old pipes."

"I've already told him you would.....says for you to meet him at the barracks' main gate at three o'clock this afternoon..or rather fifteen hundred as he put it, he'll arrange everything."

John nodded; it was almost over. But buoyant as the Commodore could rightly feel, another feather in his cap, there was still one final act to be played out. Suddenly John felt tired of it all. Retrieving the black case, he threw it inside the BMW.

"I'm goin' to borrow the German's car, after all he'll not be needin' it anymore," said John, "I'd better get back to the club, Chris'll be worried. You'll have to hang about here until everything's done and dusted, then get yerself back to the hotel and get your head down.....you've earned it."

"John!"

"Yes son?"

"Nothing really....I just wanted to say thanks, that's all."

"No need to, you did alright."

The left hand drive of the foreign car proved a little awkward at first, but once he had driven five or six miles, he became accustomed to it and then he put his foot hard on the accelerator pedal and the miles sped by. After giving Chris the pre-arranged signal, he waited by the door for her to let him in. It was now eighteen minutes past seven, the very first signs of daybreak were trying to force themselves through the darkened clouds.

"Hello, flower," he said.

The relief on her face at seeing John standing there was plain to see, she almost dragged him inside and, encircling him with her arms like bands of steel, she kissed him as hard as she could.

"I've been so worried," she said, "I couldn't bear the thought of anything happening to you....Are you alright?...Was it Beaulieu after all?....Did you get what you wanted?"

"Yes to all three questions," he smiled, "you did the trick for me."

Chris recognised the fact that if John had found out everything they needed to know, then people would have been killed.

"Timothy?" she asked.

John nodded his head. "There's a few more out of the game now," he replied, "it can't be helped."

"As long as you're safe," she smiled, "I wish that we were a thousand miles from here...away from it all. They've got what they need, why don't we just go?"

"Because we can't, flower....not yet anyway," he answered, "Come on, it's time you were home, you've had a long night. By the way, can you drive?"

"Yes I can drive...I'll have you know I used to own a VW beetle, went all over the country in it."

"Well you shouldn't 'ave any difficulty in driving that lovely BMW over there," he said pointing to the German's car and giving her the keys, "go steady because it's got left hand drive. Park it somewhere near the flat and lock it up.....take the black case which is on the passenger seat and hide it in the bedroom, there's a hell of a lot o' money inside; we'll see to it later."

Watching her drive off rather precariously, he locked the front door and sprinted back up to the living quarters. Sneaking a look into Rose's bedroom, he saw that she was still dead to the world; whatever was in the little white pill had certainly worked. Removing his heavy sheepskin coat, he soon realised that he now had two handguns, his own Colt and the nine millimetre automatic which used to belong to Timothy. Placing one in each of the deep pockets of his overcoat, he arranged it on the rack in such a way it didn't look conspicuous. After removing his boots and putting the lights out, not forgetting to reset the burglar alarm, he stretched out on the sofa and gratefully closed his aching eyes. One thing he was not getting on this so-called holiday of his was much sleep; not that he was complaining as he thought of the major reason.

He had accomplished it with almost an hour and a half to spare.

"Morning John," said Rose, entering the living room.

John moaned and groaned, twisted and stretched himself. "Mmmmmm, my bloody 'ead," he said, rubbing his eyes, "Mornin' Rose...sleep well?"

She appeared in front of him, she looked shattered; her hair was dishevelled and her dress was all crumpled. He decided it had to be genuine, no-one could arrange themselves to look that bad; it was too authentic to be anything else.

"I can't remember if I've slept well or not," she replied, "what happened?"

Swinging his feet onto the floor, he began to put on his boots. "It was about two o'clock when you finally began to fizzle out," he said, "you'd just finished tap dancing on top of the table. You said you wanted another drink, but when I got back with it..you'd flaked out on me; so I carried you into the bedroom and laid you on the bed....you didn't move a muscle; dead to the world."

"I must have died," she moaned, "I'm normally up before this....would you like some breakfast?"

"No thanks, flower, I couldn't face up to food just yet....a nice walk along the sea front will do me good, it might clear me' head."

Rose came over to him, looking a bit embarrassed. "I think I can remember coming on a bit strong to you last night, when we were dancing," she said, "if I did and I shocked you....then I'm sorry, John."

"No need to be sorry, Rose," he smiled , "you were the perfect hostess."

"Thanks," she said, returning his smile.

As he put his overcoat back on, the inner lining was still warm. He walked over to the box on the wall and switched the alarm off yet again. Turning, he looked at Rose and winked at her. "Ta-ra flower," he said, "thanks for a smashin' time......I'll see yer later on tonight."

Chapter Twelve

The large stone pillars holding the massive steel gates had always presented a daunting atmosphere in the past, as if to warn all those who ventured through them 'to fear to tread'. But, standing back from them today, they did not seem so bad after all; passing through them voluntarily was far better than being drafted to the Naval barracks.

"Can I 'elp you, sir?" asked the duty quartermaster on the gate, noticing John's interest.

"I've got an appointment to meet a Commodore Ward," he replied, "but I'm a few minutes early.......and thinking over old times."

"You been in the barracks before?" asked the quartermaster.

"Lots of times, years ago."

"Would you like me to ring the wardroom an' tell him you're here?"

"No thanks, I'll wait.......it'll give me the chance to reminisce for a while."

After returning to the hotel, he had eventually managed to get a couple of hours' sleep; not finding it practicable to return to Chris's flat. Much as he had wanted to go and be with her, the need to sleep was too great; a definite sign of middle age, to prefer a warm bed to a warm body. If the sea trip the Commodore had planned turned out as expected, there would be time enough to be with her tonight and show her just how much she meant to him.

The voice of the quartermaster interrupted his train of thought.

"'Ere's the Commodore coming now, sir," he called.

John looked up and was surprised to see the old man looking

so resplendent in his naval uniform, the quartermaster and his gate staff snapped smartly to attention and saluted him.

"On time I see, John," he smiled and, after shaking hands with him, he added, "I must congratulate you on a splendid night's work...all we have to do is to carry on from where you left off."

"I was surprised to see you in uniform," said John.

"Officially I'm retired, but on occasions when the need arises, I'm still permitted the pomp and splendour my rank allows," explained the old man, "on and off like Prince Philip I suppose....the uniform to suit the occasion."

John accompanied the Commodore across the massive parade ground, where two huge gunnery instructors were attempting to teach their platoons the art of rifle drill. As they neared, the two instructors shouted out simultaneously.

"Platoons, 'shun'.......General salute, present arms!"

The Commodore politely acknowledged the recognition.

"Slo..ope arms!......Order arms!.....Stand at ease...Stand easy. That was bloody terrible," screamed one of the G.I.'s, "that officer must be wonderin' what we've got 'ere!"

"It doesn't change much, does it, John?" smiled the Commodore.

"Only the faces sir....the G.I.'s still frighten the life out of me after twenty years."

"A Wessex helicopter should be arriving shortly to take us to Milford Haven, where we'll be joining the minesweeper *H.M.S. Wisperton*," explained the officer, "there's already a section of the Royal Marines Special Boat Squad on board. Hopefully, just having them with us should prevent any argument, and we'll arrest both crews without any trouble at all...Then your job is almost over."

John realised the significance of the word 'almost'.

'Almost, but not quite,' he thought sadly.

The Commodore invited him into the wardroom and ordered two large drinks; this was a new experience for him; John Williams actually sitting in the officer's mess and having a drink. At three forty five the barracks emergency fire party assembled on the parade ground with the necessary fire-fighting equipment, ushering the two platoons of trainees out of the immediate vicinity.

Five minutes later the terrific roar of the helicopter could be heard approaching, the loud swishing of the rotor blades unmistakeable, and then it came into sight; the sound was deafening as it landed forty yards from the wardroom.

"Time for us to move," said the Commodore, standing up and putting on his heavy navy blue overcoat.

"Getting ready to face the elements?" asked John, with a smile.

"We can't all afford coats like that," he replied, indicating the sheepskin coat which John was fastening.

The helicopter's winchman assisted both men into the aircraft and fastened them into their seats, offering ear protectors as well. The roar of the engines increased and suddenly John's stomach seemed to drop through the floor as the helicopter rose vertically, the towering mast and the fluttering white ensign left behind as the power was transferred forward.

"Next stop Milford Haven," shouted the young flight lieutenant over his shoulder.

The longer the flight went on, the more John began to enjoy the new experience; he spent his time looking down at the snow covered countryside below. The flight took just over an hour before the pilot landed with a gentle bump and switched the engines off. No sooner had they clambered down than they were whisked away in a staff car which took them to the small jetty where the minesweeper was tied up alongside awaiting their arrival, its twin Deltic diesel engines idling away in readiness. Standing together in small groups along the upper-deck, were the dozen or so members of the renowned S.B.S. and, looking at them it was comforting to know that these elite fighting men were here to assist and not resist in the operation. At the end of the gangway stood the 'piping party' waiting apprehensively to complete the age old custom bestowed upon high ranking dignitaries, retired or not, the Commodore came into that category. The welcoming party comprised the ship's captain, first lieutenant, the coxswain and other members of the quartermaster's staff. "Pipes ready!" ordered the first lieutenant, or 'Jimmy' as he was more commonly called.

Respectfully, John remained on the jetty until the piercing shrill of the pipes was over and the ensuing handshakes had taken place between fellow officers; when it was completed he walked across the gangway and halted.

"Permission to come aboard, sir?" he asked of the captain.

"Permission granted, Mr. Williams, welcome on board *H.M.S. Wisperton.*"

Stepping onto the wooden upper deck of the minesweeper, as a token of his own respect, John turned to face aft and saluted the quarter-deck. Although relatively small in size, this and her sister ships were an essential part of our coastal defences.

"We'll be under way in a few minutes," said the captain then, turning to John in particular, he added, "it must be rewarding to see the result of your efforts....I hope we can do them justice."

"I'm expecting it to be a formality," smiled John, "with your gun crew on one hand and the marines on the other...only fools would try and make a run for it."

"I hope you're right," replied the officer.

Last minute preparations were being carried out to get the small ship ready for leaving harbour, the gangway was being taken away and two harbour workers were standing by to slip the restraining hawsers.

The first lieutenant approached John, looking slightly embarrassed. "Excuse me, Mr. Williams...but do you happen to be armed?"

"As a matter of fact I am," replied John.

"I'm sorry to have to ask, but would you please hand it over," said the officer, "you can collect it when you leave the ship."

"Of course, I understand."

"Thank you," said the captain, "but I'm afraid Queen's Regulations dictate the procedure."

Delving into his pocket, John produced the Walther automatic he had taken from Timothy and handed it to the first lieutenant; the Colt remained tucked firmly inside his left boot.

"It's not as if you'll be needing it, John," smiled the Commodore, "you're here to enjoy a relaxing trip to sea and act as a casual observer."

As the minesweeper left the calm of the breakwater, the sea roughened a little, causing it to pitch and roll slightly.

"If my memory serves me right," said the Commodore, "you once served on board a coastal minesweeper."

"Yes sir, in 1960....*H.M.S. Wolverston,* we were engaged on East Coast fishery patrol; based at Great Yarmouth and Lowestoft...seems like another life."

301

"What did you think of 'sweepers'?" asked the first lieutenant.

"I loved it, " replied John, "always found that small ships were the happiest ones to be on.....but a little rough in a force six."

"I can't promise you a force six tonight," smiled the captain, "I'm afraid all we can rustle up is a three to four."

"That'll be enough for me," said John, "my stomach hasn't been to sea for over twenty years."

The deck of the small warship began to vibrate as the captain increased the revolutions and the diesel engines answered the call. Once clear of the harbour restrictions and inshore hazards, the coxswain handed over the responsibility of the ship's wheel to the duty able seaman.

"Permission for able seaman Jones to take the wheel, sir?" he asked.

"Permission granted," replied the first lieutenant.

"Able seaman Jones on the wheel, sir, course to steer two eight zero."

The Irish Sea looked stark and unfriendly and, although there was not much of a wind blowing, the white horses broke against the wooden superstructure as the vessel forged its way ahead.

"We'll arrange our E.T.A. for twenty fifteen, and we will go to darken ship stations at nineteen hundred," said the captain, "hopefully we can give them an unpleasant surprise."

The Commodore looked across the bridge to where John stood huddled against the cold.

"I'm forgetting that you had no sleep last night," he said, "I don't suppose the captain will mind you going down into the wardroom and stretching out for a couple of hours or so."

"Of course, Mr. Williams," agreed the skipper, "you remember the way?"

"I remember...thanks."

He made his way from the bridge to the wardroom, pausing for a moment to look in at the stoker's mess which was on the same level; all the coastal minesweepers were identical. The wardroom was a confined area, large enough to seat half a dozen people comfortably and, as with other officers' living areas, lavishly furnished. John took off his overcoat and relaxed in one of the soft red leather chairs and within minutes he was asleep.

At seven thirty, the first lieutenant roused him by gently shaking him by the shoulder; in the Navy it was well known that you never touched anybody when waking them up, the odd matelot was known to lash out at the intruder. But there again John was quiet by nature.

"We'll be in position in thirty minutes," said the officer, "there's a mug of coffee and a few sandwiches for you to get through. Come up to the bridge whenever you're ready, but be careful, we're at darken ship."

"Thanks," replied John, stretching himself and stifling a yawn. Soon he left the warmth of the wardroom and made his way up to the bridge in the darkness; carefully negotiating the water tight door and blackout sheets.

"Feel better, John?" asked the Commodore.

"Smashin'."

There was movement on the fo'c'sle, the marines were getting into position and carrying out their last minute checks. The crew members manning the Bofors gun were at action stations, awaiting orders; a very young sub-lieutenant in charge of the gun crew. This was to be a special night for all of them, their own opportunity to strike at the dreaded I.R.A.

The captain of the minesweeper looked over at John and the Commodore standing together side by side in the darkness, he mused at these two strange bedfellows, one a high ranking Naval officer and the other a Geordie; but whatever the connection, the pairing obviously came up with the results.

"The I.R.A. would dearly like to get their hands on him," the Commodore had told the captain earlier, "he's inflicted quite a bit of damage on them lately."

"Radar reports two bearings approximately five miles ahead of us, both stationary," said the officer, "it looks as if we've found them, gentlemen."

"Good," replied the commodore.

"Slow ahead both engines!"

"Gun's crew, ready to fire starshell."

The little minesweeper slowly closed the gap, hunter closing in on its quarry.

"Stop both engines!"

Suddenly the rhythmic beat of the propellers stopped and only the ship's momentum carried it forward, taking them closer to the two suspect ships.

Voices carried over the distance as men transferred the arms from one vessel to the other; every now and then a loud curse in broad Irish could be heard. Turning to the Commodore, the captain whispered his plan of action. "We'll be illuminating the area with starshell and searchlight, then the gun's crew have been instructed to put a live round across their bows and sterns; this should act as a deterrent to them."

"Excellent," replied the senior officer.

Every man on board that little minesweeper was ready, the Royal Marine S.B.S. with their automatic weapons poised and threatening; the distance was minimal.

"Illuminate!" shouted the captain.

The Bofors gun erupted twice in quick succession and suddenly the whole vicinity was bathed in brilliant light, men who seconds ago were talking and urging each other stopped in their tracks, disbelief on their faces. There was the sight of the dark-clad marines pointing their weapons at them, combined with the ominous sight of the Bofors barrel moving slowly from left to right, as if inviting them to put up a show of resistance. Twice more the Bofors fired, and a large plume of water from bow and stern sections cascaded over the beleaguered men.

"Switch on!" ordered the captain; and four massive searchlights were suddenly switched onto the crew members of the two vessels, who were now in a delayed state of panic. Crates and cargo were abandoned where they lay, the men made foolhardy attempts at scampering to their own ships, and for a short while confusion reigned.

The captain handed the microphone to the Commodore. "Ready sir," he said, "just press the button and speak."

"Attention!" the old man's voice echoed across the sea. "This is her Majesty's ship *Wolverston*, and I am an authorised representative of her government....Both vessels and their respective crews are suspected of being engaged in the illegal purchasing of arms and explosives, to be used against British subjects. It is my duty to warn you against any attempt to resist arrest....the action would be ill advised....As you have already seen, the men of the gun crew are more than capable of halting you if this should prove necessary.....We also have on board a detachment of the Royal Marines Special Boat Squadron. These men, along with members of the Royal Navy, will be boarding you shortly and I feel the importance of stressing the seriousness of the situation you now find yourselves in......No obstruction or resistance will be tolerated, any indication of such and these men have been authorised to shoot. If it is found that the accusations against you are well founded...then both captains and all crew members will be placed under immediate arrest, the vessels impounded and the cargo confiscated.......To minimize the effects of confusion, as well as the possibility of injury, I must insist on you all remaining where you are until instructed to move.....Do not resist my men as they carry out their search procedure, and do everything you are told to do.''

The Commodore passed the microphone back to the captain.

''Out fenders port side!........Board!''

On hearing the command to board, two dozen armed servicemen leapt into action, jumping from the deck of the minesweeper onto the other two vessels and beginning to round up the prisoners like sheep dogs gathering stray lambs and penning them together. The young first lieutenant in charge of the boarding party levered open the nearest crates and immediately confirmed that they were full of assorted weapons, including a number of Armalite rifles and two-man rocket launchers.

''Quite an arsenal, Sir,'' reported the young officer, his face flushed with the excitement of the find.

''Bring both captains to me and place everyone else under armed guard,'' instructed the Commodore, then added, ''Man all essential posts, we'll be getting under way as soon as possible.''

It did not take too long to transfer two very despondent looking individuals to the bridge of the minesweeper, escorted by a burly looking marine who kept nudging them in the spine with the barrel of his rifle.

"Gentleman," said the Commodore, "I thank you both for your co-operation, but it appears that you're both guilty of illegally trafficking arms for the Provisional I.R.A.....You will now be taken to Milford Haven where there are members of the Special Branch waiting to interview you, no doubt with a view to bringing other charges against you."

"Bollocks to you," snarled one of the men, in a thick Irish accent. "you'll get fuck all from me."

"I've already got what I came after," smiled the Commodore, then turning to the marine, he said, "Take them down to the galley flat and stay with them until we get alongside.....no doubt someone will arrange a relief."

"Yes sir," snapped the marine, "you can leave 'em to me."

As the cortege left the bridge, the Commodore turned to John, who had silently observed the efficiency of every man involved. "Well," he said, "what did you think....as a casual observer, of course?"

"Very impressive sir, very impressive."

"I think we can leave the Captain to finalise things up here," smiled the old man, "the warmth and hospitality of the wardroom beckons us.....a nice drop of something or other would be appreciated."

"I won't disagree with that," replied John.

Later, sitting together, after a couple of large rums to thaw themselves out, the Commodore returned to the matter in hand. "This whole operation has gone better than I'd dared hope," he said, "thanks to you, John...it's almost over." Once again the phrase 'almost over'.

"Is the rest really necessary, sir?" asked John, almost pleading with the old man, "after all we've done everything we set out to do....You've got the arms shipment and most of the guilty people are either dead or locked up, plus two of the I.R.A.'s bombers who weren't on the schedule.....Can't we just leave things as they are? After all, when the I.R.A. find out about this...I doubt if they'll let Michael leave Ireland...he'll take the can for the lot."

Placing his empty glass on the table, the Commodore looked at him, a man whom he himself had groomed for the job. John Williams had repeatedly proved his immense value to the section; even the Minister who had been against his recall was now impressed by what he had done in such a short time. "Listen John," he said quietly, "I can appreciate your feelings and I honestly sympathize with the situation you find yourself in; but things can't be left incomplete. Michael Reagan will return to Portsmouth, he's left too much of his life behind to abandon it....there's the woman to consider; you yourself said that he always returns to her. As long as there's one rotten apple left, it will find a way to contaminate others around it......sentiment must not be allowed to rule your head. If you wish, you can call it a day....go back to Durham until things are finished here and then I'll get in touch with you because, now that you're back in the field, I don't want to lose you again."

"What about Michael?"

"I'll instruct young Bright to take care of it," replied the Commodore.

John sat silently remonstrating with himself, trying to accept the fact that if he chose to, he could walk away and leave his responsibilities behind. Maybe now Chris and himself could put everything behind them and start that new life they spoke of; the temptation was strong. But in his heart he knew it was useless, he could not accept this escape clause the old man had offered him; he could not allow Steve to complete something which had been his responsibility from the beginning.

"No sir," he said, "thanks for the chance to run...but we both know whose job it is."

"I respect the bond of friendship you share with this man," said the Commodore, "but you must realise what has occurred since the days you were young men together.....your lives have virtually gone in opposite directions."

"I know that, sir.....and you're right as usual."

On their arrival at Milford Haven, the apprehended members of the two vessels were received by agents of the Special Branch, who accompanied the marines in their transportation of the prisoners back to London.

"Congratulations, sir," said the senior Special Branch officer, "once we get them into custody, we'll get them sorted out and find out who's who."

"You're welcome to them," replied the Commodore, "but keep the news from the media for forty eight hours...we need the time to wrap up all the loose ends."

"I'll do my best sir," agreed the officer, "but won't the I.R.A. realise that something's gone wrong with their plans?"

"I don't think they'll be too keen to brag about this....it's going to be another embarrassing pill for them to swallow."

The two men shook hands, and the Special Branch officer left the wardroom;

"Another drink, John?"

"Don't mind if a' do."

It was shortly after two a.m. when the same Wessex helicopter landed on the barracks parade ground; John felt sorry for the unfortunate fire and emergency party gathered. Once the two weary passengers had alighted and were well clear of those menacing rotor blades, the helicopter lifted off and disappeared into the night, returning to its base at *H.M.S. Culdrose* in Cornwall.

"I bet we're bein' called some ripe old names," said John.

"You're quite possibly right," smiled the Commodore.

The emergency party gathered up their fire-fighting equipment and hurried back to their bunks in the duty room, and the two men were left alone in the centre of the parade ground.

"Well sir, I'll be off," said John, "if Michael does come back...I'll finish it; hopefully I still hold the element of surprise."

"Take care, John...I'll be close by should you need any assistance."

The two men shook hands, and went their separate ways; the Commodore to the lavish setting of the wardroom and John over to the main gate where the duty quartermaster bade him goodnight.

Twenty minutes later, after finding a taxi, he put the key in the lock and quietly opened the door to Chris's flat; she was fast asleep on the sofa. After removing his coat, he tip-toed over to her and looked down at that angelic face; asleep and at peace with the world. Kneeling down beside her, he kissed her gently on the lips; it brought about a gradual response from her. Opening her eyes, she smiled at him, placed her arms about his neck and pulled him to her. "You look tired," she said, "you alright?"

"I am now...now that I'm back here with you."

"Things go alright.?"

He nodded. "No trouble at all......How did things go at the

club?''

"Just as normal," she replied, "except that Tom was expecting Timothy back last night......He's expecting Michael back sometime tomorrow..or should I say today. I called in to see Rose and explained that your mother-in-law had took bad and you'd gone over to Havant to see her..She seemed to believe me, told me to tell you she'd be alright."

"All that's left is Michael," said John, "once he's out of the way, we can all go home."

"As long as we're together, I don't mind where we go," said Chris, kissing him. Getting up from the sofa, she led him by the hand. "I'll turn on the shower, get yourself undressed and under it," she said.

"Any chance of gettin' my back washed?"

"None at all," she smiled, "but I can promise you a lot better when you come to bed."

"It's definitely worth lookin' forward to," he said, "you've been on my mind all day."

It did not take him long to take a shower, it not only acted to wash him, but also revived his senses. With that kind of offer beckoning, he had to be able to justify himself. If there was a tiredness in his limbs when he had entered the flat, it soon dissolved when he gazed appreciatively at that beautiful body which called out to him. He discarded the towel which was wrapped around his waist and climbed into bed next to her; she came to him with a passion which took him by surprise, covering him with her kisses.

"I love you, John, so very much," she cried.

"I love you as well," he assured her, "you're all I have."

After they had given each other their love, they fell asleep entwined in one another's arms.

311

Today was going to be judgement day.

Chapter Thirteen

The continuous sound of the phone ringing brought Rose from out of a deep drink-induced sleep and, after struggling about in the darkness to find her dressing gown, she eventually went into the living room and picked up the receiver.

"Rose..is that you?"

"Michael," she answered, recognising the voice instantly, "is anything wrong?"

"Anything wrong," he replied, "everything's wrong..Where the fuck is Timothy?"

"I don't know, he never came back yesterday like you said he would, and I didn't know what to think......what's happening? Where are you?"

"I'm in London, on my way there," he explained, "something's gone wrong with the deal.....the shipment never turned up as expected, and even the boat which went out to collect the merchandise has disappeared....Something smells rotten about the whole thing, that's why I've got to talk to Timothy..he was supposed to hand over the money to Schumaker. There's all kinds of accusations being bandied about..they're suggestin' that Timothy's done a runner with the money and I'm to blame for trusting him with so much; nearly half a million quid. Me 'n Herman were bloody lucky to get out of Ireland in one piece...an old friend o' mine give me the buzz that they were out to get their pound of flesh, and guess whose flesh they wanted. Jesus! I even got up the nerve to get on a plane..I had to get out of there somehow and try to sort this mess out."

"What's going to happen to us, Michael?" cried Rose, fearing the worst, "if the I.R.A. are after you, no place will be safe from them."

Michael was aware she was on the point of hysteria, he had to pacify her somehow. "Listen, sweetheart," he coaxed, "it won't come to that, I'll be able to calm things over....I'll be home in about two hours, so please keep calm and don't panic. We have too much wrapped up in the club to just pack our bags and run; there had to be some valid explanation to all of this...I just have to find out what it is, that's all."

"Be careful, Michael, I'll be waiting for you."

"If by some miracle Timothy does turn up," added Michael, "tell 'im what's goin' on and to stay put until I get there."

"Oh, Michael," said Rose reluctantly, as if just remembering something, "there's something you should know about, it could be important....it's about John."

"There's not the time, Rose," he shouted, "I'm goin' to have to make a dash for the train...tell me when I get there...love you!"

"I love you too," she replied, but Michael had hung up.

It was too late for him to have heard her last few words. Was it possible that her growing suspicions about their good friend, John Williams, were true? She kept remembering little bits more about their night together, though most of it was still very hazy; but it had to be more than just coincidental.

Even though he was exhausted, John had a restless night, his mind once again over active. Faces kept reappearing in front of him, the fountain of blood spouting from Lurch's head onto the terrified Timothy; the look of astonishment on Timothy's face as he realised his own fate. Michael and Rose laughing together, not as they were now, but as they were twenty odd years ago...and somehow Chris was with them making up the foursome. But he could not find Angela anywhere; the past was confused with the present. Andy and Lillian were there also, and the Commodore stood at one side looking on; but still he could not find Angela. Suddenly they were all standing round that little graveside hundreds of miles away in that little village in Durham, and now he could see her; she held her arms as if beckoning him to her, arms held out to him to hold her. He had woken with tears in his eyes, plus a desperate longing to be far away from the awful reality of what he had to finish today.

Slipping out of the bed, careful not to rouse Chris, he dressed and went through into the lounge where he lit the fire to take the chill off the room. Opening the blinds, he found it was dull and overcast with a heavy frost outside, these winter mornings were always cold and miserable looking. Turning away from the window, he suddenly found Chris standing near him, her dressing gown tied tightly about her slim waist, which served to accentuate the desirable body hidden underneath.

"Sorry if I've woke you," he said.

"Couldn't you sleep?"

"Too much on my mind," he replied.

It was plain enough for her to see that he was a worried man, this was the only time she had seen him actually look his age; but it only increased her love for him. She sensed a vulnerability in his confidence and yearned to give him her own strength in support.

"What's wrong, John?"

"Nothing for you to worry yourself about, flower," he said,

with a sad smile, "it's just that I'm not too overjoyed at the prospect of having to kill Michael; but at the same time I do understand the need for it......I promise you this much, once this is over and done with, you and me are out of this altogether. Another problem which has to be faced up to is Rose...what happens to her? She's relied entirely on being with Michael, nothin' else matters to her; she's been caught up in all of this and turned a blind eye to the truth. Suddenly, yours truly turns up and uses her weakness to prise the information out of her which will destroy her life.....Rose couldn't put up with being sent to some prison or other kind of institution, it would kill her. I've done all the Commodore has asked of me, and more; but deep down I feel like a right bastard who's done wrong. Last night I was given the chance to pack it all in...could pack me' bags and get off home..he even suggested young Steve could finish things off here. Do you know what....I said no, it was my responsibility. Jesus bloody Christ! I must've seen too many bloody pictures; real life isn't like that.....I should have grabbed the chance when he offered it to me."

Chris held him in her arms, trying to comfort him. "Don't you realise you've done more damage to the I.R.A. in a couple of weeks than all of them put together? It's the age old battle of right against wrong...of good against evil. Rose was unfortunate in her choice of men to fall in love with but, during all those years, she must have had the opportunity to walk away from it; but she chose to stay, as I now choose to stay with you. As for the Commodore suggesting that Steve would finish things off, that was purely hypothetical; he knew John Williams, and he knew you wouldn't just get up and walk away from it...and he was right."

"You're right there...it had to be me, but as long as you're here for me to come back to, then it will have been worth-while."

"You won't get rid of me in a hurry," she smiled.

Untying the belt which secured her dressing gown, he stared at her beautiful body, her breasts rising and falling as she breathed. "I don't think I want to get rid of you at all," he said.

"Prove it to me."

Later, as they lay snuggled together by the fire, the phone rang. Chris jumped to her feet and once more put on her dressing gown.

"Hello," she said, then signalling John, she added, "it's the Commodore."

"Morning John," he said, "I've rung you to keep you up to date with the situation as it stands. Our Special Branch colleagues inform us that Michael Reagan and his bodyguard are out of Ireland and on their way to Portsmouth. Somehow they got wind of the War Council placing a contract on them and managed to elude whoever it was that was handed it. The news of the arms deal and the subsequent apprehension will be publicised in the press tomorrow..this gives you twenty four hours to complete what you have to do."

"It will be done," said John, replacing the phone, then turning to Chris, he added, "Michael's on his way back...I was secretly hoping that he would never leave Ireland, but it seems like the I.R.A.'s put a contract out on him, so he's finished either way.

"Try and forget about Michael for the time being," she said, "we have our own plans to make...Second thing we have to do is get you checked out of the hotel and bring your things to

317

the flat, so we can leave as soon as possible."

"If that's the second thing....what's the first?"

"Can't you guess?"

By midday, John had packed his belongings into his suitcase and moved out of the hotel, assuring the receptionist that he had enjoyed his stay in Portsmouth but it was time for him to return to the North East, now that the weather had returned to somewhere near normal.

He phoned Steve Bright.

"I hope to finish this tonight, son," he said, "what I want you to do is stand by in the club, and when it's over I'll give you a ring. Tell Tom the barman who you are and for him to close up shop and get everybody out without too much fuss or bother."

"OK John, it looks as if we're in the final furlong."

"You could be right about that," said John, "but this is only one race in a busy racing calendar...there'll be other meetings in the future."

"If you need me," said Steve, "give out a yell. One thing I want to tell you, you old bastard, is to take care of yourself....I'm getting quite used to working with you."

John smiled as he replaced the phone. "Cheeky young sod," he said.

At last all the loose ends were almost tied up, like bonfire night twenty two years ago, his target was there; it was left up to him to eliminate him. The old Gunnery Instructor's words came back to him, 'Never consider the human factor..concentrate on the target.' Michael was that target and he had to put all personal feelings aside. Removing the two handguns from his pockets, he checked them; Timothy's Walther automatic was fully loaded, and he replaced the three spent cartridges in his own Colt. Once he was satisfied with them, he placed the automatic in his right hand coat pocket and the Colt back into his left boot.

Chris had sat silent as he had completed his arrangements, fully understanding the diligence John brought to the task.

"How about after lunch we go for a nice walk along the seafront?" she asked. "It might help relieve the tension....later we can come back and you can take a nap until it's time to go to the club."

"Just the job," he smiled.

The rest of the afternoon passed too quickly for them, they walked arm in arm for miles; the cold and dampness were secondary, they were together and that was all that mattered. As it so often happens, when you wanted the time to drag by, it did the opposite. By six p.m. they returned to the flat and John lay on the sofa, whilst Chris busied herself packing her clothes and getting herself ready for her last night at the club; her final performance.

"Come on John..it's nine o'clock, almost time to go."

"I must've dozed off," he said.

"You needed it," she replied, handing him a strong cup of coffee.

"Thanks, flower........Tell you what, how about coming up to Durham with me tomorrow? I'll have to make arrangements to sell the house and say my ta-ra's to everybody....How's Cornwall sound to you....a nice little village near the beach where we can drink scrumpy all day and make love all night?"

"It sounds fine to me," she smiled, "Cornwall it is....a nice place to bring up a baby."

"A what?"

"I know it's a bit premature," she said, blushing a little, "but

I know neither one of us have been taking any precautions, and you know what should have started a few days ago..but there's no sign of that happening; so anything's possible.''

John was completely overwhelmed by her news. After all these years of accepting that he would never know the joys of being a father, here he was being given the chance.

"How long before you know for sure?" he asked.

"I don't know, I've never been pregnant before..we'll just have to wait and see, but the chances must be good.''

Taking her into his arms, he placed the palm of his hand on her flat stomach and hugged her tightly. "It would be fantastic Chris...you and a baby, I couldn't ask for more than that. After tonight, the Commodore and his section can go fuck themselves....John Williams and his new family are retiring permanently.''

"Hear hear," added Chris.

At nine forty five p.m. they entered the club and, after exchanging the customary pleasantries with Bill the friendly doorman, they went upstairs into the lounge.

"Mr. Reagan asked me to extend his invitation, says will you go straight upstairs," said Tom.

"Certainly," replied John, then kissing Chris on the cheek, he added, "See you soon, flower.''

"Please be careful," she whispered, her eyes betraying the concern she felt for him.

Out of the corner of his eye, John noticed Tom pick up the internal phone, no doubt informing Michael of his arrival; his right hand gripped the Walther in his pocket. Had he known what the reception would be, he would have prepared himself entirely different; as it was he intended playing it as it came.

Herman was stationed outside the door of the flat.

"Evening Mr. Williams," he said, "Mr. Reagan's waiting for you inside."

Herman knocked on the door and opened it. There were three people inside the room; Michael and Rose were two of them, but the third one, a man John had never seen before, stood gazing unconcernedly out of the window into the street below. It was only then the alarm bells began to sound in John's head and he realised he had walked into this obvious set-up like some sacrificial lamb to the slaughter; but it was too late to take any evasive action. His head suddenly felt as if it had exploded, agonising pains shot through his brain and a kaleidoscope of brilliant colours appeared before his eyes; his legs seemed to lose all their strength and he sagged helplessly to the floor, finally coming to rest in a kneeling position as if in prayer.

"Jesus Christ!" yelled Michael, "Don't fuckin' kill him... I need to get some answers from him. The ultimate pleasure of killing him belongs to me..it's me he's made look like an idiot."

Herman had used his huge balled fist as a club and had brought his full weight of almost eighteen stones down with a terrific force to the side of John's head; he had used this same effective method on frequent occasions in the past.

"Get him to his feet!" snarled Michael.

Two enormous hands the size of miner's shovels then grabbed hold of John and hoisted him bodily into the air, slamming him not too gently back onto his unsteady feet; the room appeared to be spinning round and he was the axis.

"Search him!"

The same two shovels began their rough search of his person and it wasn't long before Herman discovered the automatic in

321

his pocket.

"What's this bastard, then?" the big man shouted in glee, smashing the steel barrel into John's mouth.

The unexpectedness of the move hurled John backwards into the wall, where he remained, dazed and with blood streaming from between burst lips; fresh pains speared through his brain. Herman was not finished with him yet; reaching out he grabbed him by the testicles and dragged him back into the centre of the room, squeezing so hard that John vomited. Getting vomit over his shoes only served to intensify Herman's anger; stretching his long arm to its furthest extremity, he smashed his massive fist into John's unprotected face. More blood spurted forth and it now seemed possible that, along with several teeth, his nose and cheekbone could be broken. John was not allowed to fall, the large man prevented him from doing so; the fist hit him again, and even then there was no respite. One of those shovel sized hands grabbed his bruised testicles once again, and he kept him upright; the whole of John's body seemed to be racked with pain.

Herman was thoroughly enjoying himself, he was putting John through the mill; gaining sweet revenge for his friend's embarrassment, a pity he wasn't here to see it.

"How do you like your balls crushed, Geordie?" he sneered into John's face, "Oh I'm sorry, you're not a Geordie are you...you come from Durham, another shit pile. Well then 'Geordie', you're not so tough now are you; not when it's your balls that's gettin' the treatment."

With a final squeeze, the pressure was suddenly released, and John staggered about, but once again Herman steadied him and smashed two vicious blows into his kidneys. John collapsed onto the floor in grateful release, the pain too much for him to endure.

"That's enough," ordered Michael, "he's had enough for the time being. Put him in the chair and leave us..but stay in the corridor outside in case I need you. Let nobody in, unless it's my brother."

Unknown to John, Herman picked him up and dumped him into the easy chair, where he slowly regained his senses, attempting to take stock of a seemingly hopeless situation by keeping his eyes closed, thus allowing himself that little extra time to recover. The only possible advantage he still held in his favour was that, because Herman had been so overjoyed at discovering the Walther in his pocket, he discontinued the search; the Colt was still safely tucked away in his left boot. He had to be alert to the slightest opportunity which would allow him time to make a last desperate grab for it. This was the only occasion when he actually needed the services of the Commodore's back-up team, and they were all totally ignorant of his plight. His face felt as if it resembled a piece of meat which had been roughly tenderised on some butcher's block but, as long as there was the faintest of chances, there had to be hope. Although feeling very weak from the well-executed beating he had taken, he had to give them the impression that he was hurt even more than he actually was; anything that could possibly work to his advantage had to be grasped at. His left eye was almost completely closed and his vision was impaired due to the terrific force of Herman's blows to his head. John forced himself to raise his head and look into Michael's eyes and, even at this stage of the proceedings, could feel no intense hatred towards him.

Michael saw the movement, and walked over to him. "Why John?" he asked, "Of all the people...why you?"

"Why what, Michael?" The answer came with great difficulty, the salty taste of blood on his split lips mingled with fragments of calcium which had broken from his teeth.

"Don't take me for a fool any longer," said Michael.

The stranger who had stood by the window observing what had taken place, finally decided to take part himself and show his hand. "Get on with it," he instructed Michael, "the only reason you aren't dead yourself is because you contacted the Council and told them you would come up with some answers....now fuckin' get them!"

It took a few seconds for John to realise that the stranger was not referring to himself, but Michael. This had to be the I.R.A.'s executioner and he was here to carry out the contract on the brothers. If the opportunity did present itself to him he would have to concentrate on the stranger first; he posed the greater threat.

"There's no hurry," insisted Michael, "he must have valuable information the War Council would be very interested in....we've got to find out just how much he knows."

"Shoot the bastard's kneecaps off," said the stranger, "he'll soon be beggin' to tell us everything he knows; and then I can get to fuck out o' this country."

John took an instant dislike to him.

"Here'" said Michael, offering John a glass of whiskey, "take a drink of this."

The stranger spat in disgust.

"Thanks, Michael," croaked John.

"Don't bother to thank anybody," he replied, "I want to know who you're workin' for.....who sent you here?"

Attempting to take a sip from the glass, John spilled most of the contents over himself, but the few drops that did go in his mouth stung his lips and gums.

Walking to the far side of the room Michael opened a drawer and removed an automatic pistol almost identical to the one John had confiscated from his brother and, after making a show of checking that it was loaded, he returned to where John sat and levelled it at his head.

"Old mate or not," said Michael, "you are going to tell me what I want to know...Are you with the S.A.S. or some other secret service branch?....Whoever you're with has to be top drawer, because we had you checked out by experts and you came up clean. You must've come to Portsmouth with some specific job to do......was it the arms shipment you're after?"

"You've got it all wrong," said John, with extreme difficulty.

"I've got nothin' wrong, you lying bastard," shouted Michael, "if I've got everything wrong as you say I have....why the gun? Why were you carryin' a gun..you frightened of the dark all of a sudden?"

"Rose told me the other night," said John "she said you would be in a lot of bother if the shipment didn't get through....that's why I made up the story about my mother-in-law takin' a bad turn; it gave me the time to go up to the Smoke and buy the gun.....I wanted to help you, Michael, not go against you."

John's idea was to try and introduce an element of doubt into Michael's mind.

"You're lyin' through your teeth; what you have left of them," shouted Michael into John's face, "after you got Rose well and truly pissed out of her mind, you questioned her about the meetin' with the German...You see John, one thing about my Rose; pissed as she gets..she always remembers what goes on.

325

It seems like you've slipped up, so you'd better come up with the truth..or I'll have Herman come back to 'persuade' you; I'm sure he'll enjoy doin' just that.''

For a brief instant through the confusion, and hearing her name mentioned, Rose lifted her eyes and stared impassionately into the bleeding face of her old friend John Williams but her expression was blank, as if she was suffering some emotional breakdown.

''Don't blame Rose,'' said John, ''I used her weakness for the drink to find out what I needed to know. Blame yourself, Michael, you're the sole cause of her vulnerability by being involved in what you are...she took to the bottle to ease the pain and the shame of loving you.''

''How did you find out about the shipment.....how did you know where to go?'' asked Michael, then suddenly an expression of enlightenment came across his face, ''Where's Timothy?....'Ave you bastards got my brother? That's what you did...you followed him to the meetin' and got it out of him...didn't you?''

''How he did it doesn't matter any more,'' interrupted the stranger, ''this whole operation's been one massive balls up from the word go....you've all been so fuckin' incompetent it's unbelievable. Take the woman out of the room if you prefer it, but I'm executing the Brit bastard....and just maybe the Council might give you one last chance to redeem yourself.''

''You'll do fuck all of the sort,'' shouted Michael, ''this is my operation and I'll decide when he dies; furthermore, it will be me who pulls the trigger, so stay out of it.''

''What I'm tryin' to get through to you is all this talkin' and arguing is unnecessary,'' said the stranger, ''he's admitted his

326

involvement and that should be the end of the discussion......he dies and then we dump his body somewhere."

John's head was almost clear and he was conscious of the difference in opinion; he realised they fully intended to kill him. The only question remaining to be answered was, when? Turning to face his old friend again, Michael slowly pressed the barrel of his automatic into John's left eye. "How long have you known of my organisation?" he asked.

John realised that the time for pretence was over, the truth had to be told in hope of gaining himself a little more time; he prayed he would be given the chance to get at the Colt.

"You mean about the club bein' the H.Q. for all I.R.A. activity in this country?" he replied. "I only found out about it a few weeks ago...but they've known about you for months. It sickened me to my stomach when I found out about one of the best friends I ever had....how you had joined the Provisional I.R.A. and helped to slaughter dozens of innocent people...women and kids included. At first there was no way I would believe them...not Michael Reagan, not the Michael Reagan I knew. But they showed me pictures of you with the German and other well known I.R.A. bombers.....then I believed them alright."

"But why you, John?" shouted Michael.

"Sheer coincidence......they dig deep these people, they accidently found in the files that you 'n' me were good friends and they decided to use this to their advantage.....and it worked, Michael.....we got the shipment, and you're finished now."

The barrel of Michael's pistol was thrust harder into John's eye, he thought his eyeball was going to burst and he tried to force his head away.

"I'm finished am I?" yelled Michael, beginning to lose control, "You've got it all wrong...it's you that's finished now. What have you bastards done to my brother?....Where's Timothy?"

John remained silent. Michael removed the barrel from his eye and savagely raked the sights down the side of John's face, causing a renewed flow of blood to mingle with the already congealed blood of earlier blows. John was almost unrecognisable as the person who had walked through the door a relatively short while ago.

"I said where's my brother?" screamed Michael.

"He's dead," stated John.

"What did you say?"

"I said he's dead......him, his mate Lurch; and the German....they're all dead. If you're still interested in how I found out about the time and the place of shipment....Timothy told me. He told me, hopin' to save himself...but in the end it did him no good at all. My orders were explicit...I had to find out everything and then I had to eliminate you and your brother, plus anybody else that happened to get in the way......You're the only one left, Michael, they're all gone. It doesn't matter to them if you kill me, I'm just another one of their statistics.....there are others waiting outside. It's over mate, there's no place for you to go...you're knackered one way or another; and your mate over there'll be an unexpected bonus for them."

Instead of this frank admission sending Michael into an uncontrollable rage, his reactions were entirely the opposite; his shoulders sagged forward and he looked into John's eyes.

"Who are you, John..just who the fuck are you?"

"Believe it or not," replied John, "we're very much alike you 'n' me..the only difference is that I do my killing and you have others do yours for you. We both obey our superiors, and now it looks like the end of the road for both of us......has it been worth it all, mate?''

Suddenly without any warning, Michael reverted to his former rantings; his eyes filled with hate. "What a pure load of bollocks," he shouted, his face red with effort, "if there were others outside like you reckon, you wouldn't have just waltzed in here on your 'Jack Jones'..you would've had them with you....You're tryin' to bluff your way out of this, but you've got no fuckin' chance, it hasn't worked; the only one who's going to die here tonight is you!''

"I've had enough of this crap," announced the stranger, pulling a silenced revolver from his pocket, "get out of the way."

"I've already told you I don't need any help from you," yelled Michael, "it's my brother he's killed...it's my responsibility to finish him." Barging into the stranger, Michael yanked the gun out of his hand and, after staring at the silencer he threw his own gun onto the sofa; narrowly missing Rose.

Meanwhile, because of all the excessive shouting going on inside the flat, Herman opened the door and peered inside; thinking he might be needed.

"Get out of here," shouted Michael, "and fuckin' stay out like I told you."

For those few short seconds, all attention was suddenly switched from John to the unfortunate Herman; this was surely the only chance John would be likely to get. He made a desperate bid to reach the Colt, but the heavy toll of the combined beatings he had been subjected to proved to be too much for him; and he failed hopelessly. It had been a futile effort, and his options were quickly running out.

Aware of John's sudden movement, Michael spun round to face him, the revolver in his hand quietly coughing twice in succession without him being conscious of having pulled the trigger. Two terrific burning sensations forced a way through John's upper body, and the impact flung him against the back of the easy chair, almost causing it to topple over. It felt as if his entire body was on fire, he found himself powerless to move; surprised that he had not lost consciousness, he sat with his head forward resting on his chest. He opened his eyes gradually, even having difficulty with that small task, and saw his life blood pumping out of him, soaking into the much loved sheepskin coat. It was about past redemption; as he feared he was himself.

Rose screamed at the sight of John being shot, so much so that the stranger ran across to her and slapped her hard across the face to stop her. Michael looked stunned, staring at the smoking gun as if not believing what he had done; then he looked at the bloody figure of his old friend. It took a while before he accepted what he had done, this was the first time he had killed, and he could not remember doing it. He gazed about the room, at the stranger who had silenced Rose, at Rose herself and saw the look of horror on her face; and then once again at the supposedly dead body of John Williams. Michael allowed the revolver to fall from his fingers, then turned slowly away and went over to the bar to pour himself a drink; he seemed to be in a semi-daze. John was motionless, experiencing difficulty in managing to draw air into his lungs, and not being too sure of the damage the bullets had done to him. It was the general opinion that John was dead, and none of the three people in the room seemed to be taking the slightest bit of interest in him; he wondered himself if he was too far gone to be able to do any more. Somehow, from some-where deep within himself, he had to summon together what remaining strength he had left before it drained out of his body altogether. He also found, to his dismay, that his eye-sight was failing him, he was finding it difficult to focus on anything. It seemed to him that it was possible that he could be slipping out of this life, faintly in the distance he could hear a woman crying; there was only one woman in the room and that was Rose. Could it be possible that she was crying for him?

'Oway yer useless bastard!' he scolded himself, 'you can't just sit here and fade away. Come on..move yer bloody self and get this job finished with; people are relyin' on you...people have faith in you. Think of Chris and what she told you; there might even be a baby on the way....you promised to look after them!'

Making one final and supreme effort to gather what strength he had left, John finally managed to move his fingers; and then very gradually his right arm moved agonisingly across his body towards that elusive left boot. Excruciating pain racked his entire body and all he wanted to do was close his eyes and rest for a while; but he resisted the strong temptation and concentrated on his sole objective. At last his hand made contact with the butt of the Colt, its cool firmness reassuring and, with extra determination, he brought the weapon clear of its concealment.

The whimpering Rose had sat and observed John's every pain-ful second in sheer disbelief; from the moment the blood-stained body had taken a massive breath until she saw the gun appear from his boot into his hand.

"Michael!" she screamed.

331

Both Michael and the stranger spun simultaneously to find the reason behind Rose's cry, both instantly aware of the threatening Colt now in John's hand.

'Impossible,' thought Michael, in that split second, 'he's dead...he has to be.'

Unfortunately for him he was wrong!

The ensuing actions were automatic, John Williams' self preservation was at risk; he brought the Colt to bear upon the stranger and fired once; then it arced towards the bewildered figure of Michael and fired a second time; the twin explosions echoing around the room. It looked slightly comical to John, the way the stranger staggered backwards into the wall as if smitten by some giant hand; the .38 calibre bullet hitting him in the throat. John's second shot was a little wayward, entering the lower regions of his old friend's stomach; knocking Michael off his feet and onto the floor, where he was now attempting to drag himself towards the weapon he had dropped. John looked at the pathetic figure, even now it was still the old friend from the past; their eyes met. "I'm sorry, mate," he whispered, squeezing the trigger for a final time. Michael's head snapped back as the second bullet entered his brain via his left eye, and he lay still on the floor.

It was over!

The extreme effort proved too much for John, he dropped the gun onto the floor and closed his eyes, searching for the respite he longed for.

Outside in the corridor, hearing the sound of gunfire, Herman opened the door and looked in the room; his eyes opened wide as he was suddenly confronted with the bloody aftermath. The Geordie was still seated in the chair where he had put him, but now he was absolutely covered in blood and his head hung forward. The I.R.A. exterminator lay against the wall, his eyes wide open and frothy blood gurgled from a gaping wound in his throat. Finally his eyes found his employer, a nasty looking hole in his face and very obviously dead. Rose sat next to him on the floor, cradling his head in her arms and crying; but it was a useless gesture.

"Jesus Christ!" exclaimed Herman and, ignoring her pleas for help, he turned and ran from the devastation, deciding that it was time to get as far away from there as possible.

Herman was not the only person to hear the sound of the three gunshots, they were easily distinguishable above Chris's singing down in the nightclub lounge. She suddenly stopped and her eyes sought out Steve, but he was already out of his seat and sprinting through the crowd towards her.

"Ring this number," he said, pushing a piece of paper into her hand, "tell the Commodore we need assistance, and to cordon off the club."

After stopping briefly to give Chris the instructions, Steve ran to the door marked private and through the changing room towards the door which led up to the living accommodation. It was at that precise moment that the huge figure of Herman burst through the door, and the two running men collided heavily with one another, causing both of them to fall to the ground. Steve's reactions were well rehearsed, he instinctively fell into a controlled sideways roll and sprung back onto his feet almost instantly; his hand removing his own Colt from its shoulder harness. Herman, being that much bigger and heavier than the younger man, struggled to get himself upright again; he too made a grab for the gun he carried. Steve Bright found himself with no alternative but to squeeze the trigger, the subsequent explosion reverberated around the confines of the small space, almost deafening him. An expression of surprise appeared on the face of Herman as the bullet entered his temple, blood trickled from the fatal wound, down his oversized Roman nose and dripped from its extremities onto his chin. His eyes were still open as he toppled backwards like a mighty oak tree being felled; the floor shaking under the impact. This was the first time Steve had been called upon to kill, and he remembered the words of advice given to him by John; his initiation was now complete. Upstairs, amidst the carnage and death, Rose had lapsed into a state of disbelief, accumulating and reaching its climax at the acceptance of Michael's death; she had tried so hard to bring him back to her, but all of her tears and prayers had been in vain. The person who was responsible for causing her this pain sat in the chair and, unlikely as it seemed, she was positive he was still alive. Slowly she climbed to her feet and stepped warily away from Michael's lifeless body, walking towards John, pausing only to pick up the gun which had fallen from his bloody hand. This was the gun he had used to kill the only man she had ever loved and nudging John in the head with the barrel produced a slight moan from between those swollen lips. This reaction brought a twisted smile to her face; she knew that he was still alive, and she did not intend him to cheat her out of claiming her revenge. Grasping the Colt in both hands, she used her thumb to pull back the hammer and pointed it at John's head.

Through the pain and misty red haze which completely engulfed him, John was able to hear the distinctive sound of the cocking action of the Colt and, after forcing his undamaged left eye open and lifting his head, he saw Rose standing in front of him with the gun in her hands. He was totally powerless to prevent her from doing whatever she intended, there was insufficient strength in his body to raise any objection; never mind anything else. Fortunately for John, fate stepped in and took a hand in the proceedings; Steve burst into the room and instantly evaluated the crisis in front of him. His sudden appearance startled Rose and, forgetting about her revenge on John, she automatically turned towards this new-comer who she had never seen before; inadvertently bringing the Colt to bear upon him, her mind now in total confusion.

Straining to see what was going on, John immediately appreciated the tragic sequence of events which followed; he tried so desperately to call out to his young friend.

'No Steve, don't !' he wanted to shout, but nothing emerged; not even a whimper. As far as Steve was concerned, he had only a split second to decide on what course of action to take; the woman had a gun in her hand and she had turned it on himself. He fired! a bright red crimson stain appeared over the left breast of Rose's dress and her mouth opened in amazement as she was flung backwards like some discarded rag doll. With a pitiful cry, she fell dead by John's feet; the question of Rose was resolved.

'I'm so sorry, sweetheart,' he wanted to tell her, and he felt the tears come to his eyes. It was too late for recriminations, though in spite of the pain and damage they had inflicted upon him, he had not wanted anything to happen to her. As they had been for most of their adult lives, Michael and Rose were united in death.

"John," said Steve, gently shaking him by the shoulder, "hang on a bit longer; I'll soon get someone here to help you."

It did not take a specialist to realise that John had endured a terrific beating before being shot, his face was so badly swollen and out of proportion; covered in deep lacerations, the congealed blood only adding to the horrifying effect. Yet still he had been able to kill two men.

"Bastards!....Rotten bastards!" cursed the young man as he ran to the phone and dialled the section's emergency number. "This is code nine official," he spoke into the receiver, "one of ours is hurt; we need an ambulance and a doctor at the *Four Leaf Clover Club* as soon as possible."

"Assistance is on its way," replied the operator; the words code nine official explaining the seriousness of the call.

Steve looked over at John again, and he was saddened by the lack of life in him; accepting that it was some kind of miracle that he had been able to hang on for so long. Becoming aware of the sound of running feet, he went into the passage and saw Chris and another man who he knew belonged to the section's back up squad. Stepping in front of her, he prevented her from going into the room.

"Don't go in, Chris," he said quietly, holding her by her shoulders, "he wouldn't like you to see him as he is; there's an ambulance on its way...it shouldn't be much longer."

Chris stopped struggling, her eyes filled with tears and she began to cry.

"How bad is he?" she asked, fearing the worst.

"It looks bad, there's no point in lying to you," admitted Steve, "but as long as there's a breath left in that man's body...then he'll put up a hell of a fight, that's how he's made."

"What about the others?"

"I honestly don't know how he did it...but Michael and some other bloke are both dead...the woman was going to finish John off altogether when I got here; I had to stop her."

336

Chris tried to wipe the tears from her eyes and to compose herself, but she was finding it difficult. The member of the back up squad came from the room and nodded to Steve. "It doesn't look as if we're needed up here," he said, "I'll have my men concentrate on the customers and staff; see if anyone interesting turns up.....and by the way, do you know who the man lying over by the window is? He's Adam Slattery, one of the I.R.A.'s top gunmen. There'll be a lot of people more than pleased he's out of the way."

Escaping Steve's restraining arms, Chris pushed past him and ran into the room, where not so many hours ago she had enjoyed being with John; but the sight of him slumped in the chair soaked in blood was almost devastating. His face was a deathly shade of grey, how could he possibly still be alive? Once again the tears came and she cried openly as she rushed to his side, picking up his bloodstained hands and pressing them to her lips.

"Don't leave me, John," she begged of him, "please don't leave me."

The sound of her voice brought the merest hint of response from him, she was positive that his lips moved as if trying to smile; it was there for only an instant, but she saw it.

"Yes John," she cried, "you're going to be alright, I know you are...keep on fighting, you can do it; I love you."

The distinctive sound of the two-tone klaxons could be heard in the distance, louder and louder with every second.

"They're coming," she told him, her tears dripping onto his hands, "it won't be long now."

Steve entered the room and knelt by her. "It's all over John," he said into his friend's ear, "you can get yourself back to that bloody Geordieland you love so much; and take Chris

337

with you.''

''We've decided on Cornwall, haven't we John,'' she said, trying to raise a further response from him.

The ambulance screeched to a halt outside the club and within a matter of moments the emergency team stormed into the room carrying a stretcher and other necessary equipment.

''Right,'' said one of the men in a white overall coat, ''you can leave him to us.''

''Please doctor,'' pleaded Chris, ''you've got to save him.''

''We'll do our best,'' he answered, gently opening the front of John's sheepskin coat.

The next sensation John became aware of was the renewal of those agonising pains throughout his entire body as he was lifted onto the stretcher; then someone stuck a large needle into his arm and attached a long tube leading up to a bottle with liquid inside. Then he was being carried down the stairs and through the club, endless rows of inquisitive faces peering down at him. He had been here before, but where was the young subby? He was carried past the piano where he had first seen Chris's beautiful face and heard her dulcet voice; and then he was outside in the open, the bitter cold air acting to revive him a little. Once again he had the sensation of being lifted, and the stretcher was slid into the ambulance; the doors slammed closed. Almost immediately they were moving and he could feel the momentum rapidly increasing, the sound of the klaxon, coupled with the blue light flashing, clearing the way ahead. During the whole time he was aware someone had held on to his hand tightly and spoken words of encouragement to him. Forcing he eyes open, he saw her tearful face staring down at him.

''Chris,'' he whispered.

"I'm with you, my love," she said, "I'll always be with you."

John smiled and closed his eyes, he felt so tired; all he wanted to do was to go to sleep. The flashing light and the sound of the klaxon were gradually becoming fainter. What was happening to him? The pain was subsiding and he felt alright again; why could he not get up and walk away from here? Why was Angela beckoning to him, just as she had in his dreams? Did she want him to go to her?

"I'm coming," he whispered, "wait for me."

Chris felt his hand go limp in her own, and the whole of his body seemed to relax; suddenly John was still. She searched desperately for some sign, but could not find any. "Doctor," she cried, "please don't let him leave me now."

Commodore Ward arrived on the scene as they were putting John in the ambulance, he stood silently as it roared away into the distance on its way to the hospital; a feeling of sadness came over him.

"How is he, Bright?" he asked the young man, who was also staring after the disappearing blue lights.

The Commodore had successfully restrained himself from showing his true emotions, Steve wrongly misinterpreted this as a lack of concern for the seriously injured man. It was safe enough for the likes of the senior officer and the Minister, all they involved themselves in was the issue of commands to others who did the actual ground work; regardless of the possible consequences or inner feelings and doubts of ordinary mortals. They took it for granted that whatever it was they decided upon in their joint wisdom, some patriotic fool such as John Williams would carry out their every whim. Up until the short space of a few weeks ago, his new and much respected friend had been well out of this, but they had decided to drag him back. Maybe the life he was leading at the time, and the sadness surrounding it, had not been too happy an existence; but at least he had been alive, now even this hung in the balance.

"As well as can be expected," he snapped, "after almost being beaten to death and having a couple of fucking great holes blown in him......But you trained him well, sir, he did everything you wanted of him...they're all dead, even one of their top killers we didn't even know was in the country."

Understanding the young man's emotional ties with John, the Commodore chose to ignore the sudden outburst. "Ease up a little, Bright," he advised, "there's no need for you to sound off like that. You can't tell me anything about John Williams.....I selected him at the very beginning and we started this section together. We go back a long time, and he's more than just another operative to me.....he's an idealist, the kind of person who accepts what has to be done for the good, and dangers associated with the job.......he realised what he was up against and he still chose to do it."

Steve Bright quickly recognised that he had been completely mistaken about the Commodore, he too had this special feeling for John. "I'm sorry sir," he apologised, "I was out of order....I should have known. It will interest you to know that the other man John killed was Adam Slattery, I don't know how he got inside the club, but he did.......It's absolutely incredible how John's managed to do what he's done, he must have just walked into their trap."

"He's an incredible man," smiled the old man then, turning

340

his attention to the large numbers of police, he added, "The local police have been informed that this is a government operation which overrides their authority; but they'll remain here until things have been finalised. I appreciate that you yourself would prefer to be at the hospital at this moment, so get yourself off and give support to that young woman; I'll make sure his in-laws are brought as soon as possible....they have the right."

"Yes sir, thanks," called Steve, as he sprinted towards his little sports car. He had almost reached it when he was suddenly stopped in mid-stride by a stocky figure stepping from the shadows; his hand went to the Colt and whipped it from its shoulder harness.

"No sir!" shouted a worried voice, "don't shoot."

It was the doorman from the nightclub.

"Jesus!" gasped Steve, "how did you manage to get away?"

"As soon as I 'eard the shootings, I tried to get away then, but I saw all those men running towards the club," he replied, "so I sneaked into the garage and waited till it was clear....then I was out of the club in a flash....I didn't know what the fuck was goin' on and I didn't fancy hanging about the place to find out. I waited over here and saw them carrying Mr. Williams out on the stretcher, and Chris cryin'.....he didn't look too good, will he be alright?"

"I don't know," replied Steve, becoming impatient, "but one thing I do know, and that is you have to get back to the club and tell the people in there who you are and what you did.....they'll want to check everybody out."

"Check everybody out?......Why's that?"

"Because the I.R.A. are involved here," said Steve, "and you don't want to be roped in among them, do you?"

341

"You're kidding...the I.R.A.?" gasped the astonished doorman, "Me with the fuckin' I.R.A...you have to be kiddin'.....Jesus Christ, you're not safe anywhere."

"That's why you must get back to the club..help sort things out, they'll be checking on everything and everybody."

"Are you 'n' Mr. Williams with the law?"

"Something like that," said Steve, "but there's one thing I want you to promise me..forget the name John Williams; as far as you're concerned..he never existed, OK?"

"OK sir," he agreed, "I'll get back to the club straightaway ... but when you see him..tell him Bill was askin' after him. Told me he was a lover, you know..not a fighter...he's alright that Mr. Williams."

"I'll tell him...now please excuse me, I have to go."

The two men parted, Bill on his way back to the club and Steve running to the little car which John had never been too impressed with. As he drove through the quiet night traffic of the city, his mind unconsciously drifted back to John's natural ability to befriend so many people from so many different walks of life. Smiling to himself, he recollected their initial meeting on Waterloo station and the gentle rebuke he had received for his apparent impertinence.

"Geordie accent isn't it?" he had asked.

"No it isn't," John had answered, "I come from Durham and, I'm pleased to say, not a Geordie."